MW00614769

Praise for The Turrim Archive

"A web of piracy, betrayal, and wizardry upon a world in peril: Just wait until the story starts to move ... and then hold on for the ride!"

—Kathy Tyers, award-winning author of the *Firebird* series

"Firefly meets steampunk with hints of fantasy in this adventure series. Jenelle Leanne Schmidt deftly weaves together sky pirates, academy students, and a mystical guardian into a riveting story. Definitely recommend for fantasy and steampunk readers!"

—Morgan L. Busse, award-winning author of the *Ravenwood Saga* and *Skyworld series*

"Dazzling steampunk adventures with a practical wizard and an evil warlord."

—BookLife

ALSO BY JENELLE LEANNE SCHMIDT

Turrim Archive

The Orb and the Airship

Mantles of Oak and Iron

Hearts of Stone and Steel

The Prisoner and the Pirate

Towers of Might and Memory

A Classic Retold

Steal the Morrow: a Turrim story

The Minstrel's Song

King's Warrior

Second Son

Yorien's Hand

Minstrel's Call

The Faelands

An Echo of the Fae

Children's Picture Books

'Twas an Evening in Bethlehem

THE ORB AND THE AIRSHIP

BOOK 1 OF THE TURRIM ARCHIVE

JENELLE LEANNE SCHMIDT

STORMCAVE

The Orb and the Airship

Volume 1 of The Turrim Archive

By Jenelle Leanne Schmidt

Copyright © 2023 by Jenelle Leanne Schmidt

Published by Stormcave

www.jenelleschmidt.com

The Orb and the Airship

All rights reserved.

No part of this book may be reproduced in any form or by any electronic or mechanical means, including information storage and retrieval systems without written permission from the author, except for uses of brief quotations when due credit is given.

ISBN-13: 978-0-9884512-4-7

This is a work of fiction. All of the characters, organizations, and events portrayed in this novel are either products of the author's rather large and vivid imagination, or are used fictitiously. Any resemblance to persons real or historical is purely coincidental.

Cover art by Dragonpen Designs

Book design and maps by Declan Rowe

To Derek
Thanks for giving me the world

THE WORLD OF TURRIM

Turrim is a single-continent world with six separate cultures and a calendar that looks slightly different from our own.

Turrim's year is only 336 days long, separated into twelve lunats (what we would call months) and each lunat is exactly 28 days long, separated into 4 sennights (what we would call weeks). Their seasons are much as our own, following the same pattern of fall, winter, spring, and summer.

Their new year begins on what would for us be September 21st, or the Fall Equinox.

The months of the year (starting at the beginning of their calendar year) are named thus:

Chanjar	**October**
Deepthen	**November**
Darkthen	**December**
Edrian	**January**
Tella	**February**
Malla	**March**
Urin	**April**
Paute	**May**
Avar	**June**
Mirad	**July**
Avest	**August**
Felling	**September**

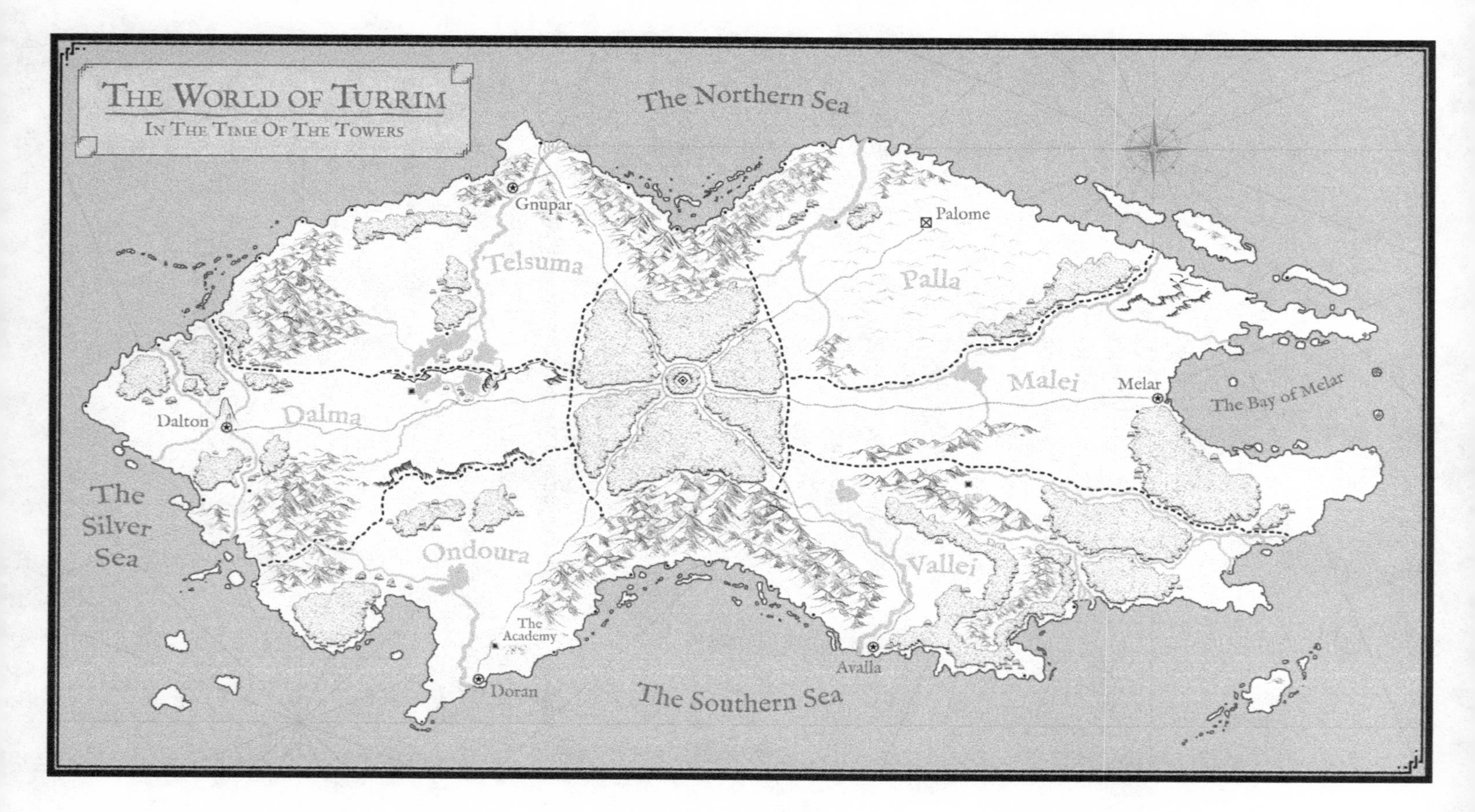
THE WORLD OF TURRIM
IN THE TIME OF THE TOWERS
The Northern Sea
Gnupar
Palome
Telsuma
Palla
Malei
Melar
The Bay of Melar
Dalton
Dalma
The Silver Sea
Ondoura
Vallei
The Academy
Doran
Avalla
The Southern Sea

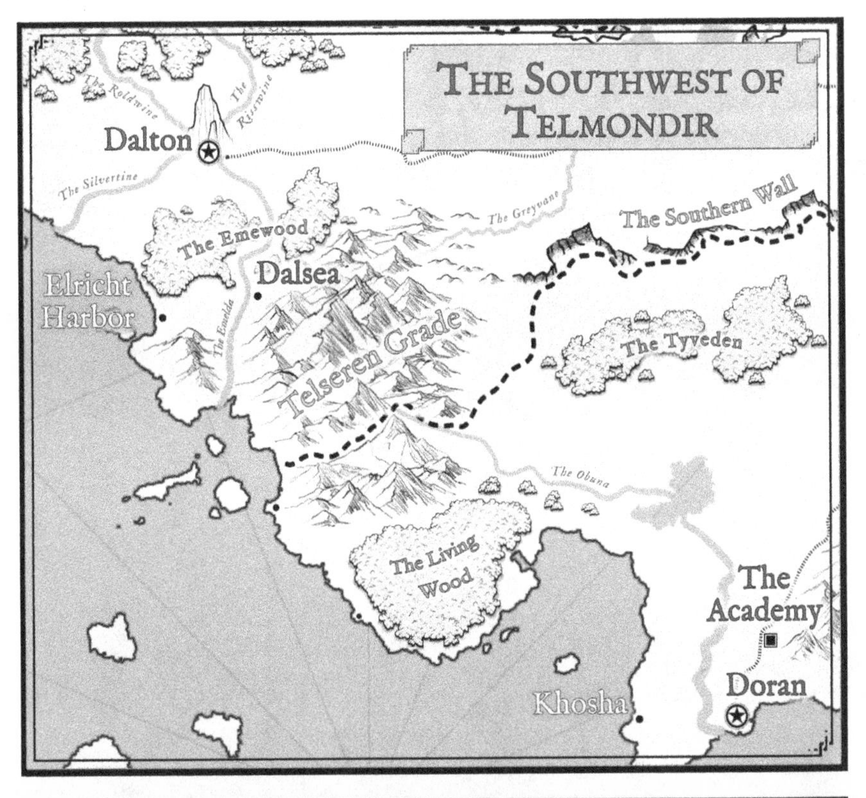

THE SOUTHWEST OF TELMONDIR
The Roldwine
The Risswine
Dalton
The Silvertine
The Greyvane
The Southern Wall
The Emewood
Dalsea
Elricht Harbor
The Emelda
Telseren Grade
The Tyveden
The Obuna
The Living Wood
The Academy
Doran
Khosha

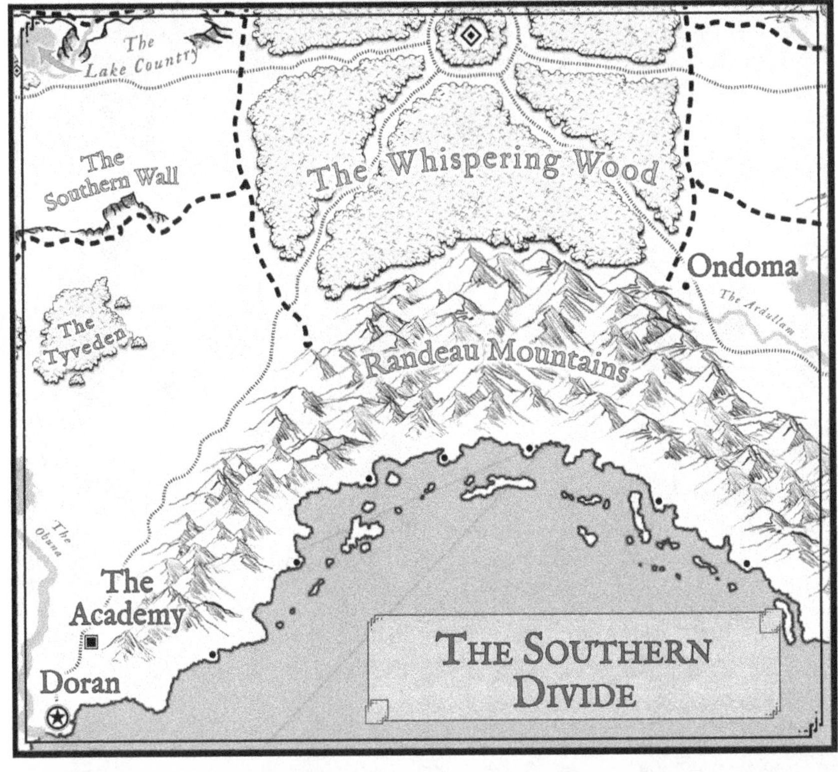

The Lake Country
The Southern Wall
The Whispering Wood
Ondoma
The Ardullam
The Tyveden
Randeau Mountains
The Obuna
The Academy
Doran
THE SOUTHERN DIVIDE

PROLOGUE

Firelight flickered across the old man's face. The shadows made his wrinkles seem deep, deeper than they were. The small room boasted worn furnishings: a small, faded rug, a stone hearth, and the wooden chair in which he sat staring into the dying fire. One wall held a bookshelf full of ancient, hardbound books dusty from disuse.

The man hunched forward, wrapped in a tattered cloak. His white beard hung in snarls nearly to his waist. In a different time he had kept his beard short and neatly combed, but what, really, was the point anymore?

They were all gone. He was alone. Perhaps if Shiori were here... but no, she had long since abandoned him, as well. Surely he deserved this aching, lonely despair? After all, he had survived where better men had died.

The fire burned down to a handful of glowing embers and the air in the room took on a chill. The man sighed and shifted, glancing out the window above the washbasin at the rising silver moon. He could get more firewood, now that it was dark. Restarting the fire would require little effort, and yet he remained sitting, immobile as stone. What was the point? What point in keeping it burning? What point in maintaining his post? All was well. All had been well. All would most likely continue to be well. The world did not need him.

For over five hundred years nothing had required his attention. Outside the tower, time marched on without him. He had long since abandoned his practice of leaving periodically to check on the goings-on of the world.

Not for the first time, he wished for the luxury of death. If only he could slip into oblivion. It would not be a desertion of his duties in a world that no longer needed him, would it? Dalmir longed to sleep, to be reunited with his brothers. He glanced guiltily at the table as though to reassure himself, suddenly afraid that his thoughts might cause some change.

The orb, however, did not flicker.

The orb was the only decoration in the room: a small, spherical ball made of blown glass that looked so delicate a breath might cause it to shatter. It would not, of course; the object was far sturdier than it appeared. Unbreakable, even. It rested on the stem of a candlestick and glowed a steady, reassuring blue.

The man sighed again, the sound filled with a mixture of relief and weariness. If all were not well, the jewel would become streaked with orange and red. But even then, there would still be time, time to stop the darkness. If the streaks grew until the surface of the jewel grew overwhelmed.... The old man shook away the unpleasant thoughts, not liking to think what that might mean.

Ultimate failure. That would be the ultimate failure in his assigned task.

It would not happen. It could not happen; he had seen to that. He pulled his shabby cloak around his shoulders and snapped his fingers, expending very little energy, but more than it would have taken to actually go retrieve the wood from the nearby forest. Firelight blazed forth, warming the room once more and chasing away the shadows threatening to overwhelm him.

Dalmir blinked back tears at the sudden onslaught of memories and scowled into the flames.

1

Marik strode into the dimly lit tavern and made his way to an empty table in the corner. He scanned the room as he pushed his long coat back and sat in the chair that gave him the clearest view of the door. He had spent time in worse establishments, though he couldn't call any of them to mind at the moment. The entire room gave an impression of grime. Paper covering the windows let in a hazy gray light that made everything look dim and dusty. Glancing at the table before him, he realized it wasn't just the lighting. Glops of a sticky substance dappled the wooden surface. He wondered if he dared order anything to eat.

The murky room only held a few other patrons. Several solitary figures sat by themselves at two tables near windows, while two others boasted slightly larger groups. Half a dozen older men played dice and cards in the center of the room. Marik noticed and dismissed these in a singular, sweeping glance, his attention caught and held by the final group. At a table in the far corner, conversing in low tones sat five men: Igyeum soldiers. Even without their uniforms and weapons, Marik would have spotted them by their bearing. One of them glanced his way, and Marik acknowledged his notice with a small nod. The soldier narrowed his eyes, then returned his attention to his companions.

A sour-faced woman headed toward Marik, wiping greasy hands on her stained apron. Under the apron, she wore a plain brown robe of a dress that was far from flattering. She stared icily at him.

"Whaddya want?" she asked, her tone bored and disagreeable.

"A tankard of your finest ale, good lady." He flashed his best smile, the one legends had been written about, but this woman seemed immune. She glowered and Marik continued, more tentatively, "And a loaf of your softest bread, if it's not too much trouble."

"I'll see your coin first," she demanded, pursing thin lips that were out of place in her round face.

He pulled out his pouch and dumped a handful of small, square coins in an even mix of stin and bars onto the table. Several of them accidentally landed in one of the sticky patches. Marik wrinkled his nose.

"Be right back." The woman's tone, if not her demeanor, turned a shade more pleasant.

Marik tried to relax, but the atmosphere in the tavern made it difficult. A strong, unpleasant scent of sulphur wafted in through the open doorway, making him reluctant to breathe through his nose. He risked another glance at the soldiers, but they ignored him.

The tavern sat on the edge of a lake fed by the Pello River, which, if the smell was anything to go by, clearly originated somewhere volcanic. A thick layer of grime covered the entire town, and the people he saw all wore sour expressions and drooping shoulders, as though weighed down by the heavy load of far too many cares and worries. Marik wondered again why Arrio had insisted on meeting here.

The woman returned with a pewter tankard and set it down, sloshing it carelessly. Drops of ale splashed across Marik and he frowned at the droplets of liquid now seeping into his sleeve. The forest green was his favorite shirt, and the ale seemed inclined to leave a stain. He rubbed at the spots in exasperation as the woman slapped a tin plate in front of him with a clang. He stared in disbelief at the small, crusty slice of bread. Whatever else it might be, he could tell any attempt to bite into it would be bad for his teeth.

"That'll be forty stin."

Marik's head snapped up. "For that?" He gestured at the disappointing repast.

"Forty stin or you can take your business elsewhere," the woman growled, staring pointedly at the coins.

"My good woman, what have I done to earn such unkindness? In most other establishments, that much coin would buy me a full meal and a room for the night. Some might be tempted to term your price robbery." He cast a meaningful glance at the soldiers.

She ignored his implication. "We're not 'most other establishments,' and I don't give a sulphur-stone what 'some' might say. We don't like strangers here in Ondoma, and we'd just as soon see you leave." She held out an impatient hand.

"Peace, Criselda." A well-dressed man suddenly appeared, putting his hand on the woman's shoulder. "Marik here is with me."

The woman's frown eased slightly. "Well, then. Twenty stin for the both of you, Arrio, but you vouch for 'im. If he causes any trouble, he's your responsibility."

"He won't cause any trouble, desert flower. You have my word of honor on that. Marik is a business partner. Bring me a mug of whatever he's having. There's a sweet lass." Arrio poured a handful of rectangular coins into Criselda's apron pocket.

Marik wrinkled his nose and retrieved ten of the coins he had dropped, targeting the ones that had landed in the sticky substance. He plucked them up gingerly and took private delight in dumping them into the disagreeable woman's pocket. Spitefully, he hoped they stuck to the cloth and that the ooze stained every other article of clothing she owned when she washed the apron. He scooped up the clean coins and deposited them back into his pouch.

Criselda departed, and the newcomer sat down. Marik noticed that Arrio held himself away from the table and divined that the other man had noticed the lack of cleanliness as well.

"I was starting to think you wouldn't make it," Marik drawled.

"I got held up. I see you found the place." Arrio's voice held a hint of a Pallan accent.

"It wasn't hard. May I ask what prompted this choice?" Marik let his eyes drift back to the table surrounded by soldiers.

"I am well liked here."

"So I see." Marik eyed the man warily. Arrio was tall and thin, with a nose just slightly too big for his face. He looked down it upon the world through his dark eyes. Unlike Marik, he wore no coat. The sleeves of his blindingly white shirt billowed out from shoulder to wrist, where cleverly knotted leather drawstrings held them in place. Like Marik, he wore dark pants and high boots and had a sword strapped to his waist. Marik wondered if the man knew how to use it; many men wore swords these days, but most were just for show. Every stitch of his apparel bespoke wealth and power.

Arrio gave a serene smile and then lowered his voice to a conspiratorial whisper. "Pay no mind to the soldiers. They have no reason to bother with us."

Marik pursed his lips and took a swig from his mug. He instantly regretted it. If they could turn cooled lava into liquid, he imagined it would taste quite similar to this. He tried to keep his expression placid, but Arrio grinned at him knowingly. Marik winced and set the mug down, wishing for a glass of cool water.

"I'm told you have a knack for... acquiring things of value," Arrio whispered.

"I have certain skills in that area," Marik replied. "What particular valuable has caught your fancy?"

"I hear you've even acquired airships."

Marik gave a lazy shrug. "Allegedly."

Criselda returned and set a mug in front of Arrio. Marik

noticed that she took far more care with his drink, none of it spilled. Marik glared daggers at her back as she returned to the kitchen.

"You are among friends here, Marik," Arrio soothed.

"Caution and I are old friends," Marik replied. "She's kept me alive and out from behind prison bars. I trust her. You and I are not friends. Just because some of my associates know you doesn't mean I trust you."

"Fine." Arrio's tone grew clipped. "You don't need to trust me. But are you willing to take the job?"

"You don't think I can do it, hire someone else," Marik said in a bored tone as he took a long, lazy swig of the repellent liquid in his cup. Perhaps it was brewed after being strained through a mixture of dirt and pepper flakes? He managed to keep his eyes from watering, anyway. He made an impatient gesture at Arrio, hoping to wrap up the haggling. Marik hid his annoyance. "This isn't how I work, Arrio. You can hire me to do the job, but I will do it my way or I walk."

"No, no, forgive me." Arrio's tone grew oily and Marik suppressed a contemptuous grimace. "I meant not to offend. My apologies. You can have it for me by the Autumn Equinox, then?" At Marik's nod, he dropped a bag full of coins on the table. "Very good." He stretched out his hand for Marik to shake and then stalked out.

Marik touched a finger to his right eyebrow at the man's retreating back. Criselda shot Marik a fractious glance from behind the bar, but Marik ignored her. Instead, he unfolded the pieces of paper Arrio had given him, being careful not to let them touch the table. The corners of his lips turned up in excitement at the puzzle before him, as well as the promised reward if they could pull it off. This could be it: a payout like this could keep him and his crew living comfortably for a long time. It would be risky, of course, but it looked as though the risk might be worth it.

Marik refolded the papers and tucked them away. Resting his elbows on the edge of the table, he grinned into his mug. He lingered for a few minutes, solely to annoy Criselda as she bustled about the other tables, refilling cups. If she glared at him any harder, her eyes might light on fire, and that would almost be worth seeing. At length, however, he could come up with no good reason to remain. He refused to drink any more of whatever vile brew sloshed in his mug, nor was he planning to touch the crusty bread. Ordering more food was out of the question.

As he rose from his seat, he heard a commotion from the far side of the room. He glanced over to see Criselda's wrist clenched in the fist of one soldier as he used his other to backhand her across the face in a resounding slap.

"I told you I wanted my food hot!" the soldier raged, looming over her. "Do you think you can defy the Ar'Mol's troops and get away with it?"

Criselda cowered away from him, gibbering frantic apologies, cringing in his grasp, but the man held her fast. As the soldier raised his fist for another blow, Marik slid smoothly between him and the woman. In an instant, the tip of his sword hovered at the officer's throat.

Unflinchingly, the officer gave Marik a withering look. "Best sit back down before you end up swinging from the gallows," the man growled. "What business is this of yours?"

Marik didn't blink. "I've had dealings with your sort before, and I'm just aching for any opportunity to avenge that memory," he drawled. "Please, give me an excuse." He narrowed his eyes at the man, whose face reddened slightly. The officer looked ready to claw Marik's face off with his bare hands, but with the sword still hovering dangerously near his throat, he did not dare move.

"Criselda." Marik jerked his head at the still-blubbering waitress. "You've got a good fire going over there; gather their weapons and heap them in the hearth."

The soldiers near the officer half rose in protest, but Marik pressed the point of his sword harder against the man's throat, causing him to gasp. At the sound, the soldiers relaxed into their seats and did not argue as Criselda gathered up their swords and daggers and bows and piled them into the fire. The flames leaped around the weapons, blackening the steel edges and lapping hungrily at the wooden bows. The swords would probably be salvageable, but the heat of the flames would make them difficult to retrieve in a hurry.

Still holding his sword to the officer's throat, Marik reached over and picked up a mug. He moved with deliberate slowness, his expression placid. All eyes were on him as he casually overturned the mug and emptied the horrible liquid onto the officer's plate of food.

Righting the mug, he held it out to them. "Empty your pockets," he commanded. "Now."

Grudgingly, they dug into their pockets and coin purses. The clink of rods of various denominations sounded loudly in the tavern as the soldiers placed every stin they had inside the mug. Marik gestured to the waitress to come closer. Criselda edged nearer, her dark eyes wide and terrified.

"Hold out your apron," he instructed. With trembling hands, she complied and Marik poured the clinking coins into the fabric. It made a good pile. He looked her straight in the eye. "If you ever come crawling back to this life, it will be your own fault," he hissed. Then his voice turned to a roar. "Now get out!"

The woman blanched. Gathering up her apron around the precious coins, she fairly fled through the doors.

With a bored expression on his face, Marik returned his attention to the dumbfounded soldiers. "The Ar'Mol's finest," he drawled. "Now... I am going to walk out of here, and you all are going to sit on your hands until I am gone. Rest assured, gentlemen, if our paths ever cross again, it won't just be your weapons that burn."

2

The first rays of sunlight crept over the horizon, illuminating the thin layer of frost covering the ground. Each blade of grass glistened in the nacreous light of dawn. As the sun rose higher in the sky, the warmth of its rays gradually melted the frost into crystal beads.

"Grayden! Wake up! Wake up! Today is Harvest Festival!"

Grayden groaned and threw an arm above his head, squeezing his eyes shut and pulling his blanket over his face. He wasn't sure what time it was, but he was certain it was earlier than he wanted it to be. A small but powerful force landed on his stomach.

"Oof," he grunted.

The covers pulled away, and he squinted blearily into a pair of bright green eyes. He sighed. He would never get back to sleep now.

"What time is it, Seren?"

"The sun is up. Come on, Grayden! Today is the big celebration!"

"I know that, Seren," Grayden groaned. "Do you know what is special about today?"

She sat back, looking thoughtful. "We celebrate the crops we've grown and the hard work that brought them to fru... fru..." Her brow wrinkled with deep concentration. "Fruit-shon. And this year we're throwing a party for you and Wynn!" Her excitement could not be contained, and she bounced up and down on his stomach.

"And we also generally rest, Seren. That means we get to *sleep in.*"

"I slept in... well, a little. Ma said I couldn't wake you till the sun was all the way up. I waited a whole hour." Seren's eyes widened dramatically. "The chronometer moves *so slowly.*"

Grayden couldn't help but chuckle. "Well, for that incredible feat of patience, I suppose I should thank you."

Seren nodded, her brown curls bouncing around her small face. "You're welcome."

Now that Grayden had woken up more, he grew impish. "Know what else happens on Harvest Festival?"

"No."

"Big brothers are allowed to tickle their annoying little sisters who wake them up too early!"

"No!" Seren shrieked as Grayden grinned and formed his hands into claws. He growled and tossed his covers off as Seren dove toward the edge of the bed. He caught her leg and started tickling the bottom of her foot, causing her to squirm and giggle. She kicked at him with her other foot, but her six-year-old strength was no match for him.

The door to Grayden's bedroom swung open and Grayden paused, looking up at the cheerful face of his mother. He let go of Seren, who half-clambered, half-fell out of the bed. Their mother put her hands on her hips.

"Grayden is demonstrating one of the Festival traditions, I see," she said.

"Mother!" Seren scrambled to the doorway. "You mean it's true?"

"I'm afraid so," their mother replied. "But only once during the day." She winked at her son, and Grayden beamed back at her.

"Come on, Seren, I need your help with the biscuits, and Grayden needs to get up and ready for his big day."

Grayden felt a strange prickle of tangled emotions skitter through his mind at her words. Seren bounced out of the room and Dara smiled after the little girl, then looked over at Grayden. He saw many of his own emotions peering out at him through her eyes: pride, joy, fear, sorrow, and a little wistfulness.

"Your father's out milking the cow. He thought you should get to sleep in, but he also mentioned a pile of wood that needs chopping."

"Yes, Mother."

Dara left and Grayden swung his legs out of bed. His bare feet hit the floorboards and he gasped at the cold. It seemed they had gotten the last of the cherry harvest in just in time. Apple-picking would begin soon. He pulled on his brown trousers and blue tunic, stuffing his feet into socks and pulling on his worn shoes. Then he went outside to the pump and splashed water on his face and hair. Toweling off with the rough cloth hanging by the pump, Grayden looked in the plate-glass window and examined his faint reflection. A tall boy stood looking back at him: square jaw, blue-gray eyes, sandy brown hair that gave his mother fits trying to keep it tidy it grew so fast, broad shoulders, and strong arms, deeply tanned skin from working long hours in the orchards. He wore clothes that had been patched several times in various places. He shrugged at the reflection. He would change his shirt for the festival, but there was no point in wearing his best clothes while he did his daily chores. Finished with washing up, he stepped inside the kitchen.

"Can I help with anything?"

Dara smiled. "Not today. Just sit down and keep Seren company. Breakfast is ready."

Grayden sat down at the table, his insides hopping about like the little frogs down at the pond. His mother brought over a plate of warm biscuits slathered with freshly churned butter and blackberry preserves. He helped get one for Seren before taking one himself. Dara brought over another platter of thickly sliced ham and hard-cooked eggs. Seren bounced in her seat while Grayden filled her plate.

"Can't sit still?" Grayden teased his little sister.

Seren made a face at him, but she did stop wiggling as she focused on her plate. Grayden dug into his food with enthusiasm. There was nothing like his mother's cooking. He would miss it. A lump formed in his throat, but he shook his head, swallowing past it. He would not focus on that today. Today was about celebrating. Blessedly, he was distracted from his thoughts by the door opening and his father striding in, a bucket of fresh, frothy milk in each hand. He set them both on the counter and ladled out tall glasses of the smooth liquid.

"Thought you could use fresh milk for breakfast," he said, setting the glasses on the table and sitting down next to Grayden. "Sleep well, son?"

"Until Seren jumped on me."

"Seren..." Their father's voice held a note of warning.

"I waited!" Seren protested. "I waited until the sun was up, just like Mother said."

Their father gave her a look and Seren hung her head. "Sorry, Gray."

Grayden reached over and mussed her hair. "Not to worry, it's what you're best at."

"My hair!" Seren screeched. "Now I have to brush it all over again! Mother, will you help me tie ribbons in my braids for the Festival?"

They all laughed together and set to their meal in the easy companionship of family. Once the dishes had been cleared and washed, Dara sat down with Seren and began twisting her curls into two short braids, twining purple ribbons through them, while Grayden and his father headed outside to finish the morning chores.

"You didn't have to let me sleep in," Grayden said. "I should have helped with feeding the animals and the milking."

"How many times do young farm boys get honored like you will today?" his father asked. "I can't give you much, Grayden. But I could give you a few extra hours of sleep this morning."

"Da..." Grayden found himself suddenly overwhelmed. "You've given me so much."

"Well, you can make it up to me by studying all the harder at the Academy, then," Bevan replied.

Grayden smiled, nerves making his stomach feel queasy. He suddenly wished he hadn't eaten such a big breakfast. He wanted to make a quip or turn the conversation to a lighter tone, like he usually did, but the words wouldn't come.

"Nervous?"

Grayden nodded.

"About the trip, or the Academy itself?"

"I'm not sure," Grayden said. "I've never been outside of Dalsea, not really, and the Academy's in an entirely different nation."

"A nation of allies and brothers," his father reminded him. "Ondoura is not so different from Dalma."

"I know. It's just... well, it's just so far away, and I'm going to miss you and mother and Seren. I'm going to miss getting to watch Seren grow up."

"Seren's only six winters old; she's not going to grow up too fast," Bevan reminded him. "Conspectus is only two years."

"But I don't get to come home until I graduate. And if I decide to advance into the Experyus program, that's another two years. And if I join the Defenders... that's another two years I'll owe them before my first furlough. She'll be twelve before I can come home for good. I... I'll miss everything."

Bevan gave his son a sidelong glance. "Do you want to join the Defenders?"

"I don't know," Grayden admitted.

"Are you regretting your decision? All the work you've done? The studying, the practicing?"

"No..." Grayden searched for the right words. "I'm just realizing that maybe I didn't think it through—what it would be like if I were chosen. I mean, I never thought that far ahead. The goal was always just to be the one they picked. Beyond that... I knew it would be difficult for the village to raise the entrance fee, and I didn't know if they'd even be willing to, so I never really thought beyond that. And when I started, Seren was just a baby. Now... she's... well..." He gave a little chuckle. "She's a sister. I guess I'm just wondering why I didn't consider any of this before."

"That's the way dreams can be, son. The reality of them can sneak up on you. Doesn't mean you shouldn't follow them, though. It just means that sometimes there are things you have to give up in order to do so."

"So you think I should go."

"I'm saying it would be a shame to waste all that effort, and the scholarship money. But even more than that, it would be a shame for you to short-change yourself that way. It will be good for you to see the world, get an education, and even make a difference beyond our small village. Whether you join the Defenders or not, this opportunity doesn't come to everyone. But no matter what I think, it is still your choice. Always has been. Your mother and I will be proud of you, no matter what you decide."

Grayden remained silent for several breaths as he considered. "I made my choice the moment I started training with Master Farley. I can't turn back now, and I guess I don't really want to."

"I didn't figure you would." Bevan smiled. "It's never been in your nature to quit."

They reached the woodshed. Grayden grabbed the axe and headed toward the wood pile as Bevan made his way to the barn. The Festival activities would start soon, but chores on a farm were a constant that couldn't wait. They would head into town after the wood was chopped and the animals had been tended. Grayden had a feeling his father had gotten up extra early so as not to make Seren wait any longer than absolutely necessary, and a twinge of guilt for sleeping in twisted in his stomach. His father worked so hard, and would have to work even harder or find the money to hire an extra hand once Grayden was gone.

As he raised the axe, he caught a glimpse of purple ribbons down in the yard and chuckled at the sight of his impatient little sister. Seren had been looking forward to Harvest Festival since the day after *last* year's Festival. She was even more excited about it now that she understood there would be a special ceremony honoring her brother for being chosen to enter the Academy. Grayden grinned past his nerves. His best friend, Wynn Drexel, had also been accepted, and they would be traveling together, but Seren was convinced the whole celebration was solely for her big brother. He had to admit, it was nice to have someone cheering wholeheartedly for him the way that only a sibling could. It had been good to voice his fears to his father. As he swung the heavy axe, Grayden felt lighter than he had in sennights.

3

When he had chopped all the wood and stacked it neatly outside the kitchen, beneath the overhanging roof that kept it dry, Grayden took off his old shirt and washed himself more thoroughly in the cold water of the pump. The sun's rays were warm, but the morning air had a bite to it that heralded the onset of autumn. The air smelled of wood smoke and an unidentifiable scent carried on each autumn breeze. As he headed to his room to change into his good clothes, Grayden relaxed a bit. Talking with his father had put his mind at ease about the journey ahead.

He was looking forward to the Festival as much as Seren was. Time to simply relax did not happen often. He had his own share of responsibility around the orchard, and his friends all had their own duties on their farms or ranches or family businesses, as well. The Festival always gave them a unique opportunity to get away from the never-ending chores. But it was more than a simple picnic. Many activities and entertainments would fill the day. In addition to the ceremony honoring him and Wynn for their achievement, there would be contests, challenges, a horse race, and a huge bonfire and dance at the end of the night. There would be a feast to which every family contributed, and if they were lucky, perhaps a bard or storyteller would be staying at the inn and might be cajoled into entertaining during the meal, or playing music for the dance. If not, there were several youths in the village who weren't bad with a harp or flute, and Mistress Brenna could carry a passable tune.

The dance was foremost in his mind as he buttoned his dark gray shirt and shrugged into a black vest. As the honored guests at the ceremony, he and Wynn would escort two young women out onto the floor and lead the rest of the village in the first dance. He glanced in the mirror and ran his fingers through his unruly sandy-brown hair, trying to keep it from sticking up so much. Maybe Ailwen would dance with him. They had been friends forever, and her father, Master Farley, had been his and Wynn's private tutor for the past five years. He gave his own blue-gray eyes a hard stare and berated himself for a fool. Asking Ailwen for a dance would be like asking her to wait for him, but he couldn't do that. The unkindness of it would gnaw at him. Better to leave things the way they were. Giving up on his hair as a well-known lost cause, he wondered who Wynn would dance with.

"We're ready to go," Dara said when he emerged from his room. "Your father is hitching up the wagon, and I could use your help loading the food."

She gestured at several baskets, and Grayden sniffed appreciatively. His mother had been baking and cooking for days in preparation for the Festival. His mouth watered thinking about her strawberry-rhubarb pie, and he decided right then that he would definitely hit the dessert table before his meal, to make sure he got a slice. Dara's fruit pies were renowned all the way to Elricht Harbor; of course, it didn't hurt that they owned and farmed the largest orchards in Dalma. The Ormonds were famous for their apples, cherries, raspberries, blackberries, strawberries, blueberries, and pears. They also had a large crop of rhubarb in the north pasture, which wasn't a fruit, but went well in almost any fruit pie.

Dara smiled at him as he lifted two of the baskets. "I declare. Who is this handsome man in my house, and what has he done with my son?" She came over and raised a hand briefly, as though to straighten his hair, but instead brushed a stray hair from her own face, covering the habitual gesture poorly. She squeezed his arm. "I am so proud of you."

"Thanks, Ma," Grayden said. "But you know, no matter how old I get, I won't ever be able to keep my hair from sticking up. That's how you can always be sure it's me." He grinned teasingly at her, acknowledging in his own way that he didn't mind her need to mother him a bit.

"I must remember to buy you a hat at the Festival today," she shot back. "I don't want those highfalutin Academy folk to send you back on account of they think your mother never taught you how to brush your hair."

Grayden chuckled and carried the baskets out to the wagon. Soon they were ready. Bevan helped his wife up onto the seat and Grayden helped Seren into the back of the wagon before climbing in to join her. Seren wore a pale pink blouse and a bright orange skirt with tiny green flowers embroidered up one side. The purple hair-ribbons completed the strange conglomeration of hues she had adorned herself in. And yet Grayden had grown used to his sister's taste in color combinations.

"You look colorful, little sister." Grayden winked at her.

Seren preened and held herself like a fine lady, supremely confident in her choice of outfit.

His father clucked at the horses and the team started forward down the road. Corn, one of the few crops still standing in the fields, waved their golden tassels in the slight breeze, promising a good yield this year for many of their neighbors. It wasn't a long ride. The Ormond farm stood closer to the village than many, but Seren's impatience knew no limits. She kept popping up from her seat to ask their parents if they had arrived yet. Grayden kept a close eye on her. The last thing they needed today was for his sister to fall out of the cart.

The village center was already full of people by the time they arrived. Master Farley had opened up his pasture for people to let their horses graze. Wagons and carts lined the roadways. Long, oaken tables covered with pitchers and dishes filled with the long-awaited wonders that only came once a year, and the impatience of the gathering crowd to begin the day-long feast, was proof enough that the offerings of the Harvest Festival did not disappoint. It never disappointed. Harvest Festival gleamed in their hearts brighter than any jewel or gemstone could. This day of feasting, this celebration, this time with neighbors and friends would bring joy and comfort in the long chilly nights to come once winter descended.

Grayden helped his father unhitch the cart and wheel it to an out of the way spot, then he and Seren helped their mother set out her baskets on a table. When they had finished, Bevan gave his children a nod. Seren squealed with delight and made a beeline for her group of friends. Grayden watched her run, her braids and skirt billowing. Seren had begun school the year before, but all the families in their little town of Dalsea were close and so she had already known most of her classmates, and quickly befriended the rest.

Grayden looked around and quickly found Hunter, Burke, Ailwen, and Greta standing together near one of the dessert tables. He made his way to them as Mistress Ilsa began shooing them away.

"The table with snacks is over that way. These tables are for the dinner tonight." She frowned at them.

Hunter laughed and held up his hands. "As you say, Mistress Ilsa. The food smells wonderful. We'll restrain ourselves from snitching, though. We're not children anymore."

Ailwen elbowed her brother. "Well, some of us aren't, anyway," she teased.

Mistress Ilsa sniffed and looked at them with suspicion. When she caught sight of Grayden, though, her demeanor changed. "Ah,

Master Grayden." She beamed. "And how is Dalsea's honored student doing on this fine Harvest Festival day?"

"I am well, Mistress Ilsa," Grayden replied, trying to keep his smirk from showing.

"And your lovely mother, how is she?"

"My mother is well. Thank you for asking."

"That is wonderful, truly wonderful to hear." Mistress Ilsa clasped her hands together. "We are all just so proud of you and your accomplishment. You make sure to stop by before you leave. I know Jenni would want to say goodbye. We will miss you while you're gone." Her voice took on a melancholy note before she turned to snap at a group of younger children who were trying to steal cookies off the table.

Grayden used her distraction as an excuse to join his friends. Burke waved at him as they made their way across the town square.

"So, you gonna ask Jenni to marry you before you leave, Gray?" Hunter teased.

"I'm sure it would set Mistress Ilsa's heart at ease; she seems rather distressed that you're leaving," Burke joined in.

"You're the only boy in town good enough for her perfect daughter," Ailwen added with a laugh.

"I wonder how she can be so oblivious to the fact that Jenni hates me," Grayden said. "Ever since I dipped her braids in my inkwell when we were eight, she's held a grudge and won't even speak to me."

"Aw, never mind her. Who wants to watch the races?" Greta asked. "We can get corn sticks on our way over to the track."

"Sounds good to me." Grayden paused, looking around. "Have any of you seen Wynn?"

Hunter shook his head. "Not yet."

"He's probably holed up in his shed," Burke said. "You know how he gets."

"Well, let's go fetch him, then." Grayden jogged a few steps.

"We'll still have plenty of time to get corn sticks and get a good seat to watch the races."

Grayden and his friends made their way down to the Drexel home and knocked on the front door. Mistress Drexel opened the door and welcomed them in. He could hear the clatter of dishes and voices in the house behind her. Best friends since they were young, Grayden and Wynn had spent countless hours at each other's homes, especially in the past several years as they studied together for the prestigious Academy entrance exams. The Drexel home was always full of a sort of warm chaos. With six children, three of whom were still quite small, the house had a constant energy and noise about it. At times, that could be difficult, if you needed quiet, which was why they often ended up studying out in Wynn's shed or back at Grayden's home, which was smaller, but quieter.

"Hello," Wynn's mother said, her voice warm. She took in the group with a glance. "Wynn's in the shed."

"We figured." Grayden gave her a grin.

"You can go on back," she said. A small child toddled up and tugged on her skirt, crying. In the house behind her came the sounds of children squabbling, and Mistress Drexel turned her head to the noise. "Oh, dear..." Distractedly, she waved a hand at Grayden and his friends before disappearing into the house, presumably to attend to whatever conflict had arisen amongst her brood. Grayden motioned to the others and they ducked around the side of the house.

The shed door was propped open, and the friends crowded near the entrance. Wynn sat on a stool, hunched over the large, slightly slanted table that took up most of one wall, his pencil moving swiftly across the paper. His dark blond hair looked as though he hadn't bothered to brush it yet, and his clothes were rumpled as if he'd slept in them.

Every available square inch of wall space had papers tacked over it. The far end of the shed had a bookcase that held overflowing portfolios of Wynn's drawings, and several precious books written by or about scients that Wynn most admired. Above the bookcase hung one of Wynn's most prized possessions: a map detailing the voyages of Shurik Medvev, a famous archaeologist from three centuries ago.

Grayden knocked lightly on the door before walking over to stand behind his friend. He peered over Wynn's shoulder. "What are you dreaming up today?" he asked, keeping his voice quiet.

Despite all his precautions, Wynn's pencil jerked, and he straightened abruptly, turning his head to stare at Grayden in wide-eyed surprise. His nearly black eyes stood out in stark contrast to his pale face. Not for the first time, Grayden thought that his friend should probably spend more time outside.

"Oh! Hello there, I didn't hear you come in," Wynn said.

"I knocked," Grayden replied.

"You did?" Wynn frowned down at his paper, which now had a stray line on it. He carefully removed the line with an eraser, using a brush to sweep away the crumbled bits that were left behind. He looked at the precision of his drawing and the untidy mess left by the crumbly eraser, and muttered, "Now there's a tool that could use improving."

"Festival's started," Grayden interjected, sensing that he should interrupt before his friend became seized by the frenzy of a new idea.

Wynn looked up, a puzzled expression on his face, as though he had forgotten Grayden was there. "Festival?" His eyes widened. "The Harvest Festival? Today?" Wynn looked down at his rumpled, graphite-covered clothes in dismay.

"Just started," Grayden assured him. "They're still setting up tables and food. But the races are about to begin. Why don't you get changed? I'll wait for you. Hunter and everyone can go make sure we get good seats."

The others nodded and dispersed as Wynn hurriedly got up and crossed the yard to his house. Grayden entered behind him and was immediately bade to sit down, and a warm slice of freshly baked bread was set before him, along with butter and two different preserves. Wynn's youngest brother crawled over and pulled himself up on Grayden's knee. Grayden scooped the child up and settled him comfortably on his lap with one hand, eating the bread with the other.

"This is delicious, Missus Drexel," he said around the mouthful of savory goodness. She gave him a sweet smile before setting out more plates for the rest of her family members.

Master Drexel came out of another room and paused at the sight of Grayden. "Ah, young Ormond," he greeted him. "Welcome! I know I've said it before, but extra congratulations are in order this day, I believe."

The baby fussed, and Grayden bounced him on his knee. "Thank you, Master Drexel," he said.

Master Drexel came over and lifted the baby off Grayden's lap, then laid a callused hand on Grayden's shoulder. "You've been a good friend to my boy," he said softly. "You will keep an eye on him for us, won't you? At the Academy, I mean?"

Grayden swallowed his last bite of bread and nodded. "Of course," he assured the man. "Wynn and I will look out for each other, just like always."

At that moment, Wynn appeared in the doorway of the room he shared with his oldest brother. His sandy blond hair had been tamed, and he had changed into clean clothes without a hint of a wrinkle to them.

"I'm ready," he announced.

The two young men exited the house amidst a clamor of younger siblings and Wynn's assurances to his parents that he would find them and sit with them at the dinner later that evening. Then they were outside. Grayden took a deep breath through his nose, savoring the mixture of crisp breeze and sun-warmed air in this time between seasons. Soon, the bitter winds would whip up over the mountains, first bringing frosty nights and later thick blankets of snow. He would not be here to see either this year. A melancholy ball with the weight of iron settled in the pit of his stomach until Wynn distracted him by dragging him over to a booth selling food.

Munching on their corn sticks—ears of salted corn skewered on long wooden rods and slathered in butter—they made their way over to the field where the races were to take place. The men of the village had constructed long, raised benches for ideal viewing of the events. Just in time, Grayden and Wynn edged into the spaces their friends had saved them.

The children's races came first. The sack race, which Wynn and Grayden had won a few times in their younger years. Next, there would be the egg race. After that would come several foot races. Finally, there would be the horse race, which was everyone's favorite event.

Grayden and his friends ate their treats and cheered and shouted for their friends and family participating in the various competitions. Two young girls won the sack race. Seren was in the egg race, and Grayden jumped up and down and cheered louder than anyone else during her round. She came in third and waved her ribbon proudly, her cheeks flushed and her braids coming undone. Grayden pressed his way through the crowd so that he could congratulate her and missed the first two foot races.

The day wore on and the events grew more and more competitive until, at long last, it was time for the horse race. Grayden settled in with his friends, eager to see which of the noble creatures would win this year. The race was for younger horses only, ones that were old enough to be saddle-broken but had not yet carried a rider, which was part of what made it so much fun. The race comprised a single circuit of the track, but it was more than a simple examination of speed: it also tested the rider's skill with an untrained animal.

As the trainers led the horses to the starting line, Grayden looked around. "Where's Hunter?"

Burke gave him a puzzled look that quickly cleared. "That's right. You were congratulating Seren when he told us. Hunter's riding in the race this year."

Grayden let out an exclamation of surprise and delight. "So he finally convinced his father! Which horse is he riding?"

"The tall bay." Ailwen pointed.

"Well, then I know who I'm cheering for this year," Grayden replied, picking his friend out of the group of men and youths leading their horses out onto the track.

As the racers lined up, the crowd fell into a hush. The first challenge would be simply to mount their steeds, something none of the horses would have experienced before. Grayden watched Hunter as he stood near his horse's head, whispering to it. Hunter had a way with animals and had wanted to be in this race ever since he could stand.

The bell clanged, and the riders tried to mount their skittish horses. A few made it up on the first try; their mounts stood, twitching their muscles in response to the strange situation. A few lost control of their horses and had to chase them around the track, herding them back to the starting line. One or two got on, only to be bucked off immediately.

Those who had managed to mount now urged their horses forward. This caused even more chaos as the young horses took off in various directions or backed up or spun around in a circle, uncertain what was being asked of them. Grayden lost sight of Hunter for a minute, but the pack parted a little and he spotted him again. His friend had not tried to mount his horse yet; he still stood near the bay's head, patting his nose, his lips moving as he spoke gently to the animal. Quietly, he moved back along the horse's body, then eased himself into the saddle. The horse flicked an ear, but did not seem overly concerned by this additional burden. Hunter sat still, his lips still moving. The bay nodded its head a few times, one hoof pawing nervously at the earth. After another few breaths, the horse walked forward slowly. Most of the other trainers had mounted their horses by now. A few were still going in circles, while the leaders now moved in the correct direction, though still in jolts and starts. Hunter's bay trotted forward.

"I don't believe it," Grayden said. He raised himself up on his tiptoes to get a better view. Around him, the crowd took notice of the young man riding the well-behaved bay. A murmur rippled through the audience.

The bay's trot turned into a canter before moving into a smooth gallop. A minute later, it was all over. Hunter had won easily, crossing the finish line before anyone else had made it halfway around the track, though his ride seemed to have instructed a few of the other horses in what they were supposed to do, and an actual race for second place was developing farther down the track.

Beyond the finish line, the bay kicked up his heels a bit, refusing to slow at first, but Hunter gradually reined him in until the horse came to a quivering halt. The young man dismounted and grinned triumphantly up at his friends. Grayden and the others raced down through the stands and ran out onto the track to congratulate their friend. The rest of the crowd burst into an enthusiastic cheer and surged after them. When everyone had calmed down, Master Elhearn, who had been Master of the Festival every year for as long as Grayden could remember, came over and awarded Hunter his ribbon.

"You sure this horse has never been ridden, son?" he asked.

Hunter beamed with pride, understanding that the question was a compliment for the display of horsemanship and not one of suspicion. "I'm certain, sir. Just saddle-broken, like the rules say. But Storm here is my horse, and he trusts me."

"I've never seen anything like that. You have a gift, lad."

"Thank you, sir."

When they could pry Hunter away from his newfound town full of fans, Grayden and the others left the track, congratulating Hunter and talking about the races. Usually they went from the races straight to the inventing tent. Wynn entered a device every year and usually won a prize. He had a keen mind for clever contraptions, and a passion for building whatever interesting idea sprang into his head. His bedroom was often buried under schematics and drawings, though his parents had given him the shed to contain his mess somewhere other than their small house. With all the excitement about the Academy, however, Wynn had reluctantly decided not to enter the competition this year. He simply hadn't had the time or ability to focus on building anything.

4

Riding the sleek malkyn he had hired, Marik made good time getting back to his crew. The cavern, hidden in the side of one of the deep ravines distinctive to the Temnia River Valley, was one of Marik's many havens. Difficult to reach except by airship, hard to see unless one already knew of its existence, and large enough for Marik's pride and joy, the *Valdeun Hawk,* to rest inside, this particular cave was the closest thing to a home he'd had in nearly twenty years, ever since he had left his childhood home at the tender age of seventeen. He grimaced at the memory. He had expected to win glory and honor. Instead... He cut the thought off abruptly.

His crew greeted him as he stepped through the opening and Marik nodded at them, swinging the lead-line for the enormous cat over the rail that served as a hitching post. They were a good crew. There was tall, broad-shouldered Oleck, with his black hair pulled severely back from his narrow face and wrapped in a leather cord. He wore a sleeveless chain-mail vest covered by a sleeveless, long leather jacket, and his bare, tawny arms rippled with muscles. He greeted Marik with a solemn nod, which was almost emotional, for Oleck. Marik hid a grin at the thought and turned to Raisa, the more energetic of the group. Tall and thin,

Raisa greeted him with a gentle smile lighting her warm hazel eyes. Her dark hair hung over her shoulder in a messy braid, complementing her beige skin. She wore dark brown breeches with tall dark boots that came to her knee, a gray blouse with billowing sleeves, and a long, short-sleeved jacket overtop it all. A sword and several daggers were belted at her waist.

Something small and determined affixed itself to his leg and Marik tousled the blond mop of hair attached to the smallest member of his crew.

"Mouse, did you miss me?"

The small boy stared up at him with adoring eyes. "Did you bring me anything?"

Marik grimaced. "Sorry, kid, there's not a thing worth stealing in Ondoma."

Mouse shrugged, taking the disappointment stoically. He released Marik's leg and trotted over to his small corner of the cave, plopping down onto a pile of worn blankets and picking up a battered book. Marik studied the boy. That book signified his only clue to Mouse's past, but it didn't tell him much. A book of strange tales, it had been the only possession Mouse brought with him, aside from the worn—but neatly patched—clothes on his back. Marik's conscience pricked him. Mouse had never been willing to talk about his parents, or the people he had been living with, in Melar. He had simply attached himself to Marik's crew. Not for the first time, Marik wondered if he had done the right thing. He couldn't very well have left the kid alone on the streets, could he? A vision of that gaunt, pleading face, white as moonlight staring up at him with blue eyes that begged for adventure flashed through Marik's memory. He hadn't had a choice. The kid refused to tell him where he came from, only that he had been loved there but needed to strike out on his own. Marik huffed a sigh. At least the kid seemed healthier now that he'd gotten some wind and sunshine. One day, he swore to himself, he would find out where Mouse belonged and take him back there.

"Did you get us a job?" Raisa asked.

Marik nodded. He handed over the papers from Arrio, wondering how his crew would react. Oleck and Raisa bent their heads over the papers, reading them carefully.

Raisa bit her lip. "We'll need a few extra crew for a job like this," she said, ever practical. "And quite a few supplies."

"Think you can get Shaesta to join?" Marik asked.

"I'm sure she will be interested," Raisa replied. "Especially since it was her tip in the first place. But according to your plan, we'll need at least half a dozen extra hands to pull this off."

"Don't worry about that." Marik waved a hand. "I know where we can pick up more crew."

"The crew isn't what has me worried," Oleck said, his expression turning apologetic. He flashed a grimace. "It's—"

"The *Hawk*," Raisa said. "Marik, how are we going to do any of this when our own ship is barely flying? She came back from that last job pretty beat up. You never did tell us what happened. And besides that, she's only got the one cynder left, and that's nearly used up. Look, you know I love the *Hawk*. But in order to pull this off we need her to be flight-ready and she's—"

"Just a little under the weather," Marik assured them both. "We've got plenty of time to make the repairs. We only need a few parts, a couple of cynders, and we'll be ready for the next stage of the plan."

"Marik..." Raisa's tone held a note of warning.

"She'll be ready!"

"He always says that," Oleck grumbled.

Raisa sighed. "He's always right."

Marik gave them both a smug nod. "That's right, I am."

Oleck tossed another log into the hearth. "Looks like you and I are going to market tomorrow, Ray. We'll let the captain here get the old boat running."

Marik's hackles rose defensively at the "old boat" comment, but he was too busy mulling over the finer aspects of his plan to be upset with his oldest friend.

THE NEXT DAY, Raisa and Oleck made their way through the forest and down to the River Temnia where the town of Viklund had gathered itself down by the watery banks. At first glance, the town was visible only to those who knew it was there. Although the buildings were walled with heavy timber and stone, making them sturdy shelters against the sweeping storms that could spring up across the Maleian plains without warning, the long grasses of the river valley covered the roofs and sidled down the short walls, giving them the appearance of short hills or tall mounds of earth. Not until a traveler stood on the village path and espied the wooden doorways and the brightly painted signs hanging over shop doors and caught the glint of sunshine reflecting off windowpanes could the town truly be recognized.

Outside the main thoroughfare, many of the dwellings themselves were constructed entirely of sod and bricks of mud, and these dotted the prairie spreading out away from the river where the farmers made what meager living they could.

Raisa took a moment to survey the area before she and Oleck descended from the edge of the wood and down into Viklund. They did not make for the main street, however, but skirted around the village and came up at it between two shabby little yards, dodging chickens and the occasional small child.

They had just reached their destination when a contingent of soldiers turned the corner and came marching down the street toward them. Oleck linked his arm through hers and steered her along the alley toward the soldiers.

"What's your business in this part of town?" one of the soldiers demanded.

"Please." Oleck kept his eyes on the ground. "We were visiting a sick relative and bringing them food. The missus here"—he gestured at Raisa—"has a little skill with healing herbs. We're on our way home now."

The soldier stared at them suspiciously. "I haven't seen either of you before, have I?"

"Don't know why you would have, sir," Oleck replied. "I've been out in the fields with our flock of sheep these past several sennights, and me wife's been staying in another village with her sister. Helping with the new baby and all."

The soldier peered at them. "I see." He glanced up the road toward the farmland that started at the edge of town. "I will be stopping in to ask after your sick relative, later. Just to make sure you're telling the truth."

"Very good, sir," Oleck replied, still keeping his eyes fixed on the muddy street.

"On your way," the soldier finally barked. The rest of the contingent marched past, and Oleck and Raisa kept walking until they could duck around a corner. Oleck's fists clenched at his sides, but he remained silent as they waited and then doubled back once the soldiers were out of sight.

Wasting no time, Raisa knocked once on the wooden door, waited three seconds, and knocked again in a rapid staccato pattern. The door swung open at once.

"Raisa! You're back!" The friendly voice preceded a sudden flurry of color and Raisa found herself wrapped in an enthusiastic embrace.

"Shaesta, you're smothering me," Raisa complained. "We need to get inside. A group of soldiers just went through here."

"Quickly!" Shaesta urged, pulling Raisa through the door.

They stood in the cramped entrance to the building while Shaesta carefully locked the door. She turned and flung herself at Oleck. The man stood ramrod straight, his arms pressed against his sides as she threw her arms around him. He shot a desperate glance at Raisa, who smothered a chuckle and gave a little shrug. No defense against Shaesta's hugs had ever been formulated.

She released him and beckoned them further into the building. "Come in, come in," Shaesta enthused, turning and sashaying down the hall, her long, brightly colored skirts swishing and swirling around her legs.

Oleck gave a long-suffering sigh and followed, with Raisa bringing up the rear. Shaesta led them down a flight of stairs into a hollowed-out cellar below.

"Has this patrol been here long?" Raisa commented as Shaesta lit a lantern and set it on a table.

"They arrived in Viklund a few days ago. But do not worry, we had plenty of advance notice," Shaesta replied cheerfully. She sat down in a chair, gesturing for them to join her. When they were all seated, she propped her elbows on the table. "Now, what can I help you with?"

"We need cynders," Oleck began.

Raisa studied the younger woman carefully as Oleck spoke. As always in Shaesta's presence, Raisa felt drab and everyday. Shaesta's perfectly clear umber complexion with undertones of bronze shone with health. Her coarse, curling twists of onyx and gold hair framed her face, and her eyes gleamed with golden-brown humor and energy. Large, delicate hoops hung from her ears and jangled when she spoke. Thin bracelets of gold and silver banded her arms from wrist nearly to elbow, where the sleeves of her cream-colored blouse ended in a ruffle. Shaesta barely blinked at Oleck's request.

"We don't currently have any cynders in stock. Did Marik take a new job?"

Oleck nodded.

"Are you looking for more crew?" Shaesta's voice sounded hopeful.

"Yes," Raisa replied. "This is a big one."

Shaesta grinned, her teeth glinting white in the lantern light. "How many do you need and when? I can ask my contacts, but I can already tell you it won't be easy."

"You want to sign on for this one?" Oleck asked.

Shaesta drew back slightly, an expression of hurt flicking through her eyes. "Do you have to ask?"

"Kind of," Raisa said, keeping her tone apologetic. "You know the routine."

"After all this time, after so many jobs"—Shaesta gave her head a shake—"I'm a little hurt to discover I'm not part of the crew yet."

"Marik trusts you with his life," Raisa assured her. "Look, you understand we can't be too—"

"Careful," Shaesta finished. She heaved a sigh. "I know, I know, I'm in the business, too. But come on, do you really need to ask?"

"I do," Oleck said, his voice firm. "I've only ever trusted two people beyond question in my entire life, and I'm too old to add a third. What's your problem with answering the question?"

"I'm in! You happy, you old grouch?" Shaesta snapped. A teasing light danced in her brown eyes. "Too old, huh? It's not like you're on death's door; you've only got, what, ten, fifteen years on Marik?"

"Excuse me," Oleck huffed. "Marik is four years *older* than me. I'm only thirty-three, but in our business... that's old. Life as a pirate isn't exactly one of safety. Odds say I should either be living comfortably in retirement, or rotting in prison, or dead. Most people in our trade at my age... well... let's just say there aren't many of us."

"I didn't realize you were such a relic," Shaesta sniffed. "Does Marik realize you're about to keel over? And him, too, apparently. And to think, I used to find you attractive."

"What?" Oleck's eyes widened in alarm.

"Never mind," Shaesta said in a breezy tone, "I wouldn't want to saddle myself with an *old man*."

Oleck grumbled and pushed away from the table, stalking over to peer at the shelves lining the walls.

"Oh, Oleck, Shaesta's only teasing you," Raisa called, but he refused to rejoin them. Rolling her eyes, she gave Shaesta an exasperated look. "You really shouldn't, you know."

Shaesta laughed. "I can't seem to help it, somehow. Now, tell me about this job."

Raisa outlined the plan briefly. When she finished, Shaesta leaned back and let out a long, low whistle.

"Quite the risky venture. But with the shortage right now, the cynders alone would be worth it," she said.

"Shortage?" Oleck turned to stare at her. "What shortage?"

Shaesta shot him a puzzled frown, all amusement gone from her face. "Haven't you heard? I thought I mentioned..."

"You said you didn't currently have any cynders in stock," Oleck approached the table and leaned his hands on its surface. "You didn't say a word about a *shortage*."

"It started a few lunats back," Shaesta replied, unintimidated by Oleck's looming presence. "A raid on the Ar'Mol's refinery in Venua. From the reports I heard, the saboteurs caused a landslide and the entire operation was buried. All the miners were killed." Shaesta glanced back and forth between them. "You really hadn't heard about it?"

Both Oleck and Raisa shook their heads.

"Strange. Everyone is talking about it. Nobody knows what happened, exactly, or who pulled it off, but the Igyeum is scrambling to recover what it can." Shaesta toyed with one of the many bracelets adorning her arms. "Thousands of cynders were lost, both the cut and uncut stones were buried or destroyed, and the rumors say that all the tools and equipment were also lost. The Ar'Mol has been covering up what he can, but the rumors can't be quenched completely, especially when cynder shipments suddenly ceased."

Raisa chewed on her lower lip. "So we might not be able to fuel the *Hawk*?"

Shaesta shrugged. "Like I said, let me ask around. How many does Marik want?"

"Play it safe and go with three," Raisa replied. "I'm sure Marik would like to stock up, especially if there's a shortage, but three is probably all we can afford, and should get us through."

"How much are they running these days?" Oleck asked.

Shaesta grimaced. "I'm not sure, exactly. Supply lines have been more heavily guarded, for obvious reasons. They'll probably go for no less than five bars a piece."

Oleck made a sour face. "This job better go well." He pulled a leather pouch out of his sleeve and poured a handful of square coins of different denominations into his hand. He counted slowly before sighing and handing three of them over to Shaesta.

"Tavs?" Shaesta's eyes widened. "This could buy you over twenty cynders!"

Oleck stood. "I don't have enough bars. Besides, we're going to need other supplies, too, legitimate ones. Raisa's made a list. And we'll need to convert some of our coin into Telmondir runes. If there's any change left over, I trust you'll get it to me. And if you come up short, let me know what I owe you."

Dimples formed in Shaesta's cheeks. "Does this mean you really do trust me, Oleck?"

The big man rolled his eyes, but stiffened when Shaesta went up on her tiptoes and pecked him on his cheek. He grumbled about "never being too careful," and tramped out through the door.

Raisa chuckled, then frowned, mock reprovingly. "You're never going to change your tactics, are you?"

"Whatever do you mean?" Shaesta flipped a hand through her curly hair, tossing a few locks carelessly over her shoulder.

"He thinks you're just teasing him. If you want him to see you're in earnest, you're going to have to tell him right out. Oleck's a straightforward sort of man; he doesn't understand subtle."

Shaesta sighed dramatically. "You're right... but teasing him is easy, and nobody gets hurt that way."

"I see." Raisa pursed her lips, and her tone hardened. "Be careful. Oleck's been like a brother to me, and I'd hate to have to come after you if you accidentally break his heart."

Shaesta stared into her eyes, a startled expression crossing her face for a moment. She gave a sort of forced-sounding laugh. "I can't break the heart of a man who barely sees me. Here, let me see that list." Raisa handed it over. Shaesta perused it and waved a casual hand. "I'll bring the supplies to the cavern in a day or two, and I'll let you know what I find out about the cynders."

"Thanks, Shaesta," Raisa replied.

"Ray?"

Raisa paused, halfway out of her chair. "Yes?"

"You don't have to worry about me and Oleck. With eleven years between us, he'd never see me as anything other than the kid who tags along with you, anyway."

Raisa narrowed her eyes, then gave a short nod. It was probably true, she allowed to herself. Oleck did seem immune to Shaesta's charms. But after so many years, feeling fiercely protective of him just came naturally to her. He might not be her brother by blood, but he'd been the only family she had ever since that terrible day... Raisa flinched away from the memories, not wanting to relive the nightmare she had been forced to witness fifteen years ago.

Instead, she gave Shaesta a wink. "Oh, I don't know about that. Even Oleck might notice someday that you've gotten a bit taller over the years." With an airy wave, she traipsed out the door. She had promised Marik that she'd stop by and give Flare a treat. She shook her head with a rueful smirk. He always hated returning the beast to its owner. If there were a way to fit the malkyn on the *Hawk*, she was sure Marik would insist on taking the huge cat everywhere with them.

5

The air had warmed considerably since the morning, and Grayden suggested they get drinks and find a spot to eat their lunches. They wandered over to tables that held enormous crystal bowls filled with shimmering rose-colored liquid. The punch was cold and sweet and quenched the thirst they had worked up after an hour of cheering in the sun. They found a shady spot under a tall oak tree and settled down with their food. Nobody had brought anything extravagant; they all wanted to save room for dinner later in the evening—the activities and events were fun, but it was the feast most people looked forward to the most—but it was a long day to go without lunch.

"Remember the time you brought a raccoon into the schoolhouse?" Burke asked Grayden.

Grayden leaned back, remembering. "Yeah, he was a cute little guy."

Hunter laughed. "He made the girls scream."

"He skittered around the room and we thought it was a mouse at first," Greta retorted defensively.

"Master Becker tanned my hide so hard, I couldn't sit down for a sennight." He grimaced as the others chuckled. "I'm not exaggerating. Seven whole days! Had to take my lessons standing at the back of the classroom."

They passed the next hour chatting and reminiscing, sprawled comfortably in the soft grass. Grayden grinned as the stories continued, most revolving around various pranks he had pulled, and yet he felt strangely distant and disconnected. It was an uncomfortable and unfamiliar sensation for him, so often the center of any gathering.

A bell chimed, signaling the time, and Grayden sat up restlessly. He no longer wished to sit still, but he found himself at a loss for what to do. It would be several hours until the dinner and ceremony and dancing, but he had no interest in exploring the various tents to see the familiar quilts and jams and inventions.

"Are you feeling well, Gray?" Ailwen asked, looking up at him.

She was pretty, Grayden realized. The prettiest girl in town. How had he never noticed that before? They had been friends their entire lives, and yet he had never quite cared before about how she looked. He wondered if he should ask her to dance later, maybe try to steal a kiss during the sweethearts reel? He shook his head, angry at himself. That would never be fair to her, not with him leaving tomorrow.

"Yeah." Burke rose and gave Grayden a curious look. "You've barely said a word. Something on your mind?"

"Dunno," Grayden replied, not sure how to gather his thoughts together into anything coherent. "Guess I've just been thinking."

"Regretting that you never got around to climbing the tower? There's plenty of time before dinner."

Grayden chuckled. "Nah, just realizing how time is funny."

"What do you mean?" Wynn asked. He had been scratching a crude drawing in the dirt, and now barely looked up from it.

"Just that when I was studying with Master Farley and doing what I could to earn my part of the tuition fees, it seemed like time was crawling by, like a worm trying to burrow through a rock. Each minute lasted a year, as if my anxiety and impatience didn't matter at all. But now that it's actually today, now that I have the time to reflect, I sort of want it all to slow down a little, but it's racing past me like Hunter on that young colt of his. I can't grab hold of a single moment. I blink and half the day is gone already."

"Isn't that how it always is when you've been waiting for something?" Burke groaned. "It can't get here fast enough, and then you barely have time to enjoy it before it's over?"

"Just like a horse race," Hunter agreed.

"I suppose," Grayden said. "There's just... I feel like I missed out on a lot in the past five years, stuff I didn't even realize I was missing because I was so focused on passing the entrance exams. But now... there's so much I wanted to do, so much I thought I still had time for."

Ailwen swatted his shoulder. "Quit that!"

"Ouch! Quit what?"

"Talking like you're dying. You're not, you know," she chided. "You're going to school. It's only two years, unless you decide to join the Defenders."

"Yeah, you're right."

"Are you?" Hunter gave him a keen look.

"Am I what?"

"Going to join the Defenders?"

Grayden shrugged, suddenly uncomfortable. "I haven't decided yet. Figured I'd see what Conspectus is like before committing to more."

"Makes sense." Burke nodded.

"What about you, Wynn?" Greta asked.

Wynn looked up, his expression startled. "Oh! I... I don't know," he mumbled. "I guess Grayden has it right. See what the Academy is like first."

"The Defenders get to see the world," Burke said, flopping onto his back and staring up at the sky, his voice dreamy. "I hope they pick me next year."

Greta gave a little huff. "Who says that anyone will even come to Dalsea next year to administer the test? They don't go to every town every year, you know."

"That's just because there isn't always a big enough group of young men and the entrance fee is so steep most towns can't afford it two years in a row," Burke said, a little defensively. "But we'll have enough of us next spring, same as we did this year. Our class is even bigger than Wynn and Grayden's. And with the entrance fee waived for you, the town could afford to send a student next year, too."

"Did the scout ever tell you why they waived the fee?" Ailwen asked.

Grayden shook his head, sticking a blade of grass between his teeth. "Nope."

"Enough of this." Hunter burst to his feet. "Come on, let's go to the tents. Even though Wynn doesn't have an invention in the contest, I'd still like to see what everyone else came up with."

The others got to their feet and followed Hunter. Grayden trailed along behind his friends, still pensive. Ailwen noticed him falling back and slowed to join him.

"You look sad. I'm not used to this quiet side of you," she teased. "Usually, we can't get you to stop talking. Or joking."

"I just can't stop thinking about how everything will be different by the time I get back. Seren will be all grown up, Hunter will be taking on more responsibilities at the farm, Burke will probably be at the Academy." A teasing note entered his voice. "You'll probably be married to one of the village lads. I'll come back and you'll be out hanging clothes to dry with a baby on your hip."

Ailwen rolled her eyes at him. "You're wrong, you know."

"Oh?" His heart thudded ominously, but he tried to keep his tone casual. "How so?"

"We're not the ones who will change," Ailwen said, her voice oddly forceful and yet gentle at the same time. "You will. The village will go on as it always has. We'll keep growing up, taking our positions as adults in the community, but you... you're getting an education. A real education, Gray..." Her face took on a wistful expression. "You're going to learn so much. Not just how to fight, but geography, history, science, engineering, leadership. You're going to go on long journeys with your classmates. You'll travel farther than most anyone in our village has ever traveled other than Wynn's father, and even learn to fly airships. You're right. Even if you come home after just two years, you won't fit here anymore. But it won't be because we've changed. It'll be because you've outgrown us." Now her voice sounded sad. "You'll come back for a visit, wander around for a while, looking for the village you remember, and it will be here... but you won't recognize it. So you'll join the Defenders or become a Conscript in the city guard, because that is where you'll fit in—it's who you'll be when they're through with you."

"How could you possibly know that?" Grayden asked, his stomach clenching as though it had just taken a punch.

"Jessie told me that's what happened when her brother went to the Academy," Ailwen replied, her voice soft.

Jessie and her family were well known in Dalsea. They were traveling merchants who often passed through Grayden's village on their route between Elricht Harbor and Dalton. Jessie and Ailwen had become friends during their frequent stops in Dalsea, and Grayden knew they exchanged letters between visits. Vince, Jessie's brother, was several years older than Grayden, and had gone off to the Academy four years ago.

"Vince joined the Defenders?" Grayden's eyes widened. The older boy had not seemed like the type to yearn after adventure or glory on the battlefield. It had been hard to picture him at the Academy at all.

"Jessie wrote to me about two years ago when Vince decided to enter Experyus. She said she didn't think he really wanted to, but he sensed there wasn't any place left for him at home. Said he was different, seemed older, still a little shy, but more confident in who he was. But he kept talking about how everything at home had changed, but that it hadn't, really, he'd just... sort of... outgrown them."

"That won't happen to me," Grayden retorted steadfastly. How could it? Home was as much a part of him as... as... the heart beating in his chest.

"I don't think you'll be able to stop it," Ailwen replied, her tone wistful. She eyed him strangely, as though she wanted to say more, then quickened her pace to catch up with the others, leaving Grayden pondering her words with an even heavier heart.

They reached the village commons and wandered through the various tents, admiring all the different wares and artistic creations on display. They all agreed that the inventions were not nearly as interesting as anything Wynn had come up with, and Wynn accepted the praise with his usual awkward modesty, which only caused them to tease him further, but their teasing was in kindness, for Wynn truly was as brilliant as they made him out to be.

When the sun fell low in the sky, the village elderman held a brief ceremony in which he called Wynn and Grayden up to stand next to him. He said many things that Grayden could never later remember. His father also said a few short words that Grayden knew would be seared into his memory forever, about how proud he was of his son. They were words that would comfort him during the bruises he would acquire in weapons training and sustain him on long marches with a hungry belly as he learned survival skills and would ease his loneliness in the long days far from home. He also spoke about how bittersweet this celebration felt: sweet because these two young men had worked hard and deserved the honor bestowed upon them, but bitter because Dalsea was losing two of its finest young men for a while. Then there was a toast, and their friends could speak up, which many of them did. Grayden felt as though it were all happening in a dream, or to someone else. He smiled and thanked people as they came up to congratulate him or say a few words or wish him well.

Eventually, he managed to get a plate of food and return to his table, but a numbness had entered his soul. The food held little enjoyment, and even his mother's strawberry-rhubarb pie barely broke through the haze he was sliding into. People kept coming by his table, interrupting his dinner to offer their congratulations, and Grayden found it to be highly uncomfortable.

So when Wynn suggested they sneak away for a bit after dinner, before the bonfire and dance, Grayden readily agreed. The friends tiptoed away from the commons and raced across town through the small, woodsy area that stood between the village and the tower.

6

Angry shouts greeted Raisa and Oleck upon their return to the cavern. They could not make out the exact words coming from their captain's mouth, but it was fairly clear he wasn't reciting poetry. They entered the hideout in time to see Marik hurling himself over the side of the airship and sliding down the rope ladder, a stream of unintelligible fury emanating from his mouth all the way to the cavern floor. He reached the ground and dropped to his knees, hands splayed out and running back and forth across the rocky floor. He picked something up, squinted at it, then tossed it away with an impatient jerk.

"Lose something?" Raisa asked.

Marik rose and stared at them, a blank expression on his face.

"You all right, Captain?" Oleck queried.

Marik brushed his hands against his pants. "Raisa, Oleck. Yeah, I'm fine. Tattered pin dropped through a hole and fell out of the ship."

"Don't you have any others?" Raisa asked.

"Not the right length. This one's a special size and has a little double curve at the end. Help me look. Mouse!" Marik raised his voice. "Get over here and help me find that pin!"

The younger boy came scrambling across the floor as lightly as a malkyn. Not a stone skittered out of place at his approach. Raisa lifted her lantern and scanned the floor with the others.

"How'd it go with Shaesta?" Marik asked as they searched.

"Fine," Raisa replied.

"Can she get the supplies?"

Raisa leaned down to pick up something glinting in the lantern light, but it turned out to be nothing more than a bent nail. "She thinks most of them should be fairly easy to come by. The cynders, however, could be a problem." She glanced surreptitiously over at her captain to gauge his reaction. Marik barely blinked.

"How's that?"

"There's a shortage. Seems one of the Ar'Mol's refineries has been destroyed," Oleck rumbled, brushing his hand over the stones in front of him.

"I see." Marik scanned the ground with his eyes, his voice steady.

"Marik..." Raisa narrowed her eyes at him. "Is that where the *Hawk* got those?" She pointed at the deep gashes on the hull of the airship resting in its support frame above them.

Marik's face darkened.

Oleck's head jerked up. "You said you were just getting supplies and that those scratches were from flying too low in thick fog in the mountains."

"And that's the truth," Marik replied.

"But you were at the refinery, too." Raisa did not phrase it as a question.

Marik gave a curt nod.

"That's where the extra cynder came from," Oleck breathed, his eyes wide.

"Why did you destroy the refinery?" Raisa asked.

"I didn't," Marik barked shortly. "I was there when it happened, but I didn't cause the explosion. One of the workers dropped a cynder."

Raisa's eyes widened.

"He might have done it on purpose," Marik muttered. "I didn't get a chance to ask him."

"Shaesta said all the workers were killed in the landslide."

Marik's expression grew even blacker. "Everyone made it out. I was there when the foremen declared everyone had been accounted for."

"Is this what you're looking for?" Mouse popped to his feet with a long, oddly shaped pin in his hand.

Marik swept the small pin from the boy's palm. "Thanks," he said, "that's it." He stood and stretched, glancing up at the airship. "She's not cooperating with me today."

"Marik? Oleck? Raisa? Anybody here?" Shaesta's voice echoed from the mouth of the cavern.

"Shaesta!" Raisa called, recognizing the voice. "Back here."

The young woman appeared a few moments later, her skirts swishing across the stone floor of the cave. She smiled at them. "Marik, welcome back."

"Did you find any cynders?" Marik asked, his voice terse.

"I have good news and bad news on that front."

"Good first," Marik said.

"I know where we can get cynders," Shaesta said.

"And the bad?" He braced himself.

"We can't buy them, and we can't keep all of them."

"A job," Raisa stated.

Shaesta nodded. "There's a shipment of them being moved in a couple of sennights from Venua to Melar. Should be about a thousand units."

"By airship?" Marik asked, his tone bleak.

"No. By caravan."

"Wagons?" Marik turned incredulous. "Are you serious?"

"The landslide at the Venua mine is hurting the Ar'Mol. He has to keep the shipments of cynders to Telmondir running on schedule."

Marik rubbed his chin. "Or admit the shortage to them," he mused out loud.

"You know he'd never do that," Oleck rumbled. "Show weakness to our neighbors?"

"Never," Marik agreed.

"And he has his own airships to keep aloft," Shaesta continued. "The shortage is forcing him to cut corners."

"Which means he can't spare any fuel to transport fuel," Marik muttered. "Makes sense. What else do you know about the shipment?"

"My contacts can get us the map of their route and an estimate of how many guards to expect."

"And what's the split?"

"A hundred cynders from the shipment."

"A hundred cynders?" Raisa could barely imagine such wealth all in one place. "Even if we had to divide that evenly with half a dozen others our share would still power the *Hawk* for a year. Not a bad deal."

"What's the catch?" Marik asked.

"It sounds like the caravan will be heavily guarded," Shaesta replied. "A full escort of leythan and a regiment of Igyeum soldiers."

"A full escort," Marik said. He paused for a moment. Raisa knew he was weighing the cost and the risks against the feasibility of such a job. "Makes it tough, but not impossible. I'd feel better if the timing wasn't so tight, but I think it's doable."

A coil of fear wound tightly in the pit of Raisa's stomach. "Captain, it seems risky."

"We need the cynders, Ray," Marik replied. "Without fuel, the *Hawk* is grounded, a scenario that I cannot accept, at least not without a fight."

7

"No!" Grayden laughed, shoving his friend. "I'm not gonna do it, Wynn."

"Come on, Grayden," Wynn teased. "You've been talking about scaling that thing since you could walk, but you've never done it. I think it's the only thing you've ever not followed through on. If you don't do it now, you never will."

"When you come back from the Academy, you'll be too mature for pranks and antics," Hunter agreed.

Grayden gave the tower a thoughtful look. "Well..."

"You gotta do it," Burke urged. "It's your last chance. You leave tomorrow."

"I don't know." Grayden hesitated. The tower had always intrigued him. Most of the other villagers barely gave it a second glance, but Grayden had always felt drawn to it. He'd been talking about climbing it for as long as he could remember. It beckoned to him, promising hidden treasure or adventure if he would just answer its call. Yet the others were right. He often made big claims, or boasted of pranks he would pull, and he always followed through... except for when it came to the tower. He stared up at it now, suddenly pensive. "It doesn't seem right," he muttered.

"What do you mean?" Ailwen asked, a teasing gleam in her eyes. "It's just the abandoned tower. It's not like anyone's ever said it's off-limits, it's just that nobody but you has ever cared two kips about the place."

"Doesn't that seem odd to you?" Grayden asked. The fog of unrealism had lifted in the presence of the challenge. He had not known this was what his friends were planning when they had suggested a break from the festivities, but it struck him now that he should have known.

"It's all right, we understand," Burke teased. "You never meant to do it in the first place. It was all talk and now you've found a way out of it."

"That's not true!" Grayden felt an irrational anger surge through him.

"Sure."

Grayden snorted in exasperation. "Fine, I'll do it. But you warn me if you see anyone coming."

"All right!" Hunter cheered.

Grayden faced the structure, muttering irritably to himself.

"You don't really have to, you know." Wynn was at his shoulder. "We only meant it as a prank. Nobody really cares if you don't climb it."

Grayden let out a low chuckle, his irritation evaporating. "I know. I don't know what's wrong with me. I've put this off forever. And now that it comes down to it, I'm not sure why. But Hunter and Burke will pester me relentlessly if I don't."

"We leave tomorrow. They can't pester you when we're gone."

Grayden shook his head. "You know what I mean."

Wynn gave him a blank stare.

Grayden placed his hands on the uneven stones. A small part of his brain screamed at him as he touched the wall, warning him away, but he ignored it. "Too late to turn back now," he joked.

The tower boasted no door, but the stonework jutted out and provided plenty of hand- and footholds along the way to the top.

It simply begged young boys to try ascending it, and yet, none ever did.

Grayden pushed himself up, his fingers seeking out the best places to grip, his legs propelling him up the side of the massive tower. It stood on the border of Dalsea, surrounded by a thin stream. On each of the four sides, buttresses sprang from the walls and spanned the stream, wide enough for a horse to traverse them like bridges. Grayden had once speculated that perhaps the buttresses were supposed to function as bridges, but then Wynn had pointed out that it would be foolish to cross a bridge just to get to a place that had no doors, and anyway, the stream wasn't big enough to even warrant a bridge. To this, Grayden had argued that perhaps the stream used to be wider, or maybe there used to be doors, but when nobody took him seriously, he had stopped speculating, at least out loud.

He had heard that the tower resembled a miniature version of Dalton, the capital of Dalma. Grayden had never been to the capital, and Wynn's father was the only person he knew who had actually been there, but somehow he had never remembered to ask Master Drexel if the rumors were true.

Grayden's hand slipped. He tightened the fingers of his other hand, pulling himself close to the wall. His heart beat frantically and he resisted the temptation to glance down. He stared up at the wall, and a wave of dizziness washed over him. Why hadn't he insisted on a harness before attempting such a mad endeavor?

The sight of light glinting near the top of the tower interrupted his thoughts. Behind him, the sun sank down to kiss the horizon, its last fiery rays reflecting off something up there. He stared at it, blinking in disbelief, then decided he wasn't just seeing things. There really was a window! He renewed his efforts, making his way toward the window, wondering what he might see when he peered through.

The window was dark and dirty, too dirty to see through, but it opened easily and Grayden slipped through and dropped to the floor inside. No dust billowed. In fact, the entire room was far cleaner than he had expected. A small glittering object on the table caught his eye, and he stepped closer to it.

"What are you doing in my tower?" a loud voice demanded.

Grayden jerked upright, his thoughts tumbling in shock and sudden fright. He stared at the old man, taking in his shabby clothes, his long white beard, and the hard, angry eyes. "Do you... do you *live* up here?" he asked.

"You have not answered my question." The man raised his cane and pointed it threateningly at Grayden's chest. "Now, tell me truly: who are you, how did you get in, and what are you doing here?"

"I'm s-sorry, sir. I didn't know anyone lived up here." Grayden stared around, curiosity piercing his thoughts. "How... how do you get food?"

"Answer my question!" the man thundered.

"Oh, right. I... uh... well, I... my name is Grayden Ormond. I climbed up here. It was sort of a dare, I guess. Or a last prank before I leave for the Academy. I truly didn't think anyone would mind. I certainly never thought anyone would be inside!"

The old man strode over to the window and glanced down. He frowned, then turned back to Grayden. "You could *see* my tower?"

Grayden paused, confused. "Uh, yes. It's been standing on the border of our village for as long as anyone can remember."

"That's not possible," the man muttered. He glanced out the window again. "Are those your friends down there?"

"Yes."

"And they can see my tower, too?"

"Sir, everyone can see the tower. Why wouldn't we be able to?"

"Why, indeed?" the man muttered. He stood there, silent and brooding.

Grayden glanced back at the gleaming orb. It called to him, and he leaned closer... closer... A blue light flashed and the old man whirled about.

"Do not touch that!" he shouted.

Grayden jumped and snatched his half-outstretched hand back. The orb shone brightly with a sudden inner light. The old man strode to the table and snatched up the orb protectively. Blue light poured through his fingers. Then he peered into the gleaming blue surface and a shock of fear skittered across his face.

"What have you done?" he asked in a low voice.

"I... I'm not sure I know what you mean, sir?" Grayden replied, glancing to the window, gauging how swiftly he could escape.

"Look at it!" The man thrust the orb forward. The blue surface swirled with tiny hairline fractures of orange and red.

Grayden gazed into it, then glanced up again. "Please... sir... I don't understand."

"Those red lines should not be there. What did you do?"

"I didn't do anything," Grayden protested, his voice trembling. "I didn't even touch it. Look, I'm sorry for intruding. I'll leave now."

"Oh, no, you don't," the man warned softly, no longer intimidating, now simply weary. "It may not be your fault, young Grayden, but you're caught up in it now. I must find out what is happening"—he paused and his eyes darted to the window—"out there."

Grayden followed the old man down the steps and emerged from the base of the tower into the purple twilight. On the air wafted the scent of wood smoke; the bonfire had been lit. He could barely muster any amusement at the shocked and worried expressions on his friends' faces as he and the old man came through the hidden door.

"Who..." Wynn was the first to speak, his expression full of confusion, but he broke off when he saw his friend. "Grayden! We were worried..." He blinked, glancing back and forth between the two figures.

Grayden shrugged. "He hasn't said much."

The five friends all took a moment to study the man who had

come out of the tower with Grayden. He was tall: head and shoulders taller than Master Farley, the tallest man in the village. His shoulders were broader than Master Elhearn's, the village leatherworker. He wore a thin, threadbare cloak over a plain tunic belted at the waist and much-patched trousers. His boots were clearly of good leather, but well-worn. The man had a long, narrow face out of which gleamed piercing blue eyes. A white beard hung from his chin nearly to his waist, and long white hair flowed down over his shoulders. The most intimidating thing about him, however, was the massive broadsword strapped to his hip.

"I suppose you can all see my tower, too." The man's voice was deep and clear, not the voice of an old man, though he was clearly disgruntled.

The others studied Grayden as if to check if the question was serious.

"Uh... yes," Burke answered. "Gray, what on Turrim?"

Grayden shrugged again, as at a loss as his friends. "I have no idea."

The man heaved a weary sigh and suddenly he hunched over and seemed to age all at once. "I am Dalmir," the man said, catching their gazes and holding them. His eyes swam with ancient knowledge and secrets. Grayden held the man's gaze for as long as he could, but in the end, he had to look away. Wynn stared down at his own feet, refusing to look up. Dalmir stared at him for a long moment, and then, as though he could feel the eyes on him, Wynn turned and bolted away, through the trees. The others gazed after him, and Grayden felt they were all secretly wishing they could do the same.

"He's probably gone to alert the town elders," Ailwen said.

"Take me to these elders," Dalmir said, his voice soft and yet full of authority.

"This way." Grayden motioned, and his gesture set the rest of his friends free from whatever spell had held them motionless. Together, they set off toward the village, their feet padding softly along the grassy path.

8

"Well?" Marik looked up as Raisa reined her malkyn to a sudden stop. She slid off the giant cat's back and landed in a cloud of dust. Oleck handed her a canteen, and she took a long draught before answering.

"It's what we were told to expect," she replied, wiping her mouth on her sleeve. "Ten fighting leythan, each with a lancer at their heads and each bearing a rider, followed by fifty swordsmen on foot and a train of three wagons, covered in plated armor and being drawn by a team of six leythan. There are three soldiers with each wagon, all fully armed. I couldn't tell if anyone was inside the wagons. They're half a day's ride away, and will most likely reach the canyon just as the sun sets. I stopped and informed Shaesta as I passed."

Marik nodded. Shaesta was their secondary lookout, hidden in a small copse of trees at the western entrance to the canyon. Her job was to alert the rest of the crew as soon as the caravan entered the ravine.

"That's what we planned for," Marik said. "They will enter the canyon with the sun at their backs. They won't want to camp in the pass. The officers will push the men to make it to the other side before sunset, which is good for us. Does everyone know the plan?"

There were a few nods. Faces were tight and grim.

"Excellent," Marik said. "Most of you have worked with me before and you know the routine. This job requires a bit more maneuvering, but if everything goes well, we can stop the caravan, lighten their load considerably, and be on our way with no bloodshed. Understood?"

"Any more questions?" Oleck called out. "Or can we get moving?"

The crew before them dispersed. They knew the plan and their parts in it. Marik made his way to his chosen position and settled himself into a comfortable position where he began methodically sharpening his dagger.

The Temin Range was a small group of mountains that sprouted suddenly from the middle of the Plains of Temnia like a massive mesa. This point here, Merin Canyon, was the only pass through the Temin Range, and at only a mile long, was also the shortest route from the western mountains of Vallei to Melar, the capital city of Malei. Going around the Range would cost a caravan three days, and with the cynders that ran the airships in such short supply already, Marik had guessed rightly that the shipment would use this route.

The sun was already setting when Shaesta's whistle came to his ears, signaling that the caravan was now entering the canyon. He got to his knees and let out a low whistle of his own, letting Shaesta know he had heard her and their plan would proceed.

He quickly and expertly strung his bow and peered out from his hiding place. He had chosen a spot near the entrance on the north wall of the canyon. A few minutes passed and then came the heavy, trudging steps of the leythan. A moment after that, they came into view with a full complement of soldiers and wagons behind them.

This was the hardest part. Marik waited as the caravan leaders halted outside the mouth of the canyon. Dusk crept up over the sky, the last few rays of the sun blazing up over the horizon at the backs of the caravan, bathing the interior of the canyon in a shadowy orange glow. The sky had turned from a brilliant blue into a deep purple, with the brightest stars just winking into existence. Nocturnal insects woke, their buzzing and singing filling the air with an oddly harmonious cacophony. A cool breeze ruffled its way between the canyon walls as the caravan slowed.

"Shall we make camp here, sir?" A youthful voice pierced the silence.

"No, Deymash," a deeper voice, full of authority, replied, "there will be light enough to make it through the pass. It's only a mile. We will be through soon enough."

Marik grinned fiercely in the fading light as the orders were passed along and carried out. He counted silently as one, two, three of the leythan passed his hiding place. The creatures lumbered along, huffing loudly in the quietly fading twilight, followed by the tromping of heavy-booted soldiers. It took an eternity for the complement of soldiers to enter the ravine, followed by the other six leythan drawing the three wagons, and more soldiers. When all had passed by his hiding spot, he stepped out onto the canyon floor behind them. Unnoticed by the soldiers, who continued to march onward in blissful ignorance, Marik nocked an arrow. Taking his time, he made full use of the fading light as he sighted down the arrow toward his target. He held steady a heartbeat more, then released. Without waiting to see if it hit its mark, he drew and released a second bolt, sending it soaring at a different target.

The first missile flew straight and true, piercing into the unprotected section on the back of the lead creature's neck. The massive creature bellowed in pain and reared up on its hind legs, pawing at the air with its front claws before collapsing to the ground, its bulk blocking the path forward. A split second later, the head leythan hitched to the carts also collapsed, blocking the path back the way the regiment had come.

For a breath, all stood silent. The Igyeum soldiers drew their swords and grouped together, unsure of what had just happened, but aware of the fact that most of their fighting force was now boxed in with no easy route of escape.

From the canyon walls, a rain of fiery arrows fell around the soldiers. Most missed their targets, though they made an impressive showing, but a few hit their marks, igniting the small brush piles that had been strategically placed and primed with pitch to make them light more easily. The kindling flared up in the purple twilight, clearly revealing the soldiers in the dark canyon.

His crew targeted the other fighting leythan. Highlighted as they were by the fires, hemmed in by the narrow canyon and the carcasses of the leythan before and behind, and unable to get clear of the mass of soldiers, the beasts were easy targets and fell swiftly.

Marik stayed where he stood. "You are outnumbered, surrounded, and clearly visible to my archers," he called out. "If you don't put up a fight, there's no reason for anyone to get hurt."

"Thieves and pirates will get no surrender from us," one guard shouted.

A muttered argument emanated from behind the fallen leythan and then a new voice called out, "What are your terms?"

"Tell your archers to drop their bows and get out of the wagons," Marik shouted.

"And how do I know you won't slaughter us where we stand after you've taken what you want?"

Marik made a slight gesture, and an arrow embedded itself in the wooden cart just next to the head of the man who had spoken.

"If I wanted you dead, we wouldn't be having this conversation now," Marik said.

He watched warily as the archers in the wagons tossed their crossbows to the ground and then clambered down, arms raised. Oleck and the twins, Rustam and Yefrem, stole like foxes out of their hiding places and unharnessed the dead leythan while the rest of the beasts shifted nervously, but the soothing voices of their new handlers kept them docile. They got the creatures unhitched and walked around to the other side of the carts, where they hitched them back up. The canyon was too narrow to turn the carts around and the effort took far longer than Marik would have liked. He could feel his nerves fraying with every second that ticked past, could sense the rising tension of the soldiers, angry at the ease of their ambush and swearing oaths of vengeance under their breaths. Sweat beaded on his brow despite the cool night air. The fires that had flared so brightly to life had diminished to a feeble glow, the fuel nearly consumed.

Then the leythan were moving back the way they had come. As the carts moved past him, picking up speed, Marik caught hold of one and swung himself up and in, shouting at Oleck to drive them faster. One of the creatures snorted again and soon their steady trot had become an all-out run. A few arrows whizzed overhead, but none hit their marks, and soon they had left the soldiers far behind. The leythan couldn't hold this pace for long, but it would be enough to prevent the soldiers from being able to overtake them on foot. They could easily get out of sight and then take the time to hide their tracks as they headed to the prearranged meeting place to offload the cynders and take their cut of the spoils.

9

By the time they reached the center of the town, the elders were already waiting. Wynn was nowhere to be seen, but Grayden didn't begrudge the absence.

Master Farley strode to meet them as they entered the square. With him were Master Baines and Master Thwyll, the two oldest and wisest men in the village. His father strode next to them and Grayden took in their serious expressions.

"Grayden," Master Farley greeted him. "Wynn came racing through here and told his parents a mess of garbled nonsense. Said you had climbed the tower and brought an old man down with you. He was clearly unnerved. What happened?" He seemed to notice Dalmir for the first time and took a step back. "Who is this?"

"It wasn't nonsense, Master Farley," Grayden replied. "I did climb the tower. I always wanted to. But at the top, I discovered that this man was living there. His name is Dalmir."

Bevan Ormond blinked. "How is that possible? We've never seen anyone come out of that tower. There's never been the slightest hint that anyone was actually living up there."

Dalmir stepped forward. "Many things are possible. It is only your imagination that limits you. This boy speaks truth. I have been living at the top of that tower for... oh... many years now."

The elders exchanged glances, clearly out of their depth. Grayden marveled at seeing these respected men so at a loss.

"If this is true," Master Thwyll asked in a shaking voice, "how have you gotten food, water? How is it that no one has ever seen you?"

"My tower is well-stocked with the supplies I need," Dalmir replied evenly. "And as for you seeing me, I did not wish to be seen. I have not left my tower in a very long time."

Master Baines gave him a calculating stare. "Then why have you come down now? What do you want?"

"I want to be left alone," Dalmir snapped. The crowd of villagers drew back and the older man's shoulders slumped. "But that, as with all my desires, has been denied me. This boy"—Dalmir jabbed an accusing finger at Grayden—"has brought it to my attention that things have changed in the world since I last set foot in it. Things that should not have changed. I was given a charge, and it seems that I have failed in my duties. I must speak with you and the town elders and hear of your recent history. I must learn of what is going on in the world at large, if you know it."

Bevan shouldered his way through the crowd and stood before Dalmir. "You must do better than that. You have barged into the midst of our celebration, demanding information and claiming you've lived here for many years. But begging your pardon, sir, we don't know you."

Dalmir met Bevan's eyes for a long moment. Then the older man seemed to slump a little. "Forgive me, it has been a long time since I spoke with anyone. I mean you and yours no harm. I am a guardian, as it were, of an ancient and powerful being who would harm every living creature on Turrim without thought. For many years, I have thought my prisoner to be safely locked away. But this young man," Dalmir gestured at Grayden, "has brought to my attention that my locks may not have been as strong or as stable as I thought."

"Locks? Prisoner?" Bevan squinted.

"It is complicated," Dalmir replied, "and I do not have time to explain it all now. Suffice to say, I believe my prisoner has found a way to escape. I must learn what has allowed this and return him to his prison if I can."

Thwyll stepped forward. "We can tell you a little of what we know, but if it is truly knowledge you seek, then I would recommend you visit the library."

Dalmir flinched visibly and stepped back, his face turning a little gray. "How do you know of the Library?" he whispered.

Thwyll and the others exchanged puzzled looks. "Er... they built it at the same time they built the Academy. Few people use the library itself, but it is the largest repository of scrolls and books of knowledge in all Telmondir."

At these words, Dalmir's face regained a little of its color, but his eyes remained troubled. "Where can I find this... library?"

"Wynn and Grayden begin their journey to the Academy tomorrow morning," Bevan replied, his tone even and guarded. "The library is on the same grounds. If you truly mean no harm, perhaps you could journey with them."

Dalmir nodded at once. "I truly mean you no harm. I only wish to find out what has happened to my prisoner."

"You can stay with us for the night, if you wish," Bevan said, drawing the words out slowly. "Grayden can give up his room a night early. The boys plan to leave from our house in the morning." He glanced across the crowd and caught his son's eye. "You could ride with them to Dalton. There are airships to take you the rest of the way to Doran, but the fare is costly."

Dalmir pondered in silence, then nodded. "I accept your gracious offer. I must return to my tower to gather a few things, but I will meet you back here in one hour." He glanced about, taking in the food tables, the tents, and the decorations gleaming in the firelight. "Forgive me, I seem to have interrupted your festivities."

Master Farley waved a dismissive hand. "We can get back to our festival easily." The folks who had gathered around laughed and trickled away back to the bonfire, which was now blazing merrily.

Dalmir turned and was gone. Grayden let out his breath in a slow sigh and turned to find Wynn standing a few feet away. He raised an eyebrow and Wynn shuffled over, looking a little apologetic.

"Sorry for running off," he mumbled, not meeting Grayden's eyes. "I don't know what made me do that. It's just... that old man..." He shivered. "Guess I'll have to get over it, since he's going to be traveling with us. Maybe he'll be less intimidating in the daylight."

"Could be," Grayden agreed. He didn't feel any fear of the old man, just an irresistible curiosity. "He took me by surprise at first, too," he added, noting Wynn's downcast expression. "Looks like our adventure's starting a bit earlier than we planned."

"And working out a little differently, too," Wynn mumbled. "We didn't know we'd be traveling with anyone else."

Grayden studied his friend. "Are you all right with this?"

Wynn stared down at his feet. "I don't like it," he said eventually in a halting tone. "But it makes no sense for him not to travel with us, since we're going to the same place. And it's not like it'll count against us in the Academy policy, since we're the guides."

"We should look at it as our first mission," Grayden suggested.

Wynn brightened and the two friends wandered over to the bonfire, which no longer had flames leaping so high into the sky, but it radiated a pleasant warmth. They found the others and talked and laughed for a while, until Seren suddenly appeared at Grayden's elbow.

"Dad says we're gonna go home now," she announced. "Master Dalmir is back. But Mom said you could come later if you get a ride with the Carlins." She stared up at him, her expression wistful.

Grayden glanced at his friends, and for a brief, selfish mote of time he wanted to take his mother up on her offer. But a second look at Seren's face decided him. He squeezed her shoulder. "I'll come in a minute," he promised. "Can you tell Mom and Dad to wait while I say goodbye to a few people?"

Seren beamed and she nodded enthusiastically before dancing off. The fresh flowers she had wound into her hair that morning were wilting and falling out of her braids, but she didn't seem to notice.

Grayden turned to Wynn. "See you in the morning."

"Bright and early," Wynn replied.

"We'll miss you," Burke told him.

"Aw, I'll see you soon." Grayden punched his friend lightly in the shoulder. "Bet you get accepted into the Academy next year. They would have taken you this year if you'd been old enough."

Burke shrugged. "I hope so."

"Don't forget us, now," Hunter teased.

"Well, I might forget *you*," Grayden shot back, then enveloped both of his friends in a tackling sort of hug before they broke away laughing.

Greta went up on her tiptoes and pecked him on the cheek. "Take care of yourself." Her eyes shone in the firelight, and Grayden managed to stammer something awkward, though he wasn't sure it was intelligible.

The others drew back a bit, leaving him staring at Ailwen. Grayden's face suddenly grew warm, though not from the fire, as he remembered how earlier he had contemplated asking her to dance and perhaps stealing a kiss. Too late for that now. She smiled at him, blissfully unaware of the thoughts going through his head, and embraced him warmly. He hugged her back, awkward and shy.

"Take care of yourself, Gray," she said, stepping back and

looking up at him, her face earnest and friendly. He searched her expression, not sure what he hoped to see: a glimmer of hope that might hint at feeling beyond their years of friendship, a signal that could prompt him to say the words he had purposefully left unsaid. But there was nothing, just sincere, kind Ailwen, looking at him the same way she looked at her brother, Hunter.

"I'll try," he promised. "Goodbye, Ailwen."

He turned and walked away. Others, seeing him departing, jostled up to shake his hand and congratulate him. Grayden found himself hemmed in by the crowd, pushing his way through as against a sudden gale, then he was through, amidst a chorus of cheers and well-wishes. When he finally emerged, he saw his family waiting in the cart, with Dalmir behind them astride a magnificent bay horse Grayden recognized from Master Farley's stables. With a wave to the people behind them, Grayden clambered into the cart and settled himself next to Seren as his father clucked to the horses and they began the ride home.

Seren chattered at him happily, recounting everything she had seen and done during the Festival. Grayden listened with half an ear until her voice grew drowsy. Eventually, Seren's eyelids drooped and her head slowly drifted over to rest in his lap. He brushed a strand of hair away from her face with a fond hand, awed at her ability to fall asleep mid-sentence.

The rest of the ride home passed in comfortable silence. Grayden leaned back and stared up at the stars. The wind whistled through the long grasses and crickets chirped in the dark. A haunting melody of wolf song rose to meet the sky, and Grayden's heart swelled to bursting. Had he been a bit younger, he might have cried. It was all so heartbreakingly familiar and safe. He wondered what the nights at the Academy would sound like in far-off Ondoura. Would there be wolf song and crickets? Would he look up and see familiar constellations? Ondoura lay far to the south, and he knew the Academy itself stood much closer to the capital city. He had lived his whole life in the wide-open fields far outside a small village. Would he hear the familiar night song, or would he be closed up inside walls so thick that the outside night would be shut off from him completely? Would he even be allowed outside late enough to see the stars? The Academy had strict rules, especially for the Conspectus students.

A goodbye welled up within him and he suddenly wished that he could put off his leaving a little longer. He wished he could be content to remain in the village, a simple farmer, like his father. Why had he pushed so hard for this? Why couldn't he have been content with what he had?

A flicker of movement caught at his peripheral vision and he turned to study the man riding along silently beside the cart. Dalmir sat easily upon his horse, wrapped in a long cloak whose edges billowed gently in the breeze. Grayden felt again that strange draw, the same one he had felt pulling him to the tower his entire life. His thoughts paused. Maybe it wasn't the tower after all. Perhaps it was this strange man who had been pulling at him, tugging him, singling him out among all the others. Looking at Dalmir, Grayden realized he wouldn't turn back now even if he could. He wasn't content with never seeing the world. He wanted to experience adventure, command respect, learn things he could never learn in Dalsea. He would miss home, his family, his friends, but he ached to widen his world. Ailwen's words echoed in his memory, and he knew she was right. Perhaps he could return, one day, after learning all the Academy had to teach him, perhaps he would not. Either way, he wanted the opportunity to find out what lay beyond the borders of his world.

They arrived back at the Ormond farm. Seren woke up and helped their mother carry in the now-empty baskets and half a pie, as well as tablecloths and other items they had brought to the Festival. Grayden and his father cared for the horses, giving them a good brushing and making sure their water troughs were full. Grayden mixed them up a hot mash and stroked their soft noses. They had done a good day's work, hauling them to town and back, and he wanted to reward them. He also wanted them to know, in some small way, that he would miss them, too.

Usually, the family would spend the evening around the hearth, with Bevan reading a chapter of a book or sipping hot cider and talking together as a family, but they were all tired after a long day, so they turned in a bit early. Grayden took his few things that were not packed and made himself a pallet of blankets in the corner of Seren's room, giving up his own space for their guest.

"You want the bed, Gray?" Seren asked, standing barefoot on the cold floorboards, her long nightdress brushing the floor. She had undone her braids and her hair hung in bumpy waves about her shoulders.

"Nah, thanks, Ser. I'm good here. Mom gave me a few extra pillows. Might have to get used to it, anyway. I'll be camping for the next sennight, lying on the ground."

"Seven nights without a bed," Seren breathed. "You scared of the trip?" she asked, as she snuggled into her bed.

Grayden tucked her in, pulling the covers up around her chin. "A little," he admitted. "Never been much farther than Elricht Harbor. Never really been anywhere further than a half-day's journey in any direction."

"Never flown in an airship, either. That would scare me." Seren's eyes were wide above her covers. "What keeps them up, Gray?"

He chuckled. "Well, I'll find out and tell you when I come home next summer."

"You will?"

"Course I will."

"I'd like that." She yawned.

Grayden turned down the oil lamp and snuggled himself down onto his pallet. Blackness filled the room, along with silence. It was so quiet that Grayden thought his little sister had already fallen asleep. He rolled over to go to sleep himself when she spoke up again, her voice small in the vast night.

"Gray?"

"Yeah?"

"I'm gonna miss you."

Grayden's heart nearly broke. He crossed the room to sit on his sister's bed, wrapping his arms around her in a tight hug. Moonlight shone through the window and his eyes had now adjusted enough that he could see her face.

"Gonna miss you, too, little sister. More than anything."

She sniffled a little. "You'll send me letters?"

"As often as I can." He winked. "And a treat now and then, too, if I can find a reliable merchant to carry it."

"Really?"

"Really."

"Good." She settled herself back down on her pillow. "But... you *will* come home next summer, right, Gray?"

"Of course I will. What else would I do? Stay alone at that big empty Academy?"

"Kelsie says not everyone goes home on breaks. There's classes and things you can take even in the summers. Kelsie said you might leave and never come back, not ever." Reflected in the moonlight, Grayden saw tears gathering in her eyes. He took her hand and squeezed it.

"I'll be back. You can count on it. I don't know exactly when, Seren, I can't promise a specific date. But I can't miss seeing my little sister grow up, now, can I? Don't want you to forget all about me and start thinking you're an only child, now, do I? Gotta keep you from getting all uppity."

Seren mock-glared at him, but the glare turned into a watery smirk.

"Now, go to sleep and stop worrying," Grayden told her.

She sat back up and threw her small arms around his neck. "I love you, Grayden."

"Love you too, Ser," he whispered, hugging her back.

He returned to his mat on the floor and pulled the blankets up around his neck. Tomorrow he would be on the road. Tomorrow night he would sleep beneath the stars. The ground would be lumpy and uncomfortable, and he would most likely be too nervous to sleep, worried about predators lurking beyond the firelight. But for tonight, he was still at home, safe and surrounded by the people who loved him most. As he drifted off to sleep, his last regret was that he had not had the courage to ask Ailwen for a dance.

10

Raisa and the crew were waiting when Marik and the others arrived. They had taken care through most of the night to leave no trail behind en route to their well-hidden camp, and dawn approached rapidly.

Raisa and Oleck removed the heavy armor plating from the wagons. The steel alone made the job worth it, but Shaesta's contact intended to meet them for the cynders soon, and Marik wanted to make certain that the promised goods were actually in the carts. He clambered into the first wagon, opened a box, and began counting.

When he had finished, he stepped back out. Oleck glanced at him and the man's eyes narrowed in concern.

"Everything good, Cap'n?"

Marik did not answer, but silently checked each cart in turn. When he emerged from the final cart, he nodded to Oleck and Raisa, who joined him a few paces away from the others.

"It's a shipment of cynders, just like Shaesta's contact said." He kept his voice low. "I count forty boxes in each wagon, and there are fifty cynders in each box."

Oleck stared at him in silence. Marik could see him doing the calculations in his head. At length, he whistled. "Six thousand cynders."

Raisa's eyes widened. "Six thou... but that... that's..."

"Six times what we were told," Marik finished.

"No wonder it was so heavily guarded," Raisa breathed.

"Lot of good it did them," Oleck said.

Marik was about to continue, but a shout tore his attention away from the startling discovery. In an instant, two of his men were rolling on the ground, fists pummeling one another, fingers jabbing into eyes.

Marik waded in and pulled one combatant off the other by the collar of his shirt. "What's this, then?" he demanded.

The man he had by the collar glowered, but remained silent, a line of blood dripping down one cheek. The other one, a man Marik had never hired before, pushed himself to his feet, sputtering. "That whelp attacked me!" Already, the skin around his left eye was turning an interesting shade of purple.

"He deserved it," the younger man muttered. He spat blood onto the ground.

Marik eyed the man he had by the collar. "Egan, isn't it? You've worked with us before. Why don't you tell us what happened?"

Egan winced. "Bento here was disrespecting you, Captain. I couldn't stand by and let him say those things. He was getting the others all riled up, saying you should have killed all those soldiers last night, that leaving them alive was foolhardy and reckless. That you were soft. I told him to shut up, but he wouldn't."

"So you attacked him? A grown man twice your size?" Marik tried his best to sound disapproving.

The young man stared up at him. "I gave as good as I got."

Marik glanced at Bento and recognized the truth in his words. In addition to the black eye, Bento had a split lip and a torn shirt. He growled at Marik, his eyes like coals glowing with fiery hatred.

"I meant what I said!" he shouted. "Them soldiers don't deserve to live. After the things they done! You all know what they done. Every one of 'em." He swung himself around, meeting the eyes of everyone in the small circle with burning intensity. "They're murderers and thieves. They got blood on their hands, blood that's miles deep."

Raw pain infused the man's voice. Every word struck like a hammer blow. "They picked the wrong side, that's certain," Marik replied, his voice even. "But they're men, just like us. Some of them don't see the wrong they've done, and some try to ignore it, and a few have grown callous enough they even enjoy it. But can you tell which is which just by lookin'? You work on my crew, Bento, you follow my rules. Everyone knows my reputation. You knew what you were signing up for when you took this job. If killin' is your pleasure, you're in the wrong place."

Bento stood there for a long moment, his gaze digging into Marik's, blood dripping down his chin. The hatred in his eyes was threaded with palpable grief, and Marik wondered briefly who the man had lost. Then Bento broke his gaze and stomped off, muttering thickly under his breath.

"Don't hire that one again," Marik said in a quiet undertone to Oleck.

They fed and watered the leythan and after Raisa and Oleck had double-checked Marik's count of the cynders, they made camp for what was left of the night. When dawn broke a few hours later, Marik and his crew hitched up the carts once more and made their way north as quickly as they could convince the beasts to move. Trained leythan could be a terror to face in battle, but these were more domesticated and Marik was glad they were merely pack animals, and not the ones trained for war.

Even though the lighter wagons and smaller group meant they could move faster than the soldiers had, it still took the pirates a full day and a half to reach the appointed destination. They pulled to a stop in front of an enormous, burned-out blacksmith's forge. Behind the forge was a large amount of charred rubble that appeared to be the remains of a fairly sizable house. Marik and his crew approached the ruined edifice warily. The wreckage had weeds and ivy growing up through it. Clearly, the place had been abandoned for many years.

"You are punctual." The rough voice filled the yard and a tall man with deep-set brown eyes and short silver hair stepped out from behind a partially fallen wall. He wore plain gray clothing and deep wrinkles lined his face.

Shadowing the older man was a giant who looked like he could pick Marik up and break him in half without exerting himself in the slightest.

The older man continued talking. "Shaesta, always a pleasure to see you again." He surveyed the crew and caravan arrayed before him. "Well, shall we inspect the cargo?"

"They're all there in the wagon. All six thousand units," Marik said.

The man blinked. "Hmm."

"We counted every box."

The man made a slight gesture, and the giant moved forward toward the wagons and made a brief inspection of the interiors. After a few minutes, he turned and gave a silent nod.

"Mathwe here says that your count is accurate." The old man's eyes were alight with excitement and he rubbed his hands together. "This is a cause for celebration."

"Are we done?" Marik asked. Now that the job was done, he struggled against his natural impatience with the finer details of payment and congratulations. He itched to be on his way.

"Not quite," the man replied. Five more tall, broad-shouldered men, each one larger and stronger-looking than the last, stepped out from behind the ruins.

The skin on the back of Marik's neck prickled, and his hand automatically went to the hilt of his sword. "What's this?"

"Nothing, nothing. Forgive me for startling you. I have heard many stories about you, Captain, and how is a man to know which is true? Your exploits are well known, but your character is not. A certain amount of, shall we say, secrecy, surrounds you. It is only natural that I should come prepared to defend myself should the need arise."

Marik eyed the bodyguards warily. "And revealing your men now?"

"Means that I feel no need to keep them in reserve."

"And that is supposed to put me at ease?"

The man chuckled, and the bodyguards made no move to attack. Marik, however, did not release his grip on his sword.

"That won't be necessary, Captain. We are safe in each other's company."

"How could you possibly know that?"

"You could have concealed the true number of cynders you claimed from the caravan, only bringing the requested one thousand, and yet you did not." The man's lips curved up slightly. "You took on a fairly dangerous job for an agreed upon fee, and you ask nothing more. I find that unusual and worthy of trust."

Marik felt his guard relax slightly. He did not like the sensation, and tightened his fist, studying the man before him, trying to take his measure. He was well-dressed and the way he spoke suggested education beyond that normally provided in rural villages or towns.

"You have nothing to fear from me." The older man spoke again. "You may have your crew remove six hundred of the cynders as your payment."

A shock coursed through Marik at this unexpected extravagance. "Why so generous?"

The man chuckled to himself. "Let us just say that I believe integrity deserves reward. The original deal was one hundred cynders for one thousand. That is ten percent. I am simply honoring the spirit of our arrangement." He gestured to his men, who moved toward the last wagon and began removing boxes and redistributing them to the front two. The older man fixed Marik with a thoughtful gaze. "You'll need at least one of the leythan to haul your portion, I think, as it is more than you expected."

Marik, for one of the few times in his life, felt overwhelmed. "My thanks," he managed to mutter.

The five bodyguards had made short work of their task, and now the final wagon held twelve boxes with a single leythan hitched to it. The beast munched lazily on the branches of a nearby bush.

"And now, I think, our business is concluded," the man said. He swung himself up onto the cart. One bodyguard flicked the reins, and the four leythan strained at their harnesses, pulling the cart out of the clearing, through the trees, and out of sight.

Marik watched them go, a sensation of wary wonder flooding his soul. At last, he turned to his crew. "Well, you know the split. Take your shares and take care. Deadly people will notice if cynders suddenly show up in the market, so be patient. I am always in need of cynders and can give you a fair price. You know how to reach me."

Six of the hired-on crew opted to take their earnings and leave. Their eyes gleamed as they retrieved their crates and headed off on their own. Rustam and Yefrem alone joined Marik and his crew on the cart.

"How come I don't get a crate of my own?" Mouse's voice piped up as the cart wheels turned, carrying them back toward Olmei.

"What?" Marik looked up at the boy riding on the wagon. Mouse's blue eyes peeked accusingly over the rim of the wagon at him.

"The crates of cynders. You said every member of the crew would get one. But there's only six left, but there's seven of us."

"What would you do with a crate of cynders?" Marik asked, curious to see how the boy would answer.

Mouse's mouth worked silently for a long minute, his brow furrowed in concentration. Then he looked up and beamed. "I'd use it to power the *Hawk.*"

Marik chuckled. "Then you can have one of my cynders."

Mouse glanced at him sideways. "What? Really? Why?"

"That's what I was going to use them for, too."

Mouse seemed to consider that. Then his eyes lit up. "Thanks, Captain!"

Marik turned and saw Raisa, Shaesta, and Oleck all listening with eyes gleaming. Shaesta glanced at Raisa and Marik saw a stricken expression in her eyes. He wondered at it, but a moment later her face smoothed and the expression disappeared. He frowned.

"Shay? You all right?"

"Hmm? Oh, yes." She smiled brightly at him. "I was just thinking about what you said to Mouse. He's a lucky kid."

Marik watched her out of the corner of his eye. "Why do you say that?"

"He's got you looking out for him," Shaesta replied simply.

"We should head home," Marik said, his throat tight, unable to reply to Shaesta's comment. "We've got another job to prepare for and we need parts to fix the *Hawk*. Then we're headed to Dalton."

11

Morning dawned bright, cool, and clear. A breeze gusted as Grayden stepped outside. The chill air greeted him, not quite frosty, but enough to make him bundle up against the cold and pull his cloak tightly around himself as he went out to get the horses ready for their journey. The Academy had supplied mounts for him and Wynn, though they were not theirs to keep.

Dalmir sat at the table when Grayden returned from the stable.

“Biscuits and eggs for breakfast, Gray,” Dara said. “Your last home-cooked meal for a while, but I figured you’d want something you could eat quickly.”

Grayden smiled his thanks around the lump swelling in his throat. “Thanks, Ma,” he said thickly.

“Thought I heard Wynn arrive,” Bevan said, stomping mud off his feet in the doorway. “Tell him to wash up and come in for breakfast.”

“I’m sure his mother fed him before he left,” Dara said, her tone reproving.

“Would it matter if it were Grayden?” Bevan asked, a twinkle in his eye as he wrestled off his boots.

Dara considered. "You're right. I'll put more eggs on. Maybe you could get me a slice of ham from the smokehouse."

Bevan gave his boots a mournful stare, then sighed ruefully and wedged his feet back into them, tromping toward the smokehouse without protest. Grayden pulled on his own boots and made his way to the stable where Wynn was already in a stall, loosening his horse's girth strap so the animal could eat and drink a bit.

"Morning," Wynn grumbled, looking a little bleary-eyed even after the ride from his family's home.

"Good morning," Grayden replied. "You excited?"

"It's too early to be anything other than sleeping."

"It's a beautiful day, we're about to start off on our first real adventure, and you're not even a little excited? You can't make me believe that."

"You sound chipper," Wynn grumbled.

"You're not having second thoughts about the Academy?" Grayden teased.

"No..." Wynn shot him a confused look. "Why?"

"You know the schedule they keep," Grayden replied. "Mornings are as early there as on a farm, probably even earlier."

Wynn grimaced. "It's not the earliness of the morning, it's the lateness of the night. My brothers and sisters kept me up until nearly dawn."

Grayden laughed. Wynn was the second oldest of eight, and the others were all far more energetic than the studious Wynn.

"It's not funny," Wynn complained. "I was so late getting up I barely had time to eat any of the food my mother had waiting for me in the kitchen this morning."

"Come on in." Grayden gestured to the house. "Ma's got biscuits and eggs on and there's plenty. Dad's even getting more smoked ham. A few more bites of breakfast won't delay us much."

Wynn brightened considerably and followed Grayden to the pump, where they washed their hands before entering the house.

After a meal that ended far too swiftly, everyone trooped out to the stable where Grayden saddled his and Dalmir's horses, while Wynn attended to his own mount. Bevan helped Grayden affix his saddlebags, filled to the brim with clothing and food. Then he put a hand on Grayden's shoulder and produced a small, thin package wrapped in brown paper as his mother joined them.

"Your mother wasn't so sure about this, and I know it's not the most sentimental of gifts," his father said, "but you'll be traveling through big cities and across quite a bit of open road. I know you've got your sword from the Academy, and that Master Farley's taught you the basics with it, but this will be a touch more familiar, and I thought perhaps it might come in useful."

Grayden unwrapped the small package and gazed at the long knife that lay inside the brown paper. He lifted it by its leather-bound hilt and hefted it. It fit snugly in his hand and he could tell it was weighted perfectly for throwing, a skill he had honed since he was a small boy. The deceptive simplicity of the blade belied its worth, and Grayden was too overcome for words. He tucked it inside the sheath nestled in the packaging and wrapped his arms around his parents in an embrace that spoke volumes.

"I packed some extra biscuits and cookies into your bags," his mother said, her voice soft.

"One last thing, son." Bevan thrust a thin package into Grayden's hand. "Just some thoughts I wrote down. Things I want to say, things I want you to know. Much of it, you probably already know, but I thought maybe after you get to the Academy, if you need a few words from home, it might be nice to have them."

Grayden blinked, his eyesight suddenly blurred. Seren barreled into his legs and he leaned down to give her a proper hug, glad of the distraction.

Then it was time to go. Bevan gave them a few last-minute reminders about staying close to the river and not leaving the road or trying for shortcuts.

"You'll get there soon enough, and if you get delayed for any reason, well, that's why they tell you to leave for Dalton early," Bevan concluded.

Grayden nodded, then lifted Seren in his arms and gave her a big hug. She buried her face in his shoulder and he could tell that she was trying to hide her tears. He handed her over to their father, and Seren curled up in Bevan's arms, resting her face against his chest and gazing mournfully at Grayden.

"I'll miss you, squirt." Grayden ruffled her hair. She didn't even protest this, but sniffled and nodded.

The three travelers mounted their horses and started their journey, heading north and east to the great city where they would board an airship and fly the rest of the way to the Academy.

THE ROAD to Dalton followed the Emelda River in a flat, easy terrain that only wound in gentle curves. It would take them a sennight to get to the city, where they would spend approximately three days before boarding the airship. While the flying contraptions had become prevalent in the past several decades, they did not always run on a consistent schedule. The airships could travel much faster than a rider on horseback, which meant the journey to Dalton was worth the few extra days, even if it did lie in the opposite direction from the Academy. The flight itself would take two days, which was a considerable improvement over the lunat-or-more-long journey a direct line from Dalsea would have been by horse.

Grayden knew Wynn was a little nervous and queasy about the idea of flying in an airship, but all Grayden felt was excitement. He had always wanted to fly, and he secretly hoped to become an airship pilot. If he could score high enough on his exams, he could get into that specialized program. The prospect of his first flight only filled him with great anticipation.

The first day of travel was quiet. Dalmir's presence cast a pall over their journey, though neither Wynn nor Grayden could have said why. They rode in subdued silence, and Grayden felt their journey had somewhat more momentous import than it had when they were just two young men headed off to the Academy. Now they were also guides and protectors for this elderly stranger, though, if Grayden were honest with himself, he half-suspected that Dalmir was the most likely in their group to hold his own in a fight. The man carried the enormous broadsword as though he knew how to use it.

They stopped and led their horses down the riverbank to water them throughout the day and ate a simple meal along the road. As the shadows lengthened and the sky grew dim, they drew to a halt. Dalmir indicated a grassy clearing as a good place to camp.

It took a little while to set up their camp, unrolling bedrolls, digging a pit for the fire, watering the horses, and replenishing their own canteens. Grayden untacked the horses, struggling a bit more than he expected with Wynn's saddlebags.

"What did you pack in here?" he asked, lugging the bags over to a tree.

Wynn shrugged. "Just what the scout recommended."

"Then why are your bags so much heavier than mine?" Grayden demanded.

Wynn looked up from where he was laying out the bedrolls, a sheepish look on his face. "I couldn't leave behind all my books and designs," he admitted.

"You brought your portfolios?" Grayden asked.

"Not all of them." Wynn's tone grew a little defensive. "Just the most recent ones. And my biography of Shurik Medvev, and that volume that Master Daegan released earlier this year; I haven't had a chance to read it yet. He's the most brilliant mind of our time."

"You know they'll have books at the library, right?" Grayden teased.

Wynn's face grew a little dreamy. "Yes." His eyes glistened. "I think that's what I'm looking forward to the most."

Grayden laughed and finished caring for the horses. When they had finished getting the campsite ready, they foraged in a nearby stand of timber for firewood, partially to be helpful and partially to escape the oppressive silence hovering around Dalmir. As they got inside the trees, they felt more cheerful and less cautious.

"What do you think of him?" Wynn jerked his head toward the campsite.

"I dunno," Grayden replied. "He's not much for talking, is he?"

"I'd say! Has he said a word to you since last night?"

Grayden shook his head. "Other than responding when we call a stop for water, I don't think so. He spoke to my parents this morning, but I didn't hear what they were talking about."

"Too bad. It's weird, I can't think of a thing to say when I'm near him," Wynn mused.

"That's weird?" Grayden teased. "You don't exactly converse easily with anyone, you know."

Wynn threw a fake punch at his friend's shoulder and missed.

"You know what I mean, though," Wynn continued after a minute.

"Yeah, I do. Right now I've got about a million questions I'd like to ask him, but I know as soon as I'm back at the camp I won't be able to think of one of them," Grayden said.

They finished gathering firewood and returned to the campfire. Dalmir sat on a log, staring intensely into the small blaze he had managed to start with what sticks lay about in the clearing. Wynn and Grayden set down their pile of wood, and, having nothing else to say to each other in Dalmir's brooding presence, they bedded down for the night. Wynn was asleep almost immediately, but Grayden tossed and turned, unable to relax or get comfortable. After a long while, he sat up and saw Dalmir still poking the fire with a stick. Cautiously, Grayden rose and approached the older man. As he drew closer, he saw that Dalmir was staring into that strange glass ball that had been on the table in his tower. Grayden paused, more uncertain than ever about joining him. Looking too closely at the shimmering orb had already gotten him into trouble once. He paused, gripped with indecision. He had half resolved to return to his blankets when Dalmir looked up.

"You want me to tell you about this?" He held up the glittering jewel.

Grayden hesitated. "I couldn't sleep."

"I almost never sleep."

Grayden scrambled out of his blankets and joined the older man on the log. He held his hands out to the fire and the warmth crept pleasantly across his skin.

"What is it?" he asked, shrugging a shoulder at the orb.

"This object is too complicated for me to explain it well or briefly. Suffice to say that it is a warning."

"A warning about what?"

"That is the question."

Grayden waited, curiosity simmering, but held his tongue. Long experience as Wynn's friend had taught him to stay silent and wait for answers. At length, Dalmir sighed and offered him the orb. Grayden's eyebrows shot up, but when the older man nodded encouragement, he took the proffered jewel. It was heavy in his hand, heavier than he had expected for so small an object. Holding it, he realized it was nowhere near as delicate as it appeared.

"Do you see those red lines?" Dalmir asked, pointing at the spidery lines that resembled tiny fractures across the surface.

"Yes, you mentioned them in the tower," Grayden reminded him. "You said they shouldn't be there."

"Ah, yes, I had forgotten."

"What do they mean?"

"That is a long story."

"Oh." Disappointment curled at the edges of his thoughts,

but Grayden stared into the orb, trying to be satisfied with this small amount of conversation.

Dalmir raised a speculative eyebrow, and in the firelight his face seemed shadowed with ancient secrets. “How to explain? This orb is how I keep tabs on an enemy I imprisoned many years ago. If the surface remains blue, I can rest assured all is well. If red lines appear on the surface, that means my prison is failing.”

“So… it’s magic?”

Dalmir let out a hoarse guffaw. “There’s no such thing as magic.” His voice was bitter as he plucked the orb out of Grayden’s hand and tucked it away. “You should try to sleep.”

Grayden returned to his bedroll, his thoughts spinning. The blue orb winked at him in his mind as he wondered what it would be like to travel by airship and what his life at the Academy would be like and what enemy Dalmir meant. His thoughts mingled together with the crackling of the fire and the symphony of the night bugs until he eventually drifted into a sleep troubled by strange and fretful dreams.

12

"I would like to know more about this Academy we're headed to."

Dalmir's voice broke through the morning silence that had been reigning since the three travelers had broken camp. Wynn and Grayden shared a startled glance.

"Well, sir," Grayden began.

"Please, just call me Dalmir." The man's voice sounded weary. "It makes me feel less old."

"Very well, Dalmir," Grayden said, the name tasting strange and uncomfortable in his mouth. "What do you wish to know?"

"Everything," Dalmir replied. "Start at the beginning. When was it built? Which country created it? How are students accepted?"

Grayden rode in silence, digesting the question. "The beginning," he mused. "Well, the ruins were discovered after the Treaty of Telmondir—"

"The Treaty of what?" Dalmir interrupted.

"Telmondir," Wynn supplied. "You know, the treaty that was signed between the three western regions: Telsuma, Dalma, and Ondoura?"

"Telmondir." Dalmir stretched the word out as though

chewing a particularly tough piece of meat. "I had not heard of that. Why was a treaty necessary?"

Wynn looked at him sideways. "How long have you been in that tower?" he asked. "We studied that in the first year of school."

Dalmir pressed his lips together.

Wynn cleared his throat and blurted, "There was a war. A big one. Not here. It happened in the three eastern regions. Clans were rising up and attacking their neighbors, alliances were being created and broken faster than our spies could report. In the books at school, it's called the Time of Madness. It wasn't just regular factions fighting; this was a real bid for power."

Grayden interjected, "Eventually, one faction came out on top. They had this leader, called himself the Ar'Mol, and he was always one step ahead of everyone else. It was like he knew his enemies' strategies in advance. Anyway, he kept winning. Eventually, he had enough of the other clans and warlords conquered that he declared himself ruler over Palla, Malei, and Vallei. He renamed his kingdom the Igyeum and the kings of the West got a bit nervous, you know?"

"They thought maybe they should prepare to defend against an invasion," Wynn took over. "So they talked to their advisors and eventually gathered for a council to discuss the potential threat. It took lunats, nearly a year, but they came to an agreement and signed the Treaty of Telmondir."

"And what was in this treaty?" Dalmir asked.

Grayden shrugged, sharing an incredulous glance with Wynn. "It ended up being pretty basic, for how long it took to write. Mostly, it was just a lot of stuff about how the three kings were agreeing to regard each other as friends and allies. They swore to never attack each other, to respect each other's borders, and gave their oath to send help if anyone outside the treaty attacked any of them."

"Like the Ar'Mol," Dalmir said.

"Exactly," Wynn confirmed.

"I see." Dalmir fell silent. He shook himself. "I want to hear more, but we should probably pick up the pace for a bit."

They kicked their horses into a trot, and conversation halted. They spent the rest of the day alternating between walking, trotting, and a faster, league-eating canter. Dalmir asked no more questions, but the strange silence that had coalesced around the group had broken and Grayden and Wynn no longer felt any compulsion to remain silent.

The rest of their second day on the road passed in quiet contemplation. Grayden found he had plenty of time to think. As they rode, he considered his life so far and wondered what the future held. He had now traveled farther from home than he had ever been before, and he wondered at his rising excitement. Though he had trained and worked hard to be chosen for the Academy, he had expected to be more wistful about leaving home so far behind.

"Grayden, did you ever believe we'd travel so far from Dalsea?" Wynn's voice broke Grayden out of his pondering.

"I was just thinking about that," he replied. "Do you remember that trip to Elricht Harbor?"

"I still can't believe my parents let me go with you."

"If I close my eyes, sometimes I can smell the sea."

Wynn wrinkled his nose. "I just remember the stench of the goat stall next to us, and how the rug merchant your father was sharing a booth with complained every day about the reek of goats getting into his wares."

They both laughed at the memory.

"Elricht Harbor is the biggest city I've ever been to," Grayden mused. "The first couple of days were so overwhelming. I remember thinking I'd never get used to the scent of fish."

"I remember being constantly worried about getting lost, or crushed by all the people," Wynn said.

There had been so many people. Grayden remembered the sweltering heat of the late autumn days, and the crush of people in the market. He remembered gazing longingly at the sea and wishing he could go out on one of the ships moored in the harbor, out toward the horizon and far away from the shouting of the merchants and the babble of voices demanding fair prices and seeking wares.

Evenings had been better, though. The crowds thinned out as the booths shut down. The noise of a thousand conversations subsided, leaving a kind of peace behind. It wasn't the peaceful song of home—crickets and frogs and the wind rustling through the orchards—but it still brought relief.

His horse shook its head, making the leather and metal fasteners jangle slightly, pulling Grayden back to the present. The open road stretched out before them, with the river winding along beside them like a velvet ribbon beneath the darkening sky. Far off on the horizon, a harvest moon rose above the hills and hung in a blaze of orange glory, signaling to the travelers that it was time to make camp.

Grayden swung down from his horse, tired and sore from two days in the saddle. His companions seemed to feel the same, for they quietly cared for their horses, set up camp, ate a cold meal, and bedded down without conversation.

Later that night, Grayden lay in his bedroll, staring up at the glittering stars, and let his mind drift home. The lunats ahead stretched before him, as endless and cold as the night sky. A choking sensation welled within his throat as he pictured his parents and little Seren. An ache clutched at his heart and the stars blurred as his eyes grew damp. He blinked and clutched at the dagger his father had given him, clinging to it the way a small child might cling to his mother's skirts.

THE NEXT MORNING, while walking their horses, Dalmir rode up between the boys. "So, the Council met and signed the treaty. What happened next?" he asked.

The question caught Grayden by surprise, and he shared a

startled look with Wynn before remembering the subject of conversation from the previous day.

"Er, nothing, really," Grayden stammered, finding his tongue. "At least, not for a while. After they signed the treaty, the kings returned to their respective countries, and everyone sort of waited to see what the Ar'Mol would do next."

"And?"

"He didn't seem to be doing anything. There were rumors everywhere, but no evidence. After a year of waiting, King Arthfael of Dalma sent a spy into the Igyeum to gather information and bring back word on whether the Ar'Mol was planning an invasion."

Wynn interjected, "The spy's name was Talbot. He spent lunats traveling from Dalma down across the Broken Wall and through the Randeau Mountains. He crossed the river Temnia and then set out to cross the southern plains of Temsa. The journey took him many lunats, but he finally arrived in one of the Ar'Mol's camps in Malei in the dead of winter. He was bone weary and on the brink of starvation because his supplies had run out and he'd been forced to live on what he could beg or forage, but he never stopped until he reached his destination."

"When he arrived, he found that the Ar'Mol was building a palace in Melar," Grayden said.

"But that wasn't all," Wynn practically shouted. "They were building something else, something Talbot couldn't even begin to understand. It scared him. He stayed in Melar for nearly a year, watching and gathering information. When he finally returned to Dalma, he brought with him a strange report."

"What was it?" Dalmir leaned forward in his saddle.

Grayden took over. "You have to understand, the Igyeum had been at war with itself for nearly three hundred years. Unlike Telmondir, which had experienced centuries of peace, the eastern regions had been tearing themselves apart. While we were building cities out of wood and stone, the people of the Igyeum lived a nomadic lifestyle. Mud huts and tents were the most permanent structures they had. And yet..."

"And yet they were building this huge thing," Wynn interjected. "Talbot returned to Dalma and King Arthfael with news that the Ar'Mol was constructing something incredible. Talbot could barely describe it, but he had discovered that it would be a sort of transportation device. They were building a giant road for it, set a hundred feet in the air on massive stilts. The device was made of steel with giant wheels attached to each other by huge metal straps. None of it was close to being finished, even by the time Talbot returned, but he insisted it would be operational within a few years. However, the most disturbing thing about his story was that Talbot insisted that the thing would be powered by magic."

"What?" Dalmir's voice resounded loudly in the quiet morning air.

"Magic," Grayden repeated.

Dalmir's face darkened and his expression grew furious. His eyes blazed and one hand moved as though reaching for his broadsword. Then he kicked his horse and cantered ahead without another word. Grayden and Wynn shared a shocked look.

"What'd I say?" Grayden asked.

"I dunno." Wynn looked mystified. "Was he angry?"

Grayden shook his head. "He sure looked it."

"Think we should go catch him?" Wynn asked. "Find out what's wrong?"

Grayden eyed his friend. Wynn wasn't known for his tact. "Let's just follow at a discreet distance for now."

Wynn shrugged. "If you say so."

They urged their mounts into a steady trot, but hung back from Dalmir for the rest of the day.

13

The following morning, Wynn groaned loudly as they mounted up. "I had no idea how weak my back and ankles are. You'd think those muscles would be pretty strong, from, you know, standing up every day, but they're not!"

Grayden couldn't even muster a smile at his friend's joke. "It's my shoulders and neck." He grimaced, reaching his hand around to dig his fingers into a muscle, trying to work out the kink that had developed. "But I think part of my problem is that I slept on a rock last night. I was too sore to notice it, though."

Dalmir chuckled and shook his head, swinging up onto his horse without a trace of stiffness. Grayden frowned at the older man's back, but followed suit without comment, grateful that Dalmir had lost his angry look of the day before.

The road now turned away from the river and they spent the morning in a long, slow climb out of the valley. When they finally emerged from the deep bowl in which they had been traveling, Dalmir, who led the way, reined his horse to a sudden stop. Wynn and Grayden pulled up next to him, staring in silent awe at the view that greeted them.

"I can't believe I'm finally seeing it," Wynn breathed.

"It's huge." A sensation of falling gripped Grayden as he

stared at the massive structure ahead of them. "Way bigger than I imagined."

The structure jutted up from the landscape like a massive pier. A hundred feet above their heads, parallel iron beams attached to one another by massive wooden planks stretched off in either direction, disappearing beyond either horizon. The road above them curved with the road upon which they stood, mirroring its path and supported by soaring colonnades every several hundred paces. The sight of it took his breath away.

"What is it?" Dalmir's voice was tight, and Grayden glanced at him sideways.

"Er... it's the train road. We'll be traveling next to it for the remainder of the journey." He wondered how the older man could have missed recognizing what stood before them. It was an iconic landmark, and the fact that they had reached it so quickly said they were making exceptionally good time.

"The what?" Dalmir asked.

"The train road." Grayden floundered, unsure of how else to describe it. "The... you know... the road they built for the trains to drive on."

There was a long pause, and then Dalmir turned to Grayden. Speaking slowly, as though to a small child, Dalmir asked, "And what, exactly, is a train?"

Grayden's mouth opened and closed several times as his mind reeled beneath the absurdity of such a question. Eventually, he gathered his thoughts enough to stammer, "It's like a cart... but bigger. And... and it doesn't need horses to pull it."

"Way bigger than a cart," Wynn said. "And usually there are several of them strung together. My Da rode on one when he was young—right before they stopped using the trains—he said he'd never forget it. He used to tell us stories about his travels, and he always said riding in the train was like riding a thunderstorm. He said the part you rode in was like being inside a giant covered wagon, except it was all made of metal. I used to have a toy version of one, but it didn't run."

"It ran after you got done tinkering with it," Grayden said.

"Yeah... that gave me a bit of trouble until I figured out..."

"How long has it been here?" Dalmir demanded, cutting into Wynn's memories.

"About a hundred and fifty years," Wynn answered. "Give or take. It went up around 810, but they stopped running the trains about... oh... twenty years ago."

"That's what Talbot saw the Ar'Mol building. The report he brought back described the trains," Grayden added.

He braced himself for the quiet anger he had seen in Dalmir's eyes the day before at the mention of magic. Instead, Dalmir's shoulders slumped and his face drained of color, turning a sickly gray. He shook his head from side to side, his expression one of extreme weariness. After a long moment, he urged his horse forward, leaving the boys to follow behind him, their eyes still studying the great wonder of the world that was the train road.

When they caught up to Dalmir, he did not speak. He kept his eyes fixed on the road ahead, his jaw set with anger. And yet, as Grayden threw surreptitious glances at the man, he saw something else shadowed in his expression: a sorrow that hinted at something so painful, so elemental in its rawness, that it made Grayden's heart ache in sympathy.

The day passed in uncomfortable silence. As the shadows blended into the darkness of night, the travelers found themselves entering Barghei, the first of the outlying villages surrounding Dalton.

Grayden strained his eyes, trying to see a glimpse of the city in the distance, but the lack of light and the cramped construction of Barghei's buildings obstructed any view of the mountain-city beyond.

They found a clean inn and bartered for dinner and a room. The innkeeper, a sallow-skinned woman with a pinched face, eyed them suspiciously until Grayden produced his letter of acceptance to the Academy. After that, the woman's manner became courteous as she hastened to order her serving lads and lasses to see to their horses and bring them supper.

Grayden, weary from days of travel and overwhelmed by the sudden onslaught of human interaction after the quiet of the road, turned in early. He thought he would fall asleep immediately, but lying on his straw pallet, he found it difficult to quiet his mind without the comforting melody of the wind and the occasional popping of the fire soothing him to sleep. He tossed and turned restlessly for a long while before finally drifting into unconsciousness.

In the morning, Grayden woke to find Dalmir already gone from their room. He woke Wynn, who snarled at him blearily, but cheered up considerably when Grayden mentioned heading back to the common area for breakfast. The young men washed up and made their way to where they saw Dalmir at the counter talking to the innkeeper. They took the table nearest the fire, for the morning air held a chill upon its back. A girl brought them two steaming bowls of porridge laced with cinnamon, brown sugar, and small bits of apple. It wasn't as good as Dara's cooking, but it was a sight better than anything they'd had on the road.

"I'm ready to be done with this portion of our journey," Wynn commented over his bowl.

"Hmm?" Grayden quirked an eyebrow at his friend. "But you were so excited about traveling and seeing things we'd never seen before."

"Well..." Wynn tapped his spoon on the rim of his bowl. "It's different than I expected." His eyes darted around the room, seeming to cringe at every stranger's face. "I miss my workshop."

"I miss home, too," Grayden replied.

Wynn pulled a handful of parts out of his pocket, arranging them on the table. His spoon continued to beat a rhythm on the rim of his bowl. *Tap! Tap-tap-tap. Tap!* His free hand danced through the bits and pieces, sorting them by type: screws, bolts, washers, nails, a tiny coil of thin wire.

Grayden ate his porridge slowly, his thoughts tumbling

together, kept in time by Wynn's drumbeat. He wondered what Dalmir had found to discuss at such length with the innkeeper. He considered the various travelers sharing the common room with them, trying to gauge what each individual's business might be by the clothes they wore or the way they held themselves at their tables. The tapping paused as Wynn took a bite of porridge, then continued while he chewed and swallowed. Grayden's thoughts drifted home. His mother would be in the kitchen, cleaning up after an early breakfast, while his father headed out to the orchards to check the apples. In a few weeks, mother and Seren would join him for the early harvesting. Soon, as the weather grew cooler, they would hire half the town for the job of picking apples. The Ormonds would host a celebration at the end of the picking as a thank-you to their neighbors. The house and yard would overflow with people. There would be apple pies and homemade bread slathered with apple butter. The children would get the first piping hot spoonfuls of applesauce spiced with cloves and nutmeg before it was sealed away in jars to be rationed out through the coming wintry lunats. Apple harvest was his favorite time of year, and this would be the first time he would miss it.

"Are you two ready?" Dalmir's voice broke Grayden out of his reverie.

"Just a minute," Grayden replied, quickly shoveling the last few bites of porridge into his mouth and downing the mug of fresh milk that had accompanied it. Wiping a hand across his upper lip, he grinned. "Now I am."

Wynn scooped up the bits and pieces of metal he had been playing with and re-pocketed them before joining Grayden and Dalmir as they retrieved their horses.

It took them no time at all to cross the town and emerge on the other side, back on the open road once more. However, although the road continued on in similar fashion before and behind them, the view changed dramatically as they crested the hill on the far side of town. Where before they had been riding across empty, open plains and sweeping grassy hills, now farms and small houses dotted the landscape, along with thick stands of trees here and there. Grayden even spotted a few orchards, and his heart gave a mournful squeeze at the sight.

But above it all, far off in the distance, they could see the hazy outline of Dalton rising out of the horizon. Grayden's stomach flip-flopped at the sight: Dalton, the mountain city, the great metropolis of Dalma. He wondered what it would be like. The only point of reference he had was his one visit to Elricht Harbor. He remembered the way the unfamiliar sights and sounds and smells had overwhelmed his senses. He remembered the crowded, busy streets; the buildings clustered together for as far as the eye could see; the hawkers shouting about their wares to every passerby; the conglomeration of unidentifiable scents, most of them unpleasant; and the overwhelming aroma of fish and brine. At least Dalton stood nowhere near the sea.

14

"So, the kings of the West met and signed the Treaty of Telmondir," Dalmir's voice broke into Grayden's musings, startling him. "They sent a spy into the East and learned that the Ar'Mol was building the train road. What happened next?"

Grayden shook his head, struggling with the abrupt change in topic as thoughts of Dalton collided together in an effort to make room for comprehending Dalmir's sudden question. "Next? Nothing happened next. Not for a while, anyway. The peace held, but uneasily at first, especially with the knowledge of the trains. Each king continued to increase the size of his army, but it was hard for them to coordinate peace between the lands from such a distance, and the people were growing nervous, fearful that their kings meant to go to war against each other. Eventually, one of the kings... I think it was King Obrecht of Telsuma?" Grayden glanced at Wynn, who scrunched up his forehead and then gave a nod of confirmation. "He decided to call a Second Council where he presented an idea of his to the other rulers. The kings argued about the unorthodox idea for years, but they could come up with no better plan, and they finally agreed. Each king created a group of advisors from the leaders of all the towns in his region. These advisors were meant to represent everyone in their care and bring their concerns to the king, and bring the king's rulings back to villages, towns, and cities. After a few years of working with these leaders, the kings called a Third Council—which came to be known as the First Arxis—where they handed their power over to their advisors and abdicated their thrones. The advisors voted to elect a Councilman from each of the regions to be that country's spokesman, and they gave the people a major voice in the election."

"Did it work?" Dalmir asked.

"It seemed to," Grayden answered. "Everyone stopped worrying about the king taking them to war against their neighbors. They knew their Councilman could not do so without the approval of the advisors, who in turn relied on the approval of the people. The histories indicate that it took a long period of adjustment, but in the end, it worked better. It's the system we still have to this day."

"The Councilors and Advisors still hold Arxis three times a year," Wynn added. "They meet to discuss various problems or complaints that come to their attention, or to request aid from one another."

"I never lived under a king," Grayden mused. "But I believe it's better this way. Everyone has a voice now."

"Yes." Dalmir's face remained a puzzle. He looked thoughtful, perhaps a little sad. "And the train road?"

"It took years to build," Wynn replied, his voice hushed with awe. "But when it was finished, it stretched from one end of the world to the other. Each capital city had a station. My da said that it made the world instantly seem smaller. After the kings abdicated, the Council of Three made the Ar'Mol sign a treaty before they let his train road cross the Uaran River. There's been a sort of peace between Telmondir and the Igyeum ever since. Oh, there have been some minor conflicts here and there. My da said there was a really big conflict when he was in his early teens, but he wasn't quite old enough to join the defenders. That war didn't last long, not even a year, but a lot of men died on both sides.

Since then, everything's been pretty quiet. There's even been a little trade—like the airships—but it's delicate, like war could break out over a single wrong word."

"Airships," Dalmir muttered. "The Igyeum built those, too?"

The young men nodded.

"You said there were ports in each of the seven major cities?" Dalmir asked, his voice strangely hoarse.

Grayden and Wynn shared a confused glance.

"Seven?" Grayden asked. "You mean six: Telus, Dalton, Doran, Palome, Melar, and Ayalla." He ticked them off on his fingers.

Dalmir breathed an imperceptible sigh of relief. Then he cocked his head. "So when was this Academy of yours built?"

"A few years after the kings stepped down from their thrones," Grayden said. "A scholar in Ondoura—wasn't his name Farzal?" He turned to Wynn and once again received a nod. "Farzal, right. He discovered a ruin in a valley at the base of the Randeau Mountains, just inside the borders of Ondoura."

"Technically, he rediscovered it," Wynn interjected. "Shurik Medvev found it first in 684."

Grayden suppressed a small smile. "Right. But Farzal had the idea to rebuild the place. He led a team to dig through the ruins, where they discovered scrolls and books and other artifacts that dated all the way back to the Enlightenment Era. They got really excited, especially when they found a scroll that outlined the idea of creating an academy for young men to come and train as warriors. As soon as the leaders of each region approved it, Farzal started building the Academy right next to the ruins."

"It's the perfect site," Wynn interjected. "It's well-protected by the mountains and hard to reach without mounting a massive invasion force. Even by air, it would be hard to take the Academy."

"It also meant they didn't have very far to move all the scrolls and artifacts," Grayden added.

"The University of Csethel, it has to be," Dalmir murmured, then asked, "what of the library you spoke of?"

"It's a resource for the people of Telmondir," Grayden replied. "I think it's mostly just used by students, but the Council decided to make it free access to any who seek knowledge so that the people wouldn't fear the Academy or doubt its purpose in protecting them. Scholars have worked for years on restoring and copying the original scrolls. They are still working. They have added our own written histories to the library as well, of course, but the vast majority of the library is comprised of the writings found in the ruins."

"So simple in its elegance," Dalmir whispered. "And it's happening without any of us. Was there any purpose in our punishment at all?"

"Sorry?" Grayden's ears perked up. "What punishment?"

"Nothing," Dalmir snapped. Then his tone changed. "How is it that both of you came to be enrolled at the Academy?"

"They send out scouts to every town," Wynn said. "The elders of a town send word whenever there are young men in their town between the ages of thirteen and sixteen. Anyone in that age range may undergo the trial, but if you fail three times, your name doesn't go on the list. Those who pass get the best apprenticeships."

"The scouts keep track of those who pass the trials and they return each year to administer entrance exams to those who have reached seventeen years of age. If you pass, you're accepted. Then you have a year to raise the first year's entrance fees."

"Which isn't cheap," Wynn put in. "A thousand sigyls could buy a herd of good horses. Maybe even the supplies to build a barn for them, too."

Dalmir looked at them sharply. "I can't imagine many villagers being able to raise that much."

"The whole village usually helps," Grayden explained. "It's a mark of prestige to have a villager accepted into Conspectus. After the first year, each additional year is only ten sigyls. And if you graduate from Conspectus..."

"Conspectus?" Dalmir asked.

"The two-year general program at the Academy," Wynn explained. "If you complete that, you're given a choice: you can return home, or you can advance into the Experyus program, another two-year course of study to become a Defender, followed by two years of mandatory service."

"Being a Defender is a prestigious and well-paid position," Grayden took over. "You get a horse, weapons, armor, and food and lodging plus five hundred sigyls a year. If you choose not to continue after Conspectus, you still get a horse and a fourth of your entrance fee back. It's enough to get a man on his feet in any business he wants. Plus, with all the additional learning—math, science, history, strategy, politics, shoeing horses, forging, piloting, and the like—you could easily start out as a Master Apprentice in a variety of fields. Most of our airship pilots completed their Conspectus years."

"Or you can join the Conscripts," Wynn added.

"The Conscripts?" Dalmir asked.

"Sure," Wynn replied. "They're not Defenders, more like guards. They have their own ranks, even though they can never outrank an Experyus graduate. It's their job to stand watch at the city gates, enforce the laws, and keep the peace, that sort of thing. The job doesn't pay as much, but it's nothing to turn your nose up at."

"I see," Dalmir said. "And how did Dalsea manage to send two of its young men to the Academy this year? The village never struck me as being quite that prosperous."

"It's not," Grayden admitted. "If it hadn't been for the scholarship, the town would have had to choose between us."

"No, it wouldn't," Wynn muttered. "I'd have pulled out if it came to that."

"Wynn," Grayden began, ready to restart the old argument they'd been having for the past five years.

"Gray." Wynn's voice was sharp. "I know what you're going to say, but if I had to go to the Academy alone, I'd rather not go. You worked harder than anyone to pass those tests, harder than me... and we both know it. Besides, I wouldn't..." Wynn's gaze drifted away. "Wouldn't do well. Not... by myself."

Grayden pressed his lips together, wanting to argue, but knowing his friend well enough to leave it alone. The argument had sprung up between them many times before, and he'd learned it was one of those things Wynn simply wouldn't let go. Wynn came across as the kind of person over whom the world sort of rolled, barely impacting him, but when he got stubborn about something, there was no changing his mind.

"What about the scholarship?" Dalmir pressed.

"The scout offered to take us both for the price of a single admission fee."

"That must have been quite the honor," Dalmir mused.

"My da busted two buttons off his shirt," Wynn said, his tone that of earnest honesty. He wasn't boasting, just telling the events the way they had happened.

"We've sort of been the town heroes all summer." Grayden grinned.

"Are scholarships fairly common, then?"

Grayden wrinkled his nose. "Never heard of one before, but that doesn't mean anything. We didn't ask the scout, but he didn't act like it was out of the ordinary."

"Hmm," Dalmir said. And that was the end of his questions for the day.

They continued to ride northeast, the towering shape of Dalton ever-present on the horizon, but never seeming to grow any closer. The longer they rode, the more Grayden comprehended the sheer size of this city in the distance. He thought over the conversation with Dalmir. Why had he never questioned the scholarship before? Surely if it were a common occurrence, he would have heard about it before? Merchants traveled through their village often on their way from Dalton to the harbor. They brought news from all over Dalma, and even from outside their borders. Why had none of them ever mentioned the possibility?

Grayden remembered all the sleepless nights he had spent, fretting about competing against his best friend for a spot at the Academy. How much more soundly might he have slept had he known they could both afford to go?

Could there be more to it than simple generosity? He had assumed it meant they had both done so well on the exams that the scout felt it was in the Academy's best interests to have both recruits. Had he been wrong? Perhaps one of them had far outshone the other and the scout didn't want to risk the town choosing the wrong applicant? But if it had been that, Grayden reasoned, surely the scout would have mentioned it to the elders. So then, what? Either scholarships were common, but secret, or something more ominous was at work. Dalsea was remote; they didn't get much news from year to year. Could it be that tensions with the Igyeum were reaching a critical point? Was the Academy stepping up their recruitment efforts, sacrificing tuition to gain able-bodied men for a possible war?

These were troubling thoughts—ones Grayden did not want to dwell on—but he could not shake them from his mind. Wrapped in his own rumination, surprise snaked through him when Dalmir suddenly called a halt. Looking around, he realized that the sun had set without him noticing.

"We won't reach any of the towns on the outskirts of Dalton tonight," Dalmir said. "We've already ridden further past sunset than we ought."

The young men slid down from their mounts without complaint. Grayden felt oddly tired. The day had passed him by, and he wasn't completely sure how it had happened. He helped his companions make camp and after a quiet supper, he rolled himself up in his blanket and lay staring up at the sky, too deep in thought to find sleep easily.

MORNING CAME FAR TOO SOON for Grayden's liking, but he did his best to keep his lack of sleep from affecting his companions. Traveling so far from home and abandoning his normal routine had to be difficult enough for Wynn; Grayden didn't want to give him any excuse to turn around and gallop for home.

Around midday, they stopped for lunch in a town called Aberdan. The owner of the tavern, happy to have the custom of travelers, informed them that they were just a few leagues from Dalton and they should be able to reach the city long before dusk.

"You can see it from here real well on a clear day like today." The innkeeper pointed, and they gazed north and a little east, seeing the tall, shadowy form in the distance, much larger than they had seen it from the road the day before. It didn't look like a city, Grayden thought, more like a mountain, if it were standing in the middle of nowhere, all by itself. But that was silly. Lone mountains didn't just sprout up out of the ground by themselves.

The innkeeper was still speaking. "If you don't reach the gates before dusk, you may not get inside until morning, but there are quite a few smaller settlements where you can spend a quiet night."

After thanking the innkeeper, they mounted up and rode on, following the train road as the late summer sun beat down on their heads. The air was still and thick, and Grayden wondered if it was going to rain. If it did, he hoped it held off until they were inside, though he suspected the train road above them would provide a modicum of protection from the elements. The lack of sleep had caught up to him, and although he was glad that their trip would be shortened by the airship, he was also beginning to feel jittery and nervous about the experiences he was about to have. Being away from his family, riding in an airship, training at the Academy—all of these things weighed on his mind as they rode. However, toward the end of the afternoon, they crested a hill and all future worries were overshadowed.

Grayden had always thought of Elricht Harbor as a vast seaport. Compared to Dalton, Elricht Harbor was a tiny village not worth being on a map. Dalton had been carved into the side of a towering white mountain. It was impossible to tell if the mountain was natural or man-made. Though far too large to have been constructed, Grayden could not believe the mountain was a naturally occurring part of the landscape, jutting up alone in the landscape as it did. Dalton towered high into the sky, with gently rolling hills and flat plains spreading out in every direction around its base. The city rose up in levels cut into the face of the massive tower, hundreds of feet into the air. From the sides of the spire, four giant causeways arced, one in each of the four directions on a compass. Each causeway was covered in a shimmering white stone that Grayden could not identify. The path they were on led up to the causeway, which they would have to cross in order to get to the east gate, where they would enter. The causeways were not simple ornamentation; they were structurally necessary, and they also served as bridges for anyone wanting to enter or leave the city.

Beneath the mountain, four great rivers met and collided, forming waterfalls that flowed down the base of the mountain on four sides below the causeways. The train road veered away to the left and circled the mountain, and now Grayden saw that the colonnades holding the train road up mirrored the marble-white colonnades that helped to support the causeways around Dalton. Despite the grandeur and the massive size of the city before them, Grayden found the structure comfortingly familiar. He had heard that the tower in Dalsea resembled the structure beneath the capital city, but now he saw with his own eyes that the Dalsea tower was a perfect replica of the mountain that Dalton was built upon, though considerably smaller.

"Whoa," Wynn whistled.

Grayden shook his head in awed silence. Dalmir remained silent, but his expression was wistful.

"That's Dalton?" the old man asked.

"Guess so..." Grayden replied, feeling a bit unnerved.

"Interesting." He did not sound impressed. His tone was more sad than anything else. He spurred his horse forward.

Wynn and Grayden trailed after him, at a loss for words. Although the city looked close, it still took them over an hour to reach the causeway. The sun was just beginning to kiss the horizon, but the guards waved them through without even asking them about their business. Inside the gates, Grayden found himself instantly overwhelmed. Before them stretched a maze of major streets and side alleys, markets and common areas, inns and shops of every kind imaginable; the sheer number of people was enough to make him long for the quiet of home. Every main street curved around the mountain, and the side streets all sloped upwards. Grayden spent a few moments blinking in confusion, then Wynn reached over and punched him in the shoulder.

"Grayden, wake up! Dalmir is going to ask around in the market about directions to the inn."

Grayden shook himself and nodded. The Academy reserved a wing of rooms at an inn in Dalton where new recruits could wait to board their airship to Ondoura. The airships were mostly reliable, but the recruits were always told to arrive in Dalton at least three days before their scheduled flight, in case there were timetable changes.

Dalmir returned a moment later. "A woman at the fruit stand says that the Black Arms is just a few blocks up on Willow Street. Come on."

They rode their horses slowly through the streets, following Dalmir and instinctively trusting his sense of direction. The man led them through the winding streets with an air of confidence. Before too long, just as Grayden realized he was hopelessly lost, Dalmir stopped. Above their heads hung a sign that declared itself the "Black Arms." Under the words, it boasted a picture of two crossed arms coated in black armor. The building was old, but after they stabled their horses and entered the common room, they found themselves in a brightly lit, open space that was clean and cheerful. A woman greeted them as they came inside.

"My name is Martie. What can I do for you?" she asked cheerfully.

Grayden pulled out the papers the scout had given them and handed them to her. She studied them and then beamed.

"New recruits for the Academy, I see. Welcome to the Black Arms. My husband owns the inn, but he is out for the moment. I'll just lead you to your rooms." She looked at Dalmir and hesitated.

Dalmir bowed smoothly. "These young recruits have allowed me to travel with them to Ondoura. I am prepared to pay for my room and board." He produced a small satchel of coins and handed them to the woman.

She hefted it, then handed it back. "Our discount rates usually only apply to Academy students, but customers are scarce this time of year. Rooms are eight kips a night, meals are three, which is better than you'll do in the market. We'll stable your horse as well."

Dalmir pulled out two sigyls. "I'll be dining with the boys each day. Divide the change between the stable boys and your maids."

Martie's eyes widened. "You are very generous, sir; are you sure you don't want your change?"

"Very sure." Dalmir bowed from the shoulders. "This is a fine establishment, and your prices are honest. I like to encourage that. Besides, if the airship is delayed, I don't want to be bothered with figuring out how much to add to my bill."

Martie pocketed the coins. "I'll just show you to your rooms. We don't have many recruits here, so I'll put you up in the Academy wing with the boys... Master..." She hesitated.

"Dalmir."

"Dalmir. Right this way."

She led them up the stairs and around a corner to a pair of comfortable rooms. Each had two narrow beds, a floor rug between them, a table and chair, and behind a tall folding curtain was a tub for washing. Grayden had never seen anything so luxurious in all his life.

"If you want your own rooms each, we have the space now,

but I know that it can feel more like home to share, and this wing will get crowded in the next few days as others arrive..."

"This is fine," Grayden assured her.

"Very well." She gave a relieved smile. "Dinner is in an hour. I can have bath water drawn up for you after dinner if you wish it. I'll let you get settled for now, though."

They thanked her and then Dalmir retired to his own room, leaving Wynn and Grayden to exclaim over their room.

"Do you think the rooms at the Academy are like this?" Wynn asked, sitting on his bed and bouncing experimentally.

"Surely not," Grayden replied. "What good would a warrior be if he got used to this sort of comfort?"

"True." Wynn pulled off his boots and began unpacking his bags. He laid out each item with precise care. "But I think I could handle it."

Grayden grinned at him. "I'm going to take a nap before dinner. I really didn't sleep well."

"Boring. I'm going down to the common room and maybe explore around outside a bit."

"Suit yourself. Don't get lost," Grayden teased as he pulled off his boots and fell onto the other bed.

15

Grayden slept straight through dinner and woke the next morning as the first rays of sunlight peeked through the window to their room. He felt rested, but groggy, as he crossed the room and leaned on the ledge. The city glistened in the morning light. The streets below were empty and silent, not yet bustling with the morning activity that would surely begin within a few hours. In the other bed, Wynn snored loudly. Grayden wondered how late he had stayed out. Quietly, he tugged on his boots and wandered downstairs to the common area. A pretty girl about his age was wiping down tables. She glanced up as he entered the room.

"Breakfast isn't for another hour," she said.

"Okay," Grayden replied, feeling awkward. "I was wondering if I could get directions to the airship dock."

"The Docks? I can write the directions for you... You *can* read?"

"I can read."

"That makes it easier." She wiped her hands on her apron. "Let me just finish up here and I'll get the directions in a minute. Would you like anything to drink while you wait?"

"Is there any milk?"

"In the morning? Always." She hustled through a swinging door and returned a moment later with a large mug filled with foaming white milk. Grayden sipped it, savoring the cool freshness of it—probably straight from where the bottles were stored in the springhouse—and the way it relieved the hunger he was feeling from having skipped dinner the night before.

The girl busied herself about the common room, wiping down tables, sweeping the floor, stoking the fireplace, and arranging the benches. When she finished, she disappeared through the swinging door again. This time, she came back with a sheet of rumpled paper and a stubby pencil. She wrote on it, mouthing the words as she wrote. She handed it to Grayden. He stared at the directions, reading them silently, wondering how he was going to manage his way through the unfamiliar streets. He looked up to see the girl studying him.

"I'm almost done here," she said, breaking the silence. "I can ask Martie if she'd mind me taking you to the Docks."

"That would be very helpful. I've never been in a city this big before."

"Most of the Academy students who stay here never have." The girl grinned. "I'm Nia, by the way."

"And my name's Grayden."

Nia's eyes widened and her hands flew up to her head. "I'm so sorry! I had no idea—Martie said you slept through dinner and I was to make sure you had something to eat as soon as you came down—why didn't you tell me you were hungry?"

"You said breakfast wasn't ready—"

"Here." She dipped behind a counter and came back with a plate containing bread and cheese and a small apple. She took his mug and swiftly refilled it. "Eat up while I go ask Martie if I can take a break."

Grayden sat down with his food. Though not warm, the bread was fresh, laced with cinnamon and raisins. It tasted delicious. The cheese was a good yellow that looked new-made. The apple left much to be desired, but growing up on an orchard had spoiled him, so he tried not to be too critical in his thoughts and ate it anyway. Nia returned as he was finishing his food.

"Martie says I can take my break now. Let's go."

Grayden followed her out into the city; its sweeping might immediately overwhelmed him. He had been too tired the night before to take much note of his surroundings, but now, after a good night's rest and a solid breakfast, he had the cognizance to fully take in the city's vastness. There was an elegance to every building, whether it was decorative arches or beautifully stained glass windows depicting scenes from every myth and legend Grayden had ever encountered, and quite a few he hadn't. He would have been instantly lost had it not been for Nia. She led him through the winding streets with unfaltering confidence.

"The Docks are a bit of a hike," Nia informed him. "They're up near the top, well, about three-quarters of the way up the mountain, but above the main part of the city. It's the only place they could build them without endangering the other buildings. I've been told they had the same problem in other cities, but not as bad because their buildings aren't so tall as ours. We can hire a rickshaw if you'd like." She gestured at a group of men standing about with two-wheeled carts, ready to race products or passengers through the narrow streets to wherever they pleased.

Grayden contemplated racing up the mountain in one of the rickety-looking vehicles and shook his head. "I don't mind walking."

Nia did not press the matter. "Tell me about your home," she said.

As they walked, Grayden told her about his family, the orchards, the trip to Dalton, and a little about his homesickness. He was grateful for the distraction as they climbed higher and higher up the city levels. Nia listened avidly. Grayden found her easy to talk to, a little like Seren. She laughed easily and swung her arms carelessly as she walked. When he had answered all of her questions, he asked her about herself.

She chuckled. "There's nothing interesting about me. I was

born here in Dalton, got the job at the Black Arms two years ago. Martie's my aunt. I've heard good stories though, mostly from the Academy students. They're the only customers not too uppity to chat with a serving girl."

"What're they like, the other Academy students you've met?"

"Mostly, they're a lot like you. Many come from farms. Some are apprentice blacksmiths or other tradesmen, a few come from other cities, though not even the other capitals are as big as Dalton. Mostly we get native Dallans, though occasionally we get a few Telsumans, if their homes are closer to Dalton than to Telus. You'll probably meet a lot of them in the next couple of days: this time of year we usually get quite a few students at the inn. You and your friends made good time; you're a bit earlier than we usually see students arriving, I know they tell you to get here a few days early, but the airships are almost never on time, and I've never seen one arrive early. There has been a lot of pirate activity lately." She paused at the alarm on his face. "They don't generally attack the Academy transports, don't worry."

He thought about the things Dalmir had said and wondered again about Telmondir's relations with the Igyeum. Perhaps Nia, here in the capital, knew more current news than little Dalsea was privy to.

"Have you had any news from the East?" he asked.

Nia's face turned thoughtful. "There hasn't been much news recently. It's a little strange, but—I don't know. No news is good news, right?"

"Maybe," Grayden said, letting the subject drop.

Nia plucked at her apron. "It's just a few more blocks. We'll have to take the lift."

As they reached the narrow streets at the top of the mountain into which the city was built, Grayden caught his first glimpse of the docks and halted, speechless.

He had thought he had seen wonders. The train road and Dalton itself had filled him with awe and overwhelmed his spirit. The Docks were the most elegant creations he had ever seen, though all he could see currently were the bottoms of ships as they glided in and out of a great opening above him. There were no streets leading up to the Docks, and he looked questioningly at Nia. Grinning, the girl led him to a rectangular opening in the mountain's face. Together, they stepped inside, and Grayden found himself in what appeared to be a large steel crate. The walls of the crate were not solid, but rather woven together in a crisscross pattern. Nia pressed a button, and the crate jerked a bit and then rose. Grayden's eyes widened.

"It's perfectly safe," Nia assured him. "There's a pulley that raises and lowers the lift, and they use chains instead of ropes. That's why it's so loud. We'll be up to the Docks in a minute."

Grayden watched the world drop out from under him as the crate creaked up the shaft that had been carved for it. He felt that they were not going so much straight up, as up and a bit back, into the heart of the mountain itself. The angle of ascent wasn't so steep that they couldn't stand on the bottom of the crate, but it was enough that he noticed a slight leaning to their journey. His suspicions were confirmed when he noticed that the shaft was gradually enclosing them on all four sides, instead of three. The air pulsed around him, and he was tempted to reach through the side of the crate to touch the rock that surrounded them. In a fit of fancy, he envisioned the rock itself pulsing with life, and he wondered if the mountain hadn't been sculpted so much as it had been grown, as though it were a living thing, like a tree. Even as he laughed at his own speculation, he could not shake the idea that Dalton had been carved from living rock.

Thankfully, before he could get too claustrophobic, the lift jerked to a halt, and they stepped out onto solid ground once more. Grayden blinked as his eyes adjusted to the lack of daylight and found himself standing inside a great cavern. A glance up showed him only darkness, and he found that no matter how hard he stared, he could not see the cavern ceiling. He felt strangely small, standing there. Nia touched his arm and led him up a long, metal staircase. At the top, he caught his breath in amazement.

Before him, a long, straight jetty stretched out across the cavern, jutting out a few feet beyond the opening of the cave, held up, he knew, by braces and joists, which he had seen from below. These jetties lined the cave, with large gullies between them, where various sized airships were moored.

The airships themselves were spectacular in their own right. With graceful prows and elegant lines, they closely resembled sailing ships that Grayden had seen berthed in Elricht Harbor. These ships, however, were far more colorful, and their masts were taller, their sails more complex, and they had an additional set of sails extending horizontally from their sides, which acted like wings and allowed the great ships to fly. He had looked at enough of Wynn's schematics to understand what he was seeing. Nia led him up to one of the larger airships.

"You'll fly on one like this," she said.

The bottoms of the airship's trim sails gleamed with white-blue lights that shed an eerie glow throughout the cavern. He frowned. Those hadn't been noted in any of Wynn's schematics.

"What are those?" he asked Nia, pointing at the lights. "They don't look like any sort of lantern I've ever seen."

"They're not lanterns. Those lights are part of the power source that keeps the airships in the sky."

"How does it work?" Grayden asked, knowing that Wynn would want to know. His friend often lamented the lack of information on the power sources for the ancient train system as well as for the airships.

Nia shrugged. "They're called cynders, but they're heavily regulated. We've never been able to replicate them, so we have to be content with buying them from the Igyeum. The Council doesn't like it much, but there's not a lot they can do about it."

Grayden frowned. "You said something about pirates."

Nia nodded. "They exist. Not many of them. I'm sure getting ahold of an airship is even more difficult than getting the cynders to power it, but then... regulations and legality probably don't matter much to a pirate."

"True," Grayden agreed. "How do the pirates' airships stack up in speed and maneuverability?"

"They're just as fast, and more nimble," Nia admitted. "Mostly, though, it sounds like that's because they're so much smaller."

"That makes sense." Grayden studied the airships admiringly for another minute, then asked, "Who do I talk to about an extra ticket for our friend?"

Nia pointed toward the back of the cavern. "This way."

They walked over to a large wooden desk. The man behind the desk looked up.

"How can I help you?" he asked.

"My name is Grayden Ormond. I have a ticket to Doran, but a man I am traveling with does not. Can he get a ticket for the same flight?"

The man frowned and opened a book. "Academy student?"

Grayden hesitated. "I am, my friend isn't. He wants to visit the library."

"Ah. Let me see here, just one minute." The clerk flipped through a few pages and then dragged his finger down a page, peering at it closely. "Yes, I thought so. We have several cabins still available on that flight. The cost of the ticket is ten sigyls."

Grayden's eyes widened. "Ten... sigyls?"

"Well, it is rather last minute."

Grayden gaped, then shut his mouth slowly. "Thank you. We'll have to come back."

"Suit yourself. The cabin will be available for a few hours, but if it doesn't get filled by sundown today, we fill the space with cargo."

Grayden nodded. "I understand. When will the ship be leaving?"

"I was just about to send that information to the Black Arms." The man nodded at Nia. "You'd save me the cost of a messenger if you'd take it for me, Nia?"

Nia nodded. "I can do that."

"Much obliged. The ship to Doran will leave in two days."

"Two days."

"That's right, Saturday morning, ten o'clock. Here: I've already written it down." He handed Nia a slip of paper and she and Grayden turned to go.

As Nia led the way back to the lift, Grayden was silent. Dalmir had paid for his own room, but there was no telling what the limits were on his purse. Grayden himself had never seen much money. His parents took care of his needs, and what he earned he had put aside and saved for things he would need to purchase while at the Academy. Sigyls were hard to come by in Dalsea, and he had never seen a rune. Mostly, the people in his village traded in kips or by bartering goods and services. He realized now that was not how the rest of the world worked. He could never have dreamed an airship ticket would be so expensive. As they walked back to the inn, Nia tried to keep up the conversation, but she quickly picked up on Grayden's darkened mood and fell silent. She cast furtive, sympathetic glances his way, but he did not see them.

16

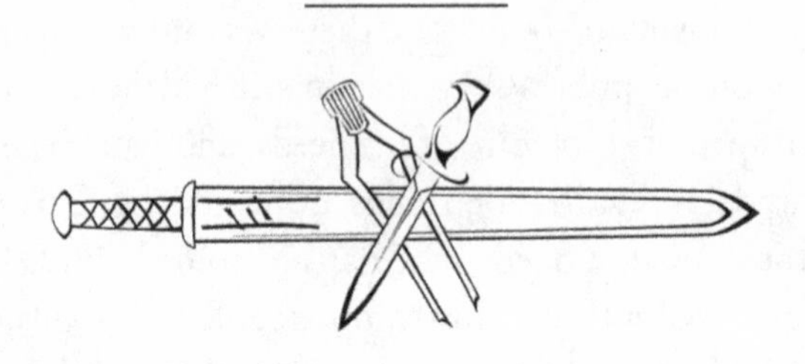

When they arrived back at the Black Arms, Martie met them at the door. She beamed pleasantly at Grayden and then turned her attention to her niece.

"We've had a few more Academy arrivals this morning, and they'll be wanting breakfast soon. I'm sorry, but your break is over."

Nia nodded. "Yes, Aunt. Oh! Master Olan sent me with a message for the Academy students about when their airship will be departing." Nia handed Martie the slip of paper.

Martie read it silently. "We'll announce this tonight at dinner, and post it up on the wall for any stragglers who get here tomorrow or the next day," she said kindly. "There are always a few latecomers."

"Thank you for showing me to the Docks, Nia," Grayden said, remembering to be polite, despite the discouraging news. "I should go find Wynn and Dalmir."

He trudged into the common room with a heavy heart. Wynn and Dalmir were sitting at a table in a corner, and Grayden joined them.

"Martie said you went to the Docks." Wynn's tone was mildly accusing. "What was it like?"

Grayden couldn't muster up the awe he had felt at seeing the Docks. "They're spectacular. You'll see them in a couple of days. Sounds like our airship is on schedule so far."

"What's eating you?" Wynn asked.

"I asked them how much an extra ticket would cost." Grayden looked apologetically at Dalmir. "A cabin will cost ten sigyls."

Wynn nearly choked on the gulp of cider he had just taken. His face turned red as he attempted not to spray his mouthful of liquid across the table. Grayden glanced at him in concern, saw he was fine, and turned his eyes back to Dalmir. The man leaned back, a look of unconcern on his face.

"That shouldn't be a problem."

This time, Wynn's cider sprayed across the table in a fine mist. Grayden thumped his friend's back as he coughed.

"Shouldn't be a problem?" Wynn wheezed out when the coughing fit ended. "That much money could buy me a whole horse in Dalsea."

"But we are not in Dalsea," Dalmir replied calmly, "and so I packed accordingly."

Grayden just stared. He couldn't think of a single thing to say, so he went to the bar to ask Nia for another mug of cider. Already at the bar stood a group of young men, about his age. A few chatted amiably. Others stood silent, simply waiting for their drinks. Nobody seemed to know each other. As Grayden walked up to the bar, he noticed that one of the young men was quite burly. He had longish dark brown hair, tied back at the nape of his neck with a black cord. He was fully half a foot taller than Dalmir, and broad across his shoulders, with a massive sword strapped to his back. Grayden had to step up next to him in order to catch Nia's eye. As he took a seat on a stool, the tall young man turned to him.

"Academy?" he asked. His voice was deep and his eyes were golden brown.

Grayden nodded. "You?"

"Yes. My name's Berenger." He pronounced it *bay-ren-zay.* "But most people just call me Beren."

"I'm Grayden. I've never heard a name like that. Where are you from?"

"I hail from Gnupar, a small village in the Naelina Mountains, just north of the Telsuma border. And yourself?"

"Dalsea, in the foothills of the Black Mountains, on the south edge of Dalma."

Beren held out his hand. "It is a pleasure to meet you, Grayden of Dalsea."

Grayden suppressed a smile at the other youth's formality as he shook his hand. He immediately decided that he liked this fellow Academy initiate, and he pointed to his table. "My friends and I are sitting over there if you need a table; it's getting crowded in here," he offered.

"Thank you," Beren replied, looking around. "I'll take you up on that offer."

With mugs in hand, they returned to the table. Wynn looked up as they approached.

"This is Beren," Grayden introduced the Telsuman. "Beren, my friend Wynn, and this is Dalmir. He's traveling with us to visit the library."

"More than visit it." Dalmir snorted. He looked up at Beren and nodded a greeting.

Grayden grinned. "Beren's from Telsuma," he told Wynn, excited to introduce his friends. Wynn's father had traveled extensively before settling down in Dalsea, and at times the only thing that could catch Wynn's interest and tear it away from whatever machine he was building were discussions of places far from home.

Wynn studied the newcomer. "You don't look Telsuman," he said bluntly. "I thought Telsumans all had blond hair and blue eyes and pale skin from living in the snow and mining in the mountains."

Grayden flinched. He often forgot how awkward Wynn could

be with strangers at times, but Beren's teeth glinted in his brown face and his eyes crinkled at the corners.

"Most are," Beren admitted. "But my mother is Pallan."

This bit of news soon had Wynn leaning forward and peppering Beren with questions, which the other answered with ease and grace. Grayden relaxed. Beren did not seem offended by Wynn's interest or his lack of social graces. His estimation of this new friend rose considerably as Beren good-naturedly answered all of Wynn's questions, and countered with a few of his own. Grayden chimed in whenever it was appropriate. After breakfast was over, Grayden offered to show them all the Docks, since Dalmir needed to buy his ticket, but Beren excused himself to find his room.

"I did not have so far to travel as you, but I have been on the road for a few days and would like to clean up. I will see you later."

Although the now crowded streets made Grayden feel hemmed in, he had always had an excellent memory, and it didn't fail him this time. He led Wynn and Dalmir straight to the lift and took them up to the Docks. Wynn was speechless at the sight of the airships and the great cavern, and even though Grayden had already seen it all that morning, he still couldn't get over the wondrous majesty of the airships and the elegance of the Docks.

Dalmir also was silent, but his eyes narrowed when he looked at the airships. Grayden showed him the way to the desk.

"I would like to buy passage on the airship taking the Academy initiates to Doran."

The man nodded at Grayden in recognition. "I told the boy the price is ten sigyls."

Dalmir didn't flinch. He simply reached into his pocket and pulled out a handful of coins. They jingled together as he poked through them, and he laid ten of the silver-banded coins on the desk. The man counted them swiftly and nodded. He handed Dalmir a form to sign and then produced a small piece of red paper. Grayden recognized it as a ticket: he and Wynn had both received one along with their acceptance letters to the Academy. Their business concluded, they returned to the lift, but Grayden caught Dalmir giving the airships a final, piercing glance. The anger in his eyes made the hair on the back of Grayden's neck stand on end. Then the lift descended and Dalmir's expression returned to its normal neutrality.

Back at the Black Arms, things were getting even more crowded, which was not unexpected, but made Grayden feel a little claustrophobic. After standing amongst a group of initiates with Wynn for a few minutes, he excused himself and headed to the kitchen, where he asked Nia for a bundle of food he could take with him for the afternoon. He wanted to go for a walk, and even though cities made him feel a bit closed in, he couldn't pass up the opportunity to explore Dalton just a little.

Since he had already traveled up the mountain to the Docks, Grayden made his way down to the lower levels of the city. He had a vague idea of getting a closer look at the waterfalls that had greeted them and poured down into the Emelda River, but he didn't have a firm destination in mind. Mostly, he just wanted to amble and sightsee.

The upper levels of the city were narrow, and the buildings carved into the face of the mountain rose many stories into the air. But the lower levels were much larger, and the buildings were shorter. The streets were wider, too, and for this Grayden was grateful. As he walked along the wide Market Street, taking in the sights and sounds, he bumped into a young boy. The child looked up at him with frightened eyes and Grayden kept his expression kind.

"No harm done, lad," he said. "As long as you give me back my knife and coins."

The boy stared at him, an expression of disbelief in his blue eyes, and then bolted. Grayden watched him go, a bemused look on his face. He was about to dash after the boy when he heard someone take up a cry.

"Stop the thief!"

Two men rushed toward him, and Grayden put his hands in the air. "Wait, I'm not a—" He didn't get a chance to finish, as the two men shouldered past him and snatched up the young boy just before he could turn a corner and disappear. They brought the boy, kicking and snarling, back to the street and set him down in front of Grayden.

"Give back what you took," one man said roughly, his hand clamped down on the boy's shoulder.

"I di'n't take nothin'!" the boy protested.

"Yes, you did," Grayden replied calmly.

"I saw him," a lady at the booth behind Grayden exclaimed. "He stole something from the young man."

The men shook the boy roughly, and he shrugged in exasperation, producing a small sack of coins and the knife that Grayden's parents had given him before he left.

"Those yours?" the men asked.

Grayden nodded. "Yes, they are. Thank you."

"Git off me," the lad yelled at the men as Grayden retrieved his possessions. "I were hungry, you know? Can't begrudge a body fer wantin' to eat."

"Would you like to press charges?" One man directed this question at Grayden.

"No," Grayden said, "but I would like the lad to show me around a bit."

The man gave him a bewildered look. "Can't trust him."

"Probably not," Grayden replied. "But I know that, now."

The men looked at each other. "Maybe we should call the guards—"

"No, please," Grayden said quickly. "I insist. I'll keep the lad out of trouble, at least for the afternoon."

"Well..."

"I'm Academy-bound," Grayden added.

The lad looked up, his eyes suddenly wide, then a strange expression crossed his face—something very much like shame—and he stopped kicking and protesting.

"If you're sure."

"I am."

"Very well." They shoved the pick-pocket at Grayden, who caught the boy by his shoulder and held him fast.

He steered the lad down the street a ways, then sat him down on a barrel. The boy looked at him warily.

"What're ya gonna do with me?"

"Just what I said. I need a guide for the afternoon. There's a meal in it for you at a nice inn, but no more stealing today."

"But..."

"You said you were stealing because you're hungry. If that's true, which I suspect it isn't, then consider your hunger for the day taken care of." He unfolded the napkin Nia had given him, displaying a mouth-watering array of grapes, bread, and cheese. "You're welcome to share my lunch as a part of the deal," he added. "But if you *do* steal anything else today, then there's nothing but the guard house for you at sundown... and I promise you this: you won't be able to pick a pocket without my noticing."

"Sure." The boy's tone turned mocking.

"I caught you picking my pocket, didn't I? Believe me, I didn't need those others to come to my aid. I would've caught you on my own."

The boy gazed at him, as though sizing him up. Perhaps he was trying to figure out whether Grayden meant what he said. Grayden stared at him steadily, and the boy seemed to decide he meant business. He reached toward the napkin and grabbed a handful of grapes.

"Deal," he said, shoving the fruit into his mouth. "What would you like to see?"

"The waterfalls," Grayden replied.

"Easy." The boy jumped to his feet. "Follow me."

The boy led the way down the side streets until they reached the widest levels. Here, most of the buildings looked like normal houses. The road, however, narrowed to a walking path, and fields filled with various crops covered all available ground.

Grayden stared in amazement at the fields. They were small compared to the ones at home, but they occupied a huge portion of land that Grayden would never have guessed could support crops of any kind.

"How is this possible?"

"The folk who live here cart in dirt every year, and I hear tell they use a lot o' fertilizer."

"Surely this isn't what feeds the entire city?"

"Nah." The boy swiped his arm under his nose. "It helps. But they grow most of the food out there." He swept his hand casually, gesturing away from the mountain, and Grayden remembered the towns and farmland they had ridden through to get to the city.

"What's your name?" he asked the boy as they continued to walk.

"Mouse."

"Seriously?"

"Eh, it's my nickname, 'cause I'm small, and I can sneak good."

"Uh huh. What's your real name?"

"Er..." The boy rolled his eyes. "Lenka."

Grayden frowned. "That's not a Dalman name, is it?"

The boy's expression grew cautious, even as he gave a casual shrug. "Dunno, don't care. Like 'Mouse' better anyway. It fits me."

"That it does. Lead on, Mouse. My name's Grayden, by the by."

Mouse led Grayden down to the massive caverns at the base of the mountain, through which the enormous waterfalls thundered. The water plunged twenty-five spans down to the river below before racing away from the mountain as though on an urgent mission. Grayden knew that by the time the rivers had run a league away from Dalton, they slowed down, becoming lazy and peaceful. Rainbows arced out from the mist that surrounded the waterfalls, and the sun dazzled off the water and hurt Grayden's eyes. They sat and listened to the thundering music for a while until the sun sank lower in the sky. Grayden glanced up. The trip to the base of the city had been quick, but he guessed it would take longer going up.

"Come on, I promised you dinner."

The common room of the Black Arms was packed by the time they returned. Grayden did not see Dalmir or Wynn anywhere, so he squeezed himself and Mouse into place around a long table filled with Academy students, and he flipped Nia a few kips.

"Feed the boy whatever he wants for dinner," he said. "If he eats more than that, I'll settle with you in the morning. I'm going to bed."

Nia nodded and hurried away to the kitchen.

"No picking the pockets of my friends, now," Grayden warned the lad. "These are Academy students, and they work hard to keep you and your kind safe, whether you abide by the law or not."

Mouse nodded gravely. "I steal to feed myself," he said. "No need tonight."

Grayden grinned at him. "Just make sure that you don't start thinking about tomorrow until you're well-fed and several streets away."

"Yes, sir."

Nia caught Grayden before he reached the stairs and pressed a napkin wrapped around a fresh loaf of bread and a block of cheese into his hands. "I know the crowd can kill an appetite, but it comes back right fierce once you're in your room and away from all the noise."

"Thanks, Nia." He took the offered food, and then hurried up the stairs to his room, where he fell into bed and was asleep almost before he could get his boots off.

17

"Is everything ready?" The pale moon shone down on the speaker, making his face appear even more angular than it already was. His voice was hushed.

"As soon as Mouse gets back with those papers, we should be good to move out," Raisa replied with equal softness. Her sable hair was pulled back from her face in a silver clip, but a few strands had escaped and fell forward across her face. She brushed them back impatiently.

"Has anyone seen that dratted boy yet?" a third voice asked gruffly.

"He'll be here, Oleck," Marik replied. "Don't worry about Mouse. He can handle himself."

"He's just a boy." Shaesta gazed toward the city, a concerned line furrowed deep between her brows.

"He'll be fine," Marik replied. "He knows how important this is."

"You sure we shouldn't go looking for him?" the third voice asked again. "Dalton's a big place, and he's just a little mite."

"Kid's good with directions, and he's been here before," Marik replied. "You keep fussing like a mother malkyn and I'll never let you hear the end of it. Two years ago, who would have thought you'd develop such a soft spot for the boy? You were dead set against him when I first brought him aboard."

"Just don't want to go back to fetching firewood for myself, is all," Oleck grumbled. "I've gotten used to the tyke."

"Shhhh." Marik held a finger to his lips and everyone fell silent.

Footsteps padded their way. As they listened, the footsteps stayed steady. Whoever was coming was not in a hurry. There was no sound except for the soft whisper of feet passing through the thick grass, and then a small shape emerged from the shadows.

"Marik?" a youthful voice asked warily.

"Mouse." Raisa relaxed as Oleck put away his knife. "You shouldn't sneak up on us."

"I weren't sneaking," the boy replied in injured tones, "I made noise on purpose as I walked. I could have crept up while you's all talking about me—your whispers aren't as quiet as you think they are—but I made sure you could hear me coming."

Marik winked at the others. "Told you he'd be fine."

"And I brought food, no less." Mouse dropped a good-sized bag in the middle of the group. "Bread, cheese, apples, all top-of-the-line."

Marik arched an eyebrow, though he knew the boy couldn't see him clearly enough for the expression to matter. "Where did you steal all this from?"

"Didn't steal it! This bloke wanted a tour of the city proper this afternoon. Said he'd buy me dinner if I kept from picking any pockets for the day. He had sharp eyes, too. I actually had to keep my end of the bargain. The maid at the inn he's staying at's taken a shine to him and gave me extras to take with me." Mouse grinned. "There's plenty for everyone whenever the others show up."

Oleck sat down on a log and opened the sack. First, he pulled out a loaf of bread. He tore off a sizable chunk and then got out his knife again and cut several thick slices of cheese. He handed several to Raisa and Marik, and would have given some to

Mouse, but the boy waved his hands in a gesture of polite rejection.

"I ate so much tonight, I think my stomach'll rebel if I try to feed it anything else." He sat down, and the others munched in silence for a bit.

"This is Black Arms bread," Marik said after a few bites. His tone was grim. "You're supposed to leave that place alone, Mouse. It's too important to our plans."

"I did leave it alone!" Mouse squeaked. "The man that wanted the tour, he was staying at the Black Arms. I swear, Marik, I'd never—"

Marik relented. "I believe you. I wasn't paying attention before. Why did this young man hire you for a tour?"

"I tried to pick his pocket," Mouse confessed.

"You tried to pick the pocket of an Academy student?" Thunder pounded between Marik's ears. "Mouse! I told you—"

"I didn't know he were Academy bound, Cap'n, I swear!" Mouse held up his hands. "By the time I realized, it were too late." The boy cringed. "I'm sorry."

"Hmm." Marik frowned. "That could pose a problem. Do you think he'd recognize you if he saw you again?"

"Probably. Like I said, he were quick and sharp-eyed. Nobody's ever caught me before. You know how good I am."

Raisa nodded. "That's true, Marik... Mouse is as good as he thinks he is."

"That's exactly why I said to stay away from that inn," Marik muttered. "Well, it doesn't change our plans much. Just means you'll have to stay well out of sight until we make our move." He gave Mouse a stern glare.

"Aye, Cap'n."

"Might have to make sure he doesn't cause trouble," Oleck said.

"We're not—" Mouse stopped himself.

"We're not going to hurt anyone, Mouse," Raisa assured him. "We have no quarrel with the Academy."

"We stick to the plan, we shouldn't have any problems," Marik added.

"Next, you'll be telling us this is going to be the easiest job we ever pulled. But you always was an optimist, Marik," Oleck said.

"Still am." Marik's teeth glinted in the firelight as he smiled fiercely. "Didn't get to the point I'm at without being a bit of an optimist."

"And a whole lotta luck," a new voice added wryly.

"Rustam, how did it go?" Marik asked the newcomer.

"Abel Karden has a broken arm and will not be reporting for duty tomorrow morning," Rustam replied. "Shaesta and Yefrem and the rest of our crew will meet us on the schooner. But plans have changed a bit."

"How so?"

"They're running on schedule for once."

Marik pursed his lips. "Unexpected, but not wholly a bad thing. Means we can be even more prepared. Mouse, you did get the papers, at least?"

"Course I did." Mouse pulled a large envelope out of his pocket. "Picked it up from Rax on my way over here. He said it's all in order: Raisa's orders, the security mandate, and the seal."

Marik examined the seal by the light of the fire, then he handed the entire packet over to Raisa. "Looks good. It would fool me, and that's saying quite a lot, actually."

Raisa shoved the envelope into her pocket. "I just wish we'd had time to read over the documents before he sealed them up."

"Rax is the best there is." Mouse's voice was confident.

"So you keep saying." Marik ruffled the boy's blond curls. "Nobody here doubts your word, lad. Though I'm still unclear about how you acquired this contact." He raised an eyebrow, waiting, but Mouse did not volunteer any extra information. Marik shrugged. Mouse had been worth his weight in gold, even if he was tight-lipped about his past and how he came by his contacts. "Everyone should try to get some sleep. I'll wake you when it's time to leave."

They all turned to their bedrolls, but Marik stayed up, staring at the fire and whittling absently at a stick. He pursed his lips and glowered into the fire. Tomorrow, they would put all their plans in place. In two days, if all proceeded according to plan, they would be the proud owners of an airship laden with enough cargo to unbind his crew from this life he had dragged them into. It wouldn't make them wealthy, though the cynders they had acquired would certainly help, but it would mean freedom. They would have to settle somewhere quiet, probably in Telmondir, probably in separate towns, but they could finally pay their debts and be free. If all went well.

He let out a harsh chuckle in the solitary darkness. When had anything ever gone as planned? But a man could dream of freedom. Even a man such as him.

18

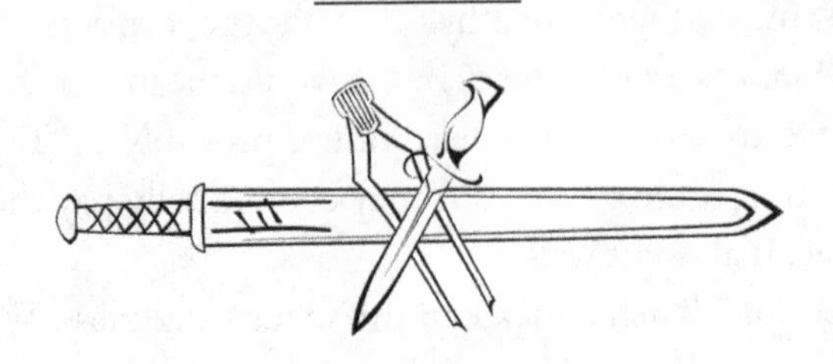

At breakfast the next morning, Nia told Grayden that the young pickpocket had eaten well, but no more than Grayden had already paid for. "I sent him away with a sack of left-overs, even," she said. "He looked like he might need them. I'm sorry, if you didn't intend for that..."

"That's just fine, Nia. I just hope it helped keep him honest."

"That was a kind thing you did. How did you run across him, anyway?"

"He tried to pick my pocket. I caught him and offered him dinner if he'd be my guide. Figured I'd be safer with him where I could see him."

Nia smiled. "Probably true."

Grayden shrugged. "He seemed like a nice enough kid, for a thief."

He took the offered mug of spiced cider and sat down at a table with Wynn and Dalmir. Wynn looked tired, and Grayden wondered how late his friend had stayed up. A few moments later, Berenger joined them. The big lad sat on the bench across from Grayden and leaned back against the wall with a sigh.

"My room is pleasant, but the furniture in this common area does not fit me well," the burly Telsuman commented. There was no hint of complaint in his voice; he was just making conversation.

"Are all Telsumans built like you, then?" Wynn asked. "I thought maybe you were Academy-bound because of your size."

Beren laughed. "You are correct on one count, but not the way you think. I'm a bit on the scrawny side in my homeland."

Grayden's eyes widened a bit as he stared at his new friend's brawny arms and shoulders. "You're joking."

"No." Beren shook his head earnestly. "Amongst other Telsumans, I am considered a runt—although I am rather taller than most—my parents think my height is the reason for the scrawniness of my arms and shoulders."

"Uh-huh." Wynn's tone was clearly disbelieving. "Yep, if I had to pick one word to describe you, Beren, I'd definitely pick 'scrawny.'"

"Truthfully." Beren's voice turned mournful. "My shoulders are only five swords wide. My brothers, though I have a full two hands in height on the tallest, can fit seven and nine swords across their backs, respectively."

Wynn looked down at his own sword and pulled it partway out of its sheath, eyed it, and then stared appreciatively at the massive weapon now hanging at Beren's hip. Shoving his own blade back into its sheath, Wynn commented, "If you used my sword as a measurement, you could probably fit ten or twelve of them."

Beren chuckled, but before he could reply, Nia arrived with their breakfast plates. For a while, they were all too busy eating to talk. Eventually satisfied, Wynn pushed his plate back and stretched his arms up over his head.

"One more day in Dalton. What do you want to do today?" Grayden asked.

"We haven't done anything really touristy yet," Wynn replied.

Grayden eyed his friend dubiously. "You want to shop?"

Wynn shrugged. "I thought I might find a few small gifts to send to my siblings."

"That sounds nice," Beren said. "How much do couriers cost if we wish to send things home?"

Grayden laughed. "A lot more than we can afford, but there are always merchants about headed toward the smaller towns to sell their wares, and they probably won't charge us much. I'll bet Nia or her aunt knows a merchant or two headed in the right directions."

"Ah." Beren nodded. "You speak wisdom, truly. I would not have considered asking a merchant."

Grayden stared, incredulous, but before he could comment, Wynn clapped the larger boy on the shoulder. "It's a good thing you're sticking close to us, Beren. I'll bet the merchants at the market will believe you're easy pickings."

Beren nodded earnestly, and Grayden wondered if they could work Beren's naïveté into some fun. But he shrugged off the desire for pranks. It wouldn't do to get in trouble here where they were strangers, especially not when they were so close to being on their way to the Academy.

The three boys finished up and headed out of the inn for a day of sightseeing. As they wound their way through the streets, they got a lot of interested stares. It was hard to blend in with their young eight-foot-tall friend. Grayden remembered arriving in Dalton and how Dalmir had blended in so well—he wondered how the man had managed it—he wasn't much shorter than Beren. Perhaps it was the cloak and the slight hunch of the older man's shoulders, or perhaps it was that they had arrived on horseback; it must be easier to hide one's height while riding a horse. Either way, Beren did not blend in, and many of the people they passed stopped to watch the young giant as he paused and peered at various booths or ducked to avoid hitting his head on painted signs above shop doors. Maybe it wasn't just his height, Grayden thought. Beren didn't attempt to hide his stature. He walked upright, his shoulders squared and his head high. He didn't swagger or come across as arrogant, he just wore his stature with extreme self-assurance.

Once they reached the open-air market, Beren grew more comfortable away from the walls and low-hanging signs. Aromas of freshly baked pastries filled the air and wafted enticingly. Jewelry sparkled on racks and tables, and bolts of cloth hung on spindle-like hangers so that people could pull out however much they needed without having to lift the entire heavy roll or worry about dropping the cloth on the dusty ground. Vendors called out to those passing along the aisles, trying to convince each person to buy their wares. Compared to the marketplace in Elricht Harbor, this experience assaulted every one of Grayden's senses.

The three of them agreed to browse before buying any trinkets for home, although they did each choose a pastry from the closest table. Munching on their freshly baked treats and getting their fingers covered in a fine, powdery sugar, they walked on, winding their way deeper and deeper into the marketplace. The long aisles and tables set with fascinating or mouth-watering items stretched on endlessly. Many of the booths boasted reasonable prices, though a few demanded costs so exorbitant they made Grayden's jaw feel as though it was about to drop off his face. Eventually, though, the boys found themselves on the far side of the market. Without truly meaning to, they entered a side street. The buildings on either side closed in upon them, and Grayden realized how free he had felt in the open air of the market, despite the cacophony and the crowds. In the close space of the alley, he felt claustrophobic and jumpy.

"What is wrong with me?" Grayden murmured.

Wynn and Beren looked at him oddly.

"Sorry, we got into the alley and I suddenly had this strange feeling like we're being followed or watched—" He rubbed his arms briskly as a chill went through him.

Wynn looked around the alley, his face suddenly serious. "We play a game back home, called Cat and Mouse," he explained in a low tone to Beren. "You split up into teams and the mice all run and hide, but they're allowed to keep moving; they don't have to stay in one place. The cats are supposed to sneak up on the mice and capture them. Nobody has ever managed to sneak up on Grayden; he's got a sixth sense."

Beren looked at Grayden with a light of respect in his eyes. "We've seen all the booths," he said. "We should probably head back."

"You're right," Grayden replied. The hair on the back of his neck prickled. "I saw a few gift ideas. Seren would go wild over just about anything I sent her."

"You sure you don't want to send something special to Ailwen?" Wynn cast him a sideways glance.

Grayden started to protest when a dark shape dropped to the ground before them. He ducked and whirled around, fumbling for his dagger. He never even got it out of its sheath because Beren shoved him, causing him to stumble into a stack of barrels. As he fell, he saw several more figures leap to the ground, surrounding the young Telsuman. Wynn was on the other side of the street, and Grayden could tell from his friend's position that Beren must have pushed him out of the way as well.

Berenger was a blur of motion as the silent warriors descended upon him from all sides. Grayden counted perhaps three or four of them, all dressed in black, with hoods pulled up over their heads, shading their faces. Steel glinted in their hands as they attacked Beren. It was hard to keep track of how many there were because they kept moving. Beren was a windmill of action himself, fighting not only with his fists, but with his elbows and knees as well. He threw one warrior over his shoulder, sending him flying into a nearby shop sign on Grayden's side of the street. The warrior cried out once as he hit the hard wooden sign and then fell to the ground where he lay, unmoving.

Since Beren had the fight well in hand, Grayden went over to the fallen assailant and pulled back his hood. The man was clearly not Dalman. His features were much sharper, his skin almost translucent. His eyes fluttered open.

"May Sevalk... be found," the man gasped, and then his eyes closed as he lapsed into unconsciousness.

Grayden frowned, puzzled at this strange exclamation. His glance fell to the man's arm, where his sleeve had fallen back, revealing a strange marking. A tattoo. He studied the marking closely, memorizing every detail. He looked up to see Beren knocking the heads of the last two assailants together. They both fell to the ground with slight groans.

Beren turned and grinned at Grayden. "That was refreshing," he said. "I have been missing a brisk morning workout since I began my journey to Dalton."

Wynn joined them. "That was the most amazing thing I've ever seen! You have to teach me how to fight like that. You never even drew your sword."

"My sword?" Beren looked aghast. "'Twould be a right dishonorable thing to draw a sword during such an exercise."

"I'm pretty sure this wasn't an exercise," Grayden said slowly, taking a dagger from the unconscious man at his feet. He wrapped it up in the paper his pastry had been in and shoved it into his pocket. "They meant business. Either way, I'd like to get out of this alley."

"Me too," Wynn agreed.

"I assumed the Academy sent these men to test new initiates," Beren said, his expression open and earnest.

Grayden shook his head slowly. "I don't think so."

Beren's brow wrinkled. "Truly?"

"I've never heard of such a practice. Wynn?"

Wynn shook his head, staring down at one of the fallen men with a studious expression in his eye. Grayden turned and paced away.

They made their way back to the marketplace. The noise and bustle of the crowd were soothing after the menacing attack in the alley. It did not take them long to choose items they could afford and make their purchases for family members and friends back home. Grayden picked out a bracelet of blue stones for Seren, a delicate vase for his mother, and a leather-bound journal with blank pages for his father to keep notes on the harvest. He eyed a sterling silver necklace with a rose charm on it and his mind drifted to Ailwen, but resisted the urge to buy it. He had no business courting a woman he would not see again for at least two years.

They then searched the market for merchants who were traveling to Dalsea or Gnupar. The merchant traveling to Dalsea was more than happy to take their gifts to their families and friends for them. He charged Wynn and Grayden twenty kips each, and promised to keep the gifts safe and deliver them in good condition. He also pointed them toward a booth where a friend of his was selling his wares.

"Ghar goes to Gnupar more frequently than any of the others I've met," the man said.

They thanked him and crossed a few aisles to where the other merchant's booth was.

"Twenty kips each?" Beren looked nonplussed. "That seems high, especially since he was going there anyway."

"It's to guarantee the items get delivered safely to the ones named on each package," Grayden explained. "A courier would probably charge us two sigyls."

"Still..." Beren shrugged. "I'm not very familiar with the practice of sending trinkets home. I believe my brothers will like the sharpening stones I found for them, though."

"You bought a lot of those," Wynn said. "How many brothers do you have?"

"Six," Beren replied. "All younger."

Wynn whistled. "Big family, and we come from a farming community. Any sisters?"

"Three," Beren nodded, "but two of them are twins."

"You're the oldest of ten?" Grayden asked.

"No, my sister, Cathrin, is eldest," Beren answered as they reached Ghar's booth.

"What do you want?" the merchant asked gruffly.

"Uh..." Beren stammered, clearly taken aback.

"Your friend, Yevor, told us you often travel to Gnupar in Telsuma," Grayden said. "We were wondering if you were heading there soon, and if you would take a package to our friend's family for him. He is willing to pay you. Yevor charged us twenty kips to take our packages home to Dalsea, but Gnupar is not as far, so fifteen might be more fair."

Ghar gave an unfriendly snort. "Yevor sent you, eh? Meddling old..." His voice turned into a low mutter for a bit, then he looked up at them. "I'll do it for thirty kips. I'll bet Yevor charged you both, swindling old..." His voice died again into a string of mutters that the boys could not make out.

"Truly, he did," Beren said. "But he has to find several homes in order to deliver the items placed in his care. All my packages are going to the same house. I'll give you not a kip over eighteen."

Ghar spat, and a stream of brown liquid sprayed onto the ground at their feet. "Twenty-five, and I'll not budge on that. Which family am I taking these precious packages to?"

"The Adelfried family," Beren replied.

Ghar's eyes widened and he stood up straighter, his entire demeanor changing in an eye-blink. "Adelfried, is it? I had heard they were sending one of their sons to the Academy. That would be you, I assume?"

Beren nodded.

"I'll take your packages at no charge, and count it a privilege, my lord." Ghar bowed from the shoulders. Wynn and Grayden shared a surprised glance.

Beren handed over the packages, each wrapped carefully in brown paper and tied with a string. He had written the names of his various family members on each package in sharp letters. The merchant handled them delicately and placed them on a shelf beneath his table.

"This is where I keep most of my personal belongings," he explained. "I swear to you that I will keep your merchandise with the utmost care and deliver it as soon as I reach Gnupar, before I even sell a single ware."

"You have my thanks," Beren replied. "And your eighteen kips," he added, pouring the money into the man's hand.

As they turned to leave, Wynn couldn't contain himself anymore. "What was that all about? He wasn't pleasant at all until you mentioned your family name."

Beren flushed and shrugged, but refused to answer the question. The three returned to the inn, where Grayden suggested they visit Dalmir's room.

"I just have a feeling he'd be interested in the 'friends' we made today," Grayden explained.

19

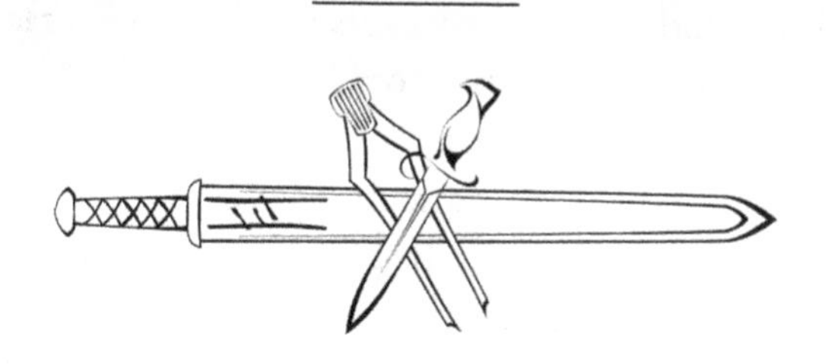

Dalmir promptly invited them into his room when they arrived at his door. They gathered around the small table and talked rapidly, their voices clamoring over each other in their excitement. The older man listened with an unfathomable expression as they poured out the tale of their adventure in the marketplace. Grayden pulled out a piece of paper and a stub of pencil, quickly sketching from memory.

"This is the tattoo the one man had on his arm, and here is the dagger he was carrying."

Dalmir glanced at the piece of paper and then his eyes darkened. He snatched it up and stared at it for a long while without speaking. Then he laid it carefully down on the table. The symbol on the paper was strange, and unfamiliar: two winged malkyns facing each other and raised up on their hind legs, noses pointed toward a seven-pointed crown. Below the crown, between the malkyns, hovered a small circle.

"Do you recognize this insignia?" Dalmir asked Beren, handing the paper to him.

Beren looked at the drawing carefully and then shook his head. "I have never seen its like before. I am sure I would remember such a unique design."

Next, Dalmir picked up the dagger. It was a plain enough thing, with no insignia or markings on its hilt. He pulled out a handkerchief and wiped the dagger on it. The white handkerchief came away stained a dark purple. Grayden stared at it, a shudder coursing through him. A coating on a blade could only mean one thing, but he held his peace while Dalmir squinted at the residue. He lifted the cloth to his nose and sniffed, then his face turned pale and he placed the blade back on the table.

"Do not touch it!" he warned, as Wynn reached to pick up the dagger. "It is poisoned with sparrack root."

Grayden's breath left his body in a sudden exhalation of alarm. Sparrack was a rare, lethal plant that grew only in small regions of Ondoura. It was so deadly, that the Council had tried to completely outlaw its use, with limited degrees of success. One scratch from a blade doused in the poison was all it would have taken to end any of their lives.

Dalmir stared hard at Beren. "Somebody wanted very badly to kill you today. Why might that be?"

Beren's face reddened. "I have not been completely honest regarding my true identity. It was because I did not wish to receive different treatment from other students. But I had no idea I might put others in harm's way because of my heritage. If not for the sparrack root on the blade, I would still consider our encounter this morning as a mere drill; I was fighting to end the fight, not to save my life. Believe me, the results would have been different had I known." He turned to Grayden and Wynn. "Please forgive me for the danger I put you in. I am the eldest son of Lord Adelfried of Gnupar. I hoped to find friends at the Academy trustworthy enough to share this information with; I am glad to have found you sooner."

"Lord Adelfried, the Council member of Telsuma?" Wynn asked, his tone incredulous. "The head of Telmondir's military?"

Grayden stared at his new friend, stunned. He kicked himself for not putting the pieces together sooner. Beren had even told them his family name in the market, but it had not registered that he was *that* Berenger Adelfried, the one whose family he had studied in primary school.

Beren nodded sheepishly. "Yes."

"So you're royalty?" Wynn asked.

"Not as you would describe it here in Dalma. My father is not a king. He still answers to the Council that rules all three of our lands. But, yes, I suppose we might appear as royalty to some. My family is wealthy and influential, not just in Gnupar, but throughout all of Telsuma."

"A good reason for someone to want you dead," Dalmir said.

"But he has six other brothers," Grayden protested. "And the position of Council member is elected, not inherited. What would killing the oldest son accomplish, other than to start a war?"

"What indeed?" Dalmir mused. He wrapped the dagger in the handkerchief.

"Your brothers, they wouldn't...?" Wynn left the question hanging.

"Never!" Beren exclaimed. "While my family owns an extensive estate in its own right, there is very little extra accorded to my inheritance that my brothers will not also receive. My father believes in equity, and set up his title, wealth, and land in such a way as to make sure that all of us will receive a fair amount."

"So it does not benefit any of your siblings to have you killed." Dalmir took the wrapped blade to the hearth and tossed it into the fire. The flames sputtered around the handkerchief and then flared to life with a purple glow that would have been beautiful had Grayden been unaware of the cause.

"No. We are all good friends as well," Beren answered. "We jest with one another, and my brothers mock the scrawniness of my shoulders, but it is all meant in good humor. I would trust any of them with my life. Our family is quite close."

"And yet the assassin bears the mark of one whose treachery against his brothers cost all but one their lives," Dalmir mused.

"You know the symbol?" Grayden asked.

"What?" Dalmir looked startled.

"You said the assassin bears the mark of one whose treachery against his brothers cost all but one their lives. You know whose mark this is?" He gestured at the drawing. "You have seen it before?"

"I did not mean to say that out loud. But, yes, I am familiar with this mark. It is the symbol of a man who will stop at nothing to gain power. I do not yet know why he wishes our friend Berenger here dead, but we shall have to disappoint him by keeping Beren very much alive. I believe that once you reach the Academy, you will all be safe, at least for a time."

"Is he from Ondoura? The man you're speaking of?" Wynn asked.

"I said nothing of Ondoura," Dalmir said, his eyebrows rising.

"No, but that's the only place sparrack root grows," Wynn said.

"Ah." Dalmir gazed approvingly at Wynn. "That is an excellent point, Wynn. But no, the man I am speaking of is not from Ondoura. However, the assassins clearly wanted to make it appear as if the threat to Berenger originates in Ondoura. We must be cautious, as we can safely assume you were never meant to see that tattoo. Can you think of anyone else who might wish you dead? What of the growing tension with the Igyeum you boys were telling me about on our journey?"

"The Ar'Mol?" Beren looked startled, then grew thoughtful. "I suppose it's possible."

"Well, the airship leaves tomorrow," Wynn said. "I guess we only have to make it through the night."

"We must keep on our guard, even on the airship." Dalmir's voice was stern. "There is no guarantee, not until we get to Csethel. For now, I would caution you all to stay inside the inn. I would insist even that you keep to your rooms, but I know it is too much to hope for that young lads such as you might heed such a warning; the young often consider themselves invincible."

He shook his head sadly. "But, please, do stay inside the Black Arms tonight."

The three boys nodded soberly, and then returned to their rooms. Grayden hung back, a question plaguing his mind.

Dalmir raised an eyebrow at him. "Yes?"

"Twice now you've mentioned a place called Csethel," Grayden said. "What is Csethel?"

"You possess sharp ears. Tell me, Wynn intimated that you had foreknowledge of the attack. How did you know you were being followed this morning?"

"I don't know. I just... felt it. It's hard to explain. I've always been able to sense when someone is watching or following me. You're not the first person to ask me that. I... it's like that feeling you get when you step too close to the edge of a cliff or a drop-off, if you know what I mean, a flutter inside warning that you're in danger." Grayden shook his head. "I'm really not good at explaining it."

"No, you explain it well. And it intrigues me, because I have never met anyone else with that ability before, not with the accuracy your friend Wynn ascribes to you, anyway. Have you ever been wrong?"

"Not that I know of." Discomfort prickled at the base of Grayden's skull. He did not like discussing his inexplicable ability.

"I see." Dalmir paused. "Very well, your honesty deserves to be repaid in kind. Csethel was a University, a place of great knowledge and wisdom. It was a cathedral of erudition, where all were welcome to venture inside with their questions and learn as many answers as they could. I believe your Academy and its library were built upon the ruins of Csethel University."

"The Academy has been there for a hundred and fifty years. And before that, it was simply a field with interesting rock formations. Not even the men who found the hidden chambers full of scrolls could figure out what its purpose had been." Grayden's voice was soft. "How could you know anything about what stood there before? You said you've never been there."

"I have not visited the library that is currently there. That is true," Dalmir replied. He hesitated, and his sharp blue eyes seemed to peer directly into Grayden's heart. The man nodded, as if making up his mind about a question that had been troubling him for a while. "But I did visit the University of Csethel, in all its former glory. Now I am tired, and the rest of your questions can wait."

Grayden understood he was being dismissed, but the rest of his questions burned in his mouth like crushed pepper pods. How old was Dalmir? How was it that the man knew history that had fallen into the blurry past, but was unaware of the most commonly known and monumental historic events of the more recent decades? Who was this strange old man? With great effort, Grayden choked down the questions—knowing he would receive no more answers—and returned to his own room. He thought about the look Dalmir had given him before revealing that he had visited Csethel during its halcyon days and realized that the man had trusted him with personal information he was not sharing widely. As he turned the knob to his door, Grayden was determined to be worthy of Dalmir's trust. He would not reveal his conversation with the strange old man, even to Wynn. At least, not yet.

When Grayden entered the room, Wynn was sitting on the bed, his face paler than usual. He remained strangely silent. Grayden looked at him askance.

"What's eating you?" he asked.

"I don't..." Wynn shook his head, and a bit of the color returned to his face. "You'll laugh at me."

"Try me."

"We're going to train for war."

Grayden frowned. "You mean at the Academy?"

"Yeah." Wynn paused. The silence stretched out between them, but Grayden held his peace and sat on his own bed, pulling his boots off and lying down. His friend would continue when he had his thoughts in order. At last, Wynn broke the quiet. "I mean,

I knew we were going to learn stuff about weapons and strategy; that's why we had to find teachers who could instruct us in the basics with swords, bows, and staves. I guess I never thought... it didn't seem real to me that the Academy was a training ground for soldiers, and that the Defenders are more than just a job you could take at graduation if you don't want to go home. There's a war coming, Grayden... and we're going to be training to fight in it."

Grayden stared up at the ceiling, unsure of how to reply.

"Someone tried to kill us today," Wynn continued after another long pause.

"Dalmir said Beren was the target."

"Maybe... maybe not. They closed in on him because he pushed us both out of the way. Perhaps they were simply after anyone who might become a future threat, say, an enemy warrior in the war that's coming."

"I hadn't thought of that," Grayden said.

"But I can't get it out of my head," Wynn continued. "If Beren was the target, the only reason anyone would have for killing him would be to start a war."

Grayden rubbed a hand across his face. He recognized the look in Wynn's eyes. His friend had come to a conclusion and would not be dissuaded from it without solid evidence. "I guess you're right. The threat from the Ar'Mol has always felt so far away. But if those assassins were his men, then we got a real taste of what we're going to be training for. I guess I'd never really thought beyond graduation before... Had you?"

"I figured I'd take the two hundred and fifty sigyls and go home," Wynn admitted.

"Me too." Grayden thought wistfully of Ailwen, and then he closed his heart. "I think I'll join the Defenders, instead." He shrugged. "But I can't join without the training, and that'll be another four years. A lot can change in four years."

Wynn didn't respond, but Grayden didn't expect him to. They both had reasons to go home at the end of their tenure.

They both had family, friends, loved ones in Dalsea. But Grayden knew, or perhaps he had always known, that he could never go back. As Ailwen had suggested, once he entered the Academy, he would never fit in Dalsea again. Though he wished he could deny it, the truth in her words rang pure. He would visit, but the ones he loved would gradually move on; they would grow comfortable without him, and he would change in the time he was gone, change in ways he could never take back. Some people, like Wynn's father, could travel the world and then slide back into their old lives and settle down, never to wander again. Grayden sensed in his heart that he was not of that kind. His was a road that would always go onward, and never back.

20

Roald, the leader of the Ar'Molon's private assassins, paced back and forth before his men, fury boiling beneath the surface of his calm exterior. Jarl had just finished giving his report on how spectacularly he and his team had failed in the Dalton marketplace.

"They saw Keir's face? The tattoo on his arm? They took one of your daggers? There were four of you. Four against one. You are supposed to be the best there is, and yet you failed." Roald stared into the eyes of his subordinate until the other looked away, a flush of shame crawling up his neck.

"There were three of them." Jarl's voice faltered as Roald's gaze froze him mid-sentence.

"From what Keir reported, only one of them actually fought back." Roald whirled on Jarl, his rapier whipping out and coming to rest with the point just barely kissing the man's throat. "Perhaps I should begin recruiting a new task force; I obviously overestimated your skills."

Jarl stiffened at the insult, but remained silent.

"Now our task is far more difficult," he muttered.

"How so? Forgive me, De'Anan, but besides the embarrassment we suffered, I do not understand how anything has changed. We can try again. Our men survived."

"You do not..." Roald's face turned a mottled shade of purple. "You imbecile! They saw Keir's face. And his tattoo. You left witnesses, they will tell others, word will spread."

"Even if they did glimpse the tattoo, it will mean nothing to them. Even if they manage to identify the poison on the dagger, it will only serve our mission. The sparrack root points directly at Ondoura," Jarl replied evenly. "They are but three youths. We are the Kotai. Even rumors will only serve us, making people jump at shadows."

"What were you thinking?" Roald hissed.

"De'Anan?"

"You knew our orders. You were to wait and observe. We were not supposed to move on the prince until after the pirates make their move. To attack in a crowded marketplace... I ask again, what were you thinking?"

Jarl hesitated. "I... I only thought that we had an opening. An opportunity that we should not allow to go to waste. I believed..."

Roald's fist backhanded across his subordinate's jaw. "You thought, you believed! You leaped upon an opportunity!" He roared the words. "You merely saw an opportunity for yourself. You expected that taking initiative like this might make the Ar'Molon smile upon you, eh? That if you brought him his prize early he might raise your rank from Koldo to Tu'Anan? Maybe give you your own ship and crew? Perhaps, had your plan worked, you might have been right. But your carelessness may have now cost us everything, the entire plan. You will spend the rest of this mission in the brig, and I will let the outcome of our assignment determine your fate."

Roald made an impatient gesture and two of his men moved forward to take Jarl by the arms, dragging him down to the small cell. Roald did not watch him go. Instead, he paced the length of his chambers, coming to a halt in front of his small porthole. He stared out at the *Crimson Eagle*, watching as its crew hurried to load their cargo in preparation for their departure on the morrow. He did not like this assignment any more than Jarl did. But the Ar'Molon had his reasons, and it was not for even a De'Anan to question them.

21

Raisa carefully chose handholds as she climbed up the wall behind Mouse. The boy glided up the wall effortlessly. How many times had he done this? Raisa wondered as she pulled her slight frame up another few feet. When Mouse disappeared over the top of the wall, she experienced a moment of panic. She heard shouting and running on the other side of the barrier. Rustam and Yefrem were doing their part, pulling the guards toward the main entrance by causing a scene.

"Come on!" Mouse hissed as she reached the top of the wall and looked down. He was dancing impatiently from one foot to the other as though the ground was hot. Raisa glared down at him.

"I'm not as good at this as you are," she hissed.

"If you're having trouble here, wait until you get on the airship," Mouse taunted. "They'll spot you as an imposter if you can't climb rigging any faster than that."

Muttering under her breath, Raisa vaulted herself over the wall and dropped the entire ten-foot distance, landing so lightly she barely made a sound. Mouse's expression changed instantly from impatient to impressed, but Raisa ignored him. She was already heading toward the large bunkhouse inside the Docks.

Her papers were in order, but they had her arriving from Telos on the *Swift Cloud*, which meant she had to present her identification to the port master from inside the Docks.

Mouse scurried to catch up with her, trying to match his strides to her long, fluid gait. She glanced down at his shabby garments and smudged face.

"You'd best make certain nobody sees you with me," she reminded him. "You look like a street urchin."

"I *am* a street urchin." He smirked up at her.

"You *were* a street urchin." She sniffed and pulled down at the bottom of her crisp, brown suede jacket that stopped at her hips in front but had elegant tails that swung down to meet the tops of her shiny brown boots in back. With a flick of her wrists, she adjusted the lacy cuffs of her dark blue blouse, making sure that her uniform was in order. She paused, brushing away a smudge of dirt from the knee of her smart brown breeches. It would not do to arrive looking as though she had clambered up and over a dusty wall. She wished she had a mirror in which she could check her appearance, but time did not allow for it. She had to make the most of Rustam and Yefrem's distraction. Striding forward, she patted absently at her hair, which Shaesta had helped her pull back from her face and plait tightly in a braid that hung down the middle of her back. The braid was so tight it felt like a headache waiting to happen, but Raisa tried to ignore the discomfort.

"Are you certain these are all in order?" Raisa asked, pulling a fat envelope out of an inside jacket pocket and tapping it nervously against her leg.

"I've told you, Rax is the best in the business."

Raisa studied the seal on the envelope dubiously. "He certainly charged enough."

Mouse shrugged.

"Well, we're almost there. We'll see if this was worth the money in a few minutes. This is where we part ways for now, little mouse."

The boy darted into the maze of barrels and boxes. Raisa

skirted her way around the bunkhouse and then strode purposefully toward the front entrance, where Rustam was holding Yefrem's arms as though trying to keep him from pummeling the officers surrounding them. Yefrem was shouting incoherently at the top of his lungs, and Rustam looked harried and apologetic.

"What is going on here?" Raisa's voice boomed out, startling everyone. The guards turned toward her, took in her uniform, and hurriedly began explaining all at once. Rustam and Yefrem also shouted as though trying to explain themselves. Raisa listened patiently for a few minutes and then her face hardened.

"This is a peaceful city and a well-to-do port of harbor. Why are these men being allowed to cause such a ruckus? Please escort them out. Gentlemen, if you wish to lodge a complaint, you may bring it to our attention through the proper channels. Then, and only then, will we consider your grievances, and I promise you we will do our best to right any wrong you may have suffered. But this is neither the time nor the place for such things."

Rustam nodded, looking cowed. Yefrem opened his mouth as though about to argue, but Raisa lifted a single finger. "I could call the city guards, if you cannot conduct yourselves like gentlemen."

Yefrem huffed out an angry breath, but turned and stomped after his brother. Raisa kept herself from grinning as she turned toward the head officer of the Docks.

"Thank you, ma'am," he said, mopping his brow with a clean handkerchief. "I believe they were about ready to draw their weapons, and who knows what might have happened."

Raisa compressed her lips. "Just doing my duty, sir. I heard the commotion all the way over on the *Swift Cloud* and decided to see if I could lend a hand. I'm here to report for my post aboard the *Crimson Eagle;* would you please convey myself and my papers to the captain of that vessel?" She held up her thick envelope. "I have an urgent message for him regarding an additional security measure."

"Of course, of course, follow me," the officer replied. "That's funny. I thought all the crew for that ship had already arrived."

"A lieutenant fell ill suddenly. When my ship arrived, a courier arrived with my new orders to replace him," Raisa explained as they walked. "Lucky my ship arrived early, or they'd be sailing out tomorrow a crewman short."

"That is fortunate," the man replied. They continued into the bunkhouse—little more than a long hallway with doors along either side of it—behind which were small rooms where the crew could rest and freshen up between assignments. "Here we are." The officer stopped in front of a door. "Captain Dagur's room."

He knocked smartly. The door opened in swift response, and a tall, well-muscled man stood before them. Raisa studied him. An intelligent gleam filled his keen hazel eyes. He was near Oleck's age, or perhaps a few years older, a seasoned captain, though clean-shaven.

"Who are you?" he asked.

"Raisa Setlander, reporting for duty, sir." She saluted smartly, clicking her heels together. "They sent me to replace Abel Karden."

"Shame about him; we've flown together before. I'll miss his bellowing," Dagur said. "You brought your orders with you?"

Raisa held out the envelope and tried to look nonchalant. Dagur examined the seal on the envelope before breaking it, pulling the papers out. He flipped through them, scanning their contents until he came to the last page. He was silent for a few long minutes as he read the last page intently before looking up at her, a question in his eyes.

"There is a new order in here for me. Are you aware of it?"

"I knew they were sending you an extra security measure, sir, but they did not tell me what it was and I never opened the envelope to find out."

"You know we set sail tomorrow for Doran?"

"Yes, sir."

"And that we will transport the Academy students along with our regular cargo and passengers?"

"I was not aware of that, sir," Raisa lied.

"You are aware of our agreement with the Academy?"

"They get a discount on airfare in exchange for helping with security."

"So that we save money by not having to hire guards, that is correct. And I've just received orders to confiscate everyone's weapons as they board the airship tomorrow and inspect them before returning them to the students and other passengers. Does that seem strange to you?"

"Yes, sir," Raisa said slowly. "Do the new orders give any explanation?"

Dagur frowned. "Says they are concerned about the quality of weapons. I suppose I can understand—most of the recruits are really nothing more than farmers—but my superiors never cared about that before. I don't like this."

Raisa shrugged. "If the orders come from our superiors, what can we do?"

Dagur eyed the paper. "Nothing. We must follow the order, but I don't have to like it. I'll make sure I assign some of the crew to 'inspect' the weapons once we're airborne and return them to our guests as quickly as possible. It's a nuisance, but like you said, what can we do?"

Raisa shrugged. "Is there a vacant room where I can get some rest?"

"Ask the officer of the Docks. Be sure to report to the *Crimson Eagle* at first bell tomorrow. We ship out as soon as we're completely loaded."

"Aye, sir."

Dagur glanced up as she turned to depart. "When you see the dock officer, could you please let him know I need to speak with him?"

"Certainly, sir," Raisa replied. She strode back into the hallway, where she found the dock officer waiting. He gave her a small smile.

"Figured you'd need someone to show you where to freshen up and rest for the evening." He led her to a vacant room and held the door for her. "We all eat together in the mess at the end of the hall. If you aren't up to it, though, you can have food brought to your room."

Raisa yawned. "I might try to join you," she lied. "But that's good to know if I decide I'm too tired. Do you need me to take a shift guarding the ship?"

"Thanks for reminding me, yes. You'll take Abel's shift, which was"—he pulled a sheet of paper out of his pocket and grimaced at it—"third watch. Sorry."

Raisa heaved a sigh. "Not a problem. I think I'll stay in my room then, if that's all right."

"Good idea. I can try to change the schedule for you—"

"Don't worry about it, sir, I'm okay."

"If you're sure?"

Raisa nodded firmly. The officer looked impressed and relieved.

"Oh, Captain Dagur said he would like to speak with you," Raisa said as he turned to leave.

"Very well. Safe voyage," he said and hurried off before she could change her mind.

Raisa let the door close behind him and opened the window that looked out into the Docks. It was not a large window, but it was big enough for Mouse to crawl through, which he did a moment later.

"Everything go okay?" he asked, dropping lightly to the floor.

"Perfectly. They gave me the third watch, just as planned. You can sneak onto the ship then and start your work. It'll give you about six hours to do the job before the passengers start boarding the ship. I'll signal you when it's time to hide. Think you'll have enough time?"

"Plenty of time."

"And you memorized the prints? You know where to find everything?"

"I could find the right room with my eyes closed."

"You have all your tools?"

"Raisa." Mouse held up his hands. "It's me. You're acting like you don't trust me or something. In the past two years, have I ever let you or the crew down?"

"Of course not. You're crew, Mouse. I'm not sure what's wrong with me. I'm a little jittery about this next bit," Raisa apologized. "No offense. I guess there's not much to do for a while. Might as well try to get a few winks, as it's going to be a long night."

22

Despite the threat of unknown assassins and the nervousness about traveling by air, Grayden slept well. He awoke refreshed and energized, ready to face whatever the new day held. He was one of the first to arrive in the common room, his belongings neatly packed up in his saddlebags. Nia smiled at him and brought him a mug of fresh milk, but did not stop to chat. Grayden sipped from his mug, feeling a little lonely, but he knew her morning would start early. The Academy students would rise soon and want their breakfast before they left for the Docks.

Dalmir emerged from his room not long after Grayden and joined the young man at their customary table. Grayden greeted him enthusiastically.

"All fresh-faced this morning, I see," Dalmir commented gruffly. "I wonder if our friend Wynn will be so chipper."

Nia swung by their table and handed Dalmir his usual morning brew of mulled cider.

Grayden shrugged, then his expression turned instantly to one of concern. "Dalmir, I forgot about your horse! Ours are included in our tickets from the Academy, but we didn't even think to ask about yours!" He looked around wildly and half got up from his bench. "Perhaps it's not too late..."

Dalmir laid a steadying hand on Grayden's arm. "Calm down there. You're skittish as an unbroken colt. My ticket." He produced it from a deep pocket in his cloak. "Read it."

Grayden looked closely at the ticket: *One passenger plus baggage and riding animal*. He sat back and breathed a slow sigh.

"That should cover it." He took a sip of his milk, then looked up, his eyes curious. "What does it mean by 'riding animal?' Why not just say 'horse'?"

"In other parts of the world, they have other types of riding animals. In Malei they ride malkyns. I suppose the closest thing you could imagine is a giant cat, but the malkyns are as like to one of your barn cats as the airships are to your horses."

"They fly?" Grayden asked.

"No. I just meant the comparison is unworthy. Malkyns are fearsome beasts, a bit shorter than a horse, with front teeth that curve down over their lower jaws. And yet they possess unparalleled grace; watching them run is like watching a river wind through its bed. In Palla they use mounts called leythan, massive beasts with great horns growing out of their faces. They are reptilian, covered in scales like a natural plated armor, and huge tails they can swing like clubs. In the regions of Vallei, it is said they ride strange horses that have horns growing out of their foreheads, or wings on their backs... but perhaps that is just a rumor. I never did spend much time in Vallei. I always assumed I'd have time to do so later. Now I wish..."

Grayden started to laugh, but stopped himself when he realized Dalmir was not teasing him. In fact, the man seemed to have ceased speaking to Grayden at all. His musings were more akin to a man talking to himself. Unsure how best to respond, and unsure if a response was even appropriate, Grayden buried his face in his mug and drank deeply. A moment later, Wynn came and deposited himself on the bench next to Grayden, swinging his belongings to the floor with a dull thud. The bags were half-packed, and clothes still hung out of the semi-open pockets. Wynn's boots were slung over his shoulder, held together by their straps. His face had a grayish pallor beneath his tousled hair.

"Are you all right?" Grayden asked, as Nia brought another mug of milk.

Wynn grimaced. "Stayed up too late... listened to far too many stories about what it's like riding on an airship and had nightmares of falling all night. I think I'm getting sick. Do you think it's too late to just go home?"

Grayden rolled his eyes. "You'll be fine. You just wait until you have a little food in you and we're on our way."

"Of course you're in a good mood. You were asleep before I even got back to the room."

"You could have gone to bed earlier."

"Eh."

"I told you before, I'm not going to be your mother at the Academy. If you're late for classes and they kick you out, it's your own fault." Grayden tried to make his voice sound stern.

"Good morning, my friends." Beren joined them, sitting on the unoccupied third bench. "Today we begin the second leg of our prodigious journey to that elite school of learning and training. I must confess, I am yearning to be done with this sitting around and waiting for airships. I would much rather have more of the sort of skirmishing that we encountered yesterday."

"Hush," Dalmir snapped. "Speak not of that, lest unfriendly ears are listening."

Color flooded into the young giant's face. "Forgive me. In sleep I did forget the gravity of yesterday's events. I meant only that I am eager to begin the intense training that the Academy promises to its recruits, not that I..." Beren trailed off, realizing that he could say no more without incurring additional wrath.

"I understand, but it would be best not to speak lightly of such things... at least not until we are aboard the airship, and perhaps not even then." Dalmir's voice was gentler now. "The technology to build the airships came from the East, after all..."

"You think the Ar'Mol might have sent them?" Wynn asked.

"I think we should not speculate on it at all while we are in any common area," Dalmir snapped.

Wynn had the grace to look ashamed. But before any of them could say more or even speak to change the subject, Nia had returned with their breakfast. She brought them plates piled high with round cakes slathered in syrup, and cooked eggs stuffed with peppers and cheese. There was even a plate with thick slabs of bacon for them to share. The boys dug into the food eagerly, and nothing more was said at all for quite some time.

When breakfast had ended, Wynn spent a while trying to stuff his things more securely into his saddlebags. At length, he gave up on getting the bags completely closed and turned his attention to pulling on his boots. While he waited for his friend, Grayden leaned back against the wall and closed his eyes. Even though they would not arrive at the Academy for a few more days, today held monumental import, and he wanted to savor the anticipation. This day he would set foot on an airship. His stomach lurched a little at the thought, and he wondered what it would be like to fly high above the ground. He hoped he would not be sick or have to spend the trip in his bunk. He wanted to explore the vessel that would carry him five hundred leagues in a mere two days, a trip that would take over a lunat on horseback.

He must have dozed off, lost in thought, because suddenly Wynn was shaking him. Grayden opened his eyes and saw that the room had filled up. Students milled about, checking to make sure they had all their belongings. An older student, with shoulders even broader than Beren's, though he was probably shorter than Grayden by a few hands, stood up on a bench and held up his hands for silence. The young men ceased talking and turned expectant eyes to their peer.

"My name is Koen," the young man said. "I'm beginning my fourth and final year at the Academy. Headmaster Freidzen sent me and a few others here to meet and give instructions to those of you who are new." He pointed out a few other older students. "If you have questions, you can ask any one of us.

"I beg the indulgence of any non-first-year students, as you've heard this before. Everyone needs to leave here in an orderly fashion, get your horses and any tack, and then meet up in the back paddock. From there we will together proceed to the Docks, where we will be told which airship to board. Handlers will take your horses aboard and they will be attended to throughout the flight. We will share quarters, two or more to a cabin, and the captain and crew expect us to keep our weapons with us at all times. The Academy gets a discount on these tickets because we can provide security during the flight that they would otherwise have to hire out. It will be a mite cramped and a few of you may experience air-sickness, but keep in mind that the flight is not even two full days. If you can survive that, you can definitely survive your first few days at the Academy."

A laugh went up from the more experienced students, and Grayden's nervousness clenched itself into a fist in the pit of his stomach. Wynn's mouth turned up at the corners in a strained smile, and Grayden noticed that his friend's face looked a little pale. Koen stepped down from the bench and chaos reigned for a few minutes. However, eventually the chaos receded and a semblance of order took over as everyone gathered their belongings and headed out toward the stables.

The boys and Dalmir retrieved their mounts and followed the line of other students as they led their horses down the street and toward the great Docks. As they proceeded through the streets, Grayden realized that there were easily three hundred of them all told. He glanced up and saw eager faces pressed up against the windows of the buildings around them as the citizens of Dalton peered out to catch a glimpse of the latest group of Academy students, most of them new recruits. A few children waved at him, and, feeling a little foolish, Grayden waved back.

When they finally reached the Docks, Grayden stood with his friends, waiting their turn to board with as much patience as he could muster. At last, they reached the man standing at the bottom of the ramp and relinquished their tickets.

"I've only got three-man rooms left," the man informed them with a wary glance, as though he expected to be shouted at for this information. "They're located in the belly of the ship. Quarters are pretty snug."

Grayden exchanged a glance with Wynn and Beren. "That'll suit us just fine."

The man relaxed visibly and pointed toward the stern. "That way." He glanced down at Dalmir's ticket and his expression changed abruptly to one of sincere politeness. "Sir, your cabin is one of the estate rooms up near the deck. You'll turn to the bow and only go down one flight of stairs. Your room number is twelve."

"Thank you," Dalmir replied.

Together, they boarded the airship. A thrill ran through Grayden as he stepped onto the deck. Another man, this one tall and muscular, with an air of authority about him like a second cloak, greeted him. There were two men flanking him as he approached Grayden and his friends.

"Academy-bound?" he asked. Grayden and his friends nodded.

"Welcome aboard the *Crimson Eagle*. I'm Captain Dagur, in charge of this fine vessel, and if you are carrying weapons, I will need to inspect them. It won't take long."

"Captain," the younger of the two other men spoke up, "the orders said..."

"I know what the orders said," Captain Dagur barked. "I am following them to the letter."

"But surely..."

"I will inspect the weapons as ordered. We will do it right here, right now, and return them to their owners. Do you have a problem with that?"

"No, sir." The younger man retreated a half step.

"Carry on." Dagur gestured at a table set up along the ramp. The two officers stepped forward and carefully handled the weaponry as they placed it on the table. Grayden expected the three officers to marvel at Beren's great sword, but they made no comment as they returned the items.

"Any other weapons?" the captain asked.

Wynn reluctantly handed over his dagger, slingshot, and an assortment of sharp-edged throwing discs. Beren turned over a long knife. But Grayden just shrugged and gestured that he had no other weapons. He thought about the knife his parents had given him, hidden under his jacket, but he was reluctant to part with it, even for a minute, and the man seemed inclined to believe that he had no other weapons. Besides, it wasn't really a weapon, Grayden assured himself. It was a memento of home, a tool. The captain nodded in satisfaction as his lieutenant visually inspected the weapons. Once they had received their swords back, the captain waved them on toward the hatch that led down to their rooms.

He stopped Dalmir and asked about the great sword he wore.

"It is merely decorative," Dalmir replied in a feeble tone. "Just a simple way for an older gentleman to delude pickpockets into believing he is not an easy target."

Grayden turned his head slightly at Dalmir's words and saw the captain's face grow indecisive. Dalmir met the man's gaze unflinchingly, but his long white beard and the way he hunched and leaned on his staff settled the captain's indecision. He waved Dalmir along.

"Welcome aboard," was all he said.

As they descended into the ship, Grayden whispered to Dalmir, "Why didn't you want him to look at your sword?"

"Why didn't you hand over your knife?" Dalmir returned, just as quietly.

Grayden fell silent. A flight down, Dalmir stopped.

"I'll head to my room now. It's number twelve if you need me."

The boys nodded and continued on down the stairs to their own room. The interior of the airship was as awe-inspiring as its exterior. The hallways were narrow, but the ceilings were high enough that Beren did not have to hunch over as he walked. Well-polished wood lined the walls and decorative lanterns hung in sconces, lighting the hallways. At length, they reached their room. Compared to their quarters at the Black Arms, the cramped cabin looked like a hovel. The room was not equipped with proper beds, but instead had canvas hammocks hanging from the ceiling. Beren eyed these apprehensively, but made no comment. There were three chairs in the room, and a small, square table. One wall had a built-in drawer unit where they could put their belongings. As they were getting settled, a knock came at their door, and Koen poked his head into the room.

"Well, here we are. You all settled?"

Wynn nodded.

"The mess is up a level, and toward the bow. They serve lunch about an hour after lift-off. Meal times are about the same as they were at the Black Arms, and the mess is usually open as a common area all day. I know quarters are tight, but you only have to deal with it for two days, and the airship quarters make the ones at the Academy seem palatial." He smirked. "Which is good, since they would seem pretty cramped compared to what you had at the Black Arms. Captain said we'd be lifting off in a few minutes, soon as everyone's settled. Is there anything you need?"

There wasn't, so Koen nodded at them and then left to check on the next room of students. When he was gone, the three young men looked at each other.

"Well?" Wynn asked.

"What?" Grayden replied.

"What do we do now?"

"I guess we wait for lift-off."

"Think we can go up on the deck and watch?" Wynn asked, his face gleaming with a wistful excitement.

"'Spose we could ask Koen..." Grayden stuck his head out the door. "Koen?" The older boy was only a few steps down the hall.

"Yes?"

"Are we allowed up on deck to watch the lift-off?"

"Sorry, yeah, I meant to tell you you could go up there. Just have to get topside before lift-off. There are places you can strap in and watch. The crew will direct you where to go."

"Thanks!"

The three young men made their way back up the stairs to the main deck of the airship. A tall, willowy woman pointed them to an area at the side of the ship where they could stand and look over the railing. "Make sure to put on the harnesses. If it's a rough take-off, we don't want anyone falling over the side. Shouldn't be a problem today, though; weather's nice out there."

They followed her instructions and found the harnesses, little more than wide leather belts with ropes strung between the belt and the railing of the airship. Grayden wasn't sure he trusted the harness with his life, but he figured it was probably better than nothing.

The crew bustled with purposeful activity from one end of the deck to the other, tying and untying ropes, unfurling sails on the massive masts in the center of the ship, and generally appearing to be in a state of chaos. It reminded Grayden a little of the orchards come harvest time. To the untrained eye, it might look like random motion, but to those who were doing the work, it all had a purpose. Without it, he suspected the airship wouldn't fly. At long last, the hustle and bustle slowed down, and Grayden held his breath.

"This is it," he whispered.

The great airship rose into the air. The floorboards beneath their feet creaked and groaned as the ship lifted out of its supports, expanding slightly as it did so. Then, slowly, and yet with building speed, the airship glided forward, out of the Docks and into the open sky above Dalton.

Wind rushed past Grayden's face, and he leaned over the railing. As they emerged from the side of the mountain that was Dalton, clear blue skies greeted his gaze. He glanced down and his head swam in a sudden rush of sick dizziness. It was easy to forget how high up they were when standing on the streets of Dalton, but from the airship he could suddenly see exactly how lofty their position had been. Wynn leaned far out over the railing, making Grayden's stomach clench; he resisted the urge to snap at his friend to be careful. It was an odd sensation. Grayden had never been afraid of heights. All his life he had longed to scale the tower; he had always been the one sent up into the highest branches of the orchard trees; he had once spent the night sleeping on the barn roof just because he had been sure the sunrise would look better from up there. But none of those structures or climbs could compare to the dizzying altitude of the airship.

"How come the crew aren't wearing harnesses?" Beren asked once they had emerged from the Docks.

One of the crew, a woman with long black hair and a twinkle in her brown eyes, stopped as she passed them. Hearing Beren's question, she changed direction and joined them. Her step was confident, but she had the air of a woman with no idea just how breathtakingly beautiful she was.

"This is what we do," she said. "The distance to the ground doesn't bother any of us. It can be quite disorienting the first time, though. I'm guessing none of you have flown before?"

The three young men all shook their heads. The woman raised an eyebrow.

"Did you react the way you expected to?"

Again, they shook their heads.

"Best to have a harness on, then, don't you think? The crew is used to it. Besides, if you can't handle the height, you can't work on an airship. The harnesses aren't to keep you from being blown overboard; there's very little danger of that, especially on a calm day like this one. And most airships can't achieve high enough speeds to need them, either. The harness is to protect you from your own reaction to the height."

"Thank you," Beren replied.

"You're welcome. My name's Raisa. If you have questions, I'm always around up here on the deck."

Grayden's thoughts turned to home as the woman strode

away across the deck. He wondered what his parents were doing this morning, and how Seren liked being an only child. How big would she have grown by the time he returned home, if he ever returned home? Would Hunter and Burke join them at the Academy next year, or would they be content to take over their fathers' businesses? Which of the young men would catch Ailwen's eye at the Mid-Winter Dance this year? He shook away the murkiness of these melancholy thoughts and turned his gaze back to the sky as they moved swiftly away from Dalton. His initial dizziness and vertigo were gone, and he now felt only exhilaration. He was flying!

23

"We need to move fast," Raisa whispered. "The students will start wondering what's wrong if they don't get their weapons back soon."

"I'm moving as fast as I can," Mouse whispered back. "These locks are a lot trickier than they look."

"Can you do it? You said you could..."

"There." Mouse stepped back, lips curved in a satisfied smirk as the door to the armory swung open. "Stroke of genius, this part of the plan, by the by."

"Thank you, now move!"

The two figures stealthily entered the armory, then stopped, aghast.

"Where are the weapons?" Raisa asked once she regained her ability to form words.

Mouse craned his neck around and then shrugged. "Not here. Captain Dagur must have disregarded the new orders."

Urgency and dismay flooded through her. "We have no way of warning Marik that the students are armed."

Mouse grimaced. "Then we'll have to figure out a way to keep the students locked inside."

"And where do you propose we do that?" Raisa snapped.

Mouse squinted. "What about the mess hall at supper?"

Raisa's panic subsided. "That might work. I'll get into the mess beforehand and get a roster of anyone ordering food directly to their rooms."

"I have my solder kit," Mouse volunteered. "I can make it impossible for anyone to get out of their rooms."

Raisa made a face. "I don't know why Marik lets you keep that. It's dangerous."

"It's not dangerous," Mouse retorted. "Besides, it's the only way to lock the doors from the outside."

"And what about when Marik wants to let everyone off the airship?"

"They can get out through their windows. Or Oleck can break down the doors. Or I can use my solder kit to re-melt the locking mechanisms enough to open them again."

Raisa sighed. "I guess we don't have any better options."

THE THREE YOUNG men stayed on the deck all morning. It seemed the novelty of flying would never wear off. Their initial discomfiture at the height soon vanished and before long, they were all leaning over the railing, peering at the ground far below. The shadow of the airship swept across fields and forests and lakes.

Grayden thought he would never tire of the view. He glanced up and then squinted.

"Hey." He nudged Wynn and pointed. "What's that?"

Wynn eyed the dark speck high above them and shrugged. "A bird?"

Beren followed his friends' gaze and made a thoughtful sound. "Too big to be a bird, I'd say. Maybe another airship on a similar course?"

"You think? It's really high up there," Wynn replied.

"I don't know what else it could be, though," Grayden

mused.

They watched the strange black dot for a long while, but it appeared to be pacing them steadily, for it never changed in shape or size. Eventually, they lost interest in it and returned their attention to other things. However, Grayden would remember and gaze upwards periodically. The black dot continued to keep pace with them, never changing course or distance from their own location. Around noon, they flew into thick clouds and he finally lost sight of whatever it was for good.

A little while before lunch-time Dalmir joined them. He did not strap himself into a harness, and he looked completely at ease. He stood at the railing and glanced over it briefly before fixing his attention on Grayden and his friends.

"Will you join me in my room for lunch?"

Grayden blinked in surprise. "We should eat with our classmates..."

"You have the next few years to get acquainted with your classmates," Dalmir countered. "I have questions for the three of you. And I would like to discuss a few other matters with you, things I would not like to say where unfriendly ears may be listening. Things we will not be able to speak of once we reach our destination."

"Well..." Grayden glanced at his friends questioningly. He enjoyed spending time with Dalmir, but he couldn't speak for his friends.

"I, for one, would be honored to dine with you," Beren said formally.

"Me too," Grayden added.

"Sure." Wynn sounded distracted, and Grayden shot a sharp glance at him. Wynn was peering over his shoulder at the crew. He glanced at Grayden and shook his head vaguely.

"Very good," Dalmir said. "I will see you there in a bit."

The tall man turned and strode away. Gone was the feeble, elderly facade Dalmir had used when they were boarding the airship. A familiar tightness in the pit of his stomach interrupted Grayden's musing, and he paused, his thoughts awhirl. Had the sensation been there all day? He couldn't be sure. The excitement of flying might have masked it, and this could be remnants of that. Or perhaps he was hungry. He would wait until after lunch. If the sensation hadn't dissipated by then, he would tell the others and they could help him decide what to do about it.

The three young men arrived at Dalmir's room a little while later and their traveling companion welcomed them into a charming space, warm and comfortable, despite its small size. Grayden had been aghast at the exorbitant ticket fare, but now he was forced to reconsider. Dalmir had gotten an excellent deal. The lines of every piece of furniture were elegant. The large window let in a good amount of sunlight, bathing the room in a golden glow. Beautiful, intricate paintings hung on the walls. In one corner stood an enormous bed that Beren eyed enviously. Nothing about the room was ostentatious, and yet every item within it bespoke luxury.

Upon the table sat a platter of roasted pheasant, bowls of red potatoes, cooked carrots, and a round loaf of soft bread. Sparkling cider filled four crystal glasses. A familiar scent tickled Grayden's nose, and he turned to see a smaller table covered in various desserts, one of which was a large bowl filled with cooked apples drenched in a thick spiced sauce. Mouth watering and memories of home filling his mind, Grayden sat down; it surprised him to find the chair immensely comfortable.

"I'm glad we took you up on your offer to dine with you. I doubt our comrades are eating this well in the mess hall!"

They piled their plates high with food and for a while, the sounds of eating filled the room. When at last they had sated their stomachs, Dalmir broke the silence.

"How are you enjoying traveling by airship so far?"

"It's better than I expected," Grayden replied. Then his stomach fluttered again, and he stared at his plate.

Wynn gave a shrug of one shoulder. "Flying is fine. But I was hoping to get a glimpse at the actual engine room. The crew said no passengers were allowed down there, though."

Grayden picked at his food.

Dalmir's sharp eyes landed on him. "Grayden? What's wrong?"

Grayden shrugged. "I've got that weird feeling again. The one that says something's not right." He exchanged a glance with the others.

"How long have you had it?"

"Why didn't you say anything?"

Grayden wasn't sure who asked which question as Wynn and Beren spoke at the same time. But he appreciated that they were taking him seriously.

"I didn't notice it until after we took off," Grayden admitted. "I have no idea how long. It must have been buried by the excitement of flying. I didn't keep it from you on purpose." Despite trying to keep calm, Grayden heard his tone become a little defensive.

"This is that same sixth sense thing you had before those assassins attacked us?" Beren asked.

"Yes."

"Then you believe we are in danger?"

"I don't know... just... there's something off here," Grayden said.

"Then we should retrieve our weapons. I left my sword in our quarters," Beren exclaimed, standing suddenly. His chair fell over as he stood, and the dishes on the table rattled together as he pushed away from it.

Dalmir raised a hand. "Yes, yes, sit back down, young giant. You can't go rushing headlong down corridors shouting for your weapons the way you would at home. If we are in danger, we need to know which direction it is coming from. We must be wary."

Beren picked up his chair a bit sheepishly and sat back down.

"Now," Dalmir continued, "did you all leave your weapons in your quarters?"

They had all left their swords in their rooms. However, all three of them had an assortment of smaller weapons with them. Beren berated himself in soft mutters about disregarding what Koen had told them earlier about keeping their weapons on them at all times.

"Good. We are not completely defenseless," Dalmir said. "Do you think you can discreetly venture to your room and back to retrieve your swords?"

"Yes," Beren replied. "Shall we go now, Dalmir?"

"Yes, I think that would be best. You and Wynn go. Grayden and I will remain. If we all go tromping through the corridors right now it might raise a few eyebrows. I think it best to be surreptitious for the moment, at least until we better know what is causing Grayden's presentiment."

24

The *Valdeun Hawk* trailed its prey like the patient predator for which it had been named. Marik kept his small vessel well below the broad cruiser's blind spot, waiting for Raisa's signal. Around him, clouds billowed, obscuring their visibility and threatening a storm; Marik paid them no mind. While he never counted on the weather, the sudden storm front worked to his advantage. The thick gray haze surrounded them like a ghost's embrace.

"There's the signal!" Shaesta called from her perch aloft the crow's nest.

"Ready the grapples!" Marik bellowed.

His crew moved swiftly to obey his orders as Marik expertly steered the *Hawk* out of the *Eagle*'s blind spot and swooped up along its starboard side, the tip of his trim sail missing their hull by inches. To the crew on the deck of the cruiser, the *Hawk* would have appeared to materialize out of nowhere.

Marik grinned, spinning the wheel in a manner that would appear reckless to the casual observer. He pulled back on the lever that controlled their altitude and the *Hawk* sprang to obey his commands, swooping up and over the *Eagle's* main mast and causing her sails to flap wildly. The crew below him erupted in shouts as their deck heaved in the sudden windstorm.

He pushed the lever and plummeted down and under the cruiser, looping beneath its belly. Marik let out an unbridled whoop of glee, ignoring the glare Shaesta was shooting him as she clung to the crow's nest. He steered the *Hawk* back into view of the other ship's deck and wove back and forth like a drunken fool around the huge cruiser. Then he sped off into the mist until the two ships had disappeared from each other's view before spinning his ship in a hairpin turn that elicited an actual shout of alarm from Oleck.

As they soared back into view of the cargo vessel, Marik's crew waved like the ridiculously wealthy passengers they were pretending to be. A few of them laughed raucously, disregarding the disapproving looks and glares coming from the crew of the larger vessel.

This was living! The wind raced through Marik's hair, sweeping it back from his face. Cold drops of mist stung his cheeks as he wove through the misty clouds. His heart soared with exhilaration as he threw his entire being into this weaving, intricate, daring flight. For just a few heartbeats, he let go of his careful calculations, his entire scheme, and immersed himself in the enjoyment of the moment. It would come to an end all too soon. But for this brief window of time, he relinquished himself to the joy of flight. He soared back and forth, crisscrossing in front of and behind, up and over, down and below and all around the *Crimson Eagle* in a display of piloting prowess by which even the angry crew of the cruiser couldn't help but be mildly impressed. From the occasional gasps and shouts from the other ship, Marik knew they were falling for the ruse. He continued for a few more minutes, reluctant to bring the glorious flight to an end too quickly, but he had a job to do.

As he swept down next to the *Eagle's* port side, he veered in a little too close, nearly scraping sides with the larger vessel. He arranged his face into a mask of terror and he strained his arms to make it look as though he was trying to turn away, though in reality he was expertly holding his schooner steady mere inches from the other vessel. The crew aboard the *Eagle* responded with shouts of anger and surprise. Marik threw a hand up in the air and let loose a scream.

"You need to move away!" one of the *Eagle*'s braver crew members shouted over the side to him. They were so close, the crewman could almost have reached over and pushed the smaller ship away. "If we collide, your ship will be lost!"

"I can't control her!" Marik shouted back, infusing his voice with terror. Deftly, he adjusted the levers, swerving a little closer and expertly hooking the *Hawk*'s figurehead into the cruiser's wing rigging. "Something's wrong with the steering mechanism!" he wailed. "Can you send someone over to help us?"

At this new crisis, a flurry of commotion and a series of panicked shouts rose up from the deck of the cruiser. Marik clenched his teeth, concentrating on keeping his ship steady and not tearing the wing off the cruiser.

Below, another man appeared. By his uniform and commanding presence, Marik decided he must be the captain.

"What's going on?" the man bellowed.

"I think I felt something snap when I turned the wheel," Marik shouted back. "I need to go below to fix the mechanism, but I can't leave my post or we'll tear the wing off your ship!"

"What about your crew?" The captain indicated the white-faced people huddled around the mainmast.

"That's not my crew!" Marik hollered, pitching his voice in terror. "They're my passengers. I was trying to impress them. It's just me and my first mate here." He pointed at Shaesta, who had descended from the crow's nest and was holding one arm close to her chest, feigning a broken wrist. "She needs a physician."

"You're up here with just the two of you?" The captain's face turned into a thundercloud of fury. "Are you daft? Tattered sails, small vessels like this shouldn't even be allowed. If you endanger my ship any further, I'll have you before the Council! If we could get away from your ship, I'd have half a mind to leave you to your fate." He turned to a crewman. "Creg!" he barked. "Take five men over there and help the man get disentangled from our rigging."

In no time at all, Creg and his small crew were standing aboard the *Hawk*. The one called Creg approached Marik.

"You said the steering seems to be stuck?" Creg asked.

Marik stared at him. "Something snapped, I think. I heard a cracking sound and then the steering went haywire. I can feel it, but I can't go belowdecks to fix it." He nodded at Shaesta. "She hurt her wrist, or she could steer while I go look at whatever's causing the problem. You have to help us, please!"

"We're here to help," Creg said. "My captain wants us to get you fixed up as quick as possible. Let me take the wheel, and you take my men down to your engine room. They'll see what they can do."

Marik took several quick breaths, keeping an expression of terror on his face. "I can do that."

"Good." Creg eased up beside him and gripped the steering mechanism. "Tell your passengers not to worry. We'll have you back on course in no time. Next time out, you might want to think about hiring more hands before you take this pretty bird into the air, right? It'd be a shame if she ended up smashed to pieces."

Marik grimaced. "It was just supposed to be a spot of fun," he mumbled. "How many should I hire on next time?"

Creg scratched his head. "Our complement is fifty. But a small vessel like this, you could probably get away with three besides yourself. Five would be better."

Marik nodded meekly and then turned and headed below, leading the men below. As they stepped off the ladder and stood in the corridor, eyes adjusting to the dim light, Oleck stepped out of the shadows and together he and Marik attacked, pushing the men into an empty cabin and pulling the door shut, locking it from the outside.

Marik nodded to his first mate. Four men neutralized, forty-six to go.

25

Wynn tried Dalmir's door handle, then paused, a strange expression crossing his face.

"What's wrong?" Grayden asked.

"It's locked. From the outside. But it's not just locked... it's... it's more like the mechanism has been fused."

"What does that mean?" Grayden asked.

"It means someone put something super hot inside the lock and melted all the important bits."

"Can't you open it?" Beren asked.

"No, that's my point," Wynn replied. "It's not just locked, it's broken. I can't pick a broken lock."

Beren reached for the door handle and tried it, but nothing happened. He tried harder, but only succeeded in bending the handle. "How is it possible? The door locks from the inside."

"The easiest way would be to drip molten tin or lead into the mechanism," Wynn said in a matter-of-fact tone. He had gone into that detached mode of his. "We're trapped in here, that's all that matters."

"But why?" Grayden asked. "Who would want to lock us in our rooms?"

"Pirates, most likely," Beren replied. "The chief advisors to the

Council have tried to argue that this whole deal the airships have with the Academy makes for a tantalizing target. Pirates would know that they are dealing with mostly untrained first-years."

"Nia said that airship pirates have been more active lately," Grayden said.

"Well, we know that at least some of the pirates are on board already," Wynn added, pointing at the door.

"And it is likely that the rest of the students are trapped somewhere as well," Dalmir added. "Their rooms would have been the first ones targeted."

"Whatever is going on, it's happening right now," Beren said.

"Is there any other way out of this room?" Grayden asked.

"There's a window!" Wynn pointed out.

Dalmir started to speak, but as the boys rushed to the window, the older man simply shrugged and inspected the door. The young men peered eagerly through the window, but it just opened out into empty sky. Beren pushed the glass open anyway and reached his arm out.

"We might be able to scale it, if the hull isn't too slick..."

"Are you insane?" Wynn asked.

"The hull is mostly made of wood. It should be soft enough. If we attach the spines of our forks to our shoes like the mountain climbers in my region do... well, they don't use forks, of course—they have their shoes specially made—but the concept is roughly the same..." Beren continued, musing out loud, as if he hadn't even heard Wynn's question.

In a less dire situation, Grayden thought he might have laughed. Instead, however, he felt his stomach lurch at Beren's suggestion. It was true he had climbed Dalmir's tower only a few sennights ago, but the two situations were infinitely different.

"Or you could simply follow me out the door." Dalmir's voice was not loud, but it got their attention. The old man stood at the door, which was now slightly open, a grim smile on his face.

"How did you... the lock was fused!" Wynn exclaimed. "It was!"

"Yes," Dalmir agreed. "Fortunately for us, I know how to deal with locked doors. Now, let's go see what is happening, shall we?"

"I'd still like to retrieve my sword," Beren said.

They peered out into the hall. Nothing moved. Grayden drew his dagger as they crept out of Dalmir's room.

"Is there another way to the deck besides the main staircase?" Dalmir asked in a whisper. "We're a bit too visible if we stick to the main hallways."

"Follow me," Wynn said suddenly as he darted into a door across the hall from Dalmir's room.

"Wynn! Wait..." Grayden whispered, but Wynn was already gone from sight. Dalmir looked questioningly at Grayden, who shrugged and followed his friend.

The door Wynn had gone through led into a narrower corridor. They followed him as he darted through one door after another, turning left, then right, then going straight on for a while. It was all they could do to keep up with him, except for the few times Wynn made them backtrack, but even then he was going too fast for them to ask questions, and none of them dared risk more than a whisper in case they were within hearing distance of unfriendly ears. Grayden was soon completely disoriented, but Wynn continued on with a determined look on his face. These smaller passageways were not completely deserted, either, and they spent a few anxious moments in several closets trying not to breathe while various members of the crew passed.

"Here it is!" Wynn exclaimed at last.

They were in a small storage locker near the crew quarters. The area was all but deserted. Most everyone would be at lunch now. Grayden peered around in bewilderment.

"What is it, exactly, that you've brought us to, Wynn?" he asked.

Wynn reached up and pulled a panel down from the ceiling. A ladder unfolded as the panel came down. Wynn beamed triumphantly.

"I knew it had to be here."

"Care to explain yourself a bit more clearly, lad?" Dalmir's voice bordered on impatient.

"Sorry. My dad—you know, Grayden, how he's traveled all over? Well, he always was getting his hands on charts and things: maps, drawings, machines, diagrams, technical things like that?"

"Yeah..."

"I spent a lot of time studying everything he got. I've always been interested in machines. Drove my ma crazy, how I was always taking things apart and putting them back together. My parents started buying broken tools for me to fix up so I wouldn't take apart anything of theirs anymore. For one birthday, my dad even got me a toy train. It didn't work, so he got it for a song. Remember that, Grayden?"

"You fixed it—we had a lot of fun with it—but, Wynn, what has that got to do with..."

"He also got his hands on schematics for different airships. I don't know how he got them, but he did. They're all pretty similar, and every one of them has these access points." Wynn pointed at the ladder.

"What does it lead to?"

"The charts were a little blurry, but mostly I'm guessing they lead to a sort of storage space between the first level and the main deck. Remember those grates on the deck?"

"No," Grayden admitted.

"You'd have seen them if you knew to look for them. Those are places the crew can use to get into the storage space without coming all the way down here."

"Won't they be able to see us through the grates, then?" Beren asked.

"No, the grates are small, and there are only a few of them. We can avoid them, I'm sure of it. Besides, we'll have to go up a few levels before we get to the compartments beneath the main deck. But we can use the storage space to find out what's happening up there without being spotted. We can get from one end of the ship to the other without having to worry about hiding every couple of steps."

"Excellent job, young man." Dalmir patted Wynn's shoulder. "Let's go retrieve your swords and see if we can reach your comrades and release them from their rooms."

The old man darted up the ladder, leaving the three boys to clamber up after him. Beren pulled the ladder up behind and they found themselves in the darkened attic of the airship.

The darkness did not fill the space as wholly as Grayden had expected, and his eyes adjusted quickly in the shadowy space between decks. Light trickled through the cracks in the planks with more concentration in a few places, giving them pinpoints to follow like guiding stars. The space was also far more cramped than Wynn had made it sound. All around them were large metal pipes that wound and stretched in every direction and blocked their path. It soon became apparent that it would be no small feat to reach the other end of the airship.

"What are these things, Wynn?" Beren asked.

"They might have something to do with the engines." Wynn's voice radiated excitement. Of the four of them, he appeared to be the most at ease in these cramped quarters. He probably barely noticed where they were, Grayden thought, feeling uncharitable toward his friend. The problem before them would consume all of Wynn's attention.

Wynn ran his hand along a pipe. "They're warm, but not hot. None of the schematics showed these, but then, the schematics never had any information about the engines at all."

"Well, it's go forward and try to navigate this maze, or go back and risk being seen by the pirates," Beren rumbled.

"I don't think it's much of a choice," Wynn muttered.

Grayden volunteered to take the lead. "I can move more easily in the tight space than Beren," he said. "And my dagger is going to be more help in a small space than Dalmir's sword, and Wynn just has his slingshot."

"I have this, too." Wynn grinned sheepishly and held up a

butter knife that he had taken from Dalmir's room. "It's not real sharp, though."

Grayden chuckled and ducked under a large pipe. Besides the pipes overhead, coils of rope and spare sails were stowed on shelves running the length of the compartment walls, along with odds and ends strewn about where crewmen had dumped them in a hurry. The space stretched out in either direction, but Grayden could not see where it ended. The low ceilings forced them to proceed on hands and knees.

Before he had gone far, they could hear strange noises above. It sounded like horses were stampeding above them. Thuds and shouts and groans continued for what felt like ages, then sudden silence.

"What do you think is going on?" Grayden asked.

"I believe we've been boarded," Dalmir replied.

"What should we do?" Beren asked.

"Shhhh," Grayden hissed.

A loud, commanding voice rang out above them, echoing faintly down the metal pipes, but they could not make out the words.

"Come on," Grayden whispered. That strange prickling sensation had returned, and he felt a sense of urgency.

They moved as quickly as they could, crawling through the gloom. They had made it perhaps a hundred paces when they felt the airship begin to angle downwards. A moment later, Grayden found himself clinging to the pipe he had just ducked under, his feet dangling. He saw the shape of one of his friends—it looked like Beren—sliding along the floor as another, most likely Wynn, tumbled away from him until he managed to catch himself on a pipe with a sickening sound and a pain-filled groan. He did not see Dalmir anywhere, but his view was limited. In his head, he knew what had happened. The airship was descending rapidly through the clouds as the pirates must have ordered. Grayden had assumed the angle of descent would make their passage more difficult, but he had not been prepared for their advance to be rendered impossible. He clung to the pipe desperately, his feet scrabbling at the floor for purchase.

"I never thought I would wish we had used Beren's idea to attach forks to our shoes," he muttered.

A snort of laughter to his right made him turn his head carefully. Dalmir clung to a pipe next to him. Despite the dim lighting, Grayden could see the gleam of the older man's teeth.

"What do we do now?" Grayden asked.

"Hang on!" Dalmir managed, as the ship continued to plummet.

26

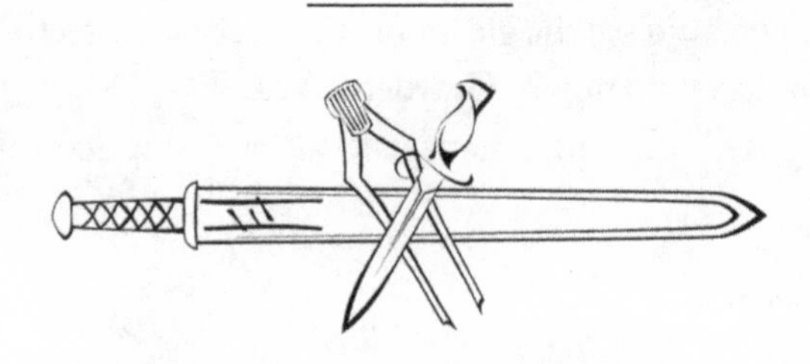

The airship dove through the clouds like a hunting falcon. Between decks, Grayden and his friends clung frantically to whatever they were holding. There was no way they could continue their journey to the other end of the ship, no way to free the other Academy students, no way to foil the pirates' plans; all they could do was hang there and hope they didn't fall.

Images flashed relentlessly through Grayden's mind of the massive airship splintering to bits upon impact with the ground. He took deep breaths to steady his nerves and gripped the pipe more tightly. Surely the pirates who had overtaken the *Crimson Eagle* had no intention of dying today? Otherwise, why stay on board while they dove to their doom?

They continued to fall. Grayden's arms shook with exhaustion. His fingers cramped. He wanted to hoist himself up and wrap an arm around the bar, but he worried that even trying to adjust would make his fingers slip and send him careening down through space. He might survive a fall, but there were so many obstacles between him and the end of the crawlspace that he would break every bone in his body on the way down.

Sweat beaded on his forehead and slicked the palms of his hands. Just as his fingers began to slip, gravity altered, and he found the floor angling more beneath him than beside him. Using his feet to push against it, he readjusted his hold on the pipe until the airship had leveled out beneath him once more. Grayden released the pipe and let himself lie sprawled on his back, gulping great gasps of relieved air and letting his shaking arms rest.

A moment later, he heard an enormous splash, and the ship shuddered with a strange bobbing sensation, and came to a halt.

"What was that?" Grayden asked.

"I imagine that we just landed," Dalmir replied.

"Landed?" Wynn asked. "Airships don't *land*. Even when they're docked, they never land. They just keep hovering. It's not like they have wheels or flat bottoms. It would be impossible to set them down on the ground—they'd fall over."

"Based on the sound we heard and the movement we are now experiencing, I suspect we have landed on a body of water," Dalmir said.

Grayden craned around to raise a questioning eyebrow at Wynn. His friend pursed his lips, looking thoughtful. He stared off into space as he always did when working on a puzzle.

"It might be possible. In theory," Wynn finally admitted.

"More than just a theory," Beren rumbled. "We are definitely afloat. I've been on a few sailing ships."

"What do we do now?" Wynn asked.

Everyone looked at Grayden. His stomach lurched as he realized they were all expecting him to have a plan. He tried to swallow, but his mouth and throat were suddenly parched.

"How close are we to the main deck?" Grayden asked.

"We're still a few levels down," Wynn replied. "Might take a while for us to get there."

Grayden wiped his palms against his trousers. "I think we need to change our strategy. We should get down to the initiates' quarters and set the other students free. Together, we might be able to take back the ship."

"And retrieve our weapons while we're at it," Beren said.

"Lead the way, Wynn," Grayden directed. "You know these

corridors better than the rest of us. How do we get to our quarters?"

Wynn pointed. With monumental effort, they got themselves turned around. Wynn snaked his way through the tunnels, leading them around corners and through tight spaces.

Grayden grew weary. How long had they been in these cramped tunnels? He wondered idly if they would ever get out again. He longed to stand and stretch his body. His back and shoulders ached and his knees throbbed from scuffing across the hard floor.

Finally, Wynn called a halt and pointed to the trapdoor before them.

"This is it," Wynn whispered. "We can drop into the hall where most of the rooms are. Dalmir, if the doors are locked like yours was, do you think you can still get them open?"

Dalmir nodded. Wynn cautiously removed the grate. Beren stuck his head through and looked around before pulling himself back up and giving them a nod. Quietly, they lowered themselves through the opening and landed in the hall. It had never felt so good to stand upright.

Wynn made his way to the first door in the hall, but stopped, frowning. He pushed on the door and it swung open easily.

"It's not even latched," Wynn said.

"Are we too late?" Beren asked. He poked his head into the room. "Nothing looks disturbed."

"Maybe they freed themselves and overpowered the pirates," Grayden said, trying to sound more optimistic than he felt.

The rest of the rooms were all the same: unlocked and empty.

"Do you think anyone survived?" Wynn asked, his voice trembling.

"I don't... Hey!" Grayden glimpsed movement at the end of the corridor and dashed after it. He heard Wynn and Beren calling behind him in hushed voices, barely registered their footsteps pounding after him, but he did not stop. He turned a corner and caught a handful of fabric.

"Ge'off me! Lemme go!" the boy hollered as he struggled in Grayden's grip.

"I thought it was you, Mouse," Grayden said.

The boy twisted around and stared up at his captor. He flushed a strange shade of purple and stopped fighting.

"This is the young pickpocket who showed you around Dalton?" Wynn asked.

"Yep. What are you doing aboard this airship?"

"Nothing." Mouse's lips turned down in a sulky pout.

Grayden gave the boy a shake. "Come on, now. You owe me."

"Don't owe you nothin'."

"I could have turned you over to the guards. I didn't."

"I showed you around the city," Mouse countered.

"I paid for that. Made sure you got a square meal... and Nia told me she gave you a sack of food to take with you, so don't argue. Tell me what you're doing on board this airship."

Mouse glowered, but pressed his lips together in stubborn silence.

"We should get out of this hallway," Dalmir commented.

They moved into one of the empty rooms, and Grayden motioned for Mouse to sit in one of the austere desk chairs. "Talk," he commanded.

Mouse wriggled uncomfortably in his seat. "What do you want me to say?"

"Are you working with the pirates?" Beren asked.

Mouse nodded.

"How many pirates are there?" Beren asked.

Mouse stared at him. "I... I'm not telling."

"Did they kill anyone?" Grayden asked, his stomach clenching.

"No, they're just making everyone get off. We locked them in the mess. Captain plans to leave them behind." Mouse's forehead scrunched up. "How did you get out of the mess hall?"

"We weren't in the mess," Beren said.

"How do we know you're not lying?" Grayden asked. "How do we know your crew hasn't just murdered everyone?"

"Captain's not like that." Mouse's eyes widened. "Why else would he land?"

"Where are we headed now?" Wynn asked.

"Not tellin' you." Mouse crossed his arms.

Grayden turned to his friends. "He can be pretty stubborn. Maybe we can retrieve our weapons and stop the crew from forcing everyone off the airship—"

"Mouse?" A woman's voice in the hallway made them all freeze. "Mouse, where are you hiding? Captain wants you."

"Who's that?" Beren hissed.

"That's Raisa," Mouse whispered back. "Marik's right hand. She'll get suspicious if I don't answer."

"Raisa!" Beren's eyebrows shot up at the familiar name.

Grayden stared at the boy, wondering how far he could trust the young thief. The woman's voice sounded again, getting nearer with every call. At last, he sighed.

"All right, answer her. But I'm warning you, if you give us away..."

Mouse stood up and walked to the door, glancing nervously up at Beren and Dalmir as he passed between them. He opened the door and leaned his head out.

"I'm over here, Raisa. Trying to get a little sleep." He rubbed his eyes, stretched an arm up over his head, and rolled his neck. "It was a long night. What's Marik want?"

"We're almost ready to take off again, but we've ripped one of the trim sails. Captain needs someone small to get into the storage compartment and find a replacement."

"Okay. I'll be right up."

There was a sound of retreating footsteps, then they stopped. "Any reason you chose a room on this level for a nap?" Raisa asked.

"Uh... nothing in particular."

"Because there are much nicer rooms up in the bow, you know," she called out.

"Yeah..." Mouse hesitated, shooting a panicked look at Grayden's dagger leveled at his throat. "I... uh... looked at those, but the beds were too soft."

"Too soft?" Raisa's voice sounded startled.

"Yeah, I felt like they were going to swallow me while I slept."

"Ah." A chuckle sounded. "Well, whatever you prefer. I'll let Marik know you're coming."

Mouse grinned at Grayden behind the door as Raisa's footsteps retreated. "We're even now." He ducked under Grayden's dagger and out into the hallway before anyone could move to grab him, and scampered away toward the stairs leading up to the main deck. The little thief disappeared through a door and the companions looked at each other in dismay.

"Will he give us away?" Wynn asked.

"I don't know," Grayden replied grimly.

They stepped out into the hallway and stared in the direction that Mouse had fled.

"Either way, we need to rescue the rest of the students before Marik forces them all off the ship. With their help and a little surprise, we should be able to retake the airship," Beren said.

But just as he finished speaking, the airship gave a mighty shudder. The hallway tilted nearly vertically, and they all had to grab hold of the doorway to prevent themselves from sliding and rolling down the hall. Grayden clung to the doorframe, his feet scrabbling at the suddenly steep floor until the airship leveled out again.

"Looks like we're too late," Wynn said grimly. "We just took off."

They stared at each other helplessly.

"We can hide in the crawlways again," Wynn suggested. "Wait until we get a better read on the situation."

"Hiding is a coward's option," Beren spat.

"Thought you might say that." Wynn grimaced. "I suppose we could..."

"Go on, what have you thought of?" Grayden asked, recognizing the look on his friend's face.

"We could sabotage the airship."

"How?" Beren asked.

"Why would we want to do that?" Grayden asked at the same time.

"If we can force the pirates to land, maybe we can take the ship back, or put them in a position where they have to do what we tell them to. It would be the heroic thing to do," Wynn replied.

Grayden looked at Dalmir, but the old man just shrugged. "There are only four of us, and we have no idea how many pirates there are, but I don't relish the idea of hiding in this airship forever, either. Who knows where they're headed?"

"All right," Grayden said, making a decision. "Wynn, can you get us to the engines?"

"Yep."

"Then lead the way," Grayden said, then thought better of it. "But while we're here, let's get our weapons."

27

They should have named this thing the Sky Whale, Marik thought as the enormous airship lumbered through the clouds. Perhaps it wasn't fair for him to compare the bulky cruiser to the sleek elegance of his own personal ship, but he couldn't help but wish he was aboard the *Hawk* instead. *If this is the best they have, the Ar'Mol will have no troubles at all when he decides to invade.*

And he would invade. Marik knew that for a certainty. The Ar'Mol was biding his time, carefully quelling the fires of rebellion amongst his own people and slowly infiltrating Telmondir with the appearance of gifts and favors: first the trains, and now the airships. But it would take a blind man not to notice that the Ar'Mol had not shared the secrets of how to power those gifts. Oh yes, he was planning to invade.

And just what are you going to do about it? a nagging little voice inside his head suddenly asked. Marik let out a slow breath. It was none of his business. He had his own concerns.

"Raisa, has Mouse found that extra canvas yet?" he called out, silencing the troublesome voice. He was doing what little he could while trying to stay alive and two steps ahead of the Igyeum forces that would see him hung if they caught him. He had others depending on him as well, that his crew knew nothing about. Whatever happened, he would safeguard those in his care.

"We're just bringing it up now," Raisa said.

"Good, hopefully repairing that wing will make this old crate fly a little more like the eagle it's named for and less like a bucket."

Raisa winked at him as she leaned down over the grate to help pull the bright red canvas up onto the deck. "She does wobble a bit, doesn't she?"

"A bit." Marik chuckled to himself. Raisa had a gift for understatement.

Just then, the airship lurched oddly. Marik clutched at the wheel and frowned as they evened out. He glanced at Rustam and Yefrem, who were getting ready to take down the damaged sail. They returned his gaze and threw their hands up in the air.

"We hadn't even begun yet, Cap'n," Rustam shouted.

"Engines malfunctioning?" Marik muttered to himself. "Or just a fluke?"

Mouse crawled out of a hole in the deck, pushing at the large, folded piece of canvas he was helping Raisa with. He staggered and nearly fell as the airship lurched sideways and then dropped a degree of altitude. Marik narrowed his eyes.

"Rustam!"

The giant, red-haired man bounded up to where Marik was standing. "Yeah, Cap'n?"

The ship lurched again and Shaesta came onto the deck, her eyes wide. She stared up at Marik, her expression one of terror and confusion. He watched her stumble over to Raisa, and saw her lips move, most likely asking what was going on. Something seemed odd about Shaesta. Even with that expression of semi-alarm in her eyes, she looked troubled... and angry. But why Shaesta should be angry was a mystery to him.

"Can Yefrem and Raisa take care of the wing without you?"

"Prob'ly. What do you want me to do?" Rustam replied.

"Go check the engine room. Quietly."

"You think we missed a crewman or a student?"

"Not sure... but this doesn't feel normal."

"Aye, Cap'n."

Marik glanced down at the deck. "Ah, Rustam... take Shaesta with you."

"Okay... mind if I ask why?"

"She just... looks like she could use a distraction."

Rustam glanced at Shaesta, who had made her way over to stand near Raisa; she looked a little green. The corners of her mouth pulled down.

"Aye, Cap'n, I see what you mean." Rustam turned and bounded down the steps. "Shaesta!" he called out, beckoning with one hand. "Cap'n's got a job for us."

Every pipe winding its way through the crawlways must eventually find its way down into this single, surprisingly tiny room. Brass plating covered the walls, and in the center of the room stood a hexagonally shaped, silver-plated plinth with four deep apertures hollowed down into the top surface. A pulsating glow emanated from these apertures with a rhythm that intensified and abated like a steady heartbeat.

Grayden entered the room first, giving his friends the all-clear wave when he realized the room was empty. Wynn followed close behind, his eyes lighting up as he entered the tiny chamber. He strode straight over to the pedestal and stared down at the light emanating from it, bending close and examining the etchings on its top and sides like an archaeologist. Grayden smirked. Same old Wynn. Pirates could descend from the rafters now, but they wouldn't bother Wynn one bit. He'd probably just absentmindedly ask them if they would mind keeping their swashbuckling down a bit. Beren ducked through the doorway and halted, hovering just inside the entrance as though afraid he might break something if he moved too quickly.

Dalmir paced around the room, his eyes darting from object

to object, taking in every bit of machinery, every detail. He took no notice of the three young men with him. After his thorough, but hasty perusal of the room, he joined Wynn at the plinth and his face puckered into an angry scowl.

From a pocket deep inside his outer robe, Dalmir withdrew the palm-sized orb that Grayden had seen twice before. He lifted it in his hand and held it directly above one of the glowing crevices. The orb flared a bright red. The glow from the plinth blazed with a golden aura that flooded the room and made them all wince and shield their eyes. The airship lurched beneath their feet as if the vessel itself protested the presence of the orb so near its heart. Beren stumbled inside and the door swung closed behind him, now open only a crack. Wynn fell against the pedestal, gripping it tightly to keep his feet under him. Grayden stumbled sideways and fell to his knees, bruising the left one badly. Only Dalmir remained immobile, as though rooted to the plank floorboards. The old man's blue eyes blazed. From where he had fallen, Grayden wondered how he ever could have thought the man was old. The lines of age had fallen away and his face appeared young and wrathful behind his white beard. When he pulled the orb away from the pedestal, the glow dimmed and the airship quieted. Dalmir peered into the orb, and then he held it over the plinth again. The results were the same: brilliant light filled the room; the airship bucked and swayed, stopping only when Dalmir hid the orb once more.

"What was that?" Wynn asked.

"Please, do not do that again," Beren rumbled, his face looking a shade greener than usual.

"My apologies," Dalmir replied as he tucked the orb safely back into his robe. "I had to be sure."

"Sure of what?" Grayden asked.

Dalmir stared down at the glowing plinth before answering. When he finally spoke, his voice was firm, but weary. "My prisoner has escaped."

A hundred questions welled up inside of Grayden. But before

he could formulate his thoughts or voice his curiosity, they heard footsteps in the hall outside the door. Beren drew his sword and Grayden retrieved his dagger from its sheath. Its familiar weight in his hand was comforting and helped calm the nervous lurch of his stomach as he prepared to face whoever was approaching. His sword hung at his side, but he felt it would be too cumbersome in such a small space. Wynn pulled out the butter knife he had taken from Dalmir's room and Grayden eyed him in concern. Wynn met his gaze, glanced at the knife, then shrugged a little sheepishly.

The door swung open to reveal two figures with swords drawn, their eyes wary as they peered into the room. The figure on the right was a giant of a man, with thick, well-muscled arms and a full, curly red beard. He was a head shorter than Beren, but his shoulders were broader and he held his sword in a way that suggested familiarity. The other figure was a slim, beautiful woman with bewitching brown eyes and coarse brown hair limned with bright gold hanging over her shoulder in a thick plait. She also held a sword, her expression fierce.

The bearded man's eyebrows shot up in surprise as he saw the company before him. The woman stared hard at each of them, but not a single muscle in her face so much as twitched to reveal what she was thinking, be it surprise or any other emotion.

The man spoke. "I'd ask where you came from, but I'm guessing you wouldn't tell me."

They regarded him in suspicious silence.

"Can we all agree that a violent argument in this room would result in discomfort for all of us?" The man nodded meaningfully at the glowing plinth in the center of the room. "Perhaps there is a better way to settle our differences?"

"We're willing to listen," Dalmir said carefully.

"I can guarantee your safety if you'll come along peacefully to see our captain," the man continued. "Just hand over your weapons and we promise you'll not be harmed."

"We would be happy to discuss the situation with your captain," Dalmir said. "But we are keeping our weapons. If you will just hand over *your* weapons, we will take you up to meet this captain of yours."

"Or we could have that violent argument," Grayden suggested.

"Or I could just send us plummeting to the ground from here," Wynn added, one hand hovering over the plinth, a hard look in his eyes.

"If you do that, you'll die, too," the woman said.

Wynn shrugged. "We are Academy students, on our way to become Defenders of Telmondir. It is our solemn duty to thwart the likes of you."

The two pirates drew back and held a whispered discussion. Grayden did not allow his hand to lower even a fraction of an inch. He watched the two pirates carefully and tried not to think about what would happen to them all if Wynn carried out his threat.

At length, the pirates stepped forward.

"It seems you have us cornered," the big man admitted. "Neither of us has any interest in dropping out of the sky." He unbuckled his sword belt and handed it over, hilt first. The woman also handed over her sword. Then they turned their backs. Wynn took the weapons, and Grayden stashed his dagger and drew his own sword, stepping out into the hallway.

"We'll take you up to see the captain," the woman said.

"What do you think will happen?" Wynn whispered as they marched down the hall.

"I don't know," Grayden replied in hushed tones. "But Mouse said they haven't killed anyone yet."

"Think we can we trust this Mouse?"

"Not around your valuables." The woman's interjection startled them both. She tossed a grin over her shoulder at them. "But he's got a certain amount of honor... for being a little pickpocket."

"Honor among thieves," Dalmir muttered. He also had been

listening to Grayden and Wynn's hushed conversation. "I do truly look forward to meeting this captain of yours."

The woman smiled, but her expression seemed strained. Her eyes darted about like she was looking for a way to escape before she replied. "Mouse did tell the truth. Our mission was to capture the airship. We got no quarrel with the Academy, and we wouldn't want to start one. I'm Shaesta, by the way."

"Grayden."

"Wynn."

Beren and Dalmir remained silent, but this did not seem to upset the woman.

"First years?" she asked.

Wynn nodded.

"Pretty quick of you to find a hiding place and get into the engine room." Her tone was admiring. "I'd love to know how you did it."

Wynn opened his mouth, but Grayden elbowed him, giving a slight shake of his head. Wynn fell silent. Shaesta grinned, a teasing light in her eyes. "Suit yourselves," she said.

They walked in silence for a few steps, but Shaesta was apparently not comfortable with silence.

"You two are obviously Dalman," she said. "Your big friend, am I right in guessing he's Telsuman?"

Beren rumbled something unintelligible.

"Yeah," Wynn replied.

"I thought as much. You're tall for a Telsuman, but your sword is a giveaway. It's obviously from a Telsuman forge. I've heard tell that Tel-crafted swords are the finest in the Western half of the world."

Beren frowned. "They're the finest in the whole of the world," he said through gritted teeth. "Not that I'd expect scum like you to know good craftsmanship when you see it."

"Beren!" Grayden hissed. Even with the pirates disarmed, he didn't feel it was safe to antagonize their adversaries.

"Just because she talks pretty doesn't make her anything more than a pirate. Don't forget they stole this airship and allegedly left our comrades in the middle of nowhere, probably without weapons or mounts," Beren growled.

"No weapons," the big man agreed. "But we did let them take their horses."

"And you think that somehow makes you honorable?" Beren snarled.

Shaesta held up her hands in a gesture of surrender. "Forgive me. I meant no offense to Telsuma or its craftsmen. Rustam, I'll go ahead and let Marik know the situation and offer to take the wheel for a bit. I'm sure he'll want to talk to our guests right away." Rustam nodded, and before anyone could stop her, she jogged ahead of the group and disappeared up the steps.

They followed in silence. As they emerged into the daylight, it took Grayden's eyes a moment to adjust. He blinked and looked around. There were far fewer pirates than he had expected. High above them, he caught notice of the tiny black shape that had bothered him earlier. It hovered at the edge of his vision like a great bird. He squinted at it, trying to determine the breed. It had a strange shape he could not quite make out. It had to be enormous to be seen from so far away, he thought. Wynn elbowed him, drawing his attention back down to their immediate surroundings. Wynn gestured at the sleek, smaller craft soaring elegantly off the *Crimson Eagle*'s starboard bow.

"I'd heard about private airships, but I thought they were just stories." Wynn's eyes were wide with admiration for the feat of engineering.

"They're real enough," Rustam said. "But you don't see them often here..." He trailed off as a tall man with black hair and hazel eyes strode over to them. The man walked with a confident grace, his tall boots clicking on the decking of the ship. From the slightly nicer cut of his clothes, Grayden guessed this man was the captain.

"Rustam, what's going on? Who are these kids?" the dark-haired man asked.

Rustam hesitated. "We found them in the engine room, Captain. Didn't Shaesta tell you?"

"Shaesta?"

"She said she was coming to inform you of the situation and relieve you at the wheel. Are you saying she's not up here?"

"Haven't seen her since you two went below-decks."

Rustam's expression darkened, and he turned to Grayden. "Who else is still on board? What have your friends done with Shaesta?"

"What have you done with our comrades?" Grayden replied, filling his voice with as much steel as he could muster and trying not to let anyone see how terrified he was. "You are the pirates, here."

The pirates stared menacingly at them, but before anyone could move or say anything more, the *Crimson Eagle* suddenly lurched sideways, throwing most of them from their feet. Grayden lost his grip on his sword and it slid away across the deck and under the railing to plummet from the airship and fall through the air, lost forever. An explosive cracking sound filled the air as another large ship swooped out of nowhere and rammed into the port side of the cargo cruiser.

28

The *Eagle* groaned as the other ship tore through her hull. Grayden pushed himself up from the deck and looked around in dazed confusion. The pirates were shouting and racing to the port side, weapons raised. He cast about for his sword, then remembered what had happened. Next to him, Wynn pushed himself to his feet, and Grayden idly noticed that he seemed to have lost both of the swords he had taken from the pirates. A quick glance showed him that they had slid quite a ways across the deck, but Wynn seemed not to have noticed.

Grappling hooks struck the railing and the mast with heavy clanks, and a few of them snagged in the rigging. Using the ropes, raiders swung and skittered across from this new ship, landing on the deck and drawing their own weapons.

"Outnumbered," Wynn whispered, the fingers of his left hand tapping idly against his own leg as he rose and stood next to Grayden.

Grayden tossed his friend a questioning glance, but Wynn was not looking at him. His face had gone expressionless.

"What?" Grayden asked.

"Four to one." Wynn's voice held no passion, no concern as he drew his own sword. The men before them had become nothing more than numbers to him. Grayden wished he could reduce the terror rising in his own mind to mere numbers.

Then there was no more time for words or numbers or even thought. The deck of the *Crimson Eagle* became a maelstrom of confusion and noise. Grayden lay where he had fallen, the side of his face pressed against the cool decking. His head throbbed and swam as he raised himself to a standing position. Reaching inside his jacket, his fingers found their quarry. He pulled out his long-knife and stared as a wave of attackers swung their way onto the cruiser. His heart pounded in his ears as their boots hit the boards of the deck with ominous thuds.

Grayden looked around wildly for his friends. At first, he could not find them amidst the chaos. Then he spotted Beren, towering above the rest. Desperately, Grayden made his way toward him.

Attackers blocked his path. Grayden sliced out at one of them with his dagger. He ducked and whirled away from a sword blow, his heart lurching as the wind of it ruffled his hair. He rushed another, elbowing the man in the side and hearing a grunt as he passed. A sharp pain bit into his leg and he crumpled, dropping his knife. Glancing up, he saw a man leap after him and he scrabbled desperately for his weapon. Failing to retrieve it, he rolled away just as the sword cleaved into the deck. Stumbling to his feet, he jumped at the attacker, knocking him to the deck. The man's head slammed against a barrel and he lay still.

Grayden rose, feeling sick. His leg throbbed. He retrieved the sword that had nearly killed him. It was heavier than he was used to. A strange curve to its blade made it feel awkwardly balanced, but it was better than nothing. His eyes scanned the deck until he found his dagger. He picked it up and bent over, breathing heavily, thankful for a sudden lull in his immediate vicinity. The reprieve was short-lived, however. One raider noticed him and advanced, sword swinging lazily, a knowing smile on his clean-shaven face.

Grayden lurched away from the new threat, wielding the

unfamiliar blade clumsily. His attacker slashed and cut at him with speed and precision. Grayden parried as best he could. He backed away. His thoughts whirled as he blocked blow after blow. Suddenly, his attacker grinned, a cunning light of victory in his eyes. Before he could wonder what it meant, Grayden backed into something with such force that it brought tears to his eyes and nearly knocked his breath from his lungs. It was the mast. Without thinking, he slid around it just as his attacker swung. The blade bit deeply into the wood of the mast where Grayden's head had been but a moment before. Moving swiftly, Grayden reversed direction and grabbed the back of the man's head, smashing his face into the mast. The man slumped to the deck, motionless.

"Grayden!"

Grayden jumped at the sudden nearness of the voice. When he saw who it was, he laughed in nervous relief. "Wynn!"

"You okay?" Wynn asked. Grayden noticed that his friend had a new weapon, a long staff with a lethal blade affixed to one end.

"Yeah," Grayden replied. "Where'd you get that?"

"Grabbed it from the man who knocked my sword out of my hand," Wynn said dispassionately. "Looks like Beren needs help."

Grayden followed Wynn's gaze and saw their tall friend at the other end of the ship. His own efforts to reach Beren had only resulted in him ending up farther away from his friend than at the battle's advent. The burly young man fended off half a dozen attackers at once. The Telsuman still stood, but the attackers were well-organized and obviously well-trained. Beren hammered his sword about like a blacksmith forging a particularly ornery piece of metal. The course of the battle swirled around Beren, the raiders surrounding him and isolating him from the rest of the pirates.

"Why are they—" Grayden began, but Wynn cut him off.

"Time for questions later. Come on, I think I see a way through."

The two young men made their way into the fray. Grayden

tried to keep up with Wynn, who carved a path with his glaive, but the closer they got to Beren, the more intense the fighting became. Halfway to their destination, the mass of raiders became so thick that Grayden lost sight of Wynn. He fought down the rising sensation of panic as he blocked and stumbled his way through the mass of combatants. Grayden searched, glancing about frantically, but he couldn't find either of his friends. In the midst of the chaos, he could not get his bearings. He could not tell which direction he was facing, let alone which direction he needed to go. He lost his footing and nearly fell, catching himself on the arm of a raider. The man stared at him in surprise and then shook him off, raising his sword and advancing. Grayden threw himself backwards, struggling to lift his unwieldy blade to defend himself. Terror threatened to drown him beneath its tide.

MARIK FOUGHT his way through the battle, his lips pressed together in a grim line. The cruiser was his prize, and he'd fall to his death before he let another group of marauders steal what he had rightfully commandeered. He took no pleasure in the dance of death, but he would dance to protect himself, his ship, and his crew. Angling himself toward the steerage, Marik used every weapon available to him, fighting his way across the deck with a singular purpose. He must reach the wheel and regain control of the airship. With that accomplished, more options would be available, but there was still a lot of ground to cover.

He used his fists, feet, and elbows when the crush of people became too thick for his blade to be helpful. His crew held their own reasonably well, considering the odds, but Marik knew he would most likely lose good men today. He glimpsed Raisa—who fended off her attackers with ease—but he had lost track of Rustam, Yefrem, Oleck, and the rest of the extra hands they had hired on. Mouse was nowhere to be seen, and a surge of worry mixed with relief rushed through him. He hoped the lad had found a place to hunker down and hide. Worry over Shaesta flickered through his mind. No one had seen her for far too long, but he could not spare much more than a thought or two in her direction. She could look after herself.

He cut down another raider and ducked beneath a wildly swinging cutlass. Interestingly enough, the fighting was not bearing down on himself. He kept waiting for the other crew to realize who he was and converge upon him. But it didn't happen. Marik found it curious that he was being allowed to move freely on his mission to retake the steering deck. He parried a devastatingly powerful blow from a mace and swung his fist into the wielder's stomach. His opponent doubled over in pain and Marik brought the hilt of his sword down on the back of the man's head, dropping him to the deck. And yet it was undeniable that their assailants were focused on something else entirely. For some reason, the raiders were mostly ignoring him and concentrating all of their attention on singling out the tall lad with the enormous broadsword: one of the Academy students. In the glances he could spare, as he fought his way towards the steering deck, Marik could tell the young giant was well-trained. He was holding his own splendidly. But why he was the focus of the raiders' attention was a mystery to the pirate.

A sudden noise caught his attention, and he turned to find another of the young Academy students. How had they managed to hide aboard the ship? Marik wondered briefly. Unlike his taller friend, this lad was struggling. He was fighting for his life, scrambling and stumbling away from an assailant who was pursuing him relentlessly. Even though he clearly lacked the training of his friend, this young man possessed skill and determination. A sudden pang shot through Marik at the sight. This young man had done nothing to end up in such danger, but he was acquitting himself well. He had outsmarted Marik's crew, disarmed two of his best, and bartered for his own freedom and the release of the ship without a quaver in his voice. Admiration wormed its way through his consciousness, along with the bitter tang of shame.

Deviating from his course, Marik lunged across the deck and stabbed the raider in the back just before he could take a swing that surely would have taken the young man's head off. Marik stood over the fallen foe and found himself staring straight into the young man's eyes. Fighting down the shame, he tossed the lad a grin and a casual wink.

"Looked like you could use a hand," Marik said.

"Th-thank you," the young man stammered.

Marik glimpsed a flicker of movement. "Behind you!" he shouted, and darted forward to interpose himself between a raider and the young man, catching the raider's blade on his own in a quick block. Out of the corner of his eye, he saw the young man awkwardly raise his sword to protect Marik from a spear-thrust.

And just like that, he and the young man were fighting back-to-back.

"What's your name?" Marik shouted.

"Grayden," came the reply.

"Captain Marik," Marik yelled, parrying another thrust at his stomach. "Quick thinking, turning that spear."

"Guess we're even," Grayden panted back.

Marik bit back a laugh at this sudden turn of events. Just an eye-blink before, they had been enemies on opposite sides of the law. Now they fought together, and he found his admiration for the younger man rising.

"Stay with me, Grayden," Marik yelled. "We have to get to the wheel."

He felt Grayden's nod, and once more slowly made his way to the ladder. Although he was clearly unfamiliar with the heavy, curved blade, the lad held his own as they fought their way through the raiders.

"You're not half-bad with that sword," Marik called out.

He received no reply, but he caught a tightening of the young man's jaw and a dangerous glint in the blue-gray eyes. Before he could wonder at his reaction, Marik reached the ladder. Catching hold of it, Marik hauled himself up onto the steering deck.

Striding to the wheel, he paused, relief coursing through him at the sight of Shaesta pulling herself over the top of the ladder on the other side of the steering deck.

"There you are. It's good to see you alive. I was worried..." he began.

Shaesta stared at him, a pained expression in her eyes. He hesitated, suddenly concerned, his gaze sharpening as he checked her for injuries. She moved a step in his direction, her arms reaching as if for an embrace. He approached her. Shaesta's arms looped around his neck and then a shock of betrayal coursed through him as cold steel pressed up against his throat painfully. The point of the blade bit through his skin, drawing a drop of blood. Never loosing her hold on him, Shaesta removed his sword from his grip and tossed it behind them. Then she moved to the railing overlooking the battle and let out an ear-piercing whistle.

"Shaesta... why?" Marik whispered through clenched teeth. "What are you doing?"

"Hush!" she hissed. Then she raised her free arm and shouted, "Yield! Or your captain dies!"

A shudder of shock rippled across the deck. Marik saw the disbelief and hurt in the eyes of each member of his crew. Raisa stared up at them, horrified betrayal etched across her face. She was the first to throw down her sword, dropping it from fingers that seemed numb and lifeless. The raiders had already disarmed most of his crew; only Raisa and Oleck were still fighting.

Shaesta's lips brushed Marik's ear as she whispered, "You will order your crew to leave their weapons and move to the stern of the ship. You will walk with me down those steps, and then I and my comrades will peacefully leave this vessel. You will not stop us. If you try, you will all die."

"Why? Why are you doing this?" Marik growled. "If you don't want the Eagle, what did you come for?"

"That is none of your concern," Shaesta replied. "Will you cooperate?"

Marik let out an angry rumble of noise from deep in his

throat, but he nodded slightly. Shaesta eased the pressure of her dagger a fraction and Marik gave the order to his people. Confused and disheartened, they obeyed, shuffling toward the stern of the boat, away from the attacking vessel. The raiders disembarked, swinging back onto their own ship. Shaesta prodded Marik in the back and together they descended the steps and crossed the now empty deck. They reached a rope and Shaesta swung around to face Marik, holding her dagger before her.

"Marik... I..." There was something dark and sorrowful in her eyes.

"Don't even try to apologize," Marik's voice was gruff and angry. "I will never forget this, Shaesta."

Shaesta's expression hardened. "You'll want to get back on the *Hawk*," she said. "I took all the cynders but one from the *Eagle* and transferred them to my airship. I imagine it's nearly depleted by now. You'll have to land right away, but you should have time to get to the ground safely. I'm sorry, but I can't afford to risk you following me."

Marik's face turned red with anger. "Shaesta—"

Shaesta raised her dagger in a threatening gesture, then sighed. "Tell Oleck I'm sorry," she said. "I truly am, Marik. I know you won't believe me, but... family comes first. Surely you can understand that."

She grabbed a line and swung back onto her airship, dropping lightly to the deck and striding toward the wheel. Marik watched her as she touched the controls to reverse the airship and pull away from the *Eagle*. She didn't look back.

Marik stared after her, his thoughts filled with murderous vengeance. The airship shuddered beneath him. He tucked his anger and the sting of betrayal into a corner. He would deal with this treachery later. Right now, he needed to get his remaining crew off this airship, before it plummeted from the sky.

29

Roald glowered through his spyglass as the *Crimson Eagle* limped through the sky. From their vantage point high above the wispy clouds, he had observed the entire battle between the pirates and the raiders. Roald ground his teeth in frustration. His prize had slipped away aboard the unmarked airship. His second-in-command approached cautiously.

"What should we do now?" Gunri asked.

Roald lowered the spyglass. "We were right to believe that young Adelfried did not disembark with the other Academy students."

"He was still aboard the *Crimson Eagle*?"

"Yes, but he is now aboard the unmarked airship."

"Should we move to intercept?"

"No." Roald slammed his fist down on the railing of his ship. "The Ar'Molon will not be pleased, but we must accept that our mission has failed."

"Failed?" Gunri's eyes widened in horror.

"Failed," Roald said grimly. "We have been thwarted. With the young Lord Adelfried aboard an unmarked airship, kidnapped by unknown marauders, there is now no way to frame Ondoura for his assassination. We had a brief enough window to begin with, but this unfortunate turn of events has ruined any chance we had left. Tell Mikah to plot a new course. We will follow the unmarked ship and determine the identity of the ones who have thwarted us. Ar'Molon Uun will wish to know whom to punish." He spun on his heel and stalked towards his cabin. "Tell Jarl I wish to speak with him." He threw the command over his shoulder as he departed.

He did not have to look at Gunri to know that his second-in-command was terrified. But if Gunri thought they would follow the standard directive in the event of a failure, he was wrong. They would not fall on their swords, as Kotai custom demanded. They would follow this new player and find out who had snatched their prize. Then they would return to Melar and give the Ar'Molon their full report. If Lord Uun decided to punish them for their failure, well, Roald had known the risks when he joined the elite ranks of the Kotai. But he would at the very least make the Ar'Molon look him in the eye as he gave the order.

Roald paused, a shudder coursing through his body. Although, perhaps the Ar'Molon would prefer that, anyway.

30

"We have to get back to the *Hawk*," Marik roared at what was left of his crew. "This bird is going down. No time to explain. Move, move!"

The pirates whirled into action at his orders. Raisa signaled the smaller vessel, and it swiftly soared into position close to the badly damaged *Eagle*. Grayden found himself nearly stampeded as the crew tossed ropes and hooks from one airship to the other. He spotted Dalmir quickly, then looked around for Wynn and Beren. He hadn't seen either of them since he had been separated from Wynn during the battle. His gaze swept back and forth as he searched each face. He did not find the ones he was looking for, and he scanned the crew again, worry turning to sudden fear. Grayden sprinted over to Dalmir and stared up at the old man, panic in his eyes.

"Wynn? Beren?" Grayden's eyes turned reluctantly to the deck, lingering on each of the fallen. "They're not..."

Dalmir laid a hand on Grayden's shoulder. "They're not dead, lad. The raiders took them both," he said gently.

Relief, followed by confusion, shock, and a new sort of terror, chased each other through Grayden's heart. He could not speak.

His mind reeled. He stared at Dalmir in wild, open-mouthed dismay.

"We'll find them. We'll get them back," Dalmir said. He stared reassuringly into Grayden's eyes, and Grayden noticed a difference in Dalmir's gaze. There was a calm, or perhaps a confidence, that had not been there before. "But first, we have to get off this airship."

They raced toward the rail where the pirate crew instructed them on how to swing over to the smaller ship. If he had not been so worried about his friends, Grayden might have enjoyed the thrill of sailing through the air hundreds of feet off the ground, but his trepidation overshadowed the moment.

Marik was the last one to cross over. As the pirate captain grabbed hold of the last rope, Grayden was still standing by the mast where the ropes were anchored. In a split second, and without any conscious thought in his head, Grayden acted. His decision astonished him, but once he had begun, it was impossible to stop. Moving more swiftly than he would ever have believed possible, Grayden unfastened the rope and wrapped it around his waist. The sudden jerk of Marik's weight dragged him toward the side of the airship, but his maneuver had the desired effect. Instead of swinging nimbly onto the deck, the pirate captain now clung to the rope below them and oscillated slightly in the open air between the ships. Grayden strained his muscles and came to a stop at the rail. He could not hold this position indefinitely, but work in the orchards and the additional training with Master Farley had made him strong. Unsure of what to do next, Grayden gazed wildly at the pirate crew.

"One step toward me and I drop him," he snarled.

Dalmir approached cautiously, but did not question Grayden's antics. He merely raised an eyebrow and placed himself between Grayden and the rest of the crew. The old man made no threatening gesture, but he stood in a clearly defensive position, guarding Grayden and allowing events to play out as they might.

Grayden stared over the edge of the airship and was surprised to see no hint of fear in Marik's eyes. The pirate stared up at him with wrathful intensity.

"What are you doing, lad?" he growled.

Grayden swallowed and tightened his jaw. "Those raiders kidnapped my friends. You're going to swear to help me get them back, or I drop you." Sweat trickled down the back of his neck. He hoped the pirate would not call his bluff.

"We both know you don't have it in you," Marik replied, his voice cool.

"Don't test me." Grayden let an inch of rope slip through his hands. A stunned expression in the pirate's eyes rewarded him. It wasn't quite fear, but he had managed to shake the man's confidence.

Marik narrowed his eyes in thought. "All right, lad. You haul me up, and we'll go after your friends."

"Swear it," Grayden said through gritted teeth.

"Fine!" The pirate's voice rose in exasperation. "I swear it, by those I hold most dear."

Grayden let out the breath he had been holding and took a step backward, pulling the captain up. He nodded at the crew and they rushed forward to help pull him up. When the captain once more stood on the deck, he spared a vicious glare for Grayden and then turned to Raisa.

"Our losses?"

"Rustam, Thayric, and Kauldar are dead." Raisa grimaced. "Yefrem and Hendel were wounded pretty bad; you need to order them below-decks so they'll rest. Zanic's got a head wound I'm a little concerned about. Mouse has a few scrapes, but nothing serious. The rest of us are fine."

A sliver of sadness shivered through Grayden when he found that Rustam had not made it through the battle. He wondered at that. Just a short while ago, he would have counted the big man an enemy, but now Grayden grieved at his loss.

Marik raised an eyebrow and directed his gaze at her left shoulder. Raisa flushed and touched the gash gingerly.

"It's nothing that won't heal."

"Cap'n!" Oleck bellowed, his voice strained with an emotion that Grayden couldn't identify.

They turned to look at where Oleck was pointing. The *Crimson Eagle* was no longer drifting lazily downwards. Her nose had dropped until she was almost vertical in the sky. With a mournful sputter, the lights along her trim sails flickered wildly and then fell dark. The airship plummeted toward the ground with increasing velocity. A span of heartbeats passed, and then she crashed into the rocks below with a thunderous sound. The bulkheads crumpled. The timbers split. The masts cracked in half. There was a flash of blinding light and a blast of sound. A wave of heat swept up and across their faces, even at their height. Grayden shut his eyes instinctively and then opened them, blinking. He stared, aghast. The airship was now splintered across the valley floor. The entire massive cargo cruiser had been completely obliterated.

"What... what was that?" he asked.

Dalmir frowned, but remained silent.

Marik was the first to gather his wits. "All right. Oleck, chart a course for Kinrea. We'll just have to deliver the bad news to Arrio... Besides, he might have an idea who Shaesta was working for."

"What?" Grayden shouted.

Marik stared at Grayden. "You're lucky I don't just toss you over the side and have done with you. I'll let you off when we land and you can go wherever you desire as soon as I'm through with Arrio."

"You lying scum! You swore! Beren and Wynn have been captured and who knows what's happening to them or why they were taken. You swore you'd help me track them down." Grayden's throat tightened and his vision tunneled with rage.

Marik smirked. "Never trust a pirate, lad. I swore by those I hold most dear... well, those I hold most dear are already dead. They won't mind my betrayal."

Grayden lunged at Marik, hands formed into fists. He landed a solid punch on Marik's jaw before Oleck grabbed him around the middle and hauled him away bodily. Grayden snarled and fought, kicking and flailing and refusing to go down without a fight. He shouted insults and screamed at the pirates, but Marik ignored him, staring at a chart Raisa had brought him.

"It's a good thing we had all those cynders aboard the Hawk," Grayden heard Raisa comment.

The airship shuddered beneath them. The entire craft gave a low moan, as if in pain. Then they, too, began to fall out of the sky.

Grayden found himself released as the entire crew scurried about, trying to figure out what was wrong with the airship. His argument with Marik momentarily forgotten, Grayden stared wide-eyed at Dalmir.

"What's happening?" he shouted.

One of the crew emerged from below-decks and raced to where Marik was desperately clinging to the wheel. Grayden saw the captain's face tighten with anger as they spoke. But there was something else, as well. A mixture of horror and desperation shone in Marik's eyes. The captain's lips moved, though Grayden was too far away to hear his words, and then he relinquished the wheel to the crewman. He walked steadily towards the center of the deck and motioned his crew around him.

"Men," he said, "Vand has informed me that our store of cynders is gone. Shaesta must have sabotaged the Hawk as well as the Eagle. The power in the remaining cynder is nearly depleted."

There was a brief second of stunned silence. Then everyone began speaking at once.

Mouse's thin, quavering voice rose up above the din. "There's nothing, Cap'n? Nothing we can do?"

All eyes turned toward Marik. The captain pressed his lips together grimly, his expression solemn.

"There are a few possibilities," Marik replied. "We can try to land. We may have enough left in the cynder to do so safely. The question is: where? There aren't any bodies of water large enough or close enough, and we're getting close to the mountains. We may have enough to get to the Yarbelg Pass. If we're very lucky, the snows have already started, which would give us decent landing conditions. Now, there's also the Steyrekh Forest, which is closer, and may have a pond or a lake. At the very least, I've heard that the trees grow so close together we might be able to set down in the branches and make it to the ground safely. What say you?"

The crew erupted again in a cacophony of desperation as the airship shuddered and listed beneath them. A few argued for the Pass, asserting that a safe and more known landing area was of utmost importance. Several argued for the forest, maintaining that it was closer and they might not make it to the mountains. Those in favor of the Pass spoke up again, citing the absence of any towns near the Steyrekh Forest where they might get more cynders.

"We could wander around for lunats before we found a single living soul near that wretched place," Raisa contended.

"Better that than falling to our deaths before we even see the Pass," Oleck shot back.

Grayden watched, worry for his friends rising. He knew he had no say in this dispute. He would have argued to make for the Pass, simply because it promised slightly more success to his own quest of rescuing Beren and Wynn. Another shudder rippled across the deck beneath his feet and his worry turned to alarm as the *Valdeun Hawk*'s slow decline in altitude suddenly dove into a free-fall. The arguments turned to gasps and voices raised in sudden alarm. The noise rose and Grayden felt as though something inside his head was clawing its way out.

He glanced over the side of the ship, and his stomach clenched. The ground was approaching much too fast. There was less fuel than they had realized. A scream pierced the air.

"ENOUGH!" Dalmir's voice sliced through the clamor and

he slammed his staff onto the deck of the airship with a mighty thud. Everyone turned to him, startled.

The *Hawk* trembled, then leveled out, then it shot straight up into the sky, gaining altitude at an alarming rate. When they reached the gray clouds, the airship stopped, hanging in the sky like a hovering falcon.

Raisa was the first to recover her voice. "What... how... was that you?" Her face, along with everyone else's, displayed open disbelief and a touch of fear.

"How did you do that?" Marik finally asked, his voice low.

Dalmir's face showed no expression. "It is not important how I am able to do this. What is important is that I can control your airship, despite a nearly depleted power-source. Do you agree?"

Marik nodded slowly. "That appears to be the case; however..."

"It is unimportant," Dalmir repeated. "This is the deal, sir. I will power your airship and keep it from falling from the sky. You will help us rescue our comrades, and when we have accomplished that task, you will deliver us all safely to the Academy."

"And what do I get out of this deal?" Marik asked.

The airship dropped several feet so abruptly that Grayden felt himself briefly lifting off the deck. He experienced a sensation of panic before the *Hawk* stopped once more and he fell to the deck. He, Marik, and Dalmir stayed on their feet. Others were not so lucky, and Grayden watched as half the crew crumpled, unprepared for the sudden stop.

Dalmir's eyes twinkled as he gazed impassively at the pirate captain. Marik met his gaze and Grayden again marveled at the man's composure.

Abruptly, Marik nodded his head once. "All right. I'll help you. But this is my ship, and I give the orders. Are we clear?"

"I have no problem with that at all, Captain," Dalmir replied. Grayden couldn't be sure, but it definitely appeared to him that the old man was fighting back a grin.

"Good. I need to confer with my crew about which direction

we should head in if we're going to catch Shaesta." Marik raised an eyebrow at Dalmir. "Can you help with that? Or does your control only extend to maneuvering airships in flight?"

Dalmir pointed. "They went that way."

"Excellent."

There was a lot of bustling about. Mouse brought maps up from below. Dalmir pointed to several locations, claiming he could "track" the airship with Wynn and Beren on it. The conversation was low and serious. After a while, Grayden found a barrel and sat down, feeling useless. He wanted desperately to help his friends, but there was little he could do. He had barely even maintained his hold on a weapon in the battle, much less been able to reach Beren or even keep pace with Wynn. He couldn't track an airship through the sky. He didn't even know how to fly an airship. As he sat down, he realized just how tired he was. It had been a long day. Grayden's eyelids drooped.

"You okay?" Mouse asked, coming up to sit next to him. It surprised Grayden that any of the pirates were willing to speak to him. He'd threatened to drop their captain to his death, after all.

"Yeah, just tired and worried about my friends."

"Marik'll find them, just watch." Mouse's voice held a confidence Grayden wished he shared. "You want to go lie down?"

Grayden looked over to where Dalmir and Marik hunched over the charts. He hated the idea of sleeping while his friends were in danger, but there was also very little he could offer just now.

"Yeah, is there a place I would be out of the way?"

"Follow me," Mouse said, his voice cheerful.

He led Grayden down to a small room with a hammock. Grayden smiled, thinking of Beren's distrustful gaze upon first seeing the hammocks on the *Crimson Eagle*. Had that only been this morning? It seemed like years had passed since he had boarded the airship bound for the Academy. What a fresh-faced, optimistic lad he had been all those hours ago.

Mouse left, promising he'd come wake Grayden for dinner.

Alone, Grayden looked despondently around the small quarters. He didn't even have a change of clothes. He gave a weary exhalation, as if he could expel the entire day's worth of fears and unpleasant events as easily as he could expel air from his lungs. Then he swung himself up into the hammock and instantly fell into a deep and dreamless sleep.

31

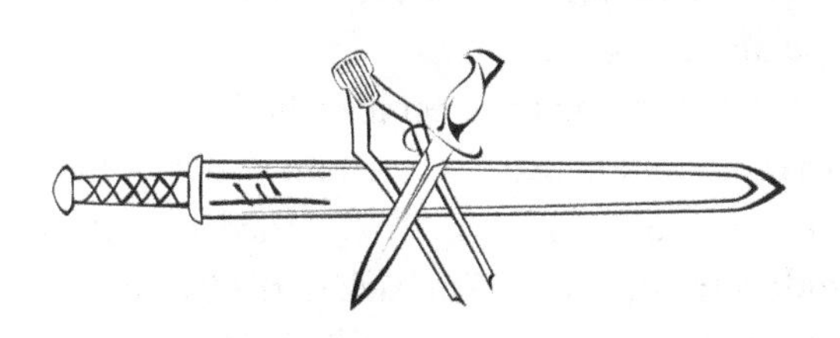

Wynn awoke groggily, his head throbbing, in complete darkness. It had all happened so fast. The battle on the airship blurred in his memory. He tried to remember, but it was like opening his eyes underwater: everything looking bleary and distorted. Rough wood beneath his hands transported him into a sudden memory.

The smooth wood of the glaive fit in his grasp with a rightness that amazed him. Despite its apparent length, it rested comfortably and perfectly balanced in his grip as he swept it from side to side. Beren was holding his own splendidly, his great broadsword slicing and chopping through his attackers. Wynn spared an awestruck glance at his friend, admiring his composure. Sweat trickled down Wynn's forehead...

The memory grew blurry.

Noise, a painful throbbing in his head...

Wynn remembered a voice shouting, "We've got him!" Beren was being overwhelmed. Something happened that Wynn couldn't see, and Beren fell to the deck, unconscious. Wynn turned to see the Telsuman being dragged away by a new onslaught of attackers.

Wynn remembered throwing himself at the men holding Beren's arms, the glaive whistling its deadly tune. Alone, he had been no match for them, but he had made them reconsider. He could see it in their eyes.

"What should we do?" one man asked. Wynn stood over his fallen friend, ready for the coming attack.

"Take them both," another voice replied.

A desperate struggle....

Wynn blinked, trying to remember the details. He had fought; he knew that much. He had been certain they would kill him and Beren if they got near enough. Wynn tried to roll over and his head pounded, transporting him back to the battle.

Something smashed into his head. Blackness. He couldn't see. Images and voices that were disconnected, jarring, danced around him.

"We've got him."

"No time! No time!"

"What about this other one?"

"Shaesta's signal!"

"Tie him up for now and bring him along."

Rough hands lifted him. He felt himself being half-carried, half-dragged. His head throbbed. Ropes were wound about his hands and legs. Wynn had just enough presence of mind to angle his wrists slightly before the bonds tightened. He could not maneuver much, but as he slipped once more into darkness he hoped it had been enough.

"Wynn?" The whisper came from his left, pulling him abruptly out of his memories. "Wynn? You awake?"

"Yeah," he whispered back. "Grayden?"

"No, it's Beren. I don't think Grayden's here. I do not believe anyone is here but us."

Wynn struggled to rise or turn his head. He instantly regretted the attempt as pain flared in his skull, bringing tears to his eyes. Fear for the fate of his friend battled with the pain in Wynn's head, each vying for predominance in his thoughts. He lay still until the throbbing subsided a little, then he tried moving again, this time more slowly. Gradually, he sat up and peered at his surroundings. As his eyes adjusted to the dim lighting filtering in through the small porthole, he realized it was not as dark as he had at first thought.

They were in a small room. The single porthole hung above a bed he could just make out in the dim light. A single glance told him it was far too small for either of them to fit through, even if they could reach it. A moment later, he realized that wooden shutters had also been nailed across the porthole on the outside, effectively discouraging them from using it as an exit as well as preventing them from being able to get their bearings. The sensation in the pit of Wynn's stomach told him they were still on an airship, and still airborne.

There was a strange thrumming sound above them. Wynn cocked his head slightly.

"Is that rain?"

Beren sighed. "Possibly."

"I've always wondered about that... airships in the rain... must be miserable up on deck." Wynn returned his attention to the ropes that secured his hands. "Can you move? Are you injured?"

Beren shifted. "I am not hurt, but my hands and legs are bound most tightly. You?"

"Mine too," Wynn replied, "and I think I got clubbed across the back of the head, but other than that, I'm all right."

Wynn fell silent as he set to work, twisting his wrists back and forth. His hands were free in a matter of minutes. He exulted silently. That was probably a record. Beren was oddly silent and Wynn squinted at him through the gloom. The Telsuman faced the wall.

"Beren? You okay?" Wynn asked as he attacked the knots restraining his legs. "You still with me?"

Beren made a dejected noise, but did not turn. Wynn strained, and the knots loosened enough for him to free his feet, though he had to remove his boots to do so. He pulled his legs out of the bonds and then stood, pulling his boots back on. He stretched, his aching muscles indicating that he had lain in the same position for several hours. Then he hurried over and placed a hand on Beren's shoulder.

"Seriously, are you all right? Give me your hands and I'll get those ropes off you."

Beren jerked slightly and rolled over. Now that he was closer, Wynn saw the surprise on his friend's face.

"How did you get loose?" Beren asked.

Wynn smirked as he worked on the knots securing Beren's wrists. "Game my brothers and I play. We take turns being tied up, then time each other to see who frees themselves the fastest. Whoever won didn't have to do chores for an hour." He grinned wider. "I was particularly good at it. After a while, you learn a few tricks, ways to hold your hands while they're being bound, things like that, that make it easier to escape. Lucky I didn't go unconscious until *after* they tied me up."

Beren's voice rumbled in a deep, soft chuckle. "How fortuitous for me to have been captured in your company."

"I never thought it'd actually be a useful skill."

Once Beren was free, the two young men examined their cell. There wasn't much to it, though they scoured it thoroughly, searching for a weakness. The door was good, solid wood, and the lock was one Wynn had never seen before.

"I can't pick it," he said after inspecting it, "even if I had something to pick it with, but they took everything."

When they had finished exploring and found nothing useful, they sat down with their backs to a wall, the door on their left. Wynn's stomach growled.

"Any idea how long we've been here?" Wynn asked.

"No."

"Any idea why they captured us?"

Beren shrugged halfheartedly. "I am the son of Lord Adelfried. I still can't think of anyone who would want to kill or abduct me, but obviously, there is someone."

"Two someones," Wynn said idly, his mind clicking over recent events faster than he could express.

Beren pulled at his lower lip. "How do you figure that?"

Wynn tapped his fingers on the floorboards beneath him, trying to keep his thoughts in order. "The men we fought in the alley had poisoned daggers. They were assassins, trying to kill you. But these marauders worked hard to merely capture you. Stands to reason there are two groups after you: one that wants you alive, one dead."

Beren rubbed his hands across his face and made an exasperated sound. "But why? Why me? And why did they take you?"

"I've been trying to think on that, but it hurts. Maybe I just got in the way... in all the fighting, maybe it was just easier to grab both of us."

"But that means you're in danger. If they didn't want you to begin with..."

"I'll just have to make myself sound as valuable as you... we'll have to figure out what they want and use it to our advantage."

Beren was pensive. "I am sorry if my friendship has put you in danger. But I must admit, I am glad to not be in this predicament alone."

The room shuddered, and there was a strange noise. The room lurched, then everything grew still. The two young men shared a nervous glance.

"We must have landed," Beren commented.

"Then we'd better be ready to meet our captors," Wynn replied.

They waited for several nerve-wracking, eternal minutes, their hearts pounding in restless apprehension. Then they heard the sound they had been dreading: footsteps in the hall. Wynn's breath caught in his throat as the door handle began to turn. He forced himself to remain still, pressing his shoulders into the wall, as if he might meld with it and render himself invisible. If only

Grayden were here, he would have known what to do. He would have acted. Wynn could only sit there, tapping his fingers on the floor, his brain sifting through a hundred different potential scenarios at the speed of light but unable to make a decision.

The door swung open. Beren struck like a blacksmith's hammer: precise and swift. He wrapped one arm around the man's neck, clapped his other hand across the man's mouth, and yanked him inside the cell, pushing the door closed with his foot. The man's eyes bulged incredulously. He struggled to get free, but Beren's hold was too powerful. After a moment, the man ceased fighting and went limp with defeat.

"If you listen up, answer our questions, and promise not to holler for help, we won't hurt you," Beren hissed into the man's ear. "Deal?"

Wynn stared at his new friend, eyes wide.

Their captor glared venomously but managed a slight nod. Beren relaxed his grip on the man's mouth hesitantly, but their prisoner kept his voice low.

"You won't..."

"Get away with this," Beren cut him off. "Well, we're going to try. Now, where are we?"

"You have arrived at His Excellency's home."

Wynn stared blankly at Beren. The Telsuman shrugged and furrowed his brow.

"What does that mean?" Wynn asked, wishing his voice didn't sound quite so terrified.

"It means you won't escape," the man replied smugly. "This is more than just His Excellency's personal home. It's also a fortress. No one gets in here unless they're invited, and no one leaves without permission."

Beren clamped his hand over the man's mouth and stared at Wynn. "We have to get out of here, now."

"Right." Wynn looked around, sure that there must be something he was overlooking.

"Hand me those ropes," Beren said, pointing.

"Right," Wynn said again, feeling slow and worse than useless. He picked up the ropes with which they had been bound, and then, using every trick he had ever learned in the game with his brothers, he tied up the man's hands and feet. He tore a strip of cloth from the man's shirt and gagged him with it. Then he and Beren slipped out of the room and into the passageway.

"Which way?" Beren asked.

"No idea," Wynn replied. "He came from that direction, though." He pointed. "Stands to reason that's the way out, unless he was just in a room and had orders to retrieve us when the airship landed. It's more likely they sent him down, though." He clamped his lips shut, aware that he was babbling.

Beren nodded. "Lead on."

The two of them crept down the passage, alert to every sound and ready to dive into one of the rooms if they ran into any more of the crew. They had a few close calls as they made their way towards the ladder that led to the upper deck. Then they ducked into an empty storage room to debate what to do next.

"We can't go up there while the crew is still around; they'll spot us too easily," Wynn said.

"But if we wait, that guard will be missed and they'll search the airship," Beren argued. "We can't stay here."

"I know, I'm thinking."

"Think faster," Beren urged.

If only I could think a bit slower. Wynn banished the thought and tried to focus. All the questions and options were making his brain itch. "Where do you think we are? I mean, where have we landed?"

"Depends on who 'His Excellency' is, I guess. Does it matter right now?"

"It might." Wynn gave half a shrug.

"Can we hide like we did on the Academy airship?" Beren asked.

"The only reason that worked is because nobody was looking

for us," Wynn replied. "These people will turn the ship inside out to find us. They went to pretty great lengths to kidnap you."

"I'm fearful for your safety more than my own, my friend."

Wynn barely kept himself from shuddering. "I'm coming to the conclusion that they never meant to capture me."

"We'll tell them you are my trusted servant, that your family has been with mine for generations, that you are like a brother to me," Beren suggested. "That might keep you safe."

"Or get me killed faster." Wynn bit his lip. "Until we know what it is they want..."

The door to the closet swung open suddenly. A pair of golden-brown eyes skewered them.

"Lying won't be necessary." Shaesta spoke with a slight quirk to her mouth. "Nobody means either of you any harm, so long as you don't try any more ridiculous stunts." The warning in her voice was clear as she stepped aside and three men moved forward to take Beren and Wynn by the arms. Shaesta rolled her eyes slightly. "Take them to the main house and get them cleaned up, and feed them." She barked the instructions. "His Excellency will want to speak with them after dinner, and you know how he is about cleanliness."

The guards snickered in a way that sent a chill of dread down Wynn's spine, but he was helpless against them. The men holding his arms were nearly as tall as Beren, and their shoulders even broader. He wondered if they were Telsuman, but did not dwell on this question long, for as they shoved him up the ladder he caught his first glimpse of the fortress.

The sight before them took Wynn's breath away. They were high in the mountains, and yet more mountains rose up on every side. Crisp, thin air filled his nostrils, and he breathed in deeply. The air did not seem to go as far and his lungs burned; this worried him and he drummed his fingers against his thigh, imagining himself sending his anxiety out through his fingertips, down his leg, and into the ground. A lightning pole, that was what he must become. The situation was too dangerous to melt into a shaking heap the way he wanted to. The wet ground squelched beneath his boots, indicating that he had been right about the thrumming noise being rain.

Whatever storm they had flown through had changed into a gently falling snow. A thin white blanket lay across the ground in every direction. The sound of running water drew his gaze to the enormous waterfalls that poured down the mountain walls behind the palace and raced into a river that encircled the entire structure. The river gurgled outside the fortress walls, moving too quickly for it to freeze or be overwhelmed by ice, and then flung itself off the plateau into a second tier waterfall. Distracted from his worries about the air, Wynn craned his neck to see if he could see the bottom of this second waterfall. He was rewarded for his efforts with a surge of dizziness.

He closed his eyes momentarily and then reopened them, focusing on the stronghold. Taking in every detail helped him forget about his shortness of breath. A high wall cut out of white rocks and polished like marble rose up before them, gleaming like silver in the dying light of day. From their vantage point on the airship, Wynn could just see over the wall. Beyond it lay a large garden and courtyard covered in a thin layer of snow. And on the other side of the garden rose a structure that could only be referred to as a fortress, and yet it was a building so exquisite in its design, so beautiful in every line, so marked by elegance in its construction that it looked more like a palace out of a fairy tale than a stronghold.

"Get moving," a guard grunted, pushing Wynn forward. He stumbled a bit and then complied, walking towards the side of the airship. They descended the rope ladder and crossed a bridge before entering the grounds of their prison.

The long trek from the airship, across the bridge, through the courtyard, and into the palace was one of awestruck wonder. Everything they passed was pristine, beautiful, and overwhelming beneath the falling snow. They were ushered inside and brought to a spacious, luxuriously outfitted set of rooms.

They were ordered to wash in large porcelain tubs filled with steaming water from faucets that could be temperature adjusted with a turn of a knob. Beren acted as if this was all quite customary. But to Wynn, who was used to bathing in the river, or in a large metal tub that had been filled with water heated one bucketful at a time over the fire, the baths were almost like magic.

When they were both clean and completely waterlogged, a pair of servants brought them fine new clothes. Beren's fit him perfectly, though Wynn's were a bit baggy in places, further assuring him that his own captivity had been unplanned. The ill-fit did not detract from the luxurious fabrics and rich cut of the clothes, however. The light tan trousers were softer than velvet, and the shirt woven from a beautiful silver silk was so thin he was surprised he could not see through it. He picked up the jacket, a long, brown suede, and tried it on. It fit a little tight across the shoulders, and the sleeves fell just short of his wrists, but it did not restrict his movements or get in his way. Wynn wondered if he would be allowed to keep the clothes, if they were ever permitted to go free. Once they were dressed, Wynn and Beren turned their attention to the table, where servants had been busying themselves for a few minutes, filling it with trays and platters.

Shaesta entered the room. She gestured at the platters with a delicate wave of her hand. "The finest Telsuman delicacies we could arrange to have are here. I hope you find the food to your liking. Please, eat, Lord Adelfried."

"I do not make a habit of partaking when I do not know the name of my host."

"You will meet him soon enough," Shaesta replied calmly. "Please, sit."

Beren scowled and looked as though he might refuse, but then he glanced at Wynn and gave a minute shrug. Beren sat and arranged the cloth napkin delicately across his lap. He hesitated and glanced at a servant meaningfully.

Shaesta simpered. "If we wanted you dead, we would have no need of using poison."

Beren did not budge or speak. He simply stared disapprovingly at Shaesta, his face like stone. Wynn stood where he had gotten dressed, feeling awkward and out of place. He was unsure of how to act and keenly aware that he was out of his element. This was a Beren he had not seen before.

The silence stretched uncomfortably between Shaesta and Beren. At length, Shaesta gestured again to one of the younger lads standing nearby.

"Aryn, you will taste the food before either Master Adelfried or his friend." She glanced at Beren. "I trust you find that satisfactorily hospitable?"

Beren inclined his head and waved Wynn over. "Come, my friend," he said, magnanimously, "we may eat at this table without fear."

Wynn sat stiffly, and waited while the boy, Aryn, tried a bite from every dish and a small sip from both pitchers. When he finished, Beren sat back and allowed the servants to fill his plate. Wynn, taking his cue from Beren, gave the servants a nod, and they filled his plate as well.

As he surveyed the food, Wynn suddenly realized that he had no idea how long ago his last meal had been. He had eaten with his friends in Dalmir's room, which was at least a whole day ago, probably more, depending on how long he had been unconscious. His stomach clenched and rumbled at the sight and smell of the food, assuring him it had been a very long time since he had last filled it. Now that Beren seemed to trust the food, Wynn dug in recklessly. Every bite tasted exquisite. Wynn had never dreamed of such a feast. Even the fare of Harvest Festival paled in comparison.

When at last both of them had eaten their fill, the table was cleared and Shaesta cleared her throat. "You will follow me now. His Lordship would like a few moments of your time."

Beren took his time, taking a long, slow sip from his glass, wiping his mouth with his napkin, and stretching. Wynn followed his friend's example, fairly certain that Beren was mostly trying to annoy his host. At length, they both stood. Beren waved his hand imperiously.

"Well, lead on. Can't keep our good host waiting, can we?"

Shaesta sniffed in exasperation, but did not speak. As she spun on her heel and stalked towards the door, Wynn caught a glimmer of amusement and perhaps even admiration crossing Beren's face.

32

Flying in the rain was a miserable and yet oddly exhilarating experience. The storm sprang upon them with all the ferocity of a late summer gale.

Grayden's first inclination had been to remain still, huddling beneath his cloak and trying to retain some semblance of dryness. However, the *Valdeun Hawk* needed every hand working, and the pirates had been none too gentle about reminding him of that.

Movement helped stave off the cold, which was surprising at first. His cloak was soaked through in ten minutes, but he kept it on as it offered minor relief from the wind. He pulled his hood up, shielding his face from the driving rain as he forced his fingers to grip the ropes that controlled the sails. Most of the steering was done at the wheel, but in weather such as this, the sails needed to be maneuvered and adjusted constantly. He threw himself into the work and found that he enjoyed it.

Airships could fly above the clouds. But Wynn had explained once that there was something wrong with the air at certain altitudes. People on the first airships hadn't known that, and several early crews perished. Nowadays, captains possessed an instrument called an aneron that was affixed to a part of the airship's engine. Wynn had explained how it worked, but Grayden did not have a mind for that sort of thing. Basically, he recalled that it prevented an airship from reaching those dangerous altitudes.

Lightning flashed nearby and thunder rumbled close on its heels. Grayden shivered. He had long since given up trying to summon up memories of warmth. The wet and the cold were far too pervasive to allow it. He glanced up at the steering deck where Marik stood.

"The captain's a madman," he muttered under his breath.

Marik refused to be relieved from his position at the wheel, even after the rain started. They had been flying through the storm for hours now, and the captain continued to wave off any and all attempts by his crew to get him to take a rest. Grayden had to admire the man's stamina, albeit grudgingly.

As he scrutinized the captain now, Marik spun the wheel and opened his mouth in a great laugh. The wind whipped through his hair as the rain poured down, drenching him. He wore no cloak to protect him from the elements. He seemed as unconcerned by the storm as he would have been by a gentle spring zephyr, or a butterfly fluttering near him.

Now the rain turned to sleet as Grayden moved to his next task. His boots slid along the deck as the surface grew icy. His toes were cold in his soggy socks. Perhaps Marik had the right of it, perhaps the best answer to this storm was to embrace the wetness of it.

The man with the thin black beard—Oleck, Grayden remembered—bellowed words he could not understand, and the entire crew set to work scraping ice from any surface they could reach. One of them thrust a strange tool into Grayden's hands, a sort of handle with a horizontal blade at one end, and directed him to help remove any ice he saw.

Getting down on his hands and knees and attacking the deck with the strange device, his mind turned toward his friends. He hoped that Wynn and Beren were safe and unharmed. Grayden regretted his self-pitying thoughts of before. Wynn and Beren were captives of an unknown enemy.

They might be enduring torture, starvation, or worse. Gripping the ice scraper in his numb fingers, he continued to work, throwing himself wholeheartedly into the chore in an attempt to banish his worries.

"Grayden." A voice broke him out of his thoughts and he looked up into Raisa's eyes.

"Yes?"

"You've been working for three hours. It's time for your break."

Grayden felt a wave of relief, followed by a surge of stubbornness. His eyes flicked back to Marik. He raised his chin.

"I'm fine."

Raisa's expression turned exasperated. "You're soaked through. You should go below, get dry, and rest while you can. Besides, the sleet has stopped. It's just snow now, not nearly so dangerous."

Grayden looked around and realized the truth of her words. The heavy sleet had turned to flurries of snow. "I'll have to get wet all over again, and I just got used to it," he argued.

Raisa waved her hands in the air. "If you fall over because of the cold or the fatigue, I'm not lifting a finger to help you, we clear?" She did not stay to hear his answer. Instead, Raisa spun on her heel and marched away.

"Mountains!" The cry went up from the lookout post. "Mountains ahead!"

Grayden leaped to his feet and ran to the bow. Peering through the gloom, he could indeed make out the hazy outlines in the distance. They were growing larger fairly quickly, as the *Hawk* was clipping along at a fairly good pace. As they sped toward the mountain range, Dalmir emerged from below. He strode across the deck and climbed the ladder to stand with Marik. Grayden eyed them, then decided his curiosity could not wait. He meandered across the airship until he stood below the steering deck, where he could overhear the conversation transpiring between the wizard and the captain.

"... Randeau Mountains." Marik's voice trickled down to Grayden's ears along with the rain.

"Not far, now," Dalmir replied. "The trail is growing stronger, so I would guess we have gained on our quarry considerably."

"Any idea when we'll catch them?"

"It depends on what course of action they take. If they continue flying, I believe we will overtake them after nightfall."

"And if they land before we overtake them?" Marik asked.

"I can follow the trail to the ship, but I won't have a way to track them once they disembark," Dalmir said.

"I thought that might be the case. Then we need to close the gap between us, and quickly. Can you do anything about our speed?"

"I will try. Your airship is fast, Captain, but even I cannot push her any faster than she is built to go."

There was silence, and the snow whipped about in a sudden breeze, stinging Grayden's face with its force. He frowned and then realized the truth. It was not snowing harder. The airship was moving faster. He glanced up towards the steering deck and then shook his head. Nobody back home would ever believe this story.

33

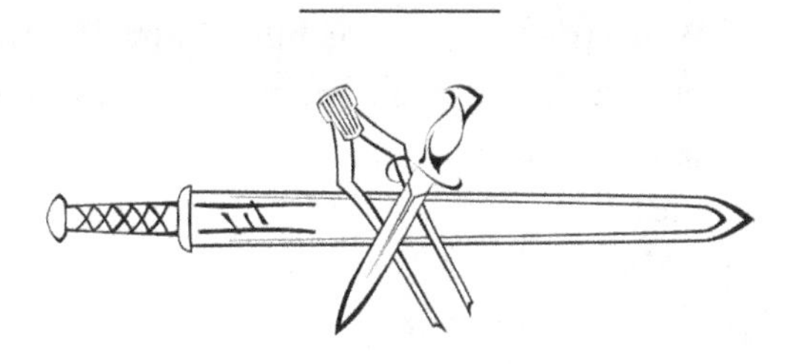

As they passed beneath arches and marched down marble halls, Wynn felt smaller and more rustic with each step. The walls sported enormous tapestries woven with brightly colored threads. The ceiling itself bore an enormous mural designed to give the impression of being under the open sky. Panes of clear glass cut in the shapes of diamonds and held together with an intricate network of gold lined the hall on both sides, letting in the warm gleam of sunlight. Wynn tried to emulate Beren's casual attitude, but—acutely aware of his ill-fitting clothes—he feared he simply looked ridiculous. At length, they reached a great, gilded door and Shaesta knocked sharply upon it three times.

The door swung inwards, revealing a lavishly decorated room. Beautiful paintings hung between elaborate stained-glass windows. Thick carpet covered the floor. At the far end of the room, a man and a woman sat on a pair of plush, velvet-covered chairs. They gazed imperiously at their visitors as Shaesta entered, leading Beren and Wynn towards them. Shaesta murmured in Beren's ear.

"Let me do the talking," Beren whispered to Wynn.

"Why?" Wynn asked, keeping his own voice low.

"Shaesta just told me who our captor is: Ericole Niveya."

"So? Does that mean anything to you?"

"Yes, I've heard of the Niveya family. My father has encountered them before."

"And?"

"None of what I know is good."

"Perfect." Wynn tried to hide the hitch in his breath and the way his heart pounded. Although Beren still held himself like a prince, Wynn had seen a flicker of fear in his friend's eyes.

When they reached the other side of the room, Shaesta curtsied gracefully. "Milord, milady, your guests."

Wynn kept himself from rolling his eyes at the use of the term "guest," but it was not without effort.

"Welcome, Lord Adelfried." The man did not rise, but he waved his hand and servants materialized with comfortable chairs for both Beren and Wynn. The two young men sat. Wynn's stomach jumped in awkward nervousness. He studied the couple before them. Ericole Niveya had a thin face, handsome in a roguish sort of way. A thin, dark goatee surrounded his mouth, trimmed to perfection. He had dark hair swept to one side and falling across his forehead above brown eyes that were almost black. The woman sitting next to him had skin as dark as Shaesta's, exotic gray eyes rimmed with just a hint of silver paint. Her black hair was twisted into a thick rope and elegantly knotted around her head in an intricate braid, and adorned with a single jeweled hair clip. She wore a long-sleeved scarlet dress banded with gold. At her throat, she wore a simple choker-style necklace adorned with a single gemstone, midnight purple in hue.

"Lord Niveya, I presume." Beren's words were stiff and offended. "You have me at a disadvantage, sir, neglecting to introduce yourself and yet calling me a guest."

"Please forgive me." The man's voice held a hint of good humor, and his lips quirked up. "You may call me Ericole, and this is my wife, Aubri. I would have us all be friends."

"What sort of friends kidnap a man, tie him up, and escort him to a prison—beautiful though it may be?"

Ericole waved his hand. "Kidnap? Prison?" The man arched an immaculate eyebrow. "All was in your best interest, of course."

"How so?"

"My dear lad, I rescued you!"

Wynn felt his jaw drop open at this pronouncement. He could not help but turn to glance at Beren to see his reaction. If Beren was surprised by this declaration, he did not show it. He barely even blinked.

"Rescued me? From the pirates, I suppose."

"No, no! Dear boy, of course not. Don't be ridiculous. You were safe with them. The pirates were working for me, not that they were aware of that fact. My nephew hired them."

"Then why attack their ship and kidnap me?"

"We planned to rescue you after the pirate made you disembark. Imagine our dismay to discover you were not among the other Academy students after Marik left them behind."

"Then Marik told the truth?" Wynn blurted. "The other students are all right?"

Niveya stretched his feet out. "Yes. They are well. They may even beat you to the Academy."

"You did not offer them transportation?" Beren asked. "That would have been the gentlemanly thing to do."

"Believe me, I wanted to," Niveya replied. "But we discovered assassins on your trail. They were there, following you, waiting for their chance. Attacking the pirates was a possible scenario from the beginning, but one I had hoped I would not have to use. It had to look convincing, don't you see? It was the only way to throw our mutual enemies off the scent. We couldn't very well have them following you to our haven, now, could we?"

"I am trying not to become angry at your rudeness." Beren's voice was calm. "But I demand you explain what is going on at once."

"Yes, yes." Ericole nodded. "Of course. You must be confused.

Bear with me, though, as this story will take some telling, and I must put it all in the proper order for you."

Beren sat back. "Very well."

"You are aware of the general state of affairs in the Igyeum Empire? You are, of course, aware of Ar'Mol Eyvind?"

Beren nodded.

"Well, here in the Igyeum, we know him better as the tyrant he is. He poses as a peaceful ruler when he interacts with Telmondir. He sends gifts to your countries: the railroad, the trains, the airships, all to assuage your fears, to make you see him as a kind and munificent neighbor, one not to be feared. But it is all a lie. The horrors he has visited upon us, his own people, would make your skin crawl to hear of them. His true goal is to gain dominance over Telmondir the way he grips the Igyeum in his fist. He knows the only way to achieve that is through war."

"We are not unprepared for war. Your Ar'Mol will not find us easy prey."

"Ah, but he is far more subtle than you realize, princeling. The Ar'Mol knows that the three nations of Telmondir will not be as easily subdued as the nations of the East were. Your united front is far more stable than the bickering tribes and warlords his father and grandfather helped to subdue. Thus, he set in motion a plot to have you assassinated. He wanted your family to believe you had been killed by Ondourans. That is why the assassins in Dalton carried blades poisoned with sparrack root."

"How could you know about that?" Wynn burst out.

Niveya arched an eyebrow at him, a faint smile upon his lips. "I have my sources."

"What would he have gained from this?" Beren asked.

"The desired effect would have been mistrust between Telsuma and Ondoura. In a perfect situation, Dalma would be caught in the middle when war breaks out across the western lands, making it ripe for invasion."

"An elaborate scheme, to be sure, though it seems a bit far-fetched to me. Assuming I believe you, how do I know you're not in on it? How can I possibly trust you?"

Ericole's face twisted into an expression of deep hurt. "You wound me, Lord Adelfried. Have I not plucked you from the midst of danger, brought you to the comfort and safety of my home, and offered you the food from my own table? I shall lavish upon you every courtesy, every luxury money can afford. Have I not saved your very life, at significant risk to my own? And yet you believe you cannot trust me? Has a hair on your head been harmed? Or on your friend's?"

"Forgive my skepticism," Beren said drily. "But your people attacked the airship I was on, forcibly kidnapped myself and my friend, and shackled us in a tiny room for the duration of our travels. I cannot help but feel like a prisoner, despite the luxury you have bestowed upon us since our arrival."

Ericole's expression turned thunderous. The woman next to him sat up straighter, glaring.

"Is this true?" Niveya directed the question at Shaesta.

The woman bowed her head. "I am afraid it is, milord. The pirates fought back most ferociously, and we feared harm would come to our guest. Several of your men were more... zealous... than they perhaps ought to have been, but only because they sought earnestly to carry out your orders. The two young men were, unfortunately, knocked unconscious in the battle. We kept them in the only room without a window, merely as a precaution. Your standing orders have always been to take every measure possible to keep the location of your home a secret, even from honored guests."

"True, true, one can never be too careful." Ericole's expression of anger faded. "I offer you my most heartfelt apologies for any discomfort you endured at the hands of my people. But surely you must understand what it is to have loyal servants who sometimes misinterpret your commands. It is frustrating, but I cannot punish mistakes that are made out of love and loyalty."

Beren nodded graciously. "Very well, Master Niveya. We understand each other perfectly."

Wynn shot his friend a surprised glance, but kept his mouth shut. Beren concealed a great yawn and blinked.

"Forgive me, my new friend," Beren said. "It seems that the events of the day and all this traveling have wearied me considerably. I am sure you have more you would like to discuss, but might we return to this conversation in the morning? I can barely keep my eyes open, and my friend here is unused to the grandeur of your home."

"Of course, of course." Ericole waved a hand magnanimously. "I look forward to breaking fast with you both in the morning." His gaze sharpened as he studied Wynn. "Good lad, I beg you to forgive the error my tailors made in outfitting you. I give you my word that you will not look a pauper on the morrow."

Wynn, unsure what to say, bowed his head slightly and murmured as polite a "thank you" as he could muster.

"Shaesta." Aubri Niveya spoke for the first time. "When you have escorted these gentlemen to their rooms, please attend to me."

"Yes, Mistress."

Shaesta led Wynn and Beren back to their rooms and left them with a cheery "goodnight." Wynn listened as she left, but heard no key turn in the lock. When her footsteps had faded away down the hall, he turned to Beren.

"You don't buy any of this, do you?" he whispered, keeping his voice low. He had seen no guards as they approached the room, but that did not mean they weren't present.

"Of course not, but I needed to buy us time."

"To do what?"

"To gather ourselves, think, strategize… perhaps escape."

"What is going on? Who are you, really? Why are people trying to assassinate and kidnap you?" Wynn blurted out the questions that had been building in his thoughts since they had landed. This was a side of Beren he did not know how to quantify.

Gone was the awkward and overly formal youth. In his place remained a polished, cultured young man who seemed more than capable of navigating these murky political waters.

Beren gazed seriously at Wynn. "I am still your friend," he said, seeming to understand what was behind Wynn's question. "I told you in Dalton who I am, and I told you the whole truth of it. There are political waters surrounding my father's title. Perhaps Niveya speaks the truth. Or perhaps he only gives part of it. But this is who I am. There is more to the world than your quiet town, Wynn, and my family has worked hard at getting a glimpse at the bigger picture. I have trained all my life for this sort of scenario. Truly, with other lads my own age, I am often awkward and inelegant. But you can trust me. My father has taught me well, and I will do my best to keep us both alive."

"They didn't lock us in," Wynn pointed out, "not that it would have been much of a problem if they had."

"Of course, they must keep up the facade of friendliness. But you can be most positive that guards will be watching all exits from these rooms at all times."

"I only saw a few guards. You could take all of them."

Beren chuckled. "Be not misled, my friend. What you see is what Ericole wants you to see. Rest assured, there are guards out of our sight, though we are not out of theirs. Whatever Ericole Niveya is up to, it is not our best interests he has at heart, but only his own."

"What do you think he is up to?"

"There are several things. First, strangely marked men with poisoned daggers attacked us in Dalton. We know the poison was sparrack root, which Dalmir says only grows in Ondoura. So, either Ericole is telling the truth, and Ar'Mol Eyvind sent the assassins to destabilize the political situation in the West..."

"Or the assassins really were from Ondoura," Wynn suggested.

"Impossible," Beren scoffed. "Regeont Roshana is like a grandmother to me and my siblings. If the Ar'Mol truly wishes to slide a knife between the members of the Council, he is doing a poor job of it."

"Well then, maybe Niveya hired the assassins himself."

"But then why bother kidnapping me?"

"Because he didn't count on the pirates attacking, and they made it more difficult."

"What would Ericole Niveya gain from having me killed by assassins who appear to be Ondouran?"

Wynn furrowed his brow, his thoughts speeding up to their normal pace. "I think it makes more sense to believe that he is telling the truth, at least so far as he knows it, about the Ar'Mol and the assassins. Telmondir already distrusts the Ar'Mol's intentions; that's the whole reason we built the Academy, to create a defense against the civil wars and unrest that we saw occurring in the Igyeum."

"All right." Beren sat down as Wynn paced around the room.

"You said you were familiar with Niveya. What do you know about him?"

"Not much," Beren admitted as Wynn drew up another chair. "My father has mentioned the Niveyan Syndicate a time or two. They are a powerful family. If I am remembering the maps correctly, we are most likely somewhere in the Randeau mountain range. The exact location of their stronghold is a secret, as Shaesta said, but it is generally understood to be located in the Valleian half of the Randeau Mountains."

"Then we're not far from the Academy?"

"It's possible, I suppose. Not that it helps us much. Even if we're only a few miles from the Ondouran border, we'd still have to cross a hundred miles of mountainous terrain to reach civilization, and that's only if we can escape this stronghold."

"I see." Wynn's voice held a note of relief. He could not sit still and rose from his chair to pace the room once more. His brain spun faster, and he had to tap his fingers against his thigh again to keep himself from talking too fast. "I know it doesn't make any sense, but here I was worrying we were way up north in the Starrow Mountains in Palla, where no one would ever see us again. Knowing we're not that far from home... I dunno, it's silly, I guess, but it makes me feel better." Wynn yawned and rubbed his eyes. The long hours of panic were taking their toll, but he did not want to sleep. He wanted to solve this problem, to find the answers. As long as he had a puzzle before him, he could stave off the debilitating fear trying to claw its way through his brain. "So what should we do? If Ericole is telling the truth about the assassins, then what is his role in all of this? Surely he's not the angelic benefactor he wants you to believe him to be, so what does he get out of helping you? He foils the Ar'Mol's plans. Perhaps that is beneficial for the Niveyan family if they want to undermine the Ar'Mol's power. He has you, the son of a wealthy chieftain, in his power; a possible ransom angle?"

"Those are both valid incentives for his actions," Beren replied. "And not mutually exclusive. Niveya strikes me as a man who is constantly running multiple angles."

Wynn grew restless. He wandered around the room and then went over to the large glass doors leading to a balcony outside and wiggled a handle idly. It held fast, locked. Wynn studied the lock. It had an intricate design that would not be easy to pick, especially without his tools. A quick glance out the window showed him they would not be escaping that way, even if he could get the doors open. The balcony was not only on the second floor, but this portion of the wall was even with a sheer cliff face that descended steeply beneath them. He reported on what he could see to Beren.

The night wore on, and they both grew tired, but sleep seemed unwise in this potentially hostile situation. Eventually, Wynn suggested they sleep in shifts.

"We won't do ourselves any good if we're too tired to think come morning," he commented. "Especially if we want to keep pace with Niveya. He's like a cat who's got hold of a mouse by the tail. And we're the mouse."

"Very well." Beren stood up. "You sleep first. I am not truly tired yet."

Wynn pulled his boots off and climbed into one of the enormous beds. The mattress was softer than pillows. He pulled the cozy blanket up under his chin and closed his eyes. A moment later, he was sound asleep.

34

Shaesta entered Aubri Niveya's solar cautiously. The woman was sitting before her mirror, lines of discontent marring her features. Her lips twitched slightly as she caught sight of Shaesta.

"Come in, child." Aubri rose and glided gracefully over to a small table that was set with delicate dishes. "Have you eaten since you arrived?"

Shaesta shook her head.

"You poor dear, you must be falling off your feet. I was so hoping you would take a small tea with me this evening. Please, sit."

Shaesta sat carefully, feeling, as she always did in Aubri's presence, strangely awkward. She reached over to pour the tea, but Aubri swatted her hand away none too gently.

"No, no, you've worked hard all day and more than earned your usual wages. I shall pour for you tonight."

A sudden lump entered Shaesta's throat, and her eyes brimmed with tears. She swallowed furiously, refusing to let the tears fall, but Aubri saw them anyway. The woman quietly passed her a handkerchief and then busied herself with the tea, giving Shaesta the chance to compose herself.

"Forgive me, Lady," Shaesta said, folding the handkerchief neatly. "It has been a difficult day."

"I am sure it has. Asked to turn on those who called you 'friend,' forced to spend time with my miscreant of a nephew for the past several hours, and now I have selfishly asked for your attendance. Forgive me, dear, I was not thinking."

"No, it is nothing. I am just a little tired."

"Do you think you burned too many bridges today? Will this mission negatively affect your daily life, or your work?"

Shaesta paused. "It could. Marik will not speak highly of me, and his opinion is worth something. However, his influence is not as broad as it could be because he keeps to himself so much. I may lose the trust of a few of my contacts, but not all."

"Marik's approval meant a lot to you, did it?"

Shaesta dropped her eyes. "His opinion impacts my work, whether it matters to me or not."

"Well." Aubri reached across the table and patted her hand, patronizingly. "He took his opinion of you to the grave, dear. Losing his approval won't harm you, if that's what you're worried about."

Years of conversations just like this one had taught Shaesta to control her expressions. "Oh?"

"Yes." Aubri's voice was brisk. "Arrio said that the *Crimson Eagle's* crash was rather spectacular. Marik and his crew are surely scattered among its remains."

Shaesta held a tight rein on every muscle in her face. "I see."

Aubri peered at her over her teacup, a cruel glint in her eyes. "Oh, Shaesta, you are such a tender-heart! It's just too precious for words. You'd think you would have learned to steel yourself after all these years." The woman walked around the table. She cupped Shaesta's chin in her hand and lifted it so Shaesta had to look into her eyes. "You know you're like the daughter I never had. Ever since you were a little girl, I've watched you, knowing you had so much more potential than any other child running through these halls, if only you could learn to be stronger." She let go of Shaesta's chin and moved away, still talking. "But you never could manage it, and you still can't, can you? Marik is another wounded animal you're bringing to your father hoping he will fix it. But your father understood, you know. Those wounded creatures were better off dead, and so he would promise you he'd nurse it back to health, and as soon as you had run off, he'd put the poor thing out of its misery. A few days later, of course, he'd point out a healthy bird or squirrel and claim it was the one you'd 'saved.' I suppose you inherited that particular frailty from him. It would have been better for you if he'd simply told you the truth. It would have made you stronger."

Shaesta managed not to flinch or even blink. "Perhaps you're right, Lady."

"Of course I'm right." Aubri took a delicate sip from her teacup and glided to a window. "So long as you know we are here for you, in this difficult time. We must come up with a good story for why you did not go down with the crew, but I'm sure we can think of something to tell any of your contacts who might question. In the meantime, you seem to have a relationship with our young guests. I would like you to make sure they are comfortable for the duration of their visit."

"Yes, Lady."

"Marvelous. Go now, I am tired and wish to retire to bed."

"Of course. Is there anything I can get you?"

"No. Get some rest. You must be exhausted, and tomorrow will be another tiresome day for you."

"I'm not truly tired yet. I might take a bit of a stroll. How long will our guests be staying?"

"Until Ericole decides upon how best to use them to our advantage, of course."

"I see. Does he have any ideas yet?"

"Ransom is his current favorite, but that might not work out. The Westerners can be strange about this sort of thing." Aubri paused, finishing her tea. "Perhaps it would be more advantageous to send their bodies to the Ar'Mol and be done with them.

Ar'Mol Eyvind wanted them dead in the first place, of course. It would assuredly send a powerful message that the Niveya family is not to be taken for granted, or ignored."

"But it could come across as a challenge," Shaesta replied carefully.

"True, one cannot be too careful in these delicate matters..." Aubri trailed off, her gaze sharpening as she turned away from the window. "But, then, you are merely the daughter of a servant—albeit a highly paid one—and none of this is your concern, dear. Just you get your rest and leave the pesky details of politics to my husband. They are too complex for you to grasp, after all."

"Yes, Lady. Goodnight, ma'am." It was all Shaesta could do to exit the room at a calm walk and not break into a run. Just when she thought she was immune to Aubri's particular brand of cold cruelty, the woman would pull out another little tidbit that froze her straight down to her bones.

35

Grayden finally gave in and went below. Dry clothes helped ease his chattering teeth, and sleep claimed him swiftly, despite it being the middle of the day.

He did not sleep long, however. When he climbed back up onto the deck, yawning and stretching, the snow had stopped and a clear, moonlit sky dappled with glittering stars stretched endlessly above. Cold bit through his clothes. Grayden's breath steamed as it left his mouth and nose. The chill entered his bones as he stamped his feet on the deck. Dalmir stood near the prow of the ship with the captain, and Grayden sauntered over to join them, curious. Far below, he glimpsed a wondrous sight: an immense and delicately crafted palace nestled up against the mountain on one side, its walls jutting out to the edge of a cliff on the other. The cliff plunged down hundreds of feet to a river. On the other side of the river, another mountain sheltered the buildings from view. The cleverness of the location and design was evident. It would be difficult, if not impossible, to even see the fortress unless one was hovering right above it.

"Do you know what you've gotten me into?" the captain growled as Grayden stared down at the structure.

Taken aback, Grayden could only gape.

"You're the one who attacked our airship in the first place," Dalmir said mildly. "The raiders would never have attacked a fully armed Academy ship if you hadn't made it easy for them."

"Easy?" Marik hissed incredulously. "You call three of my men dead 'easy'?"

Dalmir stared at the pirate captain unflinchingly. "If you hadn't forced hundreds of armed students off our ship in the first place, we would have been more than capable of defending ourselves against the kidnappers."

"Well, maybe that's true," Marik muttered. "But now you've led me straight into the heart of the Niveyan Stronghold. Nobody gets in there who isn't invited. Nobody."

"You're just going to have to figure out a way to get us invited, then," Grayden replied. He glowered at the pirate.

"You are a maddening whelp, you know that?" Marik said. Then he glanced at Dalmir and seemed to remember the reason they weren't lying in broken splinters across the rocky foothills. "I suppose we'd best find a place to land. I've already spotted a few caves that might do the trick; if they're not guarded, that is."

It took Marik the better part of an hour to find an appropriate place to land the *Hawk*. Privately, Grayden thought the pirate was being picky. He had investigated and rejected three caves before settling on one that met his exacting standards.

The cave was large and deep in the cliffs below the palace. If they had to reach the Niveyan abode on foot, they would have a bit of a climb ahead of them, but nothing that looked too difficult. Marik was happy with their location for another reason as well: in their search for the perfect cave, they had discovered the dock where the airship that had attacked them rested.

Upon landing, Marik stared daggers at Grayden as he crossed the airship and slid down the ladder to the lower decks, leaving Grayden at a loss. He was unsure what to do next. The deck of the airship was suddenly silent and lonely. He shivered.

Oleck's head popped up through the hatch. "Hey, kid, we're

all meeting in Marik's office to figure out our next move. You coming? The old man sent me to fetch you."

Grayden heaved a sudden sigh of relief at not being completely left out and followed Oleck down the ladder towards the stern where Marik's office was situated across from the engine room. The office was approximately the size of two of the cabins. A square table stood in the center of the room. Lanterns hung from every wall, filling the room with a warm glow. The wall opposite the door was covered in shelves filled with books and loose-leaf paper. There were charts tacked to the walls and scattered across the table in a haphazard mess. There were no chairs.

Grayden looked around to see who was in this meeting. Marik stood at the far wall pulling a book and a few sheets of paper off a shelf. Dalmir stood next to him, talking in a low voice. Marik shook his head at whatever Dalmir said, and the wizard threw up his hands in an expression of exasperation. Grayden frowned. What could they be arguing about? Raisa stood at the table poring over what looked like the schematics and drawings Wynn kept rolled up in his closet back home. Mouse sat unobtrusively on the floor in a corner. Oleck strode over to join the others at the table, leaving Grayden feeling awkward and out of place. Dalmir turned around and waved him over.

"We are here." He pointed to the map the others were studying. It looked vaguely like the fortress they had seen from the air.

"It's not a very good likeness, is it?" Grayden asked.

"These drawings are based on hearsay and rumor, mostly," Raisa explained.

"The Niveyan Stronghold," Oleck muttered ominously. "I knew it was up here in these mountains..."

"Everyone knows it's up in these mountains," Raisa scoffed.

"But nobody knows exactly where," Oleck continued, as if Raisa hadn't even spoken.

"Perhaps we can use that to our advantage." Marik joined them at the table. "If we can figure out exactly where Wynn and Beren are being held, we might have a chance of rescuing them."

"Haven't you heard the stories, Marik?" Oleck asked. "This place has a reputation. Nobody gets in without an invitation, nobody leaves without permission."

"And how much of that reputation is due to the secrecy of this hideout?" Marik countered. "You saw the same thing I did. It's not as much of a stronghold as the stories say."

"Excuse me," Grayden interrupted. "Could someone tell me where we are, and what a Niveyan Stronghold is?"

"I would like to know these details as well." Dalmir's voice was quiet.

"You Westerners," Oleck huffed disparagingly, but said no more as Marik and Raisa both shot him sharp looks.

"The Niveyas are an incredibly old, extremely wealthy family," Raisa replied after a brief silence. "They were originally from Palla, though they relocated to the Randeau Mountains seventy-five years ago when they first amassed true prosperity. They may have started out in a legitimate business, but for the past fifty years or so, they've been operating more and more from the shadows."

"What do they specialize in?" Dalmir asked.

"What don't they specialize in?" Oleck said darkly. "Think of every illicit or corrupt scam you can dream up; the Niveyas have their fingers in it."

"Not unlike yourselves," Dalmir interjected, earning a glare from Marik.

"Niveya's organization is far larger than a single crew. He's got his own private army," Marik corrected. "And he's only in business for himself."

"And your Ar'Mol allows this?" Dalmir asked.

"He's certainly not *our* Ar'Mol," Marik growled. "He may not like it, but the Niveyas are a powerful organization. They've earned autonomy from him, for which I applaud them. Don't have to like their methods, but that's worth something, right there."

"The Ar'Mol is smart. He knows any battle he fights up here would be on their ground, and would cost him dearly. He might be capable of winning the altercation eventually, but it would be a protracted, bitter bloodbath." Raisa took the reins of the conversation. "It's in his better interests to suffer their existence."

"He's got his sights set on bigger conquests, anyway," Marik muttered.

"I believe I can get inside." Dalmir's voice was thoughtful. "I've dealt with people like these before."

"I was hoping you might offer something like that," Marik admitted. "I have an idea you might like."

Marik outlined his plan quickly as the rest of them listened intently. When he finished, there was silence as they each mulled the idea over.

"It... could work..." Raisa broke the silence.

"Work?" Grayden asked, his tone dubious. "It sounds a bit insane to me."

"Marik specializes in insanity," Oleck grumbled. "He's got an uncanny knack for it."

Dalmir straightened, a gleam in his eyes. "I like it," he announced. "I'll do it."

"Dalmir..." Grayden began, his voice rising in pitch slightly. He paused. He did not trust these pirates. But he did not like to say so in front of them.

"I would like to offer one minor change, however," Dalmir said. "Grayden comes with me."

Marik considered, then shrugged. "Fine by me, doesn't change much, anyway. I figured you'd want him to stay with us as collateral to make sure we don't just fly off without you."

"Your cynders are depleted," Dalmir reminded him. "Your airship currently won't fly without me."

Marik grimaced. "How could I forget?" he asked wryly. He glanced around the room. "Any other suggestions? No? Very well, you all know what to do, then."

They exited the room, Grayden more reluctantly than the others.

Mouse dogged his heels. As they made their way down the

corridor, Dalmir put an arm around the boy's shoulders and spoke to him in a low, earnest tone. Grayden was curious enough to stay and eavesdrop, but Dalmir caught his eye and motioned for him to follow Raisa. Torn between his curiosity and his desire to retain the approval of the older man, Grayden wavered for a moment, then he broke into a jog and caught up with Raisa. Whatever Dalmir had to say to Mouse was none of his business. Raisa eyed Grayden critically as he joined her.

"I think a change of outfit is called for if we want you to look the part. Marik has a few things you can use," she said speculatively. As she was speaking, Dalmir rejoined them. Mouse had disappeared, but there was no time to ask what Dalmir had wanted to say to the boy. Raisa turned her gaze to Dalmir, taking in his height. "I don't know that we have anything that will fit you, though."

"I can attend to my own wardrobe," Dalmir replied.

"Of course," Raisa murmured. "Come on, Grayden."

The clothes were a bit too big, but not as much as Grayden had feared. The unfamiliar cut of the shirt felt awkward, and the loose waistband of the pants had Raisa rummaging around the closet to find him a smaller belt.

"Here we go," she announced. "A little plainer than I would have liked, but it should do the trick."

Grayden fastened the belt around his waist, and his mood improved. "I wouldn't have thought clothing that looks so similar could feel so different," he commented.

"It's a matter of where the seams are and what fabrics are used," Raisa replied, walking around him and nodding in faint approval. "It changes the whole garment. Here, try on the jacket."

Grayden shoved his arms into the sleeves, trying not to let his admiration show. In Dalsea, a coat was a luxury. Cloaks were simpler to make, and cheaper. It also never got cold enough to warrant anything more than a good, thick cloak. The recruiters who came from the Academy wore coats, though theirs had been of a more military style and cut. This jacket fell to his knees and was a little too broad across the shoulders. It had buttons, but Raisa explained that the style was to wear the jacket unbuttoned unless the weather was harsh.

She walked around him, inspecting him critically. "I think you're ready. Let's go see how Dalmir's doing."

Dalmir waited for them in the hall. Raisa halted, eyes wide as she took in his altered appearance. Grayden squinted. Something was different about the old man, something he could not quite ascertain. He circled the man, taking in Dalmir's new outfit.

Gone were the threadbare shirt and trousers of indeterminate color. Gone was the tattered old cloak and gnarled walking stick. Dalmir stood before them in a pristine white silk shirt. His trousers were a dark gray that fell sharply to gleaming, knee-high black boots that had a military sheen to them. The cloak was royal blue. The fabric alone would have caused folks in Dalsea to go out of their way to enter any store selling such an item just to handle it and dream longingly of owning material so fine.

No longer was Dalmir hunched over as though burdened by years far too numerous to count. Instead, he stood straight and tall. His blue eyes twinkled with visible amusement, and his face seemed quite youthful now that the long white beard was gone.

"Your beard!" Grayden exclaimed. "You shaved your beard."

"It was time," Dalmir replied. "You look rather dashing yourself." He bowed his head to Raisa. "Nicely done, my dear."

Raisa's cheeks flushed slightly. "You aren't as old as you look," she said, her voice composed.

"Quite the opposite, I assure you," Dalmir replied, a hint of laughter in his voice. "Well, Grayden, are you ready for our performance?"

Grayden drew a shaky breath and then squared his shoulders and nodded. "Ready."

36

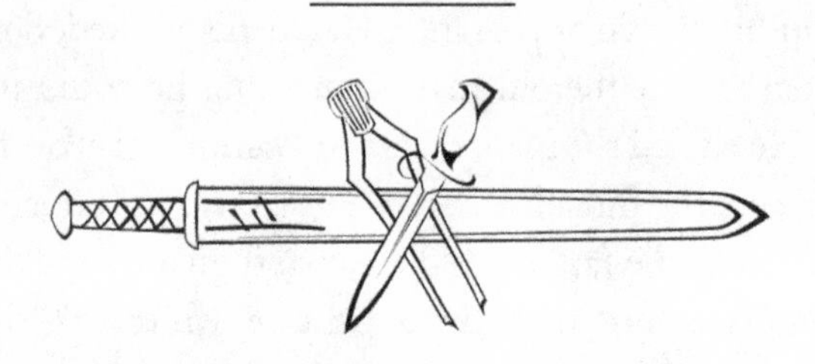

The insistent pounding on the thick wooden doors echoed down the long marble halls. A bleary-eyed servant eventually cracked the door open and peered out suspiciously.

"Who are you? How did you get past the guards?" he demanded. "How dare you disturb this household in the middle of the night?"

"My good man!" Dalmir exclaimed in an overly loud voice, causing the servant to wince and hold his hands out in a hushing motion. Dalmir took advantage of the gesture and shouldered his way inside despite vehemently whispered protestations. Grayden slipped through the door on Dalmir's heels, narrowly missing being seriously injured as the servant hurriedly slammed the door shut.

"Forgive my master," Grayden apologized. "He is not accustomed to these altitudes. It makes him slightly unreasonable."

"Who are you people?" the man asked. "I demand an explanation now."

"Who...? Are you in earnest?" Dalmir turned to Grayden and raised his eyebrows in irate indignation. "Is he serious?"

"Master, it is the middle of the night." Grayden tried to make his tone calm and placating, though it was all he could do not to laugh. He was glad they had rehearsed their parts beforehand. "The poor man is confused and cannot be expected to recognize you, as you have clearly pulled him from his sleep."

"Unacceptable!" Dalmir bellowed. "Where is Master Niveya? I demand to speak with Ericole. To think that a man I once called a friend should treat me like an unwanted beggar. Ha!" Dalmir snorted and spun around, his cape fluttering around him impressively. "Come, lad, we're leaving. I'll not darken these halls a single moment longer. If Ericole wishes for my aid in the future, he shall have to come to me!"

"Master," Grayden pleaded, "don't be hasty. Please, wait..."

The servant's eyes were wide now, and he held up his hands. "Forgive me, forgive me, please!" he cried. "Your servant is right, I was asleep, and in my sleep-fogged state I did not recognize you, Master..." he stumbled, obviously still clueless as to Dalmir's identity. "I had no idea you knew Master Ericole personally."

"Well..." Dalmir hesitated. "Well. Perhaps I could be induced to stay."

"Please, sir." The servant bowed and smiled, his entire manner now solicitous. "As it is the middle of the night, let me show you to a room where you can rest. In the morning, I will inform His Lordship that you are arrived. If you will but tell me your name?"

Now it was Grayden's turn to act surprised. "My good man, this is General Bronwin." He gave the name that Marik had suggested they use.

Grayden thought the man's eyes might pop out of his head if he opened them any wider. "General... sir! Please forgive my ignorance. Follow me, we have accommodations that I hope you will not find too humble. I give you my word. The master will be told of your presence the second he awakes."

"Very good," Dalmir said sternly. "Lead the way."

They followed the servant to a set of lavishly outfitted rooms. He showed Grayden around first, and Grayden did his best to appear bored. He peered about the rooms with a haughty expression on his face.

"These will do, sir," he said to Dalmir. "Not as grand as you're used to, of course, but adequate, for a single night."

Dalmir nodded, ignoring the gasp of disbelief at these words. "Goodnight," he said in an abrupt tone as he swept into the room. He slammed the door behind him, leaving Grayden standing in the hall with the servant.

As soon as the door swung shut, Grayden breathed a long sigh and relaxed his shoulders. He grinned conspiratorially at the servant and shrugged. "Is your master as intolerable as mine?" He jerked his head towards the now-closed door.

The servant gave a wry chuckle. "Master Ericole is often prone to certain outbursts... but it is Mistress Aubri we have to tiptoe around." He shuddered. "That one is downright scary. Crossing her is the last thing anyone ever does."

Grayden stared. "And I thought I had it bad."

"You're not terrified of him?"

"The general? No, the man is all bluster, but he'd never do anyone any harm... not off the battlefield, in any case."

"Must be nice," the servant muttered. He peered at Grayden hopefully. "Want to join me for a drink? I guarantee the general's safety while he is within these walls."

Grayden pretended to vacillate before nodding. "What's the harm?"

The servant led him through the palace down several flights of stairs into the servants' quarters. There was a quiet bustle in the kitchens even at this late hour. Grayden glanced around in wide-eyed wonder.

"When do you sleep?" he asked.

"This is the night shift," the servant replied. "I'm on it, but I usually get to sleep in the coatroom, as we never have visitors hammering on our door after midnight." He scowled pointedly, then relaxed into a chuckle. "Serves me right, I suppose. Can I offer you something to eat?"

"Perhaps a warm drink, cider, if you have it," Grayden countered. "It was quite cold outside."

"Of course." The servant disappeared into the depths of the kitchen.

Grayden picked a place to sit down near, but not too near, a table around which a small group of servants sat, sipping from large mugs and conversing. Giving off his best air of weariness, Grayden slumped his head forward and closed his eyes. The servants, who had quieted when he entered the room, decided he was no threat, and they resumed speaking in normal tones.

"... the honest truth," one servant said. "Walked in there like he owned the place and accused the master of kidnapping. I thought Master Ericole was going to have an apoplexy!"

Soft chuckles erupted from the listeners.

"What'd the master say?"

"Claimed he'd rescued them from assassins."

"Wait. Are they guests or prisoners?" another voice asked.

"Your guess is as good as mine. They're in a guest room. The doors aren't locked, but there's a rotation of guards, ostensibly for their own protection, and they're in one of the west-facing rooms."

"So they couldn't slip out through a window if they wanted to," a third voice said. "Sounds more like prisoners to me."

"At best, guests under duress," the second speaker replied softly.

"Who's that came in with Tobin?" the first voice asked.

"I don't know..."

Grayden continued to feign ignorance of their conversation until one of them tapped him on the shoulder.

"Where'd you come from?" the first speaker, a young boy, asked.

Grayden blinked and yawned. "Forgive me, I was dozing. I arrived here with my master a little bit ago. We did not mean to arrive so late, but circumstances beyond our control delayed us."

"And your master is...?" the second speaker, an elderly woman, prompted.

"General Bronwin," Grayden replied as Tobin returned, a pair of steaming mugs in his hand.

"The only thing the cook had left was steamed chocolate," Tobin apologized. "I see you've met the rest of the night crew, except for Sami, the cook, but he's busy getting the kitchen ready for breakfast. The master and mistress like to eat early."

"Did you know General Bronwin was coming here?" the elderly woman asked.

Tobin shook his head as he gulped down his own drink. "No, but then, nobody tells me nothin'. You know that, Venna."

Venna rolled her eyes and dropped the subject. Grayden sipped his drink slowly, savoring the flavor. He had never tasted a concoction like this before, but he found he liked it. He said nothing, worried that admitting ignorance about what he was drinking might give him away as not being from the Igyeum. The servants continued talking, laughing at inside jokes and reminiscing about stories he had no context for, but Grayden didn't mind. He was fairly certain he had most of the information he needed, but he remained for a while, participating in the conversation as best he could.

After nearly an hour, he decided he had learned all he could. Stretching and yawning, he stood up.

"Is there a room near my master's where I can sleep? I've been up since dawn, and the general will expect me to rise early tomorrow as well."

"I'll show you to your room. It doesn't connect to your master's, but it's just next door," Tobin offered.

"My thanks."

When they reached his room, Tobin uttered a cheery, "I should get back to my post. Get a good night's rest now!"

When he was certain the servant was gone, Grayden crept out into the hall and rapped quietly on Dalmir's door. The door swung open immediately and Grayden entered swiftly.

"They're here," he whispered in response to Dalmir's questioning look. "And I think they're prisoners, though they're being treated like honored guests. They're in a room facing west. Their doors aren't locked, but it sounds like there's a guard nearby at all times."

"The west side of the palace is right on the edge of a cliff," Dalmir mused. "Which would normally make escaping through a window impossible—" He paused.

"What are you thinking?"

"That we have an airship."

Grayden's eyes lit up. "What's our next move?"

"We have to get back to the *Hawk*," Dalmir said. "We can't risk a meeting with Ericole, since he has probably actually seen or even met this General Bronwin character."

"Our hallway is not guarded," Grayden said. "There didn't appear to be any servants about, either."

Dalmir wrinkled his nose speculatively. "I'd rather not risk being seen. Our windows do not face west, and we are on the first floor. I did not see any guards in the courtyard, either."

"Then we go out the window?"

"I believe that is our best option."

"And if we're seen?" Grayden asked nervously.

"We'll just have to deal with that if it comes, I believe. We'd best hurry. It will be morning soon."

Opening and getting through the large window was fairly easy. They soon stood outside in the courtyard. The horizon was beginning to show the very first hints of pale light and the air was still and crisp.

The two of them raced stealthily towards the front gate and freedom. Their feet barely made a sound as they swept across the courtyard as quietly as they could. They were like shadows, crossing the fortress grounds, flitting from tree to tree. The gate was only a few steps away when Grayden nearly collided with a cloaked figure.

"Oh!" The figure made a startled sound. "Forgive me." A woman's voice came from beneath the thick hood. "I did not know anyone else was out here."

Grayden made a noncommittal sound and shrugged. He stood there with his head down, wishing he had a cloak and hood of his own to shield his face. Suddenly the jacket that had seemed so classy and posh back on the airship struck him as being far less practical.

The cloaked figure peered up at him. "You!" Her hood fell back, revealing the familiar face of Shaesta. "How did you get here?"

"You!" Grayden replied, the only thing he could think to say.

Dalmir moved swiftly, clamping a hand over the woman's mouth.

"What do we do, now?" Grayden asked.

"Take her with us, of course."

Shaesta did not struggle. Her eyes wide, she walked with them calmly. They had not come in through the guarded main gates. Instead, they had scaled the wall. Grayden was a little concerned about how they were going to force Shaesta over the wall, but she surprised him by complying without any fuss or noise, even when Dalmir released her. In a very short while, they had returned to the place where the pirates had hidden their airship.

Marik looked up as they approached. "Well?" he demanded, then stopped, staring at Shaesta. His expression turned stormy, his eyes hard and angry. "Well. You found the traitor, then."

"Stumbled across her path, more accurately," Dalmir said mildly. "It seemed best to bring her along to keep her from raising the alarm."

"Yes, wisely done," Marik replied. "So, Shaesta, what do you have to say for yourself?"

"What are you doing here?" Shaesta asked, her voice soft.

"What do you think we're doing here?" Marik did not raise his voice, but the tightly controlled softness of his words made Grayden shiver. "Your people kidnapped two young men, and you stole the payload I'd been promised. I'm here to get both back."

"I can help you," she said, her eyes on the ground.

"Why would we trust anything you say? Give me one good reason not to toss you over a cliff right here and now and be done with you."

"You can't do that," Dalmir interjected. "She'll be missed, which will raise the alarm in that fortress."

"Well, what do you suggest we do, then?" Marik growled.

"I can help you," Shaesta insisted. "I had no wish to betray you, Captain. I never dreamed you'd take a job for Arrio Niveya—"

"What?" Marik interrupted her. "What did you say?"

"Arrio Niveya, he's Ericole's nephew… You didn't know?"

Marik shook his head wordlessly. "You'd better come below," he said.

Raisa and Oleck were in Marik's office when they arrived. Grayden watched as varying degrees of surprise and anger swept across their faces at the sight of Shaesta. Raisa leapt to her feet and crossed the room. Before anyone could stop her, she slapped Shaesta across the face so hard her hand left a bright red mark on the woman's cheek. Marik grabbed her arm, holding her back before she could make any further attack on their former crew mate.

"Marik?" Oleck rumbled. "What is the meaning of this?"

"Traitor!" Raisa shrieked. "Marik, let me go! She's treasonous scum. I demand you release me right now!"

"I'm as angry as you are." Marik's voice was low. "But she may be able to help us. Oleck, why didn't you tell me Arrio was part of the Niveya family?"

"What's that?" Oleck's eyes widened. "I didn't tell you because I didn't know, Marik, I swear."

"Thought you said you two went way back," Raisa hissed.

"We did a couple of jobs together back in our teens. Well, I was in my early twenties," Oleck protested. "It's not like we were friends. He always was a slimy little moldwarp."

"He's not very high in the family food chain," Shaesta commented.

"How do you fit into all of this, Shaesta?" Marik asked mildly. Grayden watched the pirate captain closely. Marik was either an excellent actor, or this entire interchange was hardly phasing him at all. Grayden wondered about that. If he had been in Marik's position, he was certain he would be the one everyone would need to be holding back to keep him from throttling the traitor.

"My family..." Shaesta faltered. "My family has worked for the Niveyas for generations. We hold high and honored positions as their most trusted servants. It's been a good life, good pay, and protection, even from the Ar'Mol himself. That is why I had to follow their orders and betray your trust." She gazed pleadingly at Marik. "If I appeared less than loyal, they would have had my entire family killed. The rumors about their brutality have not been exaggerated, I assure you."

"So the entire point of this job was to kidnap Beren?" Marik asked.

"Yes," Shaesta affirmed. "I didn't know about it until just before we boarded the *Crimson Eagle*. Arrio knew you wouldn't take hostages, so he was going to kidnap the lad when you made everyone disembark. But when we intercepted the Academy students, Beren wasn't there."

"So he had to change his plans."

"And use me, which he wasn't too pleased about. Even though I'm a servant, my family and our history with the Niveyas puts me in higher esteem than Arrio, which galls him to no end, I'm sure. He's constantly making a fool of himself over it."

"Then why isn't Arrio dead?" Marik asked. "The rumors say Ericole Niveya doesn't tolerate that sort of thing lightly."

"Arrio is his sister's son," Shaesta explained. "If there's anyone Ericole loves besides himself, it's his sister, Dianira. And if there's anyone Ericole is afraid of on this earth, it's Dianira's husband, Kale."

"Why are you telling us all this?" Raisa snarled. "How can we trust her, Marik? She betrayed us and left us to die."

"I warned you to get off the *Eagle* before it lost power," Shaesta protested.

"You didn't tell me you'd stolen all but one nearly depleted cynder from the *Hawk*," Marik countered, his voice filled with tightly controlled anger.

Shaesta stared at him dumbly.

"What? Didn't think we'd noticed?" Raisa asked sarcastically.

"I... I didn't..." Shaesta's eyes went wide. "Marik, I didn't touch the cynders on the *Hawk*, I swear! You have to believe me. I was supposed to, but I didn't. Arrio... Arrio must have realized I wouldn't do such a thing. I noticed he wasn't a part of the fighting, but I just assumed he didn't want to be recognized...."

"A likely story," Raisa snorted.

"Ray." Shaesta's voice was soft and pleading. "I would never hurt you or anyone on the crew."

"Stow it. Rustam, Thayric, Kauldar," Raisa spat. "They're dead, Shaesta, because of you. And don't you dare call me by my nickname ever again."

"I..." Shaesta swallowed. "I'm sorry. Nobody was supposed to get hurt."

"We don't have time for this," Marik said. "We need to make our plans and get out of here. Raisa, can you stay and work with her?"

Raisa wiped a hand across her eyes and then nodded firmly. "Someone's got to keep an eye on her."

"All right. To business then. Shaesta, you owe us an explanation, but right now we're more interested in where Wynn and Beren are," Marik said. "Time is short, so I will deal with your treachery later."

"They're in the west wing," Shaesta replied readily, "on the second floor. Third window from the left-hand corner of the palace. The *Hawk* could easily maneuver underneath the window for a rescue."

Dalmir nodded. "That aligns with what we discovered."

"Good, what's our time frame?" Marik asked.

"The servants will bring them down to the main dining room for breakfast around six bells," Shaesta said.

"And it's third bell already," Marik said, glancing out the window. "Doesn't give us much time."

"I might be able to stall them a bit," Shaesta offered.

Raisa gave a disbelieving laugh. "You cannot be serious."

"If we get moving right now, we should have time," Marik said. "Oleck, rouse the crew."

37

The *Valdeun Hawk* swooped in towards the fortress. All was quiet and still. Marik steered the airship expertly through the ravine until they hovered just above the balcony where Wynn and Beren's room was located. As they drew near, they could see Wynn and Beren through the windows. They were waving, and Grayden, peering through the misty morning haze, waved back.

The airship filled with activity as the pirates began the next step of Marik's plan. Yefrem descended over the side, dangling from a rope as several members of the crew lowered him carefully down to the balcony. As he slithered down the rope, Grayden glimpsed a sudden glow emanating from the roof of the fortress. He squinted at it and then decided it must be the sun rising on the other side of the palace. He turned his attention back to what was happening below him. Yefrem had reached the balcony and was gesturing through the window to Beren and Wynn. They appeared to be struggling to get the glass doors open. Grayden leaned over the side to watch. Dalmir was suddenly beside him, pulling him back.

"Can't have you falling, now," Dalmir said.

"It's almost over," Grayden replied. Elation mixed with a

sense of nervous urgency filled him. What was taking so long? Why hadn't Beren and Wynn come out on the balcony yet?

Whatever Dalmir might have said in response was lost as someone suddenly cried a warning. Grayden looked up to see what was happening. The glow on the roof had intensified, but now he could see that it had nothing to do with the sunrise. The entire top of the fortress appeared to be on fire. Flames blazed up around the edges of the balcony as well. All around the fortress, more fires raged into existence, springing up from cleverly hidden oil-filled troughs. The sudden brightness was disorienting.

The *Hawk* jerked away from the blaze slightly.

"Good thing we weren't planning to land," Dalmir muttered.

"What is the point of all that?" Grayden asked.

"Gives the fortress defenders light, fire to dip their arrows in, and prevents enemy ships from landing inside the walls," Raisa called out, having overheard Grayden's question. "Keep your wits about you. We may have to fight our way through this yet."

Below, Beren and Wynn were still inside the fortress. Yefrem suddenly stiffened and fell backwards, an arrow protruding from his chest. The burly man toppled from the balcony, and the airship rocked slightly as he swung limply from the end of his line.

Another shout pierced the night and the air suddenly exploded with the deadly hiss of flaming arrows and burning pitch hurled from mangonels, all of them converging on the *Valdeun Hawk*. As his eyes adjusted, Grayden could now see hundreds of figures standing on the roof, each holding a bow or manning a ballista. Every weapon was pointed at the airship, and Grayden realized that the mission had failed.

Marik let out a yell and spun the wheel. The airship turned swiftly and dropped in altitude. An enormous spear-like arrow whistled over Grayden's head, narrowly missing the main sail. Another arrow struck a pirate—Grayden was not sure which one—and he slumped to the deck, motionless. Dalmir yanked on Grayden's arm, pulling him down so he would not be an easy target.

The sky filled with fiery death. Grayden did not need anyone to tell him that open flames aboard the airship would be deadly. As the Hawk veered away from the fortress and began an alarmingly steep ascent, bitter sorrow welled up in his throat. He half-rose into a crouch, just enough so he could peer over the railing. He glanced back towards the balcony where Beren and Wynn had been so close to rescue. His friends stared through the window, their faces pale, their eyes wide. The airship bucked slightly and then jerked to the left. Grayden crouched down again and clung to the railing to keep from being thrown off. Dalmir, who had resumed standing, lost his balance. Grayden watched helplessly, his eyes wide with horror as Dalmir toppled over the railing and plummeted out of sight.

"DALMIR!" Grayden's scream tore its way through his throat and past his lips. "Dalmir!" Gripping the rail, he frantically scanned the darkness below the airship, but the gleam of the fires between him and the base of the cliff made it impossible to see the ground. A choking scream of despair worked its way up from the depths of Grayden's soul and lodged in his throat, making it difficult to breathe.

The airship hurtled away from the fortress rapidly, the light of the fires quickly diminishing behind them. Grayden put his forehead to the railing and remained motionless. Dalmir was gone. A long moment passed, and then his head jerked up.

Dalmir was gone! Why were they still airborne? He raced across the ship and up the ladder to the steering deck.

"How are we still airborne?" he demanded of Marik.

"What?" The pirate captain gave him a distracted glance.

"Dalmir fell off the ship," Grayden said. "So how are we still flying?"

A soft noise to his right made Grayden glance down. Mouse

sat on the deck behind Marik, his arm wrapped in a sling. His thin face was pale, but otherwise he seemed fine.

"That would be because of me," Mouse volunteered. "Before you and Dalmir scouted out the fortress, Dalmir had me sneak over to that dock we spotted, the one housing the ship that attacked us. He wanted me to steal a few of their cynders and get them powering the *Hawk* again."

Marik raised a dangerous eyebrow.

"I'm sorry I didn't tell you, Cap'n." Mouse shrugged, then winced, his arm clearly unable to handle even that small motion. "But I figured it would be the sort of thing you would have asked me to do if you'd thought of it."

Marik made a wry face. "You're forgiven. It's not you I'm mad at. I don't like that Dalmir was giving my people orders without asking, but I can't deny it was a good idea to have options."

"I see." Grayden's shoulders slumped wearily. He felt utterly defeated. His friends were still stranded at the mercy of their kidnappers. Without Dalmir, he had no influence on the pirates, and they knew it. They would probably abandon him as well, at the first opportunity.

"What's wrong, lad?" Marik asked. "Don't worry about Dalmir. That wizard is a tough old man. If he can toss an airship around in the sky like a toy, surely he can make certain his own landing is soft. I wouldn't give up on him just yet."

Grayden nodded. "I hope you're right," he replied glumly. "So, where do you think you'll be stranding me?"

Marik let go of the wheel with one hand and gripped Grayden's shoulder firmly. "Now listen here, lad," he said. "I may be a smuggler and a pirate, but I am not completely without honor. I gave you my word I'd help you rescue your friends. More than that, that old wizard saved my crew and my ship. Captain Marik doesn't leave his debts unpaid, d'you hear me?"

Grayden's spirits rose. "What are you saying?"

"I'm saying that we may have lost this round, but that doesn't mean we're abandoning your friends. And it doesn't mean I'm going back on my word."

"I... I don't know what to say." Hope surged in Grayden's chest.

"No need to say anything." Marik's voice was gruff. "Besides, Arrio Niveya tried to crash the *Hawk*, which means I've got a personal account to settle with him, anyway. Think you can stay with us and help us keep this bird flying? We're down a few good men, thanks to those archers."

Grayden nodded. He had no way to express his gratitude, and he had a sneaking suspicion the captain would probably take offense if he tried. So he merely descended the ladder and went to find out where he might help.

38

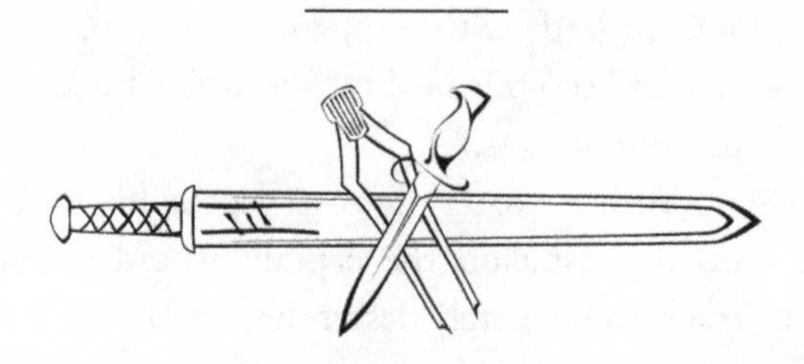

Wynn stared in horrified fascination as the arrow materialized in Yefrem's chest. Everything happened in slow motion as the man toppled backwards from the balcony. Frantically, Wynn worked harder at the lock, but the long wires he had worked out of the mattress simply weren't the right size or shape. Beren's frustrated growl made him look up. The airship leaped swiftly into the air as the lights outside dimmed once more, as the fires were simultaneously smothered all over the fortress.

Frustration welled up within Wynn, mingled with terror at the thought of their last hope of rescue disappearing into the darkness. Looking around the room for a way to give vent to his feelings, his gaze alighted on the heavy pewter pitcher resting on the nightstand. He grabbed it and hurled it through one of their windows. It made a terrific and satisfying crashing noise as the window shattered. The pitcher itself flew into the dawn and over the balcony, clanging repeatedly as it bounced down the side of the mountain in the faint light of the rising sun.

"Help!" The faint cry made the two young men stare at each other in puzzlement before cautiously creeping through the broken window. They peered about nervously, but no archers appeared and no arrows rained down upon them.

Looking down, Wynn saw a man dangling from the balcony, clinging to the ledge with white-knuckled fingers.

"Help me!" he shouted.

Without hesitation, they reached over the railing and grabbed the man's arms, pulling him from danger. He landed on the balcony in a heap of rumpled robes. He sat there, panting for breath, before looking up, a slight twinkle in his eyes.

"Dalmir?" Wynn asked in disbelief. "Is that you?"

"By the Treaty! It is you!" Beren gasped. "You shaved your beard."

"Is that what happened to it?" Dalmir asked mildly. "I wondered."

Beren looked astounded and rather taken aback, then he caught the smirk in Dalmir's eyes and he laughed softly.

"How did you come to be in such a precarious position?" Beren asked.

"When it looked as though our rescue attempt was doomed to failure, I did the only thing I could think to do," Dalmir replied. "I jumped off the airship."

"Jumped!" Both Beren and Wynn were thunderstruck.

"If we could not rescue you, I surely could not leave you here alone in the hands of your enemies," Dalmir said, as though it ought to have been obvious.

After a moment of awestruck silence, Wynn regained his voice. "What happened after they captured us? Is Grayden well? Why were the pirates trying to rescue us?" His questions came with barely a breath between them.

Dalmir held up his hand. "Hold on, young Wynn. All will be explained shortly. We should get back inside, though. It is not safe out here."

Inside the room, Dalmir sat in a chair and nodded. "Now, young Wynn, I can give you a few answers. Your friend, Grayden, is perfectly well, though I would guess he is quite concerned about me at present. He is alone among thieves and pirates, but I do not believe they will do him harm. Strangely enough, Captain

Marik seems an honorable sort. I've had the chance to take his measure over the past day or two. He may not wish to admit it, but in his own way, perhaps he can be trusted… for the moment. As for your other questions, listen closely, for we have little time."

Dalmir quickly described the last two days they had spent following Wynn and Beren's trail and how he and Grayden had visited the previous evening in order to find out where their two friends were being held so they could attempt a rescue. Wynn and Beren were both rather impressed with his story.

"When I saw we could neither land nor complete our rescue attempts, I decided I would be far more useful to you here," Dalmir concluded. "So here I am."

Beren's eyes widened. "That is more courageous a thing than I would have attempted, truly."

Dalmir waved a hand. "It was nothing. Now, tell me quickly, what have you learned about your captors?"

Beren and Wynn filled him in on their circumstances as briefly as they could. They had barely finished when the door to their room burst open. A servant entered and halted, staring at Dalmir in open-mouthed astonishment.

"How… where… how…" the servant stammered.

"How can I help you?" Dalmir asked.

"I was sent to wake the guests and help them get ready to dine with Lord and Lady Niveya," the servant managed.

"As you can see, they are already awake and perfectly capable of washing and dressing themselves. You had best return to your master and tell him to have the kitchen staff set an extra place at the table."

"Yes, sir," the servant replied automatically. He turned and left the room, no doubt wondering why he was so quick to obey an intruder.

Beren had a look of admiration in his eyes. "You reminded me of my father just now. He has that same air of authority about him." He turned to Wynn, a questioning look on his face. "I thought you said you found Dalmir living alone in a tower?"

Wynn nodded wordlessly.

"Surely not." Beren waved a hand. "For he comports himself as a king. In truth, Dalmir, without the beard you have shed quite a few years."

"I assure you, I have not. They weigh me down with or without my whiskers," Dalmir replied. "But enough of that for now. We must ready ourselves to dine with the enemy. Shaesta informed us that the Niveyas hope to ransom you, but have half a mind to kill you both if they decide ransom is not worth the effort."

Wynn felt his mouth go dry. He had already known they were in a precarious situation, possibly even in danger. But the reality of their true peril only now struck him with its full weight.

They were ready by the time the next servant arrived at their door, this one flanked by a half-dozen grim-faced guards. Nobody said anything as the three men were escorted to the large formal dining hall where Ericole and Aubri Niveya waited. Ericole rose as they entered.

"My guests," he said expansively, "please, join myself and my wife as we break fast together. I have been informed that a new arrival has joined us. Am I correct in assuming that you arrived on the airship that so rudely woke everyone up at such an unholy hour?"

Everything about his demeanor exuded confidence, but Wynn was certain that Dalmir's presence had shaken even Ericole Niveya. He wondered how much of the man's composure was an act. Ericole did not strike him as the type of man who was often out of control of a situation.

Dalmir bowed his head slightly. "Forgive me, rudeness was the farthest thing from our intentions."

"I'm sure, I'm sure." Ericole rubbed his hands together. He gestured for them to join him at the table and then he addressed Dalmir once more. "May I have the honor of knowing whom I am entertaining in my dining room this morning?"

"You may indeed. My name is Dalmir."

Niveya stared at him blankly. "Allow me to welcome you to my humble home," he said in a smooth tone. "I hope breakfast is to your liking."

BREAKFAST WAS A STRANGE, silent affair. Lord Niveya was far quieter than he had been the previous night, and nobody else seemed inclined to speak, either. Aubri sat next to her husband, eating in silence. She had not even said "good morning" to them when they entered the dining room. Wynn could not help but admire her. Despite the severe frown on her face, she was a beautiful woman. Ropes of pearls adorned her hair this morning. The jewel at her neck caught Wynn's attention again, and he stared at it in fascination. It sparkled in the dimly lit room as if filled with a light of its own, a shimmering, mesmerizing purple, the shade the air turns at dusk. Wynn stared at it, nestled against her throat, until she caught his gaze. He turned his attention back to his breakfast, wondering if he had gone mad. What had he been thinking, staring at her necklace like that?

When the food was gone and the places cleared, Ericole pushed his chair back slowly.

"My wife informs me that one of our servants appears to be missing this morning. Tell me, did your friends abduct her, or did she go of her own accord?"

Dalmir narrowed his eyes. "I'm afraid I have no idea to whom you are referring."

"Do you not?" Ericole looked as though he had more to say, but before he could, a servant entered the room.

"Forgive me, Master Ericole, but I needed to inform you—" The servant halted upon seeing Dalmir, his eyes widening in confusion. Dalmir stared at him, his expression aloof.

"Yes, Tobin? What is it?" Ericole's voice was impatient.

"Er..." Tobin took a deep breath. "The kitchen staff is short-handed this morning. I was wondering if you wanted me to help them out?"

Ericole narrowed his eyes dangerously. "You dare interrupt my breakfast for such a trivial matter?"

Tobin bowed and backed away. "Forgive me, Master. I don't know what I was thinking. What with all the goings-on last night, I'm rather flustered this morning."

"What goings-on?" Aubri asked suddenly.

"Er, the attack," Tobin stammered. "Everyone's a bit agitated about it still."

Aubri narrowed her eyes. "Don't you sleep in the closet near the front gate, Tobin?"

"Yes'm."

"And you heard the attack all the way up there, did you?"

"Er, no'm. I was going for a stroll, you know, stretching my legs a bit. I was near the west side of the palace when all the commotion started."

Aubri stared down her nose at the servant suspiciously. Tobin reddened and sort of danced from one foot to the other. Then he bowed low.

"I should go check if Cook needs anything," he gasped out and then turned and all but fled.

Aubri glanced significantly at her husband. Ericole narrowed his eyes and nodded. He turned his attention to Dalmir.

"And what was that all about?" he asked quietly.

Dalmir's eyes widened innocently. "Apparently your kitchen staff is short-handed. Others in your employ are a touch excitable," he drawled and waved a hand. "I'm not sure I can offer you aid with either situation."

Ericole raised an eyebrow. "Well," he said briskly. "I suppose we should get down to business. But not here."

Pushing away from his empty plate, he led them through the palace to the grand room in which he had received Wynn and Beren the night before. Suddenly, Ericole turned his attention to

Wynn. "I trust you find your attire of a more correct fit this morning?"

Flustered at the sudden scrutiny, Wynn looked down and nodded. The hunter-green tunic and soft brown trousers felt as though they had been made for him and he said so.

Ericole nodded. "I thought you might find the style more comfortable as well. I detected a Dalman accent in your words last night. Am I correct?" His eyes flicked quickly towards Dalmir as he spoke, then returned to Wynn.

"Yes," Wynn stammered. "Thank you."

"Forgive me for putting an end to the pleasantries, Lord Ericole," Beren interjected, "but I would like to know when I might resume my travels. My friend and I are starting classes at the Academy, and we do not wish to be late for the start of term."

"Of course, of course." Ericole nodded. "I must beg your indulgence a little while longer, I am afraid. Though I hope my hospitality more than compensates for any disruption to your plans. At least you are alive, which is reason to be thankful, no?"

"If you are referring to the assassins," Beren replied carefully, "I am sure my father will reward you handsomely for the service you have done in saving my life."

Ericole's lips drew back in a small smile. "That is most welcome news."

"I am sure it is," Beren said stiffly. "We would not wish to put you out in any way, especially since your actions may have come at substantial risk to yourself. Defying the Ar'Mol is not an insignificant act. There could be repercussions, could there not?"

"Perhaps," Ericole acknowledged. There was a light of surprise in his eyes, as if he had not expected such insight from such a young man. He appeared about to say more when another servant entered the room.

"Master Ericole," the servant gasped, "you have a guest."

Ericole's eyes grew dangerous. "For decades, the location of this fortress has been a most well-guarded secret, and in less than a day we have been discovered by not one, but two uninvited guests. Tell me, how is this possible?"

"Forgive me, Master." The servant's voice trembled.

"Who is this new intruder?"

"It is the Ar'Molon."

Ericole's face paled visibly and he stood abruptly. "Please show the Ar'Molon to the front parlor and inform him that I shall attend to him immediately."

The servant nodded and raced away to carry out his master's orders. Ericole returned his attention to his present guests. He bowed his head and rose, tugging imperceptibly at the hem of his jacket to straighten invisible wrinkles.

"Forgive me," he said, his anger under control and his voice smooth once more. "But we must continue this conversation later. It appears I have an important guest. It might be best if your paths did not cross." He glanced meaningfully at Beren. "You would not wish to be recognized. The guards will show you back to your rooms." He met his wife's eyes briefly and then strode out of the room.

Beren rumbled something deep in his throat that may or may not have been an agreement as Ericole left. When he had gone, Aubri Niveya stood.

"Forgive this rudeness." Her tone was apologetic. "But it is for your own safety that Lord Uun does not know you are here."

Dalmir's gaze sharpened. "Lord Uun? And why is his presence unsafe for us?"

"Lord Uun is the Ar'Molon," Aubri replied smoothly.

"Is he, now?" Dalmir replied thoughtfully.

"I will show you back to your room." Aubri moved to stand near the door. "If you will follow me, I can return you to your rooms without fear of Lord Uun catching sight of you."

Dalmir stood, and Wynn and Beren followed suit. As Aubri turned, Dalmir touched her shoulder.

"That is a most interesting necklace you are wearing. I cannot help but notice the jewel is of a rather unique design."

Aubri stiffened and her expression softened a shade as she touched the stone. "Ericole found this during his travels and had it made into a necklace for me. It is rather pretty."

"Then it is truly one of a kind?" Dalmir asked. Wynn thought the older man's voice held a faint touch of desperation.

"Quite unique," Aubri replied, her tone proud. "There is nothing like it anywhere. It is the envy of all the women in the Ar'Mol's court." She waved a hand, and a servant appeared from a panel in the wall that turned out to be a cleverly hidden door. "Blayne will show you the way back to your rooms," she said, dismissing them with ease.

They progressed swiftly through hallways that were far less elegant than the ones they had traversed before. These passages seemed all but forgotten. There was no ornate ironwork, no delicate tapestries, no stained-glass windows. They wound through the palace until Wynn was completely lost. When he was certain they must have walked several miles at least, Blayne pushed open a panel and then they were standing in the hallway outside their own set of rooms.

"I will leave you now," the servant said as they filed into their room.

39

Ericole entered the front parlor, head bowed respectfully. The tall man in the center of the room did not turn away from his deep scrutiny of the titles upon the ornate wooden bookshelves. He acted unaware that anyone had entered the room. Ericole stood silently, surveying the situation and his unexpected guest.

His path had crossed with Lord Uun's on a number of occasions. Ericole had never discovered what exactly Lord Uun did or where he came from. He was a man without a past. Not a single one of Ericole's sources knew where Uun had grown up. Nobody could even pinpoint the exact date he had entered the Ar'Mol's service. His accent was wholly unique. That he was cunning and ruthless, and that the Ar'Mol trusted him implicitly were the only things anyone really knew about Lord Uun with any certainty. It was whispered that the Ar'Molon actually ruled the Igyeum, though never out loud.

Uun tore his attention away from the ancient tomes slowly, almost reluctantly, and turned to face Ericole.

"You have an impressive collection here." Uun's deep, rough voice filled the room. Ericole had the sudden thought that this was not the voice of a councilor. Lord Uun had always struck him as more of a warrior, and yet he kept to the shadows, bending the Ar'Mol's ear and attaining the penultimate title of Ar'Molon with no family connections, or—seemingly—any money. Ericole's lip curled involuntarily. He never had liked Uun.

"Thank you," Ericole replied smoothly, hiding his disdain. "May I ask what has brought you to my humble abode?"

Uun tilted his head. "Your nephew was supposed to deliver an important package to one of my stewards two days ago. Yet he never arrived at the arranged location. You have not seen him, have you?"

Ericole grimaced. "My miscreant nephew is forever bungling even the simplest of tasks. I have not seen him. What was he supposed to deliver?"

Uun narrowed his eyes. "That is none of your concern."

"Surely you did not come all this way simply to check up on my nephew?"

Uun remained silent.

"Well. The package must have been of great value for your honored self to make such a journey."

"It is vital to the Ar'Mol's plans. That is all you need to know."

"If I see Arrio, I will tell him you are looking for him," Ericole offered. "Or I could send my men to look for him? He may have returned last night after the rest of the family had retired."

Uun gave Ericole a measuring glance. He seemed about to speak, then he pursed his lips. "It was a long journey, and I hate traveling by airship. Might I impose upon your hospitality?"

"Of course." Ericole snapped his fingers loudly, and a servant materialized. "Show His Lordship to our best guest suite and get him whatever he requests." He gave a deep bow. "My house is at your command, my lord. If there is anything you desire, please ask."

"Yes, sir." The servant bowed, then addressed Uun. "Follow me, sir."

Uun stared at Ericole with severe intensity, as though attempting to ferret out all his secrets with a glance. Then he grimaced and swept out of the room behind the servant. Ericole waited until they had left and then shuddered silently. He left by a different door and headed towards his wife's sitting room, where she would be waiting to find out what Uun wanted, and how much he knew.

Aubri was waiting for him, as expected. Her unease was obvious, as she was not even attempting to pretend she was doing anything but waiting for him. She rose from her chair as he entered the room.

"I cannot abide that man," Ericole said quietly as he closed the door behind him.

Aubri searched his face, her gray eyes cool. "What is he doing here?"

"Looking for Arrio, of course."

"That could be a problem."

"I ordered Arrio to remain in the servants' quarters," Ericole replied. "He should be safely hidden. Who would think to look for him there?"

"If anyone would, it would be the Ar'Molon."

Ericole made a snarling sound deep in his throat. "The only thing we can do is play the innocent host until he decides even Arrio would not be foolish enough to show up here. Then he'll leave, and we can deliver Adelfried safely to the Academy."

"Or we could simply kill Adelfried and send his body as a message to the Ar'Mol."

Ericole ran his thumb along his jaw, a thoughtful expression on his face as he considered this notion. At length, he shook his head. "No, I would prefer not to challenge the Ar'Mol so openly just yet. He is strong in men and has the advantage of the airships. Perhaps once the war with Telmondir is fully begun... but for now, I believe it is better to bide our time. We have already foiled his plans for assassination, we should not squander this opportunity. Adelfried dead is only useful once."

"Perhaps you are right," Aubri conceded. "You have always been the better tactician."

Ericole placed a gentle hand on his wife's smooth cheek. Aubri was like a marble statue: cold and aloof, but breathtakingly beautiful. She terrified and fascinated him. He was glad she was by his side. She was his equal in every way, and he loved her for it. The rumors were true: he abstained from eating anything she had touched. However, this was not because he believed for one second that she desired to murder him. She might periodically slip poison into his food, but it was simply her way of keeping him sharp, keeping his senses alert. She would be devastated if he could be killed so easily. As the head of the Niveya family, Ericole could not afford to let his guard down for one second. It was exhausting, but it was also his glory and his duty. They had not gotten where they were by being soft or naive. Aubri understood that, as so few did.

WYNN PACED AROUND THE ROOM. He felt like a horse tethered to a fence and then left outside amid a raging storm. If he had to wait any longer, he might explode out of his skin.

"What are we going to do?" he asked. He had asked the same question several times now, and both Dalmir and Beren had given up trying to give a satisfactory reply.

Dalmir reclined on a strangely shaped, but extremely comfortable couch. With his eyes closed and hands folded over his chest, he looked peaceful. Wynn wanted to throw something at him, but the servants had not replaced the pitcher. His fingers tap-tapped to a frenzied staccato rhythm that he could neither control nor slow. His breaths came in quick, frantic gulps. His brain was afire with fear and possibilities he could neither catalog nor process. He wanted to crawl out of his skin. He wanted to slide under the bed and hide in the darkness. His fingers ached for his pencil and the comfort of his shed and a stack of papers on which he could draw.

Beren stood at the window, a thoughtful frown on his face. He seemed to study the landscape outside, or perhaps he was counting the clouds. Whatever he was doing, it did not appear to be useful, at least to Wynn.

After a period of time that lasted for an eternity, a knock came at the door. Wynn darted across the room and opened it. A servant stood in the doorway.

"Excuse me, good sirs," the servant said. "Master Ericole sent me to convey his deepest regrets about cutting short your conversation this morning. An urgent and unforeseen engagement has arisen that demands all of Master Ericole's attention at present. He wishes me to assure you he desires to finish his business with you and hopes that a pleasant agreement for all parties might soon be reached."

Wynn snorted, but a surge of hope rushed through him. Surely such a message would not be necessary if Ericole had decided it would be simpler to kill them and rid himself of the nuisance of keeping prisoners?

"My master also wished me to inform you that for a little while there will be a guard posted at your door, and I am sorry to say that your door will also be kept locked. I assure you, this is merely for your own protection."

Wynn's heart plummeted. Their friendly captivity appeared to be over. Ericole was no longer even attempting to conceal the fact that they were prisoners.

Having delivered his message, the servant retreated. The loud click of the key in the lock echoed across the room and felt like an execution.

Dalmir sat up, suddenly alert. "Well, that is interesting."

Beren turned away from the window. "I must agree."

Wynn looked at them both in disbelief. "What do you mean? Is that all you can say? They've locked us in, with no hope of rescue, and all you can think to say is that this is an interesting turn of events?" A desperate need to crawl under the bed consumed him, but he fought it back with all his strength.

Dalmir looked at Wynn, his blue eyes kind. "This must have something to do with Ericole's unexpected visitor," he explained.

Beren nodded. "We had just reached the point in our conversation this morning when I would have expected Ericole to make subtle hints about how relieved my father would be to learn of my safety. We would have haggled for a bit, and then he would have sent messengers to my father. But we were interrupted before the conversation could get to that."

"And now we are locked in and guarded," Dalmir mused. "Apparently for our own protection. Ericole is taking no chances on his guest discovering that we are here."

"He told us that the Ar'Mol is the one who sent the assassins," Wynn said, calming down a bit.

"And this man is the Ar'Molon," Dalmir said. "I am not familiar with these terms, but if the Ar'Mol is the leader of the Igyeum, then I would assume the Ar'Molon is merely one step down in power?"

"That would be accurate," Beren affirmed, then heaved a sigh. "We might as well get comfortable. We may be stuck in here for a while. I do not believe rescue is imminent."

"Yes, you are correct," Dalmir replied. "But we must ready ourselves, as well. There is no guarantee that Niveya will indeed be able to keep our presence here a secret. We know little about this Lord Uun."

"Of course," Beren rumbled. "We must arm ourselves." He glanced at Wynn, a sly smirk curving his lips. "I wonder if we can get the servants to bring us a new pitcher. Wynn is deadly with one."

Dalmir raised an eyebrow as both young men burst out laughing. The laughter eased the tension that had been building in Wynn's thoughts. He wished he could find the words to thank Beren for making him laugh. Or Dalmir, for risking his life to be here in this room with them. Their present circumstances had not changed, but Wynn suddenly felt strangely confident that they would be safe so long as Dalmir remained with them.

40

Raisa glared down from her perch atop the mast. She had volunteered for sentry duty in the crow's nest for one reason only: to get away. She needed to clear her head. Truthfully, she needed to distance herself from Shaesta. Raisa glowered down at the deck where she could see the top of Shaesta's head as she stood next to Marik, her lips close to his ear as she spoke.

How could Marik trust her? What was he doing, letting her wander about the airship freely? The woman had nearly killed them all, and now she got to return as if nothing happened? Not on Raisa's watch. Her face burned as if on fire and she did not need a mirror to tell her there were angry red spots on her cheeks. Shaesta had been her friend. Perhaps that was what hurt most: that she had counted Shaesta as a friend. Blood thundered between her ears, drowning out everything else. Raisa exhaled angrily, her breath a pale steam in the frigid morning air.

The rigging swayed a bit, and she glanced down, startled out of her thoughts. The young man, Grayden, was climbing up to her. She waited, her muscles tensed, wondering why he would seek her out. As he clambered into the crow's nest, panting a bit and blowing on his fingers to warm them, she gazed at him through narrowed eyes. He reminded her a bit of Marik. Or at least, who Marik had been thirteen years ago when she and Oleck first joined his crew. There was an authority about this Grayden, an air that made others turn to him for answers and leadership. Marik had always had that same air. And the nobility the young man carried in his heart—Marik used to have that, too, before all their lives had fallen apart. Before... She pulled her thoughts away from the ancient past as Grayden reached her. His eyes were dark and troubled.

"What do you think Marik will do next?" he asked her.

"Why don't you ask him?"

Grayden's mouth quirked wryly to one side. "Not sure he'd tell me. I still don't know why he hasn't dropped me off and raced away to anywhere but here. This isn't a safe mission. It's not like my friends mean anything to him."

Raisa's eyes softened slightly. "You don't know him like I do. He may be a smuggler and a pirate, but that's just his job. It isn't who he is. He's no villain. Quite the opposite, really. Marik... Marik often takes on... causes, I suppose you could call them. He can't stand injustice, and he really... well, he cares more than he seems to. He went to great lengths to make sure nobody on the *Crimson Eagle* got hurt."

"He stranded them in the wilderness."

"We let them off less than two miles from a major town. With their mounts." Raisa's voice was defensive. "As soon as the initial shock wore off, I'm sure the captain and most of the crew realized where they were. We set down near a populated area, with plenty of landmarks. It wasn't even that far from your original destination. I'd be willing to wager that the rest of your classmates reach the Academy less than a sennight late, unless they were particularly stupid and unable to navigate their way to the village—in which case I don't believe they deserve to reach the Academy for all the good they'll do defending your precious Telmondir."

"So, if Marik cares so much, why does he choose to be a pirate?" Grayden's tone was subdued, but still held a challenge. "Surely there are far more noble endeavors he could pursue."

Raisa's eyes took on a far-away mien. For a long moment, she remained silent. At last, she muttered, "It's a long story, and I don't know all of it myself. But we haven't always been pirates."

"Oh."

Silence stretched between them. Raisa stared down at the deck. The rigging below them creaked in the wind and the crow's nest swayed comfortingly, though it made Grayden turn a bit green. She grinned at him and he chuckled.

"I've never had a problem with heights before."

"The height on an airship is different."

"True," Grayden agreed. "Do you have any idea what Marik's next move will be?"

"He's working on his plan," Raisa said. "He's got that gleam in his eye. I think he's been working on it since before our first rescue attempt, really. When he's got it all figured out, we'll act. Don't worry, Marik tends to come up with plans rather quickly, and they're usually good ones. A little crazy, but they work."

Grayden took a deep breath and nodded. "Thanks for talking to me."

She gave him a sympathetic look. He might be going to the Academy, but he was still young, she realized. He was just a boy, really, and yet he was holding his own. He was doing well, despite the fact that his life was spinning out of his control. She found that she admired him and wished him well. In quite a few ways, she wished she could be more like him.

"We'll rescue your friends. Marik keeps his promises."

Grayden squinted and swallowed with difficulty. He did not respond, but swung himself out of the crow's nest and clambered back down the rigging to the main deck. Raisa watched him as he went below. Movement attracted her gaze, and she shifted her attention to Marik. He still stood at the wheel, though Shaesta had disappeared. Marik stared up at Raisa. A look passed between them, and she nodded. He had his plan, as she knew he would, and it was time for him to let the rest of them in on it. She took a deep breath. If Marik did not think Shaesta was a problem, then she wasn't. It was as simple as that. If his judgment was flawed, so was her own. Raisa trusted Marik more than anyone else in the world. She wasn't about to change that now.

Later, as Marik outlined his plan, Raisa felt her confidence waver. It felt even crazier than usual and required a lot of faith that Dalmir had managed not to perish when he fell over the railing. Marik finished explaining the details and looked up, taking them all in with his gaze.

"Anyone who doesn't want to be part of this, speak now. I won't ask any of you to go with me. But I gave my word. I owe Dalmir my ship, and I'll not pass up a chance to spit in the Ar'Mol's eye. For whatever reason, he wants Beren dead, and I'll not see myself allowing that to happen."

There was a brief silence and a shuffling of feet.

Oleck spoke up. "I think I speak for all of us." He paused, but nobody moved to argue with him. "Those of us here, we've all worked with you before, and you've never steered us wrong. We're in this with you until the end, even if this is the end."

Raisa found herself nodding in agreement. She paused, catching a glimpse of Shaesta standing a few feet behind Oleck, and froze. But one of them had steered wrong, she thought. One of them had betrayed them all... left them to die. How could she trust a plan that Shaesta had a part in? But all around her, heads nodded. Marik graced them with a reckless smile.

"Let's go rescue us a Western lord, then."

41

"Are you leaving so soon, Lord Uun?" Ericole did his best to feign disappointment. "You have not even dined with us. My wife wished to get your thoughts on the Ar'Mol's latest maneuvers as he plots to conquer Telmondir."

Uun sneered. "You can save your pathetic lies for someone who might believe them, Ericole Niveya. I know you are most eager for my departure. I make you nervous, and make no mistake, I will discover the reason. But fortunately for you, I have had word from the Ar'Mol that I am needed back in Malei sooner than expected." The man shot a piercing gaze at Ericole that froze him through to his bones. "Know this: if I should discover that you have taken a conscious part in foiling my plans, I promise you will not enjoy the consequences."

Ericole arranged his face into a blank expression. "I have assured you already that I have no idea where my nephew is or what fate has befallen him."

"So you have said." Uun took a deep breath and rolled his shoulders. "But there is something you are not telling me, Niveya, and I will winnow it out." He shook his head with a short, jerking motion. "No matter. I will attend to discovering your secrets later."

Ericole bowed. "We look forward to your return, Ar'Molon."

Uun rolled his eyes. "Niveya."

Ericole kept his face placid, though he knew Lord Uun meant to dishonor him by withholding any honorific. However, Niveya had no use for titles, preferring for his name to be powerful on its own, inspiring necessary fear without any help. "Is there anything I can get for you or do to help you?" he asked, keeping his voice to a low purr.

Lord Uun studied him through slitted eyes, as though searching for any sign of a slight. Then he sniffed. "Send a manservant to carry my bags. I must leave immediately."

"Certainly," Ericole bowed again. "At once, Ar'Molon." He managed to keep the sneer out of his voice. Barely.

After sending a servant to attend to Lord Uun's luggage, Ericole and Aubri both walked with their guest to the front of the palace, where his airship hovered above the courtyard. Uun blinked at Ericole—denying him even a bow from the shoulders—and then bent over Aubri's hand to kiss it.

"One of your servants mentioned that your home came under attack shortly before I arrived," Uun said, his voice mild as he straightened up. "I hope that no irreparable harm was done. I found it troubling to discover that such a graceful flower as yourself might be in danger up here on these mountain slopes, so far from anyone's aid."

Ericole kept his smug grin internal. If Uun thought he might find an ally in Lady Aubri, he was in for an unpleasant surprise.

"Oh." Aubri's eyes widened, and she fluttered her lashes as though flattered by the attention and the compliment. "Your Lordship is so very kind to one so lowly as myself."

With anyone else, Niveya might have winced at such overdone acting. But he kept his face placid. Aubri knew what she was doing.

"So there was an attack?" Uun asked, his gaze sharpening.

Aubri gave a disgusted little sound. "Vicious thieves, my lord. I'm sure they meant to murder us all in our sleep. Thankfully, our home is well protected. But I must confess, I suffered a great fright. I fell into a swoon for several hours. I have never been so fearful for my life."

Uun's expression altered from interest to boredom, and Niveya inwardly congratulated his wife. She had chosen exactly the correct tack.

"Do you have any idea what they were after?" Uun asked, his tone indicating that he cared little for the answer.

Aubri waved a hand. "What weren't they after, my lord?" she demanded, her eyes wide. "We have such great wealth; so many servants; beautiful, helpless women such as myself—"

Niveya coughed into his hand, trying to cover his laughter. Schooling his face into a stern mask, he now played the part of rescuing their guest. "My dear, you have detained the Ar'Molon long enough," he said, putting his arm protectively around her shoulders and giving his guest an apologetic look. "Lord Uun has no wish to hear about our troubles."

Aubri sighed and turned her face into his shoulder.

"Good day, my lord," Ericole said.

Uun turned to leave, then paused. "I thought the location of your home was a great secret." Uun's voice held a question.

"So did we." Ericole could not contain his ire, so he let it show. "But it seems this is not as we had believed, as we are apparently to be called upon by a profusion of uninvited visitors of late."

Uun did not react except with a twitch of his lips. "Very well, then. I shall take my leave of you now. Thank you for your hospitality. I hope to enjoy it again soon."

"Please know that you are always most welcome," Aubri gushed. Ericole barely refrained from grimacing, but he admired his wife's ability to lie with such unshakable sincerity.

Uun stared at her. Then his lips curled into a sneer and he strode towards his airship. Moments later, he had climbed aboard and the vessel was swiftly winging away.

Ericole heaved a sigh of relief. "You handled that quite expertly, my dear," he said, genuine reverence in his tone.

Aubri's eyes danced. "I was rather good, wasn't I?" She giggled like a young girl, remembering their guest's sudden loss of interest in their affairs. Her face flushed and Ericole thought it strange that something so deadly could be so beautiful.

WYNN, Beren, and Dalmir had been left alone all afternoon. The sun now shone into their rooms from between the mountains as it sank towards the horizon. They had dined in their room, but had seen no signs of their captors all day. Wynn perched on the knife's edge of patience. He wanted desperately for something to happen. Even something bad—he felt—would be better than this interminable waiting. He knew better than to voice this opinion, of course. Wynn had a sneaking suspicion that Beren and Dalmir were cut from the same slab of rock. Neither seemed at all ill at ease about their situation. Beren had even taken a short nap earlier, and he had snored away as though completely unconcerned for their safety. Dalmir, as calm as a shallow stream, sat in a chair and stared into the empty hearth. The man might have been a part of the room's decorations for as much as he moved. The only thing he had done all day was get up and pour water on the fire, putting it out. When Wynn complained of a chill, Dalmir handed him his cloak.

Wynn had spent most of the morning pacing until Dalmir snapped at him to sit down and save his strength. The old man's eyes had blazed so wrathfully that Wynn dropped to the floor and remained completely immobile for half an hour before he worked up the courage to move at all.

Now, as the sun streaked the sky with fiery red, another servant entered the room.

"Master Niveya would like to inform you that his other guest will leave soon," the servant announced. "If you would please wash and dress for dinner, Master and Mistress Niveya request the privilege of your presence at their table this evening."

Wynn suddenly shook as though with weakness. Perhaps Dalmir's advice to save his strength had been wise.

Beren rose from the bed and stretched. "Inform our host and hostess that we would be honored to join them for the evening meal," he said, his tone filled with genteel deference.

The servant bobbed a shallow bow and left. As his footsteps faded away down the hall, Wynn stared at his companions.

"What are we going to do?" he asked.

"We are going to have supper," Dalmir replied.

"I meant what are we going to do about our situation," Wynn snapped. "If this Lord Uun is gone, then this might be our best chance to escape."

"I thought we had agreed to allow the negotiations to play out?" Beren said, as he splashed water on his face.

Wynn's reply was interrupted by yet another visitor to their room, though this one did not come in through the main door. A blast of soot and ash erupted out of the fireplace, and then a bundle of rags rolled out into the room. Wynn yelped in surprise and stumbled backwards as the bundle of rags stood up and stretched out.

"That was one of the less comfortable things I've ever done," the dirty figure commented, trying fruitlessly to brush the soot out of his hair.

"Mouse." Dalmir's eyes twinkled. "You owe me five kips."

Mouse rolled his eyes and grimaced. He dug his hand into his pocket and pulled out a handful of filthy odds and ends. He picked out five aged coins. "All I've got are stins."

Dalmir stared at him blankly.

"Igyeum currency," Beren said, understanding Dalmir's confusion. "The smallest coin they make."

"Ah." Dalmir eyed the handful of coins. "That will be fine."

Mouse grimaced and dropped the rectangular coins into

Dalmir's outstretched hand. "I really didn't think I'd fit," he said. "But you were right, and a wager's a wager."

Beren stared. "How did you sneak into the chimney in the middle of the day?"

Mouse's eyes brightened. "I'm just that good."

"How is the rest of the plan coming?" Dalmir asked.

Mouse shrugged. "About like you said it would. Marik sent me to tell you that everything is ready on our end. How about you?"

"Excellent." Dalmir took a deep breath. "We had a bit of a setback this morning, but it should not matter. Inform Marik that we are ready as well, and that we will meet him at the prearranged time and place."

Mouse nodded and gazed mournfully at the fireplace. He scratched behind his ear and sighed. "Going up is going to be a lot harder."

"Get moving," Dalmir barked. "You don't have much time. Besides, they'll be coming to escort us to dinner in a few minutes, and we do not want them to discover you here."

With a groan, Mouse ducked back into the fireplace and disappeared up the chimney. Before Beren or Wynn had even a moment to ask Dalmir what the plan was, their door opened once again.

"Are you ready to... great towers!" The servant gasped as she caught sight of the soot-covered room. "What happened in here?"

Wynn didn't think, he just spoke the first thing that came into his head. "I must have thrown a green log on the fire. It popped something fierce! A few coals jumped out of the hearth. They caught fire on the rug and blazed up before we realized what had happened. We had to put it out in a hurry. It didn't damage anything, but it might take an effort to get the stain out of the carpet."

The servant's eyes widened at his tale. "Why did you not call for help?"

"There was no time," Wynn replied. "We weren't ever in any

danger. It was such a little mass of coals, we put them out pretty quick. But I'm sure you know how a little soot can create a huge mess."

The servant nodded. "One time, a squirrel came down the chimney in the kitchens and ran all over the place before we managed to capture it and put it back outside. Such a little thing, but it tracked soot everywhere! We were cleaning for sennights. None of you were hurt, then?" she asked.

"No," Dalmir assured her.

"Good," she said. "And you kept your clothes clean. Are you ready for dinner then? I'll get Indie to help me clean while you dine with the master and mistress."

She led the way downstairs. As they walked, Dalmir passed a slip of paper to Beren as unobtrusively as possible. Beren concealed the paper in his sleeve. After a few paces, he gasped as if in pain and bent over. The servant stared at him in concern.

"It's nothing," Beren assured her, "just a pebble in my boot."

"We can wait if you want to take care of that."

"Thank you," Beren replied.

The big Telsuman sat down in the middle of the hall and removed his boots. Wynn stared at him, wondering if his friend had lost his senses. Dalmir nudged him with an elbow as he turned to the servant and began asking intelligent and detailed questions about the paintings hanging in this part of the castle. Though he was not sure what was going on, Wynn was not stupid. He glanced down and saw that Beren was holding a piece of paper in his hand. Wynn stepped between the servant and Beren, so that she could not see what he was doing.

"Need any help?" Wynn asked, bending over Beren's shoulder.

"Don't think so," Beren replied, passing the paper over his shoulder to Wynn. He shoved his boot back on and stood up, pacing back and forth to give Wynn a chance to read the note, under the pretense of trying to determine if he had removed the offending object from his shoe.

Wynn glanced down at the piece of paper in his hand.

Be ready to move on my mark. As soon as dinner is concluded, Beren must come up with a reason to get us outside in the main courtyard. Marik will be waiting there with his airship.

"Thank you," Beren said. "I do believe the problem has been removed. I beg your pardon for the delay."

"No apology is necessary," the girl replied. "The master commanded you to be given every courtesy."

Sitting at the massive table, Wynn was so nervous he could barely focus on what he was eating, much less keep up with the veiled politics being discussed between Ericole and Beren, with Dalmir chiming in upon occasion. On the whole, Wynn spent the entire meal battling his own racing heart and squelching his desire to fidget, hoping his face did not give away any of the strain he was feeling. The meal was interminable. Platter after platter passed in front of him, holding courses of the finest food he had ever seen, followed by the most delectable desserts imaginable, but Wynn tasted none of it. He wished he knew the actual plan. His fingers ached to twitch, to drum against the table or chair, but he knew their hosts might view it as a signal, so he sat on one hand and ate with the other. The rhythm he wished to tap pounded in his head, demanding to be let out.

At length, as the food dwindled, Beren leaned back in his chair, wiped his mouth with a napkin, and eyed Niveya. "How much?"

Niveya blinked. "How much what?"

"How much do you want for the ransom?"

Niveya's lips parted slightly, his eyes widening. "Ransom?"

"How much will it take for you to let us go?"

Ericole spread his arms wide. "Lord Adelfried, I believe you have mistaken my intentions. Ransom? Never! I merely wish to see you returned home safe after this trying ordeal. But if your father wishes to show gratitude for the men, the use of my airship, and the time it will take to escort you to the Academy... well then, so be it!"

"I am sure he will be most grateful," Beren replied.

Niveya's smile showed white teeth. "You must be anxious to be on your way, but I must beg your indulgence for a few more days. Never fear! We shall get you to your Academy before the first classes begin."

Beren growled. "May I have your word on that?"

"But of course."

"In the tradition of my people, will you shake hands at the gates of your home and make this promise to me?"

Ericole spread his hands magnanimously. "Easily done," he said.

Beren stood. "Now?"

Ericole eyed him, his pleasant expression fixed in place. "Very well." He pushed his chair back and stood. "What else is required for this custom?"

"All parties involved must be present," Beren said.

Aubri put a hand on her husband's arm, concern in her piercing eyes, but Ericole did not seem to notice. Instead, he stood and took her hand, helping her rise as well.

"My dear, we must be good hosts," Ericole said. "Come, I shall acquiesce to your request. Soon, you will be safe in your Academy and wondering why you were so eager to leave my hospitality for such arduous studies as will be demanded of you there." He let out an ingratiating chuckle and led the way with confident strides. The others trailed after him.

They strode through the massive front doors and down the path to the front gate. The night waited, dark and still. Thick clouds obscured both moon and stars. Wynn's heart careened against his ribs, pounding the word "freedom" with every step they took.

They reached the front archway and Ericole directed the guards there to open the gates. Together, he and Beren stood beneath the arch and solemnly shook hands. Ericole stepped back, his lips parting as if to speak.

Whatever he had been about to say got lost in the sudden

wind that swept across the lawn as an airship materialized above them. The *Valdeun Hawk* hovered in the air over their heads. Ropes descended from the vessel and six figures slid down them to the ground. The new arrivals stood behind Dalmir, swords ringing as they were swept out of their sheaths. Ericole's smile did not fade as Wynn had expected it to. Instead, the head of the Niveya family raised a hand, his face masked in pleasant amusement.

"Did you think it would be so easy?" he asked. "What, exactly, was your plan?"

As it had the night before, the entire estate blazed with sudden light. Fires flared to life from every direction. From inside, Wynn had been unable to appreciate the effect. Now, standing outside, he realized that the sudden flames made it appear that the entire palace was on fire. Silhouetted behind the numerous bonfires, he could see archers, their bows drawn and ready to shoot anything that moved.

Beren moved faster than Wynn had ever seen. In one fluid motion, he had an arm wrapped around Ericole's neck and held a gleaming knife to the man's neck.

"If your archers shoot a single arrow, I slit your throat," Beren growled.

"Ericole." Aubri's voice was low and held a warning.

"My death doesn't buy your freedom," Ericole replied, silencing his wife with a glance. "Ettore, my son, is ready to take my place as head of the Niveya family. My archers can take your airship down with flaming arrows. At best, you are recaptured, at worst you die here tonight. I will risk death for the good of my family; are you willing to risk the same?"

Beren hesitated. Wynn felt as if he might snap in two from the strain. His heart pounded, and he resisted the urge to wipe his sweaty palms on his pants. The men who had landed in the courtyard behind them were statues, their swords raised but their attitude as that of men awaiting orders.

"Enough." Dalmir's quiet voice filled Wynn's ears like the roar of a late summer thunderstorm.

Dalmir raised a hand and snapped his fingers. The fires all over the fortress went out as though suddenly doused by great buckets of water. The palace was plunged beneath an unexpected blanket of blackness. Wynn blinked, his eyes having a hard time adjusting to the sudden dark.

A soft but steady blue glow emanated from Dalmir's palm. He voiced a command and there was a sound like that of a chain breaking. A woman—Wynn was certain it was Aubri Niveya—gasped. Something small flew through the air and came to rest in Dalmir's open hand. In the starlight, Wynn thought he glimpsed a sparkle of lavender, and then Dalmir clasped his hand around both objects. The halo of blue gleamed around Dalmir, however, and grew until the courtyard was once again bathed in light.

Ericole, now clearly visible, stared in disbelief. He sagged, and Wynn thought that if Beren let go his hold around the man's neck, he might fall to the ground.

"I don't believe it," Aubri whispered, her voice reverent.

"I did not expect you would," Dalmir replied. His normal tone and volume were strident in the hushed stillness of the night. "And yet, you must. If you value your lives, you will let us go in peace."

Ericole regained a bit of his composure. "My archers are still ready to fire on my command," he blustered.

"Do you honestly think their arrows could damage me?"

Wynn gaped at the old man, certain he was bluffing. Dalmir's eyes, however, were clear and steady. Power and authority shrouded him. Ancient wisdom filled his eyes. As he studied the man, Wynn realized that he truly believed that no arrow would touch anything Dalmir did not want it to hit. Glancing at their captor, he saw Ericole wavering. The Dalmir who stood in the snow, bathed in the light of a tiny moon, made impossibility seem quite reasonable.

Ericole gave a slow, thoughtful nod. "Very well."

Beren made a guttural noise deep in his throat. "Can we trust him, Dalmir?"

Dalmir gazed into Ericole's eyes until the other flinched and lowered his face.

"Yes, Berenger, I believe we can, at least for now," Dalmir replied.

Beren loosened his hold on Ericole's throat and the head of the Niveya family stumbled away to stand next to his wife. Aubri stood cool and unflinching. Her chin up and cloak billowing out behind her, she appeared like a vision out of a fairy tale. She held the fingertips of one hand to her throat.

"You have made an enemy this day," she snarled, her voice icier than the frigid air. "We were prepared to be reasonable. I will make sure you regret your actions here."

Dalmir's expression shifted in a way Wynn knew he would never be able to describe or understand. It was like a great sorrow, mingled with a burning anger.

"Dear woman"—Dalmir's whisper filled the night,—"I regret so very much. Nothing you could add to that burden would even be worth my notice."

Aubri's cheeks flushed red with fury, but Dalmir neither seemed to care nor notice. Instead, he made a slight gesture with his hand.

Wynn nearly shouted in alarm and surprise. He, Beren, Dalmir, and the six men who had descended from the airship all rose into the sky, carried upwards by invisible hands. Ericole and Aubri watched them ascend, shock etched on their faces. Wynn wanted to shout with laughter, but the absolute terror he was experiencing as he flew unaided into the sky prevented it.

42

When his friends were all safely standing on the deck of the airship, Grayden ran to them with a shout of relief. Joyous laughter filled the air as the airship rose into the darkness and sped away, leaving the Niveyan stronghold far behind them. The hidden jewel of the Randeau mountain range dwindled swiftly to a mere speck in the distance as the *Valdeun Hawk* slipped gracefully through the night.

Marik barked orders, forestalling the jubilant reunion. His grim face reminded them all that they were not safe yet. There were tasks for everyone as they sailed through the sky and wove through the mountains. After several hours, they spotted a large lake that Marik deemed a good place to land for the night.

As soon as they had settled onto the water and furled the wings and sails, Marik bade everyone get some rest.

"We'll assess what damage we've taken in the morning, and then head on towards the Academy to drop off our passengers," he said.

Grayden wanted to talk to his friends. He desperately wanted to know how Dalmir had survived his fall from the airship, and what had happened to Wynn and Beren after their capture. However, his exhaustion threatened to overwhelm him, and he could see the fatigue in his friends' eyes as well. The conversations could wait until morning. He dropped into his hammock and fell instantly into a deep sleep.

Morning dawned, crisp and frosty. Grayden stamped his feet and rubbed his hands together as he made his way up to the deck. A table laid out with crackers, nuts, and dried fruit awaited them, all of which Grayden fell upon gratefully. Raisa and Oleck were already eating. The other crew members were completing tasks around the deck. Shaesta was conspicuously absent, but Grayden did not dwell too long on that bit of information. A moment later, his friends joined him. As they ate the simple but welcome rations, Marik strode up to them.

"Well, she'll fly," he announced grimly. "But she's going to need repairs when we get there."

"Where are we going to get repairs in Ondoura, Captain?" Oleck grumbled. "We don't know anyone in that region, and sure enough you know questions are going to be asked."

Marik rubbed a hand across the back of his neck. "I don't see what choice we have, Oleck."

"We could turn around and head to one of our hideouts," Oleck suggested.

"Oleck!" Raisa turned disapproving eyes on her comrade.

"I promised these lads safe passage to their destination," Marik replied steadily. "Besides, I'm not sure if the *Hawk* will make it any farther than the Academy. Even getting that far could be tricky."

"I have contacts in Thel," Beren spoke up unexpectedly. "It's a small city, a league or two south of the Academy. I can find you someone to repair your vessel. There will be no questions asked if I vouch for you."

Marik stared at the floorboards beneath his feet. "If I had known you were the real merchandise, I never would have taken the job," he said. "I don't take hostages or deal in kidnapping."

Beren dropped his chin a fraction of an inch. "I believe you. Also, I know you rescued us at great personal risk to yourself and your ship. For that, I thank you. Niveya acted like he might negotiate a ransom, but he might just as easily have decided to have me killed."

Marik acknowledged this with a somber nod, then turned to his crew that was now assembling. "We head for the Academy as soon as the *Hawk* is ready to fly. We'll be making repairs in Thel."

The bustle of activity that ensued took Grayden's breath away. He and his friends did not appear to be needed at present, so they retired below deck, where it was warmer. Grayden was extremely curious about what had happened to Beren and Wynn after their capture—as well as what had happened to Dalmir after he fell from the ship—and plied them with dozens of questions.

"When you went over the side, I thought you had died," Grayden admitted.

Dalmir's eyes crinkled at the corners. "I apologize for any anxiety that caused you. Marik and I had discussed such an option, but he wished to use it as a last resort and try his plan first."

"Did you know it wouldn't work? Is that why you sent Mouse to steal cynders?" Grayden asked.

"He told you that, did he?"

"I asked how we were still flying with you gone over the side."

"Ah, smart lad." Dalmir nodded. "Yes. Our young pickpocket did not like me giving him orders, but I convinced him of the prudence of having a back-up plan."

"And what about the two of you?" Grayden asked, turning his attention to Wynn and Beren.

"You had all the excitement," Beren rumbled. "We just kept having meals with our captors that were constantly being interrupted."

Wynn laughed. "Beren is being modest. You should have seen him staring down Shaesta as if he thought our food might be poisoned!"

"That reminds me," Dalmir said, "where is Shaesta?"

Wynn and Beren exchanged a puzzled glance.

"Marik locked her up before we settled over the Niveyan front lawn," Grayden replied. "I haven't seen her since yesterday evening."

"Shaesta is back on the *Hawk*?" Wynn asked.

"Here?" Beren demanded.

"We sort of ran into her after we infiltrated the fortress to find out which part of the palace you were being held in," Grayden explained. "She recognized me, so we had to bring her with us."

"She has been most helpful," Dalmir added.

"But she's a traitor," Beren growled.

"She had little choice," Dalmir replied. "Even her 'capture' may have put her family in danger."

"Well, just so long as Marik keeps her locked up and doesn't trust her," Wynn muttered.

"I have one question," Beren said. "Dalmir, why did you steal Aubri Niveya's necklace?"

Grayden looked up in surprise. "What?"

"She was wearing a strange gem," Beren said. "Dalmir asked her about it, and then during the rescue when he was putting out the fires and causing us to fly, he took the jewel from her necklace. I was just curious why."

"It is a long story," Dalmir said. "Suffice to say that I did not steal the jewel so much as I reclaimed it. I am its rightful owner. As to why I wished its return, that is my own business."

The three young men shared curious glances with each other, but Dalmir did not seem inclined to say any more. A few minutes later, Raisa tapped on their door.

"We're about to lift off, and we could use your help now."

They followed her back onto the deck. The sun was out, sparkling on the water and the thin layer of snow on the shores and warming the air.

"We're a day's flight from the Academy," Raisa informed them. "We should be there by the evening meal."

"With any luck, you'll beat your comrades to your destination," Oleck said, coming up behind them with a wide grin.

Wynn and Beren looked at him in confusion until Grayden explained what Raisa had told him about where the pirates had forced their fellow students to disembark. Oleck nodded, listening in.

"Aye, Captain Marik is more than he seems on the surface. Now, if you lads are able, there are a few tasks you can help me with. Dalmir, Marik would like to request your presence on the steering deck. The *Hawk* is holding together, but I think Cap'n would feel better if you were up there with him."

"Of course," Dalmir replied.

As they worked alongside Oleck for the rest of the day, a strange nervous sensation grew in the pit of Grayden's stomach. At first he thought they were in danger yet again, but eventually he recognized the feeling for what it was. They were nearing the Academy at last. Their voyage had taken a few unexpected detours, but they were finally about to reach their destination. Despite all that had happened, the peril he had encountered and the dangerous situations he had found himself in during the past sennight, Grayden found that he was still apprehensive about all that the Academy held for him. He chuckled to himself ruefully. After battling airship pirates, rescuing his friends from kidnappers, and witnessing real magic, how was it possible he was still worried about classes and the instructors he would have upon reaching the Academy?

43

Marik held true to his word. The *Valdeun Hawk* settled down on a decorative pond just behind the main Academy building before the sun disappeared beneath the horizon on the last day of Felling, the last day of the year. Here, the leaves had only begun to turn yellow or pale red at the edges, unlike the full bursts of gold and scarlet back home. Tomorrow, the new year would begin and a new moon would shine down on the lunat of Chanjar. They had arrived exactly in time for the beginning of the Academy's courses. Grayden stared at the extensive structure over the side of the airship and his breath caught as if he could not get quite enough air into his lungs.

Dalmir stood next to him, also looking down at their destination. Grayden grinned at him. It had been a far more arduous journey than they had imagined, but at last they had arrived. As his eyes lit on Dalmir's face, the excited words he had been about to speak died on his lips. The man's face had turned gray and haggard. Suddenly he seemed old, older even than he had looked the day Grayden had entered his tower. There were vast wells of sadness in the man's eyes as he looked down at the Academy.

"Dalmir?" Grayden asked hesitantly. "What is it?"

Dalmir heaved a sigh. "Nothing. It's nothing. Well, you are here at last."

The older man turned from the railing and strode purposefully away without another word. Grayden watched him go, mystified. Before he could decide whether to run after his traveling companion, Beren and Wynn jostled up next to him and pointed at the building, their voices filling his ears with stories and speculations. He joined his friends in their cheerful banter and wondered what the next days would hold for each of them.

Quite a crowd had gathered on the water's edge to see what was happening. Marik helped Grayden and his friends into the little boat that he used for such purposes, and then he clambered in himself and rowed them the short distance to the shore.

A severe-faced, authoritative looking man with graying hair strode forward to meet them as they stepped out of the boat. He carried an enormous sword on his back, and though he was no taller than Grayden, he was easily half again as broad in the shoulders as Beren.

"What is this? Who are y—" the man demanded, then he took a step back, his gray eyes widening in shock. "Beren?"

"Headmaster Freidzen." Beren's face split into a wide grin.

The imposing man before them stared in wide-eyed astonishment and then stepped forward and engulfed Beren in an enormous hug. After a long moment, he pushed Beren away and held him at arm's length, while the others stood by and watched in amazement as his entire demeanor changed from formidable to friendly in an eye-blink.

"Let me look at you, boy," he nearly shouted. "You've grown since I saw you last."

"Headmaster Freidzen is my uncle on my mother's side," Beren explained quietly to his friends. "Uncle Freid, these are my friends: Grayden, Wynn, Dalmir, and Captain Marik."

"Pleased to meet you." He looked at Grayden and Wynn with a light of recognition in his eyes. "From Dalsea, isn't it? I read your names on the roster for this year—I'm paying special attention to the students in my nephew's classes. Though it is my job every year, I do have a slightly more intense interest in this year's class." He turned his attention back to Beren. "But why are you arriving in such an unconventional manner? Your father said you were to arrive on the *Crimson Eagle*. I must confess, we are all getting rather anxious. The *Eagle* is two days overdue."

"It is a long story, Uncle," Beren replied. "I was on the *Eagle* and had every intention of arriving in Edoran on it. I am afraid I must tell you that the other students will not be arriving for another few days. Pirates attacked us, and I am afraid the *Crimson Eagle* did not survive."

Headmaster Freidzen's expression grew concerned. "Was anyone hurt?"

"Thankfully, nobody was on board the *Eagle* when it went down," Beren said quickly. "As I said, it is a long story, and it was a long journey. Perhaps we can tell it once we've gotten settled?"

"Room assignments have been finalized, but there is always a little rearranging that occurs on enrollment day. And since you three are the first to arrive, I will see what I can do to align your schedules." He turned his attention away from Beren and addressed Dalmir and Marik. "And what can I do for the two of you? I am guessing you both had parts to play in the safe return of my nephew."

Marik raised a hand, forestalling any further words. "I simply need to make a few repairs on my airship and then I will be on my way. Your nephew said he might have a contact nearby who might help with that."

To Grayden, the captain seemed to be in a hurry. He wore a strained expression, probably wondering when it would come to light that he was one of the pirates in Beren's "long story."

"And all I desire is to be allowed to visit your library," Dalmir added. "I have been told it is open to the public."

"Certainly, certainly." The headmaster nodded vigorously to Dalmir. He glanced at Marik, and a flicker of suspicion flitted through his expression. "I believe I know the person Beren was referring to, Captain Marik. You may remain here. I will send word for him to come. I will also send word to Beren's father to inform him of all that has transpired." The words held a hint of a threat, and Marik took a tiny step back.

Grayden eyed the headmaster with new respect. How much of the story did he already guess?

Freidzen turned back to Dalmir. "The library is most certainly open to the public. We rarely have anyone interested in perusing its contents. The librarians will be most pleased to help you find whatever information you are looking for."

Something shimmered in Dalmir's eyes as he bowed his head. "My most heartfelt thanks."

Marik returned to his airship while the rest of them followed the headmaster into the Academy. It was every bit as austere on the inside as it looked from the outside. The stone block walls boasted no decoration. Narrow windows lined the walls, numerous enough to let in plenty of light. Lanterns hung between windows, and Grayden assumed they were lit at dusk. After the splendor and magnificence of the Niveyan Stronghold, the Academy was drab in comparison. And yet, it held an air of comfort that Grayden could not quite express. Like the headmaster himself, the Academy appeared intimidating and overwhelming at first. But he had a feeling that as he got to know these halls and doorways and rooms over the next few years, they would grow to feel like home.

Dinner was simple fare, though to Grayden it was a veritable feast after the rations aboard the airship. Beren and Wynn were less impressed, having recently dined on the finest delicacies Ericole Niveya had to offer.

After dinner, Headmaster Freidzen bade one of the older students to lead the three young men to the room where they would be spending the next ten lunats.

"I am extremely curious to hear your story," he told them, "but I can see that the three of you are about to fall asleep at the table. Beren, you can tell your tale tomorrow."

"My thanks, Uncle," Beren yawned.

They followed the older student down several passageways, making turns that muddled Grayden's already tired head. He wondered if he would ever be able to traverse these halls without getting hopelessly lost. As he pondered this, they came to a stop before a door. It had a strange glyph on it like a sigil from an ancient and forgotten language.

Their guide pushed the door open. "The rooms aren't much to look at, but most students decorate a little with odds and ends they pick up on Market Days—which are once every third sennight. You'll get a tour of the Academy in a few days, before classes begin. Size of the room you're in, looks like you'll have another roommate in a day or so. I know this place can seem overwhelming at first, and you're going to spend the next few days wondering how you'll ever remember everything you need to remember, but you'll get used to it quickly, I promise. Pretty soon, you'll wonder how you ever thought this place was confusing." Their guide's brown eyes twinkled cheerfully. "My name's Owen. I'm a fourth year, and my room is just down the hall. If you have questions, just ask. Us older students are supposed to look out for you youngers."

They expressed their thanks and entered the room. The walls were the same bare, gray stone as the rest of the building. The room held a table, four wooden chairs, four beds, and one closet.

"Well." Wynn broke the silence. "We made it."

Grayden and Beren both burst out laughing. Wynn's brow furrowed.

"What?" he asked. "What's so funny? I don't get it."

But neither Grayden nor Beren could speak through their laughter. Every word he said made them laugh harder. Grayden tried to find the breath to tell Wynn that he did not even know *why* he was laughing, but before he calmed down enough to do so, Wynn threw him a dirty look and settled into the bed under the window.

"Fine," he grumped. "Don't explain the joke. Goodnight."

Still chuckling, Grayden followed suit, pulling off his boots and clambering into one of the empty beds. He could not explain to Wynn that nothing was funny. The relief at finally being where they had set out to be had caught up to him, and laughing was the only way to express it. As he pulled up the blanket and settled his head on the pillow, Grayden's thoughts turned towards home. He pictured his parents and Seren sitting around the fire, his father reading one of their favorite stories out loud. His mother would be knitting, perhaps a new dishrag. Seren would be sitting on the floor playing quietly with her doll. And everyone would be listening intently to the words of the story, told in his father's strong, but gentle voice. Grayden's eyes closed. He drifted off to sleep, clinging to the image of his family with a smile on his lips and an ache in his heart.

44

Roald knelt before the empty throne, waiting to hear what his punishment was to be. The silence stretched unbearably. A lesser man would have crumpled under the weight of those silent minutes, but the best warriors in the world had trained Roald. Descended from a long line of Kotai warriors, their staunch discipline pounded in his blood and strengthened him with steel in his bones. He could remain in this position for hours and never flinch or yawn or shift his weight even a fraction of an inch.

"You say that the unmarked ship landed outside the Niveyan Stronghold," Lord Uun's voice was barely a whisper, and yet it resounded throughout the stone hall.

"Yes, my lord. When we saw where they were taking young Adelfried, we headed straight to Melar to bring the news of it to you." Roald risked raising his eyes.

Lord Uun's hands clenched and unclenched reflexively. An angry light burned deep in his sapphire eyes, belying his impassive expression. Roald lowered his gaze quickly, despair filling his soul. His failure threatened to drown him in shame, and terror gnawed at the edges of his consciousness; Lord Uun had executed men for far less. Many in the Igyeum whispered that the Ar'Molon held the true power of the throne, though surely he did not hold more power than Ar'Mol Eyvind? Some rumors even accused the man of being the catalyst for the old Ar'Mol's rise to power over all the other tribal chieftains, though others dismissed this theory as ridiculous.

But the Kotai knew the truths behind the whispers. As the Ar'Molon's elite soldiers, they knew that Lord Uun did indeed hold the Igyeum in his thrall, that he was far more than he appeared, and far older. The Kotai had served Lord Uun across centuries, their ranks passed down from father to son, their secrets kept in blood.

"Rise, Lord Roald."

Here it came. Roald tensed, ready for the pronouncement of judgment that would seal his fate. He would not beg for himself, though he hoped to spare his men from being included in his punishment. Roald rose slowly, obediently; he would not tremble. He walked in the way of warriors and served an Ar'Molon. Lord Uun had bestowed the rank of De'Anan upon him, a rank of nobility given to a lowly Deymash who had risen through the ranks against all odds. Pride flooded through Roald and he held his head high, ready to accept his punishment. He had risen to the highest rank possible. That he was an assassin was no dishonor. It merely indicated how well he had inscribed the path of a warrior upon his heart.

"The Ar'Mol will be most displeased to learn this news." Lord Uun spoke, as if to himself. His soft voice seared the air. He stared over Roald's head, his expression calculating. "It would not do to leave such disloyalty unpunished. But what would be appropriate?"

Roald felt his heart beat faster. He forced his expression to remain impassive. He would take whatever punishment Lord Uun dealt him, even death. The Ar'Molon continued to mutter to himself, his voice lowering so that Roald could not hear the words clearly. This was the most excruciating moment of his life. He had never imagined how agonizing it could be to have his life and well-being so firmly held in another man's hands. Was this how his own victims often felt, just before he killed them? But no, Roald's victims never even knew he was there until the sudden instant of death came. He did not cause them to linger in the agony of waiting, of knowing their fate had come. Even Roald's warrior stoicism shuddered and cracked, threatening to shatter around him. What if Lord Uun decided not to kill him, but to keep him alive in a state of constant torment? What if he went after Roald's men? Thankfully, Roald himself possessed no family or attachments other than his men, but he could not bear the idea that they might suffer for his failure.

A wicked smile spread across Uun's face and he looked up at Roald as if suddenly remembering that he was still standing there. This was it; Roald steeled himself against whatever verdict Lord Uun decided upon.

"You... Roald, is it?"

Roald tried three times before his voice scraped out from between his dry lips. "Yes, sir."

"I have another assignment for you."

Roald tried to hide his astonishment. "Another assignment, my lord?"

"We must punish those who have thwarted the Ar'Mol's plans, don't you agree?"

Roald hesitated, unsure whether he was signing his own punishment decree. "Of course," he said carefully.

"Then I need you and your crew to do something for me. You will deliver a message, as it were, that we are not to be crossed. Do you understand?"

"I am not sure, my lord." Bewilderment at his unexpected good fortune flooded through Roald, making it hard to think.

"Then I will explain it to you." Lord Uun held out an arm. "Come, and I will give you the details of your new assignment over a glass of the Ar'Mol's wine. Ericole Niveya has grown far too bold. He presumes too much on our good nature and we must remedy his arrogance."

"Of course, my lord."

Hardly daring to breathe, to believe, Roald stepped forward. He expected at any minute to find his head being detached from his shoulders, but the death strike never came. Uun led him to a small but lavishly decorated sitting room and bade him sit on a plushly cushioned chair. As Roald sat with Uun and sipped the finest wine he had ever been privileged to taste, the Ar'Mol's advisor explained the next mission that Roald and his team would undertake.

45

Dalmir ran his fingers over the paper. This was a recently scribed document and did not have the same ancient, brittle feel of the older parchment scrolls. That did not make it any less of a wonder. It staggered him to know that the people of Telmondir had constructed this place and filled it with knowledge in the midst of a world living in the shadow of imminent invasion. Entranced, Dalmir spent days holed up in the precious room, marveling at the knowledge preserved within.

This library was nothing like that other, ethereal place he once visited. This place was gloomy and tiny in comparison. There were no sculpted columns or stained glass. No marbled walls or endless passages that echoed with the quiet voices of others lost in study and the pursuit of knowledge. No grove of fruit trees adorned its yards. This library did not even come close to comparing with that other place. Despite the drab exterior, however, the books and scrolls were every bit as beautiful and precious, and the words contained within made his heart soar with hope. Dalmir clutched at them like a drowning man clings to a passing piece of driftwood.

He hunted through the recent recorded histories, amazed at just how much he had missed. His reading confirmed the hints gleaned in the past sennights' traveling from Dalsea that all was not well. He lingered over the newer books, drinking in their words and falling under their spell. However, at long last, he reluctantly admitted that as tempting as it might be to remain in this world of knowledge forever, he could only learn so much from books.

When Dalmir emerged from the library, he discovered that nearly three sennights had passed. He blinked in the brightness outside. Twenty-one days flown by, and he was no closer to the answers he sought. The final Academy students had arrived, five days late, but safely as promised. Grayden, Wynn, and Beren were ensconced in their studies and the daily routine of their orientation. They were happy to speak with Dalmir, but their minds were preoccupied by all that they were learning. He bade them farewell and went to thank the headmaster for allowing him time in the library.

"You are most welcome," Freidzen assured him. "And where are you off to now?"

"There are many things I need to do," Dalmir replied. "Things I need to check on, and people I need to speak with." He paused, staring out the window. "I would have thought Marik and his crew would have left by now," he said, half to himself.

"They are leaving later today," the headmaster said, his voice grim. He had finally learned the entire story from Beren and it was plain from his expression that the pirate crew was no longer high in his estimation. "The repairman finished just this morning."

"Thank you," Dalmir said again, shaking the man's hand. "You take care of those young men I arrived with."

"That I will."

Dalmir strode across the lawn and down to the pond. When he reached the shore, he shouted across the water, "Captain Marik! Ahoy the airship!"

Marik leaned over the side of the airship and squinted. "Dalmir? What do you need?"

"Permission to come aboard, Captain. I have a proposition for you."

Marik's expression was unreadable at this distance, but after a slight pause he shouted, "I'll be right there."

Long minutes proceeded by as Marik got into the boat and rowed to the shore. "You mentioned a proposition?"

"I was wondering if you might be interested in a paying passenger?"

Marik closed one eye and cocked his head to the side. "I have my own business to be about, and I've already been away from it for too long."

Dalmir pulled out a small sack and held it out towards Marik. "I need passage. I'm willing to pay double what is in that pouch if you will take me on as your client."

Marik poured a few of the coins into his hand. His eyes widened and his mouth opened slightly as he stared at the wealth he was suddenly holding. Every coin was a rune. However, Marik still hesitated, fingering the golden coins stamped with the triangular symbol of Telmondir. "Where do you wish to go?"

"There are many places I need to visit," Dalmir replied. "I have interests in all the corners of the world."

Marik put the coins back and hefted the small purse.

"That purse now, and the other when I depart your airship, of course," Dalmir added. "Possibly more, if my travels take longer than expected."

"This... this is—"

"More than you can refuse, I expect."

Marik blinked. "Where do you want to go first?"

"I need to get to the remains of the Tower of Ondeou."

Marik tossed the purse back to Dalmir. "Find another airship."

It was Dalmir's turn to be surprised. "What is the matter?"

"That area is cursed. Nobody goes there. Surely you know the stories. People who enter those woods never come back out. It's a death trap."

"I have not heard the stories," Dalmir replied softly. "What if I can guarantee your safety, along with the safety of your crew and airship, so long as you are with me?"

Dalmir could see the pirate wavering. His eyes remained fixed on the bag of runes. Dalmir knew how hard it would be for Marik to turn his back on such an opportunity.

Marik heaved a deep sigh. "My crew would mutiny if they found out I walked away from such an offer. Even Mouse might doubt my sanity." He paused. "Very well. When do you want to leave?"

"I am ready this moment."

"Excellent. We were just getting ready to depart. We've nearly overstayed our welcome as it is."

THE FLIGHT from the Academy to the heart of the continent took three days. It was an uneventful flight, graced by pleasant weather. They caught sight of the top of the tower—poking up from the center of the Whispering Wood that covered most of Ondeou—a full day before they even got close to it. However, as they drew near the pinnacle on the morning of the fourth day, Dalmir asked Marik if they could descend.

"I thought you wanted to go to the Tower," Marik replied.

"I'll throw in a few extra coins if that's what you need," Dalmir snapped. "I want to check the wall first. It may take awhile, but when I get back, we will proceed to the Tower."

Marik shrugged. "Didn't know there was a wall, other than the one that surrounds the entire Wood. I spotted a clearing off to starboard. I can let you down there."

Dalmir accepted with a terse nod. Once on solid ground, he marched into the forest towards the wall he had built so many long years ago. Constructed of deep gray, almost black, shiny rocks that were streaked with white and silver, years of exposure to the elements had done their best to scratch the impassive surface. The wall itself stood fully thirty feet tall and surrounded the massive tower and all its foot-buildings, forbidding entrance to any who might take it into their heads to disturb the area. Trees grew up around the wall, obscuring it from view above, and vines now wound their way up and over its entire length, but the stones themselves appeared untouched. Dalmir smiled despite himself. He had always been fairly good at making things to pass the test of time. Running a hand across the stones, he followed them. He remembered setting the orbs in the wall itself, believing them to be safe. Seeing one of them in a necklace around Aubri Niveya's neck had disturbed him greatly.

It took him fully half the day to complete his hike. The farther he progressed, the more troubled he became. After circuiting the entire perimeter, he ascended the rope ladder back onto the airship, his expression grim. Although the structure remained mostly intact, there were several broken sections like doorways in its circumference. All five of the orbs had vanished. None of them remained in their places, though he had searched thoroughly and dug into the forest floor and through areas where the stones had fallen into rubble. Besides the two he now kept in his possession, Dalmir had no idea where the remaining five might be.

As he clambered onto the deck of the airship, Oleck greeted him with a wide grin. "We were certain something down there had eaten you," he said. "Glad to see we were wrong. I'll get the captain."

Oleck returned a few moments later with Marik striding after him. The pirate eyed Dalmir's dirt-stained, tattered robes speculatively. "I'm guessing you'll be wanting to enter the Tower now."

Dalmir glanced at the horizon. "Yes. But we should wait until morning. Some things are better left until daylight returns."

Early the next morning, Marik maneuvered the airship toward the tower. The trees thinned on the inside of the wall, and the pirate lowered the *Hawk* much closer to the ground. As he was about to hop over the railing, Dalmir felt Marik's hand on his shoulder.

"Do you need help down there?"

Dalmir had never been so astonished. He stared at the pirate. "I thought you had no desire to even fly over this place."

"Perhaps I deem it wise to protect my investment. You are paying me rather a lot of money if we get out of here alive."

Dalmir chuckled. "If whatever is inside can harm me, you certainly don't stand a chance."

"I know."

Dalmir was on the verge of brushing aside the offer. Taking Marik inside the Tower would only be a hindrance to him. However, an expression of raw pain in the man's eyes made him pause. Something in Marik's past had changed the course of his life; whatever it was had seared him straight through to his soul. Whatever Marik had been, whatever road he had been on, something had altered his course severely, turned him hard and bitter, and calloused his heart. But Dalmir could see glimmers of the man he had been before. Perhaps remnants of nobility within Marik remained intact. Dalmir could understand that sort of pain, the kind that numbed a person to their very soul; he had experienced it himself. The pirate walked a fine line between honor and villainy, but perhaps he could be tipped to the better side with a little care. And something that quailed deep within Dalmir's own heart at the thought of entering the Tower alone made him nod.

"You are most welcome to join me, so long as you understand the risks."

46

Marik followed Dalmir down the ladder, landing silently on the springy earth. Vines trailed about the place, tendrils of green dragging apart the stones. The pirate captain gazed up at the tower. From the ground, the structure appeared far more massive than it had from above. To call this place a tower was to look at a mountain and name it a stone. From the sky, the wide leafy branches of the trees hid what truly rested here. He stood in the remains of what must have once been a massive city. They stood in a courtyard between crumbling cathedrals and enormous buildings whose roofs were caving in. He could see the ruins of fountains, now dry and filled with weeds as tall as a man. The crumbling remnants of the city stretched away as far as he could see in every direction. Despite the vines and undergrowth and the trees that had taken over everything, now that he understood what he gazed upon, Marik realized this must have been a truly great metropolis, once.

"What is this place?" he breathed.

Dalmir glanced sideways at him. "This was Ondeou, the Jewel of Turrim. The city-nation stretched from the Greyklasp Mountains in the north to the Randeau Mountains we just departed, and its borders touched all six of the other nations. It was once the most beautiful city in the world, and by far the largest. People traveled here to study, though none called it home."

"Impossible," Marik whispered, but his eyes told him the truth.

"Come, we must get to the top of the tower before sunset."

Marik was hot and struggling for air by the time they finally made it through the ruined city's remains and stood before the massive doors that led into the Tower. The doors were constructed of amaranth wood and devoid of any decoration, save the rich purple color of the wood itself. A simple black knob hung unadorned and turned easily despite its obvious age. The tower itself soared above them, high into the sky, dwarfing the remains of all the other buildings.

Every line of the structure bespoke strength and military precision. Perhaps the builder had been most concerned with those aspects of character that are oft equated with a soldier, and had little use for anything of the softer or more subtle professions. The building itself was wrought of the same gray stones streaked with white and polished like marble as the wall surrounding it. Despite its enormity and hard lines, the building was, in its own way, quite beautiful.

Silently, they entered the base of the tower and found themselves in an enormous room filled with murky gloom. The air that greeted them in a sudden draft smelled of death. Marik recoiled, and Dalmir looked at him with a knowing glance.

"You may wait here, if you wish."

His voice conveyed that there would be no shame in accepting such an offer, but Marik could not stomach the idea of giving in to fear now. He squared his shoulders.

"If you're going in, I'm going with you."

They entered the great maw. Marik felt as though he was entering the jaws of a terrible beast, but he steeled his resolve to stay by Dalmir's side. The old man and his quest had piqued

Marik's curiosity, and he found himself compelled to be more than just a passive means of transportation. They traversed the length of the great room uncontested. Marik almost expected monsters to leap from every shadow, but their journey remained uneventful.

They finally reached the far side of the room and Marik followed Dalmir through an entryway into a long passage. They wound their way down hall after hall until they finally found themselves at the base of a long, winding staircase. Dalmir pulled a small gem from a pocket inside his robes and held it out. The little stone gleamed blue, lighting the staircase. Marik was relieved that they would not be climbing in the dark. Dalmir glanced at Marik.

"Lead on," Marik urged.

They climbed. Dalmir did not set a quick pace, and Marik fell into the steady rhythm. Step after step, they ascended into the unknown. The repetitive motion became all-consuming. Time ceased to have any meaning. Marik's legs ached. And still they climbed. The stairs continued with no end in sight, winding around in a spiral that went up and up and ever up.

When at last they reached a door at the top of the stairs, Marik's legs were screaming in agony. His muscles felt like they were burning from the inside out. But he ground his teeth together to keep from complaining. In the absence of all conversation and to keep his mind off the burning pain in his legs, he had counted the stairs. Dalmir seemed to have barely noticed the five thousand steps behind them, and Marik envied the man's lack of obvious physical exertion.

Dalmir pushed the door open, and Marik reeled back, stumbling down a step or two before he regained his footing. The stench that wafted out overwhelmed him and brought prickling tears to his dry eyes. Dalmir paused and then stepped through the doorway. Marik took a deep breath and then plunged into the room on the older man's heels. He nearly tripped over something small and smooth. He kicked the object and heard it skitter across the floor.

"Stop," Dalmir commanded, and Marik froze as the old man raised the glittering jewel in his hand. The light grew and illuminated the entire room. As his eyes adjusted to the glow, Marik saw what he was walking on and nearly emptied the contents of his stomach all over the floor. The floor that was covered in human bones.

47

As Dalmir stared at the piles of bones, a great sorrow welled up within him. He could hardly begin to imagine what had happened here. Before he could ponder the question, however, he heard a faint cough.

"Help me," a weak voice rasped.

In a corner nearly obscured by shadows, something moved. Dalmir stepped toward the corner with Marik on his heels. When the light from the gem in his hand touched the pitiful creature that had spoken, something crumbled deep inside him.

Hanging by emaciated wrists from black steel manacles slumped a young girl. She was no more than fourteen years old, just a child. Huge eyes devoid of hope stared at him from a hollow, sunken face. Her dress hung pathetically from her too-bony shoulders. Her breath came in ragged, desperate gasps. Dalmir wept.

So this was how Uun had concealed his escape. He ensnared these poor souls, lured them here, and then substituted their presence for his own. As Dalmir stepped closer, he sensed the power pulsing through the manacles holding the girl in place. His own power stretched toward it, pulled like iron to a magnet. With no power of her own, the manacles would simply drain this child of her life. Dalmir ground his teeth in anger. The manacles were never meant for use on a normal human; he meant them only for Uun. On him, they would not have been painful, merely restrictive: designed to hold him in this tower and deprive him of access to his own power. Dalmir had even allowed his prisoner to move freely around the tower room, which was more than Uun deserved. But on a human, the manacles were simply too powerful.

Uun! Despite all Dalmir's careful, methodical wards, Uun had escaped. But not wholly, not completely. The manacles remained. The bones covering the floor made it horribly clear that Uun was forced to return here every so often, whenever his current sacrifice was ready to expire, so that he could acquire a new locum tenens.

The girl stared up at Dalmir, a silent plea in her eyes. She did not possess the strength to beg for mercy. She was barely breathing. This child would not last another three days. Uun would need to return here at that time. Dalmir could be waiting for him —he could spring the trap and return Uun to his prison. Uun would never expect it. Surprise and greater strength would be on Dalmir's side. As long as the manacles were in place, Uun would not have access to his full power. All Dalmir needed to do was wait and it would all be over. All he had to do was wait... and let the girl die.

A terrible choice stood before him.

He could choose to let this child die. Or he could save her. It would be simple. The power that kept her here was his own, this design of his that should have kept Uun safely imprisoned. He could undo it easily. He could save the girl's life. But if he did that, it would free Uun completely. He would no longer be tied to this place, and he would regain full access to his own power. The balance of the scales would tip once again and balance. Neither would possess an advantage over the other. This chance would never come again.

Marik shuffled his feet, breaking the silence, and the wizard turned to gaze at him. The pirate looked up at him, and Dalmir felt his soul being pierced by a fiery brand. The expression in Marik's eyes said he understood. He did not know the complete story, nor did he fully realize the consequences that would come from whichever action Dalmir took. But in a flash of clarity, Dalmir saw that Marik understood with a modicum of empathy the choice that lay before him now.

With a terrible, thunderous shout, Dalmir held out the softly gleaming blue orb and thrust the shimmering gem into the manacles that held the girl aloft. Light exploded around them with a searing intensity. A hissing, crackling sound filled the room and thrummed its way into their ears, vibrating into the absolute essence of their beings. Then the light dissipated, and the manacles crumbled to dust. Released, the girl stumbled forward and into Marik's arms, where she lay in a dead faint.

Dalmir remained on his knees for a long moment. Then he quietly placed the orb back into its hidden pocket and rose. Marik rose also, holding the child in his arms.

"Will she be all right?" he asked Dalmir.

"I will see to it personally," Dalmir replied.

"Destroying those... things... that held her"—Marik's words came hesitantly—"what fell thing did you loose upon the world?"

Dalmir glanced sideways at the pirate. "Nothing that hasn't been loosed upon it before," he replied steadily. "I defeated it once."

"But it will be harder this time, won't it?"

Dalmir heaved a sigh. "Yes."

"Where would you like to go next?"

"This child needs medical attention," Dalmir replied. "She is our first priority. After that, I still need to travel to a few places; I need to investigate the state of the world. Eventually, I will need to speak to the leaders of Telmondir. But I would like to get a better idea of how Uun creates the cynders. I need more information before I approach the Council."

"I'll take you wherever you need to go."

Dalmir stared, surprised.

"After seeing this"—Marik lifted the child in his arms slightly —"well, there is more than just one monster in this world. And meeting you... I've come to understand that perhaps I cannot fight them all on my own. I know where the cynders were being created. I can take you there after we get this girl to safety."

Something within Dalmir collapsed. "You are a good man, Captain Marik."

Marik grinned lopsidedly. "Don't let my crew know."

Together they returned to the airship, Marik gently carrying the girl in his arms down every stair without complaint. When they were once more aboard the airship, Marik pointed the bow of the *Hawk* towards the west. As they soared after the sun, Dalmir spared a single glance back at the tower poking up through the clouds.

There was much work ahead, Dalmir knew. According to the documents he had read in the library and the overwhelming number of bones in the tower prison, there were over two hundred years of catching up to do since Uun first slipped from his bonds. Yes, there was plenty of work before him. First, he needed to gain the trust of the Telmondir Council. Then he would have to convince them to listen to and follow his plan. There was much he must prepare before he confronted Uun again, and in that time Uun would be working as well.

Despair should have overwhelmed him. The sorrow that had nearly engulfed him for three hundred years should have risen up and paralyzed him. And yet it didn't. Instead, for the first time since his battle with Uun so long ago, Dalmir felt hopeful. Perhaps there was a point to his existence, after all. Perhaps he was being given another chance to ameliorate the great wrong he helped perpetrate so many long years ago. With that hope welling up within his heart, Dalmir smiled. He did not know how things were going to end, but he now knew that even in the midst of the darkest night, there was always a shard of light.

EPILOGUE

A roaring fire blazed merrily in the hearth of the large room. Its light mingled with those of the torches hanging in elaborate, black iron sconces on the walls, and the tall candelabras adorning the massive oak table. A cloth of fine white linen covered the table. Crystal chalices and dishes rimmed with gold punctuated the finery. An expansive feast spread before the guests. Fruit of every variety, an entire pig, large slabs of mutton and beef, and enormous loaves of bread filled the surface of the table, along with various other delicacies and trifles.

Lords and ladies dressed in their finest splendor reclined around the table. They talked and laughed together as they ate the evening meal, lending an air of joviality and friendly conversation to the atmosphere of the lavishly adorned room. And yet an undercurrent of unease rippled beneath the layer of cheer. The smiles stretched a tiny bit too wide, hinting that the laughter was forced. Eyes darted warily, suggesting that the guests did not feel wholly safe in their current location. And a few attendees bore tiny furrows between their brows, a telltale sign that their thoughts had strayed from the lighthearted conversation.

At one end of the table, a man sat regally, enjoying all he surveyed. The young Ar'Mol wore a heavy crown upon his blond head. A scarlet cape billowed around him as he slouched in his chair with a look of bored amusement on thin lips. A young man, perhaps in his mid-thirties, Ar'Mol Eyvind watched his guests with amusement, noting which ones seemed the most anxious, wondering what secrets they attempted to hide from him. He did not engage in conversation with any of his guests but one, a tall, broad-shouldered man seated to his left. None could hear their conversation above the roar, but more than one guest wished to be privy to the contents of their hushed words.

Though the broad-shouldered guest did not sit in the seat of highest importance, nobody could enter the room without noticing him. His air of calm authority made the Ar'Mol look like a child playing at dress-up in his father's clothes. His age was indeterminable: he had brown hair streaked with a distinguished gray, and a smooth, unlined face. Muscular of body, no hunch marred his frame. His light blue eyes moved about the room lazily, but with a sharp alertness that made it clear he noted every detail, every movement, every word. Most of the guests darted guarded glances and fearful, furrowed brows his way, but if he noticed, he hid it completely.

Faint light trickled through the east-facing windows, alerting the guests that morning approached. The party had started the evening before and continued through the night. Nobody wished to draw the Ar'Mol's displeasure by begging permission to leave first.

"My liege." The tall, broad-shouldered man turned to the Ar'Mol. "It grows late, or rather, early, and I am not as young as I once was. I beg your permission to retire."

"Granted, of course," the younger man said, his brown eyes sympathetic. "Forgive us for not seeing how our revelries were wearing upon you, Ar'Molon Uun."

"Thank you, Ar'Mol. You are most gracious." Uun bowed his head and rose from the table. The conversation faltered briefly, and a smirk flickered at the corners of Uun's mouth. He nodded to the guests, not bothering to conceal the mockery in his eyes, and swept out of the room, his luxurious cloak swirling around him.

Uun climbed the stairs to his apartments in the palace, a suite of rooms that were the envy of many who attended the Ar'Mol. Uun felt his mouth curl into a sneer as he thought of how the lackeys all gazed at him with envy and admiration. They believed he lived in luxury, but if they could have only seen his tower—his true home—at the pinnacle of its glory, all the splendor of the Ar'Mol's palace would amount to less than a dirty mud hut in comparison. Uun swept the thought aside with an angry growl as he pushed his door open. At the sound, his personal attendant rose hastily from his place and hovered about, inquiring if Uun needed anything.

"Nothing just now," Uun brushed him off. Natan was useful, but sometimes the man grated on Uun's nerves with his eagerness. "In a few hours, I shall send for one of the girls. I am needed elsewhere and will want a companion for the journey."

"Yes, my lord, yes. If you need me, I will just be out in the hall."

The man left swiftly. Uun's thoughts darkened as he readied himself for bed; several of his strategies had been foiled of late, and he found himself both angry and exhilarated by the sensation of frustration. It had been a long time since he matched his wits against a worthy opponent. Had Dalmir awoken? Did he now see his own peril? Excitement and fear twinged in the pit of his stomach. At long last, his only serious opponent may have noticed his movements. At long last, vengeance lay within his grasp. But failure waited as well, in equal measure. And though he had spent many long years preparing for this conflict, Uun had to admit his disadvantage. Though he had wriggled free from the physical confines of his prison, he remained a prisoner in many ways. He lay down, pulling the warm blanket up to his chin, his thoughts moody and calculating. Losing the cynder refinery had been an unexpected blow, but a good warrior should be able to recover from surprise attacks swiftly. All was not lost. Perhaps it was a sign that the time to act drew nearer than he guessed. He closed his eyes and drifted into a deep slumber.

THE SNAPPING OF THE BONDS, the whirlwind of power, the sudden strength returned to its rightful place surged through him like resounding cymbals crashing together inside his skull. Uun bolted upright in his bed as his full power flooded through him. Pain seared down into the deepest marrow of his bones; strength roared to life within his veins. He stumbled out of his bed, tripping in his haste to get into the open air, fire boiling through his body. Reaching the balcony that overlooked the whole of the palace grounds, he convulsed as the overwhelming deluge of power coursed through his body. Uun gasped, taking in deep, gulping breaths. It was achingly familiar, and yet he had been without it for so long that its sudden presence burned like a terrible blaze as it had so long ago on that first day. He doubled over in anguish. Closing his eyes, Uun let it wash over him. For so long, he had only grasped at the barest trickle of his power, his potential. He had been like a starving man subsisting only on a single bite of food each day, and suddenly an entire feast spread before him. It was overwhelming and horribly painful, but it was also so very sweet.

After a few minutes, the pain subsided, fading to a tiny, lingering flicker. It was not enough. The flood of power had not restored him fully, and he clenched his fists tightly. Curse that Sevalk! Where had he hidden it? Why could he not find it? After all this time...

Uun straightened and stared at the western horizon. The midday sun beat down upon him and he imagined its light glinting off the top of his tower, a point of dark power in an otherwise perfectly azure sky. A cruel smile adorned his lips.

"I knew you could never abide what I had done, brother," he whispered. "So, you have put the world in peril for the sake of a single soul already broken beyond repair." He let out a loud, barking laugh that pierced the serenity of the day. "Dalmir, my brother, you have just made your first mistake."

He savored the taste of the cool morning air. Then he turned and abruptly strode to his door and flung it open.

"Natan!" he bellowed into the hallway.

"Yes, Ar'Molon Uun?" Natan sprang to a standing position instantly.

"The girls I have been collecting—"

"Yes, my lord, I shall bring you one at once, my lord."

"No, no." Uun waved a hand. "You may dispose of them."

"D-dispose of them, my lord?" Natan stared, his face scrunched into a myriad of confused wrinkles that obscured his entire visage.

"Yes. I have no further need of their kind." Uun's eyes took on a faraway gleam. He stared into the hallway, unseeing. "What would you say to that, brother? You saved one, but now many will perish. If only I could let you know all that you have to answer for this day."

Natan made a strange noise, and Uun's eyes focused on him. "What are you doing still standing there? You have your orders."

"Y-yes, Ar'Molon, it shall be as you say, Ar'Molon." Natan's expression of horror melded into a mien of utter panic and he fled down the corridor, away from his master.

Uun watched him go, and a tendril of doubt wound its way through his heart. He had seen no sign of Dalmir at work for many long years. Centuries, even. But was that because Dalmir had disappeared, or was it because he, Uun, had stayed as far away from his realm as possible? His first assumption was that this sudden freedom resulted directly from Dalmir's weak stomach, but what if it signified something more? Uun knew better than to underestimate an opponent. He was, after all, the warrior in the family. His smugness faded. Perhaps Dalmir had known of the way he had contrived to slip loose from his prison, but had merely bided his time until he discovered a new strength, a new source of power. Could such coldness, such calculation, be present in a man he had always scorned for being innocent and naive? Could he take the chance that Dalmir had remained unchanged throughout the long, lonely years?

Uun tapped a finger against his chin. He would have to proceed carefully, very carefully indeed.

ABOUT THE AUTHOR

Jenelle first fell in love with stories through her father's voice reading books aloud each night. A relentless opener-of-doors in hopes of someday finding a passage to Narnia, it was only natural that she soon began making up fantastical realms of her own. Jenelle currently resides in the wintry tundra of Wisconsin — which she maintains is almost as good as Narnia — with her knight-in-shining armor and their four hobbits. When she is not writing, she homeschools said hobbits and helps them along on their daily adventures... which she says makes her a wizard.

ACKNOWLEDGMENTS

This book, y'all.

This series.

It didn't even start out as MINE.

The World of Turrim is something that my husband began creating nearly 17 years ago, shortly after we got married. He came up with the characters of Dalmir and Grayden, the towers, the orbs... and then he asked me if I wanted to write the story for him.

I said, "No."

I was terr-i-fied that I would write the story "wrong." Remember, this was my brand-new husband of just over a year asking me to take these elements that were his brain-child and write a story. How scary of a thing!

But he kept asking. And eventually, after I had finally explained why I didn't want to, he promised that the story could be mine. I didn't have to use his history or his characters. He just wanted to build the world for me and then I could play. I could rearrange things as necessary, change them completely if I wanted. He assured me that I couldn't get it "wrong."

And so, the Turrim Archive began to blossom into something that would be nearly 15 years in the making!

So I have to begin with a massive thank you to my husband, Derek. Without him, this story wouldn't exist. Thank you for building this vast fantasy landscape and trusting it to me. Thank you for your constant support and encouragement through every step of this project. For facilitating weekend trips away to draft and edit. For the long walks around our neighborhood trouble-shooting various plot points or character arcs and helping me clamber out of deep caverns of writer's block and the moments when I despaired of ever finishing or "getting it right." For always believing in me, even when I didn't believe in myself... I thank you.

To my brother, Grant, the first true fan of this story and one of the key people whose encouragement and desire for more of this story spurred me on through all the difficult times when I thought I might just throw in the towel. Thank you. I hope that the finished product lives up to your expectations!

To Allan James, my content and developmental editor, and my most ardent cheering section, all my thanks. While I have to admit that it is always nice to read the comments where you tell me my writing is "beautiful, beautiful stuff," I have to be fair and admit that your edits that push me to greater heights and depths and make me a better author are the ones that I treasure most. (Okay, what I treasure most are the moments when we've finally ironed everything out and we're both happy with the final version).

To Nancy, my line-editor.... I don't know what I'd do without your attention to detail. You catch my overused words (THANK YOU!), and notice whenever I randomly decide to spell something the British way (I'm such a weirdo), and your comments throughout about various places where people are introduced and whether or not things are consistent are so very helpful. Thank you for letting me know when something doesn't make sense or my explanations aren't enough!

To Deborah, my final set of eyes on this project, I am so sorry about the way I abuse commas. Also, I can't seem to get the hang of em-dashes inside dialogue... but I'm so grateful that you are so much better at that than I am! I treasure your attention to detail and your keen eye that makes my final product gleam like sunshine on a rippling river. Thank you for keeping me true to my timeline and making sure that my characters' eye colors don't change constantly. This story was such a mess of rewrites and reimagined ideas and changes, and you so deftly and expertly helped me smooth out all the wrinkles. You are the best proof-reader ever!

To Savannah Jezowski, thanks for not giving up on me or this cover! Thank you for your attention to detail and the hard work you put in to help make this book cover absolutely gorgeous. I so appreciate your talent for making beautiful book covers and your willingness to put up with me and my inability to explain what I'm envisioning. And yet, you always manage to deliver. You are a wizard... or a mind-reader.

To my amazing street team of Fearless Adventurers who helped me get the word out, stayed excited about the story even though it took so many years to actually get it to you, and continued to encourage me in all my ups and downs... thank you for your support.

And to the Great Author, my Lord and Savior, Jesus Christ, thank you for the creativity you've shared with me, for the gift you've given me, and for the passion for stories you've woven into my heart and soul. Thank you for writing these stories with me.

And now, to *you* Dear Reader. The story is now in your hands. Thank you for reading. I hope that it inspired or encouraged or thrilled you. If you enjoyed this story, would you consider leaving a review somewhere? It would mean the world to me!

Printed in the USA
CPSIA information can be obtained
at www.ICGtesting.com
LVHW091127211123
764443LV00031B/371/J